"*David Lucero, who knows because he's been there, has penned an amusing and insightful look inside the retail industry with all its mysteries, intrigues and foibles. His young store manager must deal with cranky know-it-all customers, shoplifters, lazy employees, backstabbers, and dubious corporate strategies, all the while trying to keep his sanity, and be a good husband and father. There's nary a dull moment in WHO'S MINDING THE STORE.*"

— **ROGER L. CONLEE,** Author of '*SOULS ON THE WIND*,' and '*THE HINDENBURG LETTER*'

"*WHO'S MINDING THE STORE captures with uncanny realness the very familiar politics people deal with at the local Home Improvement store. Hilarious, and sometimes sarcastic. ...cunning wit and smile-making humor. I highly recommend this book!*"

— **MATT SCHOTT,** Award-winning author of '*LORD SKYLER AND THE EARTH DEFENSE FORCE*'

"*This book begs the question... "Is the customer always right?" The cast of characters will amaze you. Some come to life right before your eyes... not without the savory seasoning of a fine writer. A dry wit without match, and plenty of surprises to keep the pages turning.*"

— **L. CURT ERLER,** Author of '*SOUTHSIDE KID*'

"*Imagine the sexy hilarity of Richard Hooker's M*A*S*H, the complex political intrigue of a classic Russian novel, and the sheer wackiness of the British sitcom ARE YOU BEING SERVED. Now, imagine that all of this high-octane craziness is taking place in the strip mall right down the street from your house. David Lucero takes us on an uproarious tour of the American retail industry. You'll never look at your Home Improvement store the same way again.*"

— **JEFF EDWARDS,** Award-winning author of '*THE SEVENTH ANGEL*,' and '*SWORD OF SHIVA*'

WHO'S MINDING THE STORE?

Susie, I hope you enjoy this. Sounds
like we've both lived it.

WHO'S MINDING THE STORE?

David Lucero

NAVIGATOR BOOKS
SAN DIEGO, CALIFORNIA

WHO'S MINDING THE STORE?

Copyright © 2012 by David Lucero

Cover Art © 2012 by Jesse Martinez

Navigator Books

www.navigator-books.com

ISBN-13: 978-0-9852523-1-1

Cover design by Navigator Books, based on art by Jesse Martinez.

Printed in the United States of America

This book is dedicated to the men and women of the retail industry, where there's never a dull day. I want to add a special dedication to everyone I've had the pleasure of working with in the home improvement trade. We laughed, we cried, we fought, we made up.

I hope you look back on our time together as a special experience. I know I do.

Who says the customer is always right?

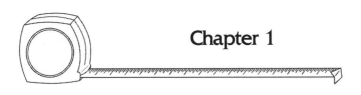

Chapter 1

The Design, Store #1129
San Diego, CA

"I want satisfaction!" the customer growled. He was a giant, burly man, determined to have his way. He glared at the cashier. "Get me the manager in charge."

Samantha stood frozen behind the counter, petrified. This was her first time working at the returns desk. Her supervisor, Teresa, insisted that each cashier train for six months before going solo, to sharpen their skills (and harden their armor). Teresa wanted her people to have the confidence to face rough customers. It was a good plan, but Burly Man had Samantha wishing that she'd waited six months and *one day* before working a shift here.

She reached for the phone, watching Burly Man cautiously, in case he lashed out like a spitting cobra.

Derrick answered the phone on the first ring. "Hello."

It was a nasty habit of his, answering the phone as quickly as possible. Christy, the phone operator, had once applauded him for answering his phone better than any other manager. Since then, he had made it a point to keep doing it. "I figure if I can look good performing something as basic as this," he told fellow managers, "why not let it ride?" But those same fellow managers got even by saying it was the *only* thing he did well.

"Derrick, I have a customer who wants to speak with you," Samantha said.

Derrick shook his head. That's what I get for answering my phone. "Did he ask for me by *name*?"

Of course, that didn't really matter. Being manager-on-duty meant being on the sales floor, available to all customers and associates, whether you liked it or not.

"He wants to speak with the manager in charge."

Derrick rolled his eyes. Lucky me. "Okay, I'll be right there."

Managers hated taking calls from the returns desk. It meant dealing with angry customers, who invariably wanted to return or cancel special-order items, which were non-returnable and non-cancelable. The no-returns/no-cancelations policy was posted on signs all over the store, and it was printed on every sales receipt. But that didn't stop customers from trying to return or cancel their special order purchases. Stop them? Hell, it didn't even slow them down.

Derrick Payton was up to his ears in cancelled orders and returns. No one at *The Design* had the backbone to tell a customer, "No, we can't cancel your order. No, we can't issue you a refund."

He knew the source of the problem. Whenever someone did get up the nerve to say no to a customer, the irate shopper would demand to speak to someone of higher authority, like a vice president, or the CEO. When the complaint hit the desk of one of the big dogs, the response was always the same... "Take care of the customer."

Translation: "Cancel the order, and refund the customer."

The Design, Your Choice for Home Improvement specialized in quality products for interior design and remodeling. The 30-store company was based in California, but had locations in Nevada, Arizona, and New Mexico. They offered appliances, kitchen and bath fixtures, indoor and outdoor furniture, cabinet hardware, draperies, lighting, décor, and a wide array of design-related specialty items.

The company motto proclaimed, 'We make your dream home a real home.' Everyone agreed that it sounded cheesy, but at least their mission statement showed a spark of imagination.

'The Design's goal is to improve the beauty and tranquility of our community by providing quality service and products to reflect the lifestyle of every home. Each customer we meet is the beginning of a relationship, and a bridge to an entire neighborhood. We will give back to the community the respect and service they deserve, by doing what is right for the customer with an entrepreneurial spirit unmatched in our industry.'

Okay, that sounded cheesy too, but at least there was a bit of substance buried in there among the fluff.

As a specialty store, *The Design* special ordered products to suit the lifestyles of individual customers. Which meant that an item ordered for Customer A would probably not fit the needs (or tastes) of Customers B, C, D, E, F, G, or H. As a result, any special order return went to the clearance section and was tagged 25% off, creating an immediate profit-loss for the store. When the item didn't sell at the reduced price, the discount would be increased to 50% off, and finally 75% off. After several months of languishing in discount limbo, the unwanted item would be marked down to zero, and tossed in the trash compactor.

The store's profit margin took a beating every quarter, because of returns. But that wasn't Burly Man's problem, and it certainly wasn't his concern. His name was PJ Nabors, a 6 foot and 3 inches tall giant, sporting a beer belly and beard reminiscent of Grizzly Adams. He liked pushing people around to get his way, and the store personnel were tired of him. He was like a monkey in the wrench, the poison pill that kept popping up in your medicine cabinet, the ex-girlfriend who kept asking why you dumped her, or the ex-boyfriend who got arrested for stalking you.

Derrick had dealt with him before. Derrick had dealt with a *lot* of people before, but PJ stood in a class of his own. He had been remodeling his kitchen for a year, and was the classic example of a do-it-yourselfer who took on more than he could handle. To save money, PJ had signed up for the fast-track program. This meant that no designer would visit the jobsite to verify measurements for flooring, cabinets, lighting, or anything else. The program required the customer to provide those details.

With the exception of the company CEO, the VP, and the district manager, everyone hated the fast-track program, because whatever *could* go wrong *did* go wrong, as PJ's kitchen makeover had repeatedly proven. From the moment he had signed up for fast-track, things had begun to go downhill.

First, he claimed that the custom cabinets he received were stained with the wrong finish. He waited four weeks for the reorder to arrive, at the expense of *The Design*. Later, he failed to order enough wood flooring to cover his entire kitchen.

Then, the refrigerator cabinet was two inches too short for the refrigerator to fit. It was obviously a measuring error on PJ's part, but he swore that *The Design* had delivered the wrong sized cabinet, and he pitched a fit until the company agreed to fix the problem. Again, he waited four weeks for the reorder to arrive, at the expense of the store.

After that, it was the granite countertop, and PJ had been in rare form that time. "I ordered *Baltic Brown*! This looks *nothing* like the slab I chose. You people are ripping me off!"

Fortunately for Derrick, he didn't usually have to deal with PJ's self-inflicted problems. That privilege fell in the lap of Paula, the project manager.

But Paula was already gone for the evening, which put Derrick on the firing line. He had no idea what PJ's problem was this time, but he was sure as hell going to hear about it now.

He entered the returns office, and Samantha sighed with relief.

"PJ, how can I help you?" The smile on Derrick's face looked as superficial as his question sounded.

"Why didn't your saleswoman tell me I'd have to upgrade my electrical for the lighting she ordered?" PJ asked. "The city inspector won't sign off on my permit, and my sub-contractor said it'll cost me two thousand bucks to get my wiring up to spec."

Derrick nodded, pretending to be empathetic. "We didn't tell you because you didn't hire us to supervise your project. You wanted to 'do it yourself,' no pun intended." And if you believe that, I'll sell you another countertop, he added silently.

PJ glared as though he were about to throw a right cross, but Derrick stood his ground.

"Is there anything else?" He hoped to shut this guy down fast.

"Hell yes there is! I want you to pay two thousand dollars for this upgrade, so I can get my permit signed off."

Derrick immediately recalled a former manager's saying, '*hope* is not a strategy.'

He shook his head. "You know we can't do that, PJ. You agreed to take on the responsibility as project manager when you signed up for our fast-track services. If you had hired us for design and install services, the responsibility would be on us. But you chose to handle the job yourself, so I'm afraid you'll have to handle it."

PJ still looked like he wanted to deck Derrick. "I shouldn't have to pay for this," he grumbled. "I'm not at fault here."

Of course you're not at fault, Derrick thought. It's *our* fault. We failed to properly qualify you as a customer. We didn't ask the right questions. We were too focused on closing the sale. We sold you what you *wanted*, instead of what you *needed*. And we see how well *that* worked out.

PJ stepped closer to Derrick. Samantha looked on, still petrified.

"How else can I help you?" Derrick asked.

The irate customer glared at him. "Did you not hear a word I said?"

"Of course," Derrick said. "And I understand your frustration. But there's not anything I can do about it. Is there something else I can do to help you?"

PJ slammed his hand on the counter again. "Damn it! *I WANT SATISFACTION!*"

Samantha took this latest outburst as her cue to leave the office.

Derrick resisted the urge to roll his eyes. Who the hell *doesn't* want satisfaction? "Have you spoken with your designer?"

"I don't want to talk to her," PJ snapped. "I want my money back. I'm taking my business elsewhere."

The words were like music to Derrick's ears. Nothing would give him more pleasure than to get this idiot out of his hair.

Don't let the door hit you on the way out, he said silently. By all means, go make life miserable for our competition.

"I'm sick of these mistakes," PJ continued. "It's been one thing after another."

Derrick agreed with him there.

"I signed a contract with you people, and you're not coming through on your end. Don't you people give a damn?"

Derrick struggled to keep from saying what he wanted to say. Instead, he kept his voice even. "PJ, you have to speak with your designer."

"She won't return my calls."

No kidding.

"Go speak with Paula," Derrick said. "She's the project manager for the designers. It's after 6:00 p.m., and they're gone for the day, so I'll ask her to call you in the morning."

Paula's going to love me for this, he thought.

"In all honesty, PJ, what you're asking for isn't in our contract with you."

He paused for effect. "Any additional costs which can arise during a remodel are the responsibility of the homeowner." The words were verbatim from the service contract, but he saw by the look in the customer's eyes this wasn't the end of it.

"This is some kind of bull—"

Derrick raised a hand, cutting PJ off. "Don't go there. You declined our project design and installation services, because you wanted to cut back on costs, remember?"

Of course he did.

"When you take on the role of project manager you take on all the baggage it comes with."

PJ stood there, huffing and puffing like he was about to explode. He was obviously searching for a properly cutting remark, but nothing seemed to be coming to him. Finally, he stormed out of the office. "You haven't heard the last of this, you sorry piece of shit!"

Then he was gone, for the time being anyway.

Derrick exhaled and shook his head. "And there goes another satisfied customer."

Chapter 2

I didn't deserve that altercation, Derrick told himself. Not on my last day. On Monday of the following week, he would officially become the operations assistant manager at *The Design's* store 1254 in Encinitas, California. After twelve years in the same building, most people would have been happy for a change, but Derrick wasn't quite sure what to make of this new development in his career.

On his last four performance reviews, he'd stated quite clearly that he wanted to be a store manager. He'd been an assistant store manager for nine years, and he was ready for greater responsibility. But it was one thing to know that he was ready. Convincing the district manager that he was ready? That was a different matter entirely.

Year after year, he heard the same thing...

"We're looking for someone else who suits the needs of our business."

"I think you need more time in your current role."

"You need to learn the project side of the business."

"You need to learn the merchandising side of the business."

"You need to work on improving your people skills."

He had done all of that, and plenty more. Still, the higher-ups told him that he wasn't ready for a store of his own.

When Judy Polakoff and Tom Elbert called Derrick upstairs for a talk, he knew that something had happened. A 'talk' meant they were planning to say something he wouldn't like.

"I need you to take charge of operations in Encinitas," Judy said. She was District Manager.

He waited for her to continue.

She waited for him to say something.

"When?" Derrick asked. What he really wanted to know was *why*.

"Monday."

Today is Friday. She's not beating around the bush. Derrick looked at Tom, store manager at 1129. Each waited for the other to say something.

"You okay with that?" Tom finally asked.

Hell no, I'm not okay, Derrick wanted to say. Driving to Encinitas would ratchet up his commute to 70 miles round trip. With gas prices skyrocketing out of control, he'd feel the pinch in his ever-shrinking wallet sooner than later.

"Sure," he said, without skipping a beat. "I'll do whatever's right for the company. You know that."

You're such a wimp, he told himself.

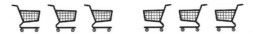

Derrick walked the sales floor when the store closed for the evening, making sure that everyone was gone, and all emergency exits were locked. A dozen questions raced through his mind.

Why are they transferring me? What did I do now? Could it be because of the complaints against me? That had to be it! Some whiner of an associate had gotten pissed off and complained again.

Tom had expressed his concerns about this over the course of several months. "People say you're out to get them," he'd told Derrick.

"What do you mean?" Derrick truly didn't know what Tom was talking about.

"Come on, you know what I'm talking about."

The hell I do. "I'm not a mind-reader, Tom."

"Okay. Have it your way." Tom looked exasperated, like he didn't want to go into details. "Kyle and a few of the others think you're trying to get them fired."

"They say I want them fired?" *What the hell is he talking about?*

Then, Derrick remembered...

Over a period of about twelve weeks, Kyle, Alma, Pete, and Lorraine had all shown problems with tardiness and absences. Derrick had approached each of them for a quiet talk about the problem. Each had acted as though they had no idea what Derrick was talking about.

Kyle worked in the plumbing department, and had been with *The Design* for four years. He was an okay employee (or "associate," as the company preferred to call them). He got along with everyone, and did as he was told, but he lacked initiative. Unless you gave him something to do, he would hang around and do nothing. It apparently never occurred to him that he should actively look for ways to be productive.

Derrick had called him to the side. "Kyle, I've been checking the time and attendance report and see you've been late three to four times a week for the past month. Is anything going on we should know about?"

Kyle stared as though Derrick was speaking a foreign language. "What do you mean?"

Here we go. "You've been late to work. I'd like to know why."

"How many times did I show up late?"

What did I say not more than 10 seconds ago? "At least three to four times a week."

Kyle tilted his head back and looked upward, as though scanning the rafters for an answer. "What exactly is late?"

The question stopped Derrick for a few seconds. Was Kyle bullshitting him? "You're not clocking in when you're scheduled to. The T&A report shows that you're 15 to 20 minutes late almost every day."

Kyle continued to search the rafters. "Maybe the time clock is wrong."

Derrick's conversation with Alma hadn't gone any better. She worked in the bath showroom, where associates special-ordered plumbing fixtures.

"Alma, I notice you haven't been coming to work on time. Is there something going on that's preventing you from working your scheduled shift?"

What he *really* wanted to ask was, why the hell can't you come to work on time? But the company's policies about political-correctness pretty much prohibited such a direct question.

Alma's eyebrows went up. "Oh, have I been *late*?"

Derrick couldn't decide which was more annoying: the woman's tardiness, or the fact that she looked surprised.

Pete worked in Hardware. He was going to college in San Marcos, and he had a long daily commute.

Derrick figured this was why he wasn't making it to work on time, but had to hear it from Pete.

"I've been staying up late," Pete said. "These early shifts are killing me."

Derrick understood where he was coming from. "Going to school takes a lot of work. I know you stay up late studying, but if you can't make it to work on time let me know now. Maybe I can schedule you for closing shifts."

Just as Kyle had done, Pete stared at Derrick like he was speaking a foreign language. "I appreciate you wanting to work with me," the young associate said. "But it would cut into my time with Wendy."

Derrick had no idea who Pete was talking about. "Who's Wendy?"

"She's my girlfriend. She doesn't believe I take our relationship seriously, so I've been crashing at her place this past month, to be with her."

Derrick was more than perplexed. "You mean you've been tardy these past weeks because you're staying up late with your girlfriend?"

Pete nodded casually. "What can I say? She's hot!"

Derrick suppressed a groan. He shouldn't really have been surprised. Every time he thought he'd heard every possible excuse, somebody threw something new at him.

Such was the case with Lorraine. She worked in flooring, where she was a solid performer. She actually enjoyed helping customers, as opposed to people who treated the retail business like an unpleasant detour on their way to better jobs.

"Lorraine," Derrick said, "I notice you've been coming late to work." He realized that he was starting to sound like a broken record. "Is there anything I can do to help?"

The woman was truly shocked. "What do you *mean*, I've been late?"

Derrick showed her the T&A report.

"This isn't right," Lorraine said.

Want to bet? "How's that?"

"I haven't been late," she replied, flatly.

Derrick looked at the report. "You can read this, right?"

"I can read the report," she said. "But it's wrong."

Of *course* it was. "How do you figure?"

Lorraine paused, searching for the right words. "Well, when I'm at home getting ready in the morning, I'm *thinking* about work. So, in a way, I'm actually working, except I haven't clocked in. Therefore, technically I'm not late, because my mind is on the job."

Derrick waited for her to laugh, and say she that was kidding. He wanted her to say that she'd make it to work on time, from now on. No such luck. She was dead serious, and farther out in left field than he had ever imagined.

In the end, Derrick did the only thing he could. He gave each of them a written notice stating that they were expected to work their scheduled shifts, and not be late. Any future tardiness or absences would result in further disciplinary action, up to, and including job termination. Of course they didn't like it. Who would?

He explained his actions to Tom. "I offered every one of them a chance to work later shifts, to better accommodate their personal schedules. Every one of them turned me down. And not one had a reasonable explanation."

Tom sighed. "Did you have to give them a write-up?"

Derrick felt his jaws tighten. He hated it when Tom played the role of good-guy vs. bad-guy. Tom knew damned well that they had to document tardiness. Store support demanded consistency when it came to holding people accountable for time and attendance. If Derrick failed to document discussions, it would be *his* ass, not Tom's.

"I gave them a game plan, just like Human Resources requires," Derrick said. "I also told them to call me if—for any reason—they aren't able to make it to work on time. I figured that would be enough to fix the problem."

Of course, it hadn't fixed the problem. Instead of knuckling down and correcting their own behavior, his devoted associates had sandbagged him as a way of escaping accountability.

In hindsight, Derrick knew that he should have seen it coming. Tom was an opportunist. Everyone knew that. He wanted a promotion to district manager, and the way to get ahead was to maintain the appearance that everything was well and good in your store.

Derrick wasn't a fan of that leadership style. If there was a problem, you were supposed to deal with it, not sweep it under the rug. Unfortunately, Tom tended to interpret Derrick's efforts as rocking the boat.

"Perception is reality," Tom often said in weekly meetings. "Take care of the customer and our associates, and don't let any complaints get to store support center. Keep them in the box. The last thing we need is for SSC to peel back the onion, and find out what we're *not* doing."

Derrick was about to pay the price for not following Tom's don't-rock-the-boat strategy. And now, he'd have plenty of time to think about it—a nice 70 mile round-trip commute every day.

But there was at least one up-side to this move. Ops managers rarely had to deal with customers. Their role was behind-the-scenes: handling the vault, the computer room, receiving and delivery issues, maintenance, supplies, and the basic infrastructure that made a store function.

The word was that operations at store 1254 were a mess. If Derrick could turn things around, it might put him in good graces with Judy. Hell, maybe she'd even reconsider him as a candidate for his own store.

One thing was sure—he didn't need *this* place any longer. He had fallen into the drudgery of routine here. Despite the 70 mile drive, maybe the change to a new store would be good for him. It was an opportunity to reinvent himself. Everything he had done wrong at this store would stay here.

No one in Encinitas knew him from Adam. All he had to do was start off on the right foot, and not make the same mistakes.

When he locked the doors to the building and headed to his car, he looked back over his shoulder, taking in the old store one last time. For some reason, the sight brought back what Julie Andrews had said in *The Sound of Music.* "When one door closes, another is opened."

"Stop being a sentimental idiot," he said aloud.

Derrick got in his car, turned on the engine and drove out of the parking lot, hoping for the best, and trying not to expect the worst.

What could go wrong? It was a new store. The people there were probably top-notch salesmen and women. Store support would've made sure to staff it with the best, so he wouldn't have to worry about having to babysit associates, or being backstabbed by his supposed team members.

A smile spread across his face. Things were going to be all right.

Then, his smile disappeared as a new thought crossed his mind. "I sure hope everyone in Encinitas comes to work on time."

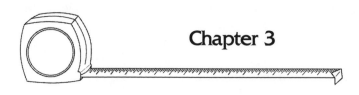

Chapter 3

Monday
5:30 AM

Derrick reached for the alarm and turned it off.

Usually he stayed in bed a few minutes listening to the radio, or he'd lean over to smell Jennifer's hair, and fondle her until she elbowed him in the ribs to stop. Today was different. It was his first day at store 1254, and he wasn't going to be late.

He kissed Jen on the cheek before climbing out of bed. He was careful closing the bathroom door, because his wife was a light sleeper. Eight years of marriage had taught him to move quietly in the morning.

"I may be a housewife," Jennifer had declared on more than one occasion, "but I still need my eight hours."

Derrick had once made the mistake of comparing the stresses of his job to her trouble-free daily routine at home. Not smart!

Jennifer's eyes had flared, and she had thrown a challenge at his feet. "If you think being a stay-at-home mom is *easy*, you're more than welcome to try it for a week! If you can cut the mustard, *then* you can make all the noise you want."

Derrick had decided to call her bluff. He had requested a week's vacation, to play the role of Mr. Mom.

Another mistake!

It turned out that maintaining a home and raising a six year old boy was a hell of a lot harder than it looked. The task took more patience and skill than Derrick could manage.

In the wake of this eye-opening experience, he made as little noise in the morning as humanly possible (as if such a thing was possible for a clumsy, self-centered husband).

He brushed his teeth, shaved, and put on deodorant. Then, he dabbed at his receding hairline with a touch of Rogaine, making sure to thoroughly wash hands after use, as the directions stated. He had come to accept hair loss as one of the consequences of aging, but his subscription to *GQ* magazine allowed him to cling to the illusion that he would eventually get his hair back.

As he ironed his shirt, a smile pursed his lips. Jen would be proud of him.

"Don't go to work looking like a slob," she would say. "It's a reflection on me."

Thank God, he had finally learned to listen to her. It had taken a few years, but better late than never.

He crept out of the bedroom and headed for the garage, where the dog slept. It was Derrick's chore to let the dog out each morning to do his thing.

The little Schipperke had been three years old when they had adopted him from the shelter, and some unimaginative former owner had saddled the dog with the name Waffle. This title had been unanimously vetoed by the Payton family, so the rescued animal had received a new name. It had taken him months to learn to respond, but—like Derrick—the dog was apparently trainable.

"Come on, Gnarly," Derrick said.

The dog jumped up and down excitedly as he was let outside.

Derrick went to the kitchen and poured himself a mug of coffee for the road. He packed the lunch he had prepared the night before, grabbed his briefcase, and headed for the door—only to be stopped short as Gnarly started barking.

Derrick let the dog back inside to keep him from waking up the whole neighborhood, and then headed for the door again.

"Aren't you going to kiss me goodbye?" Jennifer was standing on the bottom of the stairs in her nightgown.

"I didn't want to wake you up," Derrick said. "And I kissed you before I got out of bed."

"Well I'm up now."

"Yes, you are." He walked up to her, and kissed her goodbye.

She gave him a suspicious stare. "You didn't wake up Etienne, did you?"

Etienne was a light sleeper, like his mother.

"If you woke him up, it'll be *you* explaining to his teacher why he's falling asleep in class."

"I didn't wake him up," Derrick said. "Call me later."

Jen walked him to the door. "Have a nice day."

A strange feeling came over him as he walked to his car. "I'm just like the dog," he said to himself. "I've got the wrong name. I shouldn't be Derrick Payton. My name should be Ward Cleaver."

Chapter 4

6:15 AM

Derrick drove north on the 805 freeway, making sure to use his blinkers when changing lanes, and staying under the 65 MPH speed limit. The CHP was out for blood, lately. They pulled people over for even minor infractions, and if they caught you talking on your cell phone, they'd practically shoot you on the spot.

Derrick had no desire to give his insurance company an excuse to jack up his rates, so he played by the rules.

When he crossed over the I-8, merging traffic from the other freeway turned the 805 into a congested mire of cars, trucks, and highly-impatient drivers—all on a mission to get to work on time.

The far left lane was moving steady, and Derrick started to change lanes, only to be cut off by an Audi. The woman behind the wheel honked her horn longer than necessary, and Derrick barely had time to get out of her way. The look on the woman's face sent chills up his spine.

He was tempted to shout a few choice words out the window in her general direction, but he decided to let it go. No sense losing his temper, when he had everything to gain by keeping a cool head.

When he approached the Balboa Drive exit, he nearly smiled. Then he remembered that this was no longer his off ramp. He still had 20 more miles of freeway driving ahead of him.

"No problem," he said aloud. "Think positive. Think of it as an extra half-hour of privacy every day. An opportunity for solitude and peaceful thoughts."

But there wasn't much peace to be had on Southern California freeways during the morning rush hour. The pace alternated between brief intervals of violent acceleration, and total gridlock.

He was navigating the I-5 and 805 merge—known euphemistically as the 'Golden Triangle'—when a motorcyclist riding a blue Kawasaki ZX6 cut in front of him, passing so close to Derrick's front bumper that he felt his body tense for collision. Somehow, it didn't come. Still crossing the freeway on a reckless diagonal, the bike barely missed getting run over by a semi-truck in the far right lane.

The truck driver blew his horn long and angrily. Without looking up, the cyclist raised his left fist and made the time-honored 'bird' gesture. Then, he darted down the off ramp, and sped away on the East 56 freeway.

Derrick shook his head in amazement. "What the hell is *wrong* with people?"

Not more than thirty seconds later, he passed an Amber Alert sign that read, "SHARE THE ROAD. LOOK TWICE FOR MOTORCYCLES."

"You got that right," Derrick said. "Those suckers will kill you!"

He got off the I-5 at the Leucadia Boulevard East exit. He was now precisely 33 miles (and 40 minutes) from home. Two more miles to go. Not such a bad commute after all.

The poor bastards trying to make it down to San Diego had it a lot worse. The I-5 south was bumper-to-bumper, at single digit speeds. Luckily, by the time Derrick was heading south again, all those south-bound commuters would be driving north. He'd miss them again.

Store 1254 was *The Design's* newest location, sandwiched between two shopping malls and a boatload of restaurants, including a *Fuddruckers* and something called *Charlie's Bar & Grill*.

Derrick eyed grill. It looked like an excellent place to spend his lunch breaks.

He parked and checked his watch. It was 7:00 a.m. He wasn't scheduled to be here until 8:00, but he hadn't been sure how much time to allocate for the drive. No matter, he could have a look at the store and introduce himself to the receiving crew.

Derrick went through the will call pick-up and returns entrance on the right of the building. This was where associates entered the store before the doors were open to the public.

A scrawny, lanky-looking man in his mid-twenties was sitting behind the returns counter, typing away on the computer. He didn't bother looking up when Derrick entered.

"Morning," Derrick said, cheerfully. "How's it going today?"

No response from Lanky Man. He continued typing away.

"I said, good morning." Derrick was not going to be ignored.

Lanky Man looked up. "We're not open 'til ten."

"You don't say?"

Derrick had not had the pleasure of meeting Lanky Man before, but he had a strong hunch that the kid *knew* he was the new ops manager. This was Lanky Man's way of saying that he didn't give a shit.

"I'm Derrick Payton, the new OAM. And you are?"

Lanky Man turned his attention back to the computer screen. "Albert."

That was it. No, 'I'm Albert, pleased to meet you.' No handshake. He didn't even rise from his chair.

"Is Robert Morrison here?" Derrick asked. Robert was the general manager.

Albert, a.k.a. Lanky Man, shook his head without looking up.

"When will he be in?"

Lanky Man sighed. "I don't follow his schedule."

Apparently, this kid was determined to make the top of Derrick's shit-list from the very start.

Derrick resisted an urge to jerk the young idiot out of his chair. Instead, he kept his tone level and polite. "Who opened the store?"

A female voice from behind said, "Robert opened the store. But I sent him home."

He turned and saw Judy Polakoff, the District Manager, enter from the door leading to the front end cash registers.

Derrick smiled. "Judy, thanks for coming."

He was truly happy to see her. Having the DM introduce the new operations manager to store associates would help with the transition.

"I had to take care of some loose ends," Judy said. Then, she nodded toward Derrick. "Walk with me."

He followed her outside to the parking lot.

She stopped about a dozen paces outside the door, and turned to face Derrick. "A lot has happened over the weekend," she said.

Tell me about it. You transferred me to this store three days ago. "Like what?"

Judy looked him directly in the eye. "I let Robert Morrison go."

Her words took a few seconds to properly register. Did she say she had let Robert *go*? As in *fired* him?

"When?"

"This morning."

What the... "Can you tell me why?"

Judy's voice had an edge to it. "You bet your ass I'm going to tell you. Robert wasn't up to the job. So I showed him the door."

Before Derrick could respond, Judy turned and started walking again.

Derrick fell into step beside her. "He wasn't up to the job? How exactly do you mean that?"

They reached Judy's SUV and she opened the door, putting her briefcase inside. She turned to face Derrick again. "Sales have been down for the past two months. Robert had no game plan for turning things around. Or at least, no plan that I found satisfactory."

She paused and stared into Derrick's eyes, like she was trying to read his mind. "In this business we have to *drive* sales."

No kidding.

Her eyes narrowed. "What was that?"

Oh God! Had he said that *aloud*?

He shook his head. "Nothing. I understand. We have to drive sales."

Judy stuck her hand in her coat pocket and pulled out a set of keys. She held them out to Derrick. "Here, these are for you."

Before he could respond, she continued, "Congratulations. You're the new store manager."

Derrick stared at her. She must be out of her mind.

"No," Judy said. "I'm not out of my mind."

Damn! She had done it again. And this time, he *knew* that he hadn't spoken out loud.

Judy laid a hand on his shoulder and gave him a gentle shake. "Look, Derrick, I know this whole situation comes as a shock to you. But you're going to have to get past that. You're going to have to get your head in the game. I need you to focus, and drive sales. This store has potential. With the right leadership, things can get better. I read the comments you made on your last review. You want to run your own store, right?"

Derrick nodded, like a kid responding to his teacher. He could tell that his jaw had dropped, but he couldn't muster enough coherent energy to close his mouth.

"Now, you've got your chance," Judy said. "Don't waste it."

She climbed into her SUV, turned on the ignition, and rolled down the window. "We have a conference call tomorrow. Be ready. I want to know what you're going to do to drive sales."

She drove away, and left Derrick standing in the parking lot, his mouth still hanging open like an idiot.

What had just happened? Was he really the *store manager*? Was this some crazy dream? Or was it the friggin' Twilight Zone?

But he felt the weight of the keys in his hand. They were real. This really *was* happening.

He turned to face the building. Not just any building. This was *his* store.

Then, his mouth started to move—speaking words without thinking.

"She didn't say a word about a pay raise."

Chapter 5

There was no time for celebration. Derrick had to catch his breath. His heart raced. He was perspiring, and his deodorant wasn't holding up to the claims made by its advertising campaign.

I can't go to the store looking like I shit my pants.

A *Starbucks* was nearby. He practically ran to it, and headed straight for the bathroom. He locked the door, splashed water over his face at the sink, and then stared in the mirror. His breathing returned to normal, but he was red in the face. That always happened when he got nervous, and he hated it.

Why couldn't he be more confident?

His mind started going blank. He couldn't focus. He used the urinal carefully. His hands were trembling so hard that he was afraid he might pee on his own leg.

He washed his hands, took another look in the mirror, and left the bathroom, bumping into a patron waiting to use it.

"Sorry about that," he said.

The man grunted in response.

Derrick ordered tall mocha, and grabbed the table and chair in the back of the café. He needed to get a grip of himself before returning to the store.

What the hell was Judy thinking? No preparation, no warning. Just bang! You're in charge now.

He had dreamed about getting his own store, but not like this. He'd always assumed that when the magic day finally came, he would have a smooth and orderly transition. Instead, he had been handed a store where the previous manager failed.

He was in for a tough ride.

Why hadn't Judy stuck around long enough to introduce him to his store personnel? It would have been the perfect time for her to let everyone know he was now *the man*.

No matter. He'd been on his own before.

8:00 AM

Derrick got back to the store right as the morning crew was arriving. The store opened 10:00 a.m., Monday through Saturday, which gave them time to down stock, and clear the aisles of pallets and freight.

Keep calm, he said silently. You have a job to do. They have to see that you're confident and capable.

In the world of retail, managers came and managers went. Derrick had seen them all.

The weak managers were good at avoiding people, never looking you in the eye. They always made sure to be somewhere else whenever an issue for the store manager came up. If a customer needed to speak with the store manager, it was an assistant store manager they got instead. If an associate had a complaint and wanted a few minutes of the store manager's time, it was an assistant store manager they got. Weak managers were careful to only make themselves available when no one actually *needed* them.

How in hell could anyone succeed in life being like that?

The strong types were the ones with a good head for the business. These were the people who didn't have to say much, but had no trouble looking you eye to eye. They made themselves available for everyone. Even when they were bogged down with the all-consuming emails, phone calls, customer and associate issues, and anything else that came up, somehow they always had a moment to spare for whoever needed them.

That was the type of leader Derrick had tried to be as an assistant store manager. He figured he earned enough respect to show that he was headed in the right direction.

He could be impatient with customers and associates sometimes, but he was aware of this fault, and that knowledge usually allowed him to keep himself in check. Unless, of course, you had trouble coming to work on time.

Derrick could feel the stares from store associates as he followed them to the punch-in clock located in the back of the store. He smiled and said a hearty, "Good morning," to each of them.

I'm not going to be seen as *weak*, he told himself.

He stopped midway down the hall at the door labeled STORE MANAGER. This was it. This was his office. He reached for the door handle.

It wasn't locked. He opened the door slowly. The room was pitch-black. He turned on the light.

His new office was smaller than Tom's office at the old store. The furnishings consisted of a desk and chair crammed into the corner, two chairs for visitors wedged into the narrow opening in front of the desk, one file cabinet, and a coat rack. The walls were bare of pictures, but a large mirror did something to relieve the feeling of claustrophobia. The lone ornamentation was a plastic plant with leaves the color of toy soldiers.

Apparently, Robert had not been much of a decorator.

Derrick set his briefcase down and closed the door, before settling down in the chair behind the desk. *His* chair. The store manager's chair.

He was in charge. The idea still didn't seem real.

A dozen thoughts raced through his mind, until one of them brought him up short.

Wait a second... Judy *can't* promote me. The job has to be posted for three days before she can interview applicants. And she has to interview a minimum of three people before making a decision.

He recalled interviewing a year ago for store manager, but doubted that would count, since so much time had passed. That was why she hadn't mentioned a raise. This wasn't a permanent position. It was temporary. Like an interim position. Damn! He'd been screwed again!

There was a knock at the door. "Come in."

A tall woman entered the office. She looked to be in her mid-fifties, fit, but with a horsey face that made her unattractive. No, Derrick decided... *Unattractive* wasn't the word. This woman was downright *ugly.*

Still, she presented an impeccable appearance. Her long, auburn hair rested on her shoulders, and she wore a fashionable business suit. Too fashionable for *The Design*, maybe, but she might be compensating for her lack of beauty in other areas.

That wasn't a very nice thought, and Derrick regretted it immediately. He hadn't even met the woman, and it was a bit early to start forming opinions about her.

"Good morning," he said, rising from the chair.

The woman's dark brown eyes bored into Derrick. She seemed to scrutinize him, looking him up and down in a demeaning manner.

What the hell was her problem? "I'm Derrick Payton."

The woman didn't say anything right away. Instead, she leaned on the door jam, arms folded across her chest.

When she finally spoke, it was in a monotone. "I'm Tina Nodzak, human resources manager."

Ah... She was the HR. Derrick would be getting to know her well, then. Every store was assigned a human resources manager, referred to as the 'HR.'

The company had a thing for acronyms. Store managers were SM; assistant store managers were ASM; operations managers were OAM; district managers were DM; MOD meant manager-on-duty; district retail merchants were DRM; and department heads were DH. The list was practically endless.

When it came to running a store, the SM and HR were joined at the hip, at least in theory. The HR's primary function was to recruit, hire, train, and ensure consistency in following the process. Again, in theory. *The Design* had been sued enough times to learn the importance of consistency in matters of personnel policy. The company's solution was to hire a boatload of HR personnel.

Somewhere along the line, things had gotten warped. Too many HRs had started believing that they held as much authority as the store managers.

"Here's the pecking order," they would say. "Store manager, HR, and everyone else is beneath us."

For obvious reasons, that attitude did not sit well with the management teams. Over time, HRs had begun giving instructions on merchandising, signage, in-store transfers, and a lot of other subjects that didn't actually fall under the umbrella of human resources. The HRs also decided who got a pay raise and who didn't; who got hired and who didn't. Needless to say, the HRs made these decisions without consulting the management teams who were (theoretically) running the stores.

The ASMs felt slighted, because they were accountable for the success or failure of their respective areas. Consequently, they believed that they should be able to make decisions regarding the personnel, equipment, and merchandise under their control.

"If anything goes wrong it's *my* ass, not the HR's," every ASM would say.

But, there was no way around it. The beast called 'human resources' was here to stay. Everyone just had to deal with it.

I'll deal with it all right, Derrick said to himself. He'd had more than his share of run-ins with human resources.

"Nice to meet you," he said, holding out his hand.

Tina eyed him cautiously.

"I won't bite," Derrick said, still smiling. *Shake my hand. Or would you prefer I bitch-slap you?*

Tina's brow wrinkled. "What was that?"

Derrick's smile disappeared. Had he said that last part aloud? He really needed to watch that.

"I said I won't bite."

Tina finally took his hand, and gave it a desultory shake. "I learned only this morning that you would be replacing Robert. When did you get the word?"

She was fishing.

Derrick decided best not to bite. "A bit earlier than that," he replied.

Before Tina could comment, he continued. "It's good to be here. I haven't seen the whole store yet, but what I have seen looks pretty good."

Her only response was a steely stare.

"What time's the store meeting?"

"Same as always," she said. "Fifteen minutes before opening."

Derrick could already see that this woman was going to be a problem.

"Good. Would you do me a favor, and introduce me to everyone?"

Tina's laugh held a tinge of sarcasm. "Your first day here, and you're already looking for favors?"

The bitch had attitude.

"It'd be the friendly thing to do," Derrick said.

Tina shrugged. "I have enough friends."

She turned and left without another word.

Derrick whistled softly through his teeth. That woman either had serious relationship issues, or she hadn't been laid in a *long* time.

He chalked her behavior up to the latter.

Chapter 6

The Morning Meeting
9:45 AM

Around fifty associates were gathered in the flooring department's carpet showroom. Three-foot high stacks of expensive rugs were staged at various spots around the sales floor. In the open areas between these stacks, the assembled personnel drank their morning *Starbucks* coffee; or munched on egg and bagel sandwiches.

Morning meetings were *The Design's* way of starting the day off right. The managers went over the sales figures for the previous day, discussed goals for the current day, and threw in an occasional success story to boost morale.

Today, they were getting a special treat. They were being introduced to their new store manager.

"Some of you know that sales have been rather tough these past months," Tina said to the group.

She stood before them, very much at ease with being the center of attention. "We've been putting our best foot forward, but not enough to meet our store's financial goals."

At least she was being tactful.

Derrick looked around at the faces of the gathered associates. He knew what they were thinking.

Who's the new guy standing with the management team?

What's he doing here?

Where is Robert?

What's going on?

"…and so," Tina said. "Robert has moved on."

She paused.

The silence was deafening.

Everyone's attention became instantly fixed on Derrick. He could feel their eyes boring into him.

He concentrated on standing up straight, and not smiling too much. He didn't want to seem overconfident, but he didn't want to look scared either.

Then, he realized that Tina had not continued with the introduction. She was staring at Derrick, along with everyone else.

That was *it*? *Our sales figures are down, and Robert is gone?* No words of welcome. Not even a mention of Derrick's name.

That bitch was painting him out to be the *bad* guy. Like he had pulled a few strings with some buddies at corporate, and stolen Robert's job.

Tina finally continued. "Wherever Robert has gone, we wish the best for him."

Again, no mention of Derrick at all. She motioned in his general direction, and then she stepped aside. That was the sum total of her introduction.

At this point, traditional courtesy demanded that Tina clap her hands politely, to initiate a round of welcoming applause from the team. She didn't. She stood with her hands at her side, and regarded him with cold eyes.

How did that old saying go? *Keep your friends close, and your enemies closer...*

Derrick would have to keep Tina *very* close.

He pushed the thought out of his mind. "Good morning everyone, I'm Derrick Payton."

He took a nanosecond to look the group over, and continued. "As Tina just mentioned, Robert has moved on, and I've been given the position of store manager."

Silence. No smiles. No nods.

"I've waited a long time for this opportunity," Derrick said. "And I'm excited to be here."

Still no response. At least they weren't throwing things at him.

"I haven't had a chance to look over the whole store yet, but what I *have* seen shows me that you all take pride in your work. I find that to be an inspiration."

He nodded toward the HR manager. "As Tina pointed out, sales at this store have been significantly below goal for the past few months. I don't think that's any fault of this team. The entire national economy is in a slump, and overall sales performance has suffered throughout the company."

The stony silence continued.

"This store has been through a few rough spots," he said. "But I believe we can move in a direction that will turn things around. Obviously, I can't do that alone. No one can. That's why we have each other. I look forward to sharing my ideas with you, and I look forward to hearing your ideas on how we can improve sales. We can all learn from one another."

He thought that last bit was a nice touch. Telling them that he wanted to learn from them was the same as saying that he was on the same level as they were. It didn't matter what his title was. He needed them to be on his side, and he wanted them to know it.

He looked at his watch. "We'll be opening the store in a few minutes. I want everyone to have a fun day. Let's have a million customers, and a million smiles."

The applause finally came, but it was light and unenthusiastic.

The group broke up, and the associates all wandered off toward their own departments.

Derrick caught more than one of them stealing a last glance in his direction. Their expressions were not brimming with confidence.

Still, given the fact that he'd had no time to prepare himself for the job, he thought he'd given a fairly good opening speech. He hoped it hadn't sounded too corny. More importantly, he hoped that some of them had listened.

He would know soon enough.

Chapter 7

Manager's Meeting
11:00 AM

Derrick was first in the training room. This was where the weekly manager meeting was held, and he was impressed. At his old store in Kearny Mesa, the training room had been the size of a closet.

Six tables formed a u-shape in the center of the room, and Derrick sat at the middle of the horseshoe. That's how Tom, his SM at Kearny Mesa, had conducted meetings, and it seemed to make sense.

One by one, the ASMs entered the room. Each carried a binder and talked casually about personal issues that had nothing to do with work.

This is good, thought Derrick. They're not nervous about what happened to Robert. I need them confident, and self-assured.

Tina strode in with another woman close behind.

Derrick didn't recognize the second woman, but he could tell from her expression that she shared the HR's low opinion of the new store manager.

Terrific. *Two* bitches to worry about.

He shrugged off that thought. There was no sense in looking for trouble. He needed everyone on his side, and he wouldn't get there by making ungrounded assumptions about his new associates.

Everyone took a seat, and the room fell quiet, all eyes focusing on Derrick.

One of the men looked around with a puzzled expression on his face. "Where's Rob?"

Obviously, this guy had missed the morning meeting. He hadn't heard the news.

Derrick suppressed a surge of frustration. Judy had probably known a month in advance that she was going to fire Robert Morrison. You don't make a decision like that on a whim. That being the case, she should be here to introduce Derrick to everyone, and let them know she had confidence in him. Instead she was throwing him to the wolves. Leaving him to fend for himself.

He wondered if this was some sort of test. Was this Judy's way of finding out if he could stand on his own two feet?

Derrick had no idea, and he couldn't dwell on it now. He had a meeting to conduct.

"Some of you may not have heard," he started, "but Robert Morrison is no longer with the company."

More than one set of eyes bulged at the news.

Had Derrick looked that way when Judy had dropped the bomb on him? He hoped not. Perceptions were important, and he wanted to appear as confident as possible.

"I met Tina this morning," he said. "But I haven't had the pleasure of meeting the rest of you."

He looked in the direction of the woman sitting next to Tina. "Would you mind starting off by telling me your name, your position, and something about your background?"

The woman rolled her eyes. "Debbie Banks, PSM." There was a hint of exasperation in her tone. "Five years with the company. CKD for ten years. PSM for the past two years."

CKD was short for 'certified kitchen designer,' and PSM was the company acronym for 'project sales manager.' This was the person in charge of the kitchen and bath designers. They followed up with designers and installers to ensure timelines and milestones were met, called clients to ensure that they were happy with the progress of their remodel, and provided design assistance as-needed.

Their role required PSMs to be off the floor, and they were exempt from the usual salaried manager duties like opening and closing the store, working the MOD shift, and verifying the vault.

Derrick waited for more, but that was apparently all she had to say.

He nodded to the man on his right.

The man cleared his throat. "I'm JC Fuller. I've been with *The Design* for eight years now. Started out as sales associate, got promoted to DH, and later ASM. Before that, I worked in a grocery store as a meat clerk, but after we went on strike in 2003, I decided that a career change would be in my best interest."

The guy had enthusiasm. Derrick liked that.

"Glad to meet you, JC." He looked at the next man, and motioned for him to speak.

"Steve Lyons. I've been with the company for three years. My wife and I moved here from the Bay Area. We have a two-year-old daughter, and we love San Diego. I worked at *Allison's Design Studio* for three years as a designer before joining *The Design*."

"Glad to be working with you," Derrick said.

Next, it was the third and final guy's turn to speak.

"Welcome aboard, Mr. Payton. Glad to meet you. I'm Tim Lyon."

Good. A gentleman and professional on the team. Maybe this store wasn't going to be too bad. His managers looked pretty good, save for the Wicked Witches of the West.

"Please," he said. "Call me Derrick."

Tim continued. "I've been with the company five years. I started at the Oakland branch store, before transferring to New Mexico, where I stayed for two years. Then, I took a transfer to Encinitas, to help open this store."

He smiled. And I just want you to know that I'm *damned* glad to be here."

JC slapped Tim on the back. "Way to suck up to the new boss!"

Steve grinned. "Yeah… Laying it on a bit thick, aren't you Tim?"

Derrick enjoyed the tiny display of levity. A little good-natured humor was a sign of positive morale. He could see that Tina and Debbie did not approve, but he pretended not to notice. They would come around soon enough.

"I'm pleased to meet all of you," he said. "I've been with *The Design* for twelve years. I started as a sales associate like you, JC."

Derrick saw JC smile. Good, he thought. He likes that we have something in common.

"I got promoted from plumbing department to DH of bath showroom, and then promoted to ASM two years later. My entire time with *The Design* has been in San Diego's Kearny Mesa store."

He let his eyes travel around the group. "I feel fortunate to have this opportunity to work with you. I've heard good things about this store, and I'm glad to be part of a solid team."

The three ASMs, whom he had mentally dubbed the 'Three Amigos,' sat up straight, smiling broadly. The Wicked Witches of the West rolled their eyes.

"I've been married for eight years," he continued. "We have one son named Etienne. That was my mother's favorite name, so we placed that burden on our son, and we pray that he'll eventually forgive us."

He leaned back in his chair, making himself comfortable. He shouldn't talk too much. The last thing he needed was a reputation as a blow-hard.

"My goal has been to have my own store for some time now."

He regretted the words the instant they were out of his mouth. Idiot! It wasn't *his* store. It was *everyone's* store.

Not a smooth move—claiming ownership of a store where they had all worked for years. Nor was it smart to admit that he'd been waiting years for the promotion. It made him seem weak.

Great. They were all gonna see him as the tallest midget in the group.

He groped for something else to say. "I'm grateful for this opportunity—"

"Why is *that*?" asked Tina.

Derrick froze for an instant. The question had caught him off guard. By the look on Tina's face, that was precisely what she had intended to do.

Don't just sit there. *Say* something.

"I believe I can make a difference," Derrick said.

"How so?" asked Debbie.

Ah… So, they were tag-teaming him.

He nodded casually, as if he hadn't noticed the challenge. "As I said, I've been with the company twelve years. This has helped me understand the clients we serve. I was trained by the best people in the company, and I'd like to pass the benefits of my experience on to others."

"How do you plan on doing that?" It was Tina again.

Wow. This was supposed to be meet-the-manager, but the Wicked Witches were ready to turn it into a free-for-all. Derrick decided to shut them down.

"We'll discuss my plans later," he said. "For now, I'd like to talk about Judy's expectations."

Again, he instantly regretted the words coming out of his mouth. Forget about Judy. They needed to know *his* expectations.

He had to get them back on track, without pointing fingers at anyone.

"None of the stores in the district are making sales plan," he said. "Let alone comping to last year's sales."

'Comping' was the company's term for a comparison to the previous year's numbers.

"But that doesn't mean we can't make money in this economy," he continued. "It just means that we have to be intelligent and proactive."

He looked Tina straight in the eye. "I have full confidence that everyone in this room is capable of rising to the challenge."

Tina said nothing.

"Judy wants me on tomorrow's conference call," Derrick said. "She wants to hear what we're going to do to drive sales."

Again, he let his gaze travel around the table. "As I said, we'll talk about my plans later. But I want Judy to know from the start that—whatever difficulties this store may have experienced in the past—they were *not* caused by a lack of efficiency or leadership by the men and women seated at this table."

There! That didn't leave Tina and Debbie much maneuvering room, did it? Any counter-argument they made now would essentially be admitting to a failure in their own professional effectiveness.

Sorry, ladies... But *you* started it.

"I want Judy to know how sharp and forward-looking my managers are," Derrick said. "So I want each one of you to come up with one idea for how we can improve sales. I want to hear those ideas before the end of the business day."

He stood up, signaling that the meeting was over.

"In the meantime, I'd like to walk the floor and introduce myself one-on-one to everyone. I'll catch up with you later."

Steve, Tim, and JC rose to shake hands with Derrick—welcoming him again, and letting him know that he could count on each of them.

He had the feeling that they were worried for their jobs. When a store manager is let go, others frequently get the axe in the reshuffling that follows. Any one of them could be handed his hat at any moment.

Derrick looked over at the Wicked Witches of the West. Both women remained seated, their eyes smoldering.

Those two were *definitely* going to be a problem.

Chapter 8

Walking the Walk

Walking the sales floor was the best way for managers to see what went on in their store. It also happened to be the chore that every manager dreaded most.

The company had rolled out an SOP a few years ago, stating that all salaried managers were required to work the manager-on-duty shift, to ensure that associates engaged the customers. This policy was not popular with store managers.

Tom Elbert, the SM at the old Kearny Mesa store, had grumbled about it more than once. "I've got to sit in on conference calls, return phone messages and emails, and go over reports," he had said to Derrick. "When do they expect me to find the time to walk the damned floor?"

They were the DM, VP, CEO, and anyone else at the store support center who came up with hair-brained ideas that were nearly impossible to implement.

"You can't run a store from SSC," Tom had continued. "You have to be *in* the store. And if they want us to spend more time on the sales floor, they need to stop bombarding us with reports, emails, and conference calls."

All managers were in agreement there.

"Those guys have got to justify their jobs *somehow*," Derrick had said in response. "People in SSC don't want to be in the stores, and they certainly don't want to deal with customers. But they have to justify their position on the payroll. That's why they keep their noses in our business."

Tom had snorted. "More like up our *ass*, you mean."

Again, Tom had been right.

Now, it was Derrick's turn to face the onslaught of customers and associates waiting to speak with *the man*. It didn't take long, either. The moment he walked into the outdoor seasonal department, he was approached by Sylvia Sanchez, a pretty twenty-something brunette.

"Hi Mr. Payton, I'm Sylvia." She shook hands enthusiastically.

"Hi Sylvia, and please, call me Derrick."

She tightened her grip and pulled him closer. "I *need* another dollar." Their noses practically touched.

If this was her way of asking for a raise, she was not off to a good start.

Derrick pulled his hand free. "That's quite an introduction."

"I know how this sounds, but Robert *promised* me a raise. Now, he's gone. So it's up to you to come through for me."

Lucky me.

"Sylvia, this is my first day here. I can't have this conversation with you on the sales floor."

"Okay," she said. "Let's go to your office."

Derrick gestured for her to slow down. "Let's not rush into things," he said. "I'm going to walk the sales floor and introduce myself to everyone. I'll catch up with you by the end of day."

"Promise?" She sounded desperate.

"Yes, I promise."

Shit! You're never supposed to promise anyone *anything*.

Before he could further compound his mistake, Derrick excused himself and headed for the appliance showroom, trying hard not to shake his head over what had just happened.

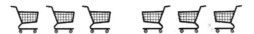

Gary was an associate specialist in appliances. He'd been in the industry nearly thirty years, and he enjoyed the thrill of the sale. His history of commission-based jobs had taught him how to survive in a cut-throat environment where your own coworkers would steal customers out from under you.

In the old days, his philosophy had been simple. "If you want to eat, you've gotta learn how to be a closer."

Now that he was in his mid-fifties, he was no longer quite so willing to swim with the sharks. *The Design* didn't pay commissions, so he didn't have to stab anyone in the back to earn a living. And no one had to stab *him* in the back. That suited him just fine.

He enjoyed qualifying a customer, versus selling them something they didn't need. For the first time in years, he felt like a professional, and not just a huckster looking to close a deal.

He was sitting at his desk, working on a written estimate, when a little old lady rounded the corner. A gentleman true to heart, Gary rose from his chair and walked toward her.

"Good morning, ma'am, how may I help you?"

The lady moved slowly, and used a cane. Her clothes resembled the fashion of the 1970s, but suited her. She looked up and smiled. "Hello."

Her face displayed the wrinkles of a person unaccustomed to face cream.

As Gary approached to a good distance for friendly conversation, his nostrils were assaulted by an overpowering floral reek. Perfume. A *lot* of it. *Too* much. And it smelled just like that horrible stuff his mother-in-law insisted on wearing. Which made it about one step short of chemical warfare.

He gritted his teeth and tried to ignore the too-sweet odor.

The woman looked to be pushing eighty. No, make that ninety!

Gary decided that he could overlook the lady's ghastly aroma, in view of her age, and her polite manner.

"Are you looking for anything in particular, ma'am?"

"Yes," the woman said. "I think I need to replace my refrigerator."

"We have lots of refrigerators on display," Gary said, motioning to the rest of the showroom. "I'm working on an order for another client, who should be here any time now. Would you mind if I excuse myself for a few minutes, while I wrap up his paperwork?"

He needed time to recover his sense of smell.

"Certainly," the old woman said. "I want to have a look for myself anyway."

"Thank you, ma'am. My name is Gary, and I'll be right over here." He pointed to his desk. "Don't hesitate to call me, if you need me."

Derrick rounded the corner, just as Gary was sitting down. The layout of the showroom was impressive. The one in Kearny Mesa was tired-looking, in need of a remodel.

He spotted the woman with the cane, browsing the refrigerators. He wondered why the salesman didn't appear to be helping her.

The lady stopped at a refrigerator with double French doors, and turned to face Gary. "May I see the inside of this one?"

"Of course you may," Gary said. "Would you like for me to open it for you?"

The old woman shook her head. "No thank you. If I can't open it without help, I surely wouldn't want to buy it."

She gripped the oversized stainless steel handle and pulled. The door didn't open.

She tried again, pulling harder. The door still didn't budge.

The old woman changed the set of her feet, and pulled with all of her strength. The door swung open, accompanied by the distinct sound of a human fart.

Gary heard it clearly. So did Derrick.

Gary gave the elderly customer a strange look. "Ma'am, did you just break wind?"

Derrick was shocked. That was *not* an appropriate question to ask a customer!

The woman turned to face Gary, her cheeks carrying the rosy tint of a blush. "It's not easy getting old. Sometimes, I lose control of my gas."

Gary smiled. "Don't worry about it, ma'am. That's nothing. When I tell you the price of that refrigerator, you're going to *shit!*"

Derrick's jaw dropped open.

The old woman began to laugh.

Before Derrick could step forward to offer an apology, she winked at Gary. "Thanks for the warning, Son. Do you think you could show me some models that won't require any participation whatsoever from my bowels?"

Gary stood up again, his smile widening. "Yes, ma'am. I'd be happy to."

Derrick shook his head as he walked away. "I'm going to like working here."

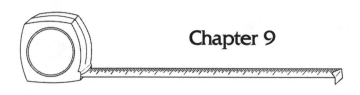

Chapter 9

6:00 PM

"What hat happened to Robert?" asked John, a plumbing department associate.

Not again, said Derrick silently. "He moved on to other things."

How many times was he going to have to answer that question?

"Kind of sudden, isn't it?"

More so for me. "I'm sure wherever he goes he'll do fine."

That was good. Neutral, but positive. Don't give them anything to run wild with.

Derrick had spent the day meeting everyone in the store; letting them know he was glad to be part of their team. For the most part, he felt welcome, but associates were shocked by the sudden departure of their store manager. Apparently, Robert Morrison had never told them that his job was on the line.

Great. Now they were all worried about getting fired.

After eleven hours, Derrick was ready to call it a day. He wanted to go home and see his wife and kid, while he still had the energy to appreciate their company.

He stopped at the doors leading to his office. Someone was watching him. He could feel it.

He turned and saw the Wicked Witches standing at the edge of the lighting department, arms folded across their chests, blank expressions on their faces. They wanted him to *know* they were keeping an eye on him.

Derrick saw the notes on his desk from his ASM team. Everyone but Tina and Debbie had followed through on his request for suggestions about how to improve sales.

Apparently, the Wicked Witches wanted to challenge him. So be it. If they wanted a war, he would give them one they wouldn't forget.

He leafed through the suggestions.

JC wrote, '*Staffing to customer demand needs to be addressed. The Whole Store Report indicates we are down 12 hours in décor, 8 hours in lighting, and 4 hours in plumbing. If we have associates on the floor, sales will follow.*'

Short and to the point. Not bad.

He read Tim's suggestion next. '*A better mix of cash-and-carry product is needed to attract customers. Right now each store in the company is expected to have the same mix of product on the shelves. Each store serves a different community with different lifestyles. Our product should be based on the needs of the community we serve.*'

A solid idea. Derrick liked it!

Then, Steve's suggestion. '*We need to address pricing. With the current state of the economy, we should offer promotional discounts to attract customers looking for quality product and low prices.*'

That was technically true, but it was also lame. The company offered promotions all the time. When one ended, another began. Steve probably hadn't spent a lot of time thinking this over.

That was okay. Derrick could spend more time with Steve, clarifying his expectations.

Derrick put the notes in his desk, and reached for his briefcase.

As he was closing the door to his office, a voice called out to him. "Can we talk now?"

It was Sylvia.

Derrick practically jumped out of his shoes. "JEEZ! You scared the sh…" He stopped short, while he was ahead.

He lowered his voice. "Sylvia, I was just leaving."

"But you said we'd talk about my raise before the end of the day."

Yes, he had. Like an idiot. And now, he was stuck with a conversation he did not want to have.

He opened the door and walked back into his office. "Come in." He motioned for her to sit. "What's on your mind?"

He really hated asking that question. It never failed to open a can of worms.

Sylvia took a deep breath, and her breasts made a fairly serious attempt at bursting through the fabric of her T-shirt. "Like I said, Robert *promised* me a raise."

Yeah, like I haven't heard *that* story before.

"You mentioned that before," Derrick said. "But you didn't tell me *why* Robert offered you a raise. I assume he had a reason."

A frown crossed Sylvia's face. "Well, the cost of living is high in San Diego, you know? It's not easy to get by."

Derrick nodded. "I won't argue with that. But most of our associates live in the San Diego area, and the cost of living affects all of us. So that doesn't really justify giving a raise to *one* person."

The young woman said nothing.

"Sylvia, you hit me with this on my first day," Derrick said. "And you know that we have a company process for managing raises in salary, don't you?"

Sylvia nodded.

When George Leaf had taken over as CEO of *The Design*, he had introduced pay-bands, as well as restrictions on *who* could get a raise, and *when* raises could be administered.

Before Leaf had taken the reins, store managers had followed their personal whims in handing out raises. Many times, Derrick had seen the SM walk up to an associate. "You've been doin' a terrific job. As of tomorrow, I'm giving you a buck more per hour, because I think you're worth it!"

Sure, it *sounded* cool. Trouble was, the managers sometimes played favorites. The company found itself neck-deep in lawsuits for racial discrimination, gender discrimination, and—in more than one instance—people who just wanted to cash in by threatening legal action.

The legal snarls had brought two lasting results: a rigid review process for managing pay raises, and the introduction of the dreaded human resources department.

Sylvia toyed with a strand of her hair. "Well, cost of living wasn't the only reason. Not the *main* reason."

"Okay," Derrick said. "What was the main reason? Why did Robert promise you a raise?"

And please keep it short. I wanna get home at a decent hour.

Again, Sylvia stretched her T-shirt with a deep breath. Was she doing that on purpose? Trying to dazzle him with her tits?

They were definitely dazzling… Okay, enough of that! He did *not* want to go down that road.

"I was hired as a part-time student in seasonal," Sylvia said. "Two months ago, I finished school and got my CBD."

Derrick was familiar with the acronym. It meant she was a certified bath designer.

"Congratulations," he said. "That's quite an achievement."

Sylvia flashed him a quick smile. "Thanks. I always wanted to be a designer."

She took another of those fabric-stretching breaths. "When I got my certificate, Robert told me he would make me a designer, and give me a dollar raise. I wanted more, because I think my CBD justifies it. But he said I need to prove myself in the design room first."

Derrick nodded. That sounded reasonable enough.

"But Debbie refused to bring me on her team," Sylvia said

Uh-oh. Derrick saw red flags waving overhead. He hated to ask, but better safe than sorry. "Did Debbie say *why* she didn't want you on her team?"

"She said she wants someone with experience."

That was reasonable too. Derrick knew that being a designer is tougher than most people realize. Do-it-yourself magazines and reality TV shows tended to glamorize design, making it seem like fun and games. What they *didn't* show was the behind-the-scenes part of the job: the complex and demanding work that took up time, and money.

Clients often thought they knew more about design than the designers did. Magazines, the internet, and those lame home improvement reality shows made it seem possible to remodel an entire home in 24 hours, on a shoestring budget.

All that Hollywood crap made homeowners believe that remodeling should be fast, and cheap. In fact, most remodeling jobs were difficult and expensive.

A designer needed to educate the customer about what to expect during a remodel. They had to have the finesse to help a customer make an informed decision, without making it obvious that they were guiding the client's choices. The designer had to understand the customer's vision well enough to formulate a realistic design, and then sell that design to the customer—all without ever seeming to exceed the role of friendly advisor.

You showed your client limited options, so as not to overwhelm them with too many choices. When you reached a roadblock you assured them this was common, but you'd help them through it. Part of the job was selling *yourself*, making the client believe in you, and trust your guidance.

All of that took experience, and that was the part that Sylvia didn't understand. Not yet, anyway.

She was too young, and too excited to listen. Derrick saw that she had passion, but that wasn't enough. Debbie needed her designers to hit the ground running. Right now, all Sylvia could offer was enthusiasm, a brand new diploma, a nice set of tits.

Derrick listened attentively, willing himself to be patient. He needed to show interest. Maintain eye contact. Avoid looking at his watch. Not make it obvious that he wanted to be somewhere else.

When Sylvia finally wound down, it was Derrick's turn to take a deep breath. His chest didn't try to explode out of his shirt.

"I'll tell you what I'm going to do," he said evenly. "I'm going to partner with Tina, and discuss the possibility of giving you an increase, to recognize your efforts to exceed expectations. You've been pursuing an education in a field that's directly related to the company's mission, and that should count for something."

Sylvia sat up straight, beaming—her chest thrusting forward.

Derrick raised a hand. "Hold on just a second. We have to wait and see what store support's position on this will be. And we have to be delicate about this, because if we give *you* a raise, you can bet *everyone* is going to want one. That's why I need you to keep this under wraps. Don't discuss it with anyone. Understand?"

She nodded excitedly.

It took a supreme act of will for Derrick to ignore the bouncing of the young woman's upper torso.

"If we *can't* get you a raise…"

Her smile disappeared, but Derrick continued talking. "If we *can't* get you a raise," he said again, "I'll talk with Debbie about the possibility of assigning you to the design room as a trainee. Maybe that way, we can justify giving you some kind of merit increase."

"I LOVE YOU!" Sylvia shouted. She practically jumped out of her chair, and ran around the desk to hug him.

Derrick held up his hands to fend off the unexpected burst of affection. And he ended up with one of Sylvia's round breasts planted firmly in each of his palms.

Their eyes locked, and they both froze in place.

This was not good. This was *NOT* good…

Sylvia lowered her eyes to Derrick's hands. His eyes followed hers.

Oh God! His hands were still resting on her tits.

He snatched his hands away, and groped blindly for his briefcase.

"Sorry," he said. "I have to go."

Chapter 10

6:30 PM

What in the hell had just happened? Derrick had no idea. After his close encounter with Big Tits Sylvia, he couldn't get out of the building fast enough.

Driving west on Leucadia Blvd to the I-5, he noticed that his hands were trembling. His hands-on experience with Sylvia had embarrassed the hell out of him. He prayed that she never repeated the incident to anyone.

He couldn't get the image out of his mind. Her eyes locked on his, the weight of her firm breasts against his palms. Were they *real*?

"Stop it!" he shouted.

He wondered if any of the other drivers had spotted his little outburst. Yelling at himself in an empty car. Yeah, *that* would make him look normal.

He grabbed the earpiece to his cell phone, and hastily fumbled it into his ear. He hated for people to catch him talking to himself. The earpiece disguised his one-sided conversations as phone calls. He hoped.

His palms still tingled from their contact with Sylvia's tits.

"Stop it!" he shouted again.

It was time to leave all the craziness behind. Go home, and be normal for a while.

He concentrated on not yelling at himself for the remainder of his drive home. He managed it.

He also tried to stop thinking about Sylvia's boobs, right in the palms of his hands. That, he did not manage nearly as well.

7:10 PM

Jennifer had dinner ready and waiting. "Wash up so you can eat," she said.

She gave him a routine kiss. More of a peck, really. Then, she pulled back and gave him a searching look. "Is something wrong?"

"No," Derrick said quickly. "Why do you ask?"

Did she *know*? How *could* she know? It was impossible!

"You look pale," Jennifer said. "And you seem nervous."

Derrick blurted out the first thing that came to mind. "I got promoted to store manager of the Encinitas store."

Now, it was Jennifer who turned pale. "Are you bullshitting me?"

Derrick was blown away by her reaction. Jen never cursed. *Never.*

"Don't leave out a thing," Jennifer said, bringing a pot of mashed potatoes to the table. "I want to know everything that happened today."

Derrick spent the next fifteen minutes going over his day. He decided to leave out his encounter with Sylvia.

He couldn't help noticing that he had his wife's full attention. Usually, she got visibly bored when he tried to tell her about work. As a rule, if she made prolonged eye contact, it was because she wanted him to do something around the house. Ah, married life...

When he finished Jennifer stared expectantly.

Derrick swallowed a mouthful of meatloaf. "What?"

"Did you get a raise?"

Uh-oh, how did he answer *that* one? "We didn't talk about salary. And I had so much stuff dumped in my lap that I didn't have time to ask."

"But you *are* going to get one?" Jennifer had that same look she got when he would forget to pick up her tampons at the store, or when he sent Etienne to school without a packed lunch.

She wasn't going to stop until he told her what she wanted to hear.

"I'm going to discuss it with Judy after the conference call tomorrow," he said, in his best reassuring voice. "You don't think I'm going to do this for nothing, do you?"

"You'd *better* not," Jennifer said.

It bothered Derrick that she knew him so well. He had never been good at standing up for himself. He hadn't been pushed around as a kid, and he didn't let people walk on him, but when it came to asking for a raise, he folded like a cheap suit.

He remembered his promotion to ASM...

He'd gone straight to the DM, and blurted it out. "I need a raise." He'd instantly regretted the bluntness of his words.

"You got a raise," the DM had replied. "The standard increase from hourly pay to salaried is anywhere from three to eight percent of your previous earnings. You jumped from thirty-three thousand to forty-three. That's a lot more than eight percent. Far above the normal rate."

Derrick hadn't been able to argue with that. A ten thousand dollar increase sounded pretty generous.

But Jennifer had balked. "They hire people from outside the company starting at fifty-five thousand," she'd said. Her tone of voice had been about a half-inch short of an accusation. "Are we supposed to pretend that they're doing you a favor?"

How in the hell did she know the starting salary for outside hires?

Derrick had not gotten the salary increase he wanted. Or rather, the salary increase that *Jennifer* wanted.

Instead, he'd gotten the standard response from human resources: '*The company is not responsible for the terms you negotiated when you were hired.*'

He'd gone back to the District Manager, and received the same answer. "*The Design* recognizes potential," the DM had said, "but unless you can tell me what you're bringing to the table that you didn't learn from us, I can't go to the VP and push for a further increase."

And that had been that.

Derrick hated not fighting harder, but he knew it was an uphill battle. Above all, he didn't want to seem unappreciative. Better to deal with an unhappy wife than a bitter DM.

10:00 PM

Derrick and Jennifer changed into pajamas and got ready for bed. She washed Etienne and put him to sleep in his room after dinner, leaving Derrick to clean up the kitchen.

"This marriage is going to be fifty-fifty," she'd said at their wedding reception, eight years earlier.

Too bad her fifty-fifty division didn't extend to work.

In truth, Derrick was proud that Jen didn't have a full-time job. From time to time, she took on a part-time job to keep busy in the afternoons, but her real job was wife and mother. Raising a six-year-old boy was challenge enough, as she frequently reminded him.

As he climbed into bed, he watched Jen wash her face in the bathroom sink. She had gained fifty pounds during her pregnancy, but lost it within four months of giving birth.

"I'm going to set an example for my kids, by living healthy," she had told her friends. As a result, exercise had become very much part of the Payton family lifestyle. Derrick appreciated this as he admired his wife's shapely figure.

When Jennifer crawled under the sheets, he suddenly imagined that it was Sylvia sliding into bed with him. In his vision, her young athletic body was draped in cherry red lingerie that revealed far more than it concealed. Derrick's imagination began to run wild.

Sylvia's breath was warm and fragrant against his ear. Her voice was pure seduction. "Oh my God, Derrick... I've wanted to do you from the moment we met."

Derrick's eyes bulged with excitement. "You're kidding!"

The voice that answered him did not belong to Sylvia. "No," Jennifer said. "I'm *not* kidding."

Derrick found himself struggling to pick up the thread of the conversation. "I'm sorry, Honey, what was that?"

Jennifer rolled her eyes. "I said, I'm not kidding. You should go straight to human resources, and demand a raise. If they're going to make you a store manager, they need to *pay* you like a store manager. Don't you think so?"

Derrick didn't answer. The image of Sylvia's nearly-naked form was still burning in his mind. He realized that he was sweating.

Jennifer frowned. "*Don't* you?"

Derrick wiped his forehead, and his fingers came away damp with perspiration. "Of course I do," he said. "I'll take care of it tomorrow."

Jennifer turned out the light, and lay on top of the bed sheets beside him. "Are you okay? You've got that nervous look again."

Derrick rolled over to face her. "It's been a long day, and I can already think of about a hundred things I need to do tomorrow."

Whoa... He needed to get a grip. He hadn't done anything wrong.

Jen cuddled up to him, and ran her hand across his chest. That felt nice, but then she raised her hand to his head, and trailed her fingers through his thinning hair. "Has the Rogaine been working?"

That was not exactly his favorite question.

"Yes," he said automatically. "Our investment is worth every penny."

"Don't worry about it," she said. "I love you just the way you are." Then she kissed him.

Her tongue slid into his mouth. It surprised him so much that he pulled his face away.

There hadn't been much passion in their sex lately. The truth was, there hadn't been much *sex* in their sex lately. Their kisses had become more like the formal pecks that a mother would give her child.

It had been a while since Jen had tried to heat things up. And here she was, trying to turn up the passion, and he was acting like an idiot. What the hell was wrong with him? Was this still about the Sylvia thing? That had been an accident. At least, he *hoped* it had been an accident.

Jennifer peered into his eyes. "What's wrong?"

Derrick suppressed a sigh. "Sorry, Honey. You caught me by surprise."

She laid her head on his chest. "I hope that's not a bad thing... Surprising you..."

She had surprised him, that was for sure. Almost as much as his accidental grope of Sylvia's tits.

Okay, that was enough of Sylvia! The only tits in his life belonged to his wife, and that was the way he wanted to keep it. Not Sylvia's tits. Jennifer's.

"I'm proud of you, Honey," Jennifer said. "You work so hard to keep our family secure."

She lifted her head to look him in the eyes. "It means a lot to me, what you do for us."

He nodded absently. "Thank you. And you have the only tits I want to touch."

Jennifer's body stiffened instantly. "Is that so?"

Oh God! What had just come out of his mouth?

"Yes!" he said desperately. "Yes, you do. You have perfect tits. Amazing tits."

He could feel his wife's muscles relax.

Jennifer giggled softly. "Amazing, huh? I guess I can live with that."

Derrick closed his eyes. He had dodged another bullet. This whole thing with Sylvia had really messed with his head. The silly bitch.

Jennifer's body went rigid again. "Did you just call me a *bitch*?"

"No, Honey! Not you—"

"Not me? You mean you're thinking of someone *else*?"

His heart nearly stopped. "Of course not, Sweetheart. You're the only woman I want." That was lame. Unbelievably lame.

They paused, their eyes locked.

Derrick waited for the explosion.

Then, Jennifer laughed. A moment later, he did too.

"You are so corny," Jennifer said. And she giggled like a teenager.

Her hand slid down to his crotch. "So, you want to touch my tits?" She squeezed gently. "Sounds like you want to play dirty."

Then, her lips were on his again, her tongue darting into his mouth. He met the passion of her kiss with a passion of his own, and their tongues swirled and darted.

It was a long kiss, and a wet one. When Jennifer pulled away, her cheek was damp with saliva. She wiped at it with the back of her hand. "You don't have to be messy about it."

"I thought we were playing dirty," Derrick said.

"There's a difference between dirty, and sloppy," Jennifer said. "*Dirty* is exciting. *Sloppy* kills the mood."

She saw the look on his face, and smiled. "You're still a helpless little boy, aren't you?"

Derrick sighed. "Well, if you want to talk about killing the mood..."

Jen nodded. "Fair enough. No little boy talk, no sloppy business. Just some nice, dirty play."

She peeled her pajama top over her head, and climbed on top of him, taking his hands and guiding them to her exposed breasts. "Touch me."

He felt the warm weight of her tits in his palms. He squeezed and began to stroke her sensitive flesh.

Jen closed her eyes, and a soft moan escaped her lips.

Derrick's hands explored territories that they hadn't visited in quite a while. He nodded to himself. "I should get promoted more often."

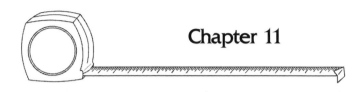

Chapter 11

**Tuesday
8:00 AM**

"Let's have a roll call," Judy's voice said over the speaker phone.

Derrick was in his office, notepad in hand, and the first person to log on the call. He knew they expected him to be eager, and he had decided to play the part to the hilt.

Judy was in her office at store support center in Orange County. In the old days, it had been called the home office, but the CEO had decided that store support center was more appropriate. After all, their role was to support the people in the stores.

The name change might have made sense, if the people who worked there had actually tried to live up to the idea. Support? That was a joke. SSC pumped out directives, and ignored the inputs of the guys who actually ran the stores.

It had taken Derrick a while to figure out that being a manager didn't mean having his way. He spent more time playing ball than he did running things.

"All of us are here to support the directives from SSC," Judy had told him once. "We want you to be creative and look for ways to drive sales. But—at the end of the day—it's your job to implement decisions from the powers-that-be."

Sadly, her words had proven to be true. He'd lost count of the times that SSC had impeded his ability to manage effectively. And now that he was SM, store support would be in his business more than ever.

Judy kicked off the call with a cheery morning voice. "I see that Derrick in Encinitas was first to hop on the call," she said. "And I want to take a moment to congratulate him on his promotion to store manager."

The ensuing silence lasted no more than a second, but the hesitation was unmistakable. Then, everyone on the call poured out their congratulations.

"Welcome to the rat pack," said Alex Quinton, store manager of 635, in Anaheim.

"Congrats on the promotion." That was Dillon Morgan, store manager of 1302, in Imperial Beach.

"Good work," Tyra Campbell said. She was SM for store 1753, in Redondo Beach.

"You have my condolences," Emerito Gomez grunted. He ran store 9566 in Huntington Beach, and he was known for his edgy sense of humor.

The group on the call laughed.

"Good for you, Derrick," said Beth White from store 4452, in Phoenix, Arizona. "You'll do fine."

"Until you do wrong," Nick Springer chimed in. He ran store 1751 in Monrovia.

Lastly there was David Lowe from store 3519, in Oakland. "Derrick Payton, right?" He paused. "Yeah, I heard of you."

What the hell did that mean?

Judy decided it was time to get down to business. "Okay everyone, we've got a lot to discuss for the upcoming holiday promotion. Our expectations are big, but we won't achieve them unless we have a plan to drive sales."

Derrick thought it strange that no one seemed concerned about what had happened to Rob Morrison. Then again, talking about it on a conference call wouldn't be appropriate. Besides, the other managers were probably just glad that none of them had gotten the axe.

When the district manager asked for a plan to drive sales, you could bet your bottom dollar you were about to be grilled for an exceptional idea. If your plan wasn't up to par, you would be asked to stay on the call after everyone else logged off. You did NOT want to be that person.

Judy said, "Let's start with you, Tyra."

Derrick breathed a sigh of relief. At least he wasn't being picked on because he was new.

Tyra spoke with confidence, but she didn't offer anything with substance. "It's going to be all hands on deck here at Redondo," she said brightly. "We're passing out flyers to inform customers that our designers will be available for free 45 minute consultations. Our project managers and installers will be here to meet customers, and explain the remodeling process. And we'll be 100% stocked in our cash-and-carry departments."

Derrick shook his head. He'd heard minor variations of that strategy at least fifty times.

Offering free design consultations was nothing new, but trying to keep a designer on hand for such events was like pulling teeth. When you asked designers to work the weekend, the response was always the same... "I was hired to work Monday through Friday."

Which was technically true, but the economy was in a shambles, and the online retailers were rapidly turning the brick and mortar stores into an endangered species. Associates didn't seem to realize that—when the company was in trouble—everyone was expected to rise to the occasion.

"Far be it for us to ask our people to step up to the plate," Derrick said.

"Who said that?" Judy asked.

Shit! Had they heard him? Derrick checked the speaker phone, and saw he had not activated the MUTE button. He was fucked.

"Listen up," Judy said, "we need to take this upcoming promo seriously. Business is tough across the board. The companies that don't..." she paused. "How was it put a moment ago? Step up to the plate? Well, the companies that don't *step up to the plate* are going to be history."

No one responded.

Judy continued. "Does everyone remember what happened to *Expo Design & Remodel*? Over seventeen years in business, and they closed their doors when the economy got tight. *San Diego Kitchen & Home Design* didn't do any better. After thirty years in the trade, they shut down too."

Derrick and the others got the point. In today's economy there were no sure things. If you wanted to succeed in retail, you had to give the customer a reason to shop during a time when people were cutting back on spending.

For the next 20 minutes, Derrick listened to the other managers provide a brief game plan that was all too common. Staffing to demand, lower prices, radio and TV advertising, and getting the merchants to buy a mix of products that suited the community. It all sounded pretty much the same.

Derrick checked his notes, and realized that he had nothing new to offer. He wondered if this was Judy's way of putting him on the spot.

"Okay, Derrick," she said, "you're up to bat."

She might as well have slugged him with a sledgehammer.

Derrick cleared his throat and searched for something to say. There was no time to come up with a new idea, so he'd have to say something generic. The trick would be to keep it from *sounding* generic.

"I heard a lot of excellent ideas from everyone," he said. "And I don't want to repeat what others have already said."

He took a deep breath. "In addition to following the excellent suggestions made by my fellow managers, at store 1254, we're going to emphasize the importance of sticking to basics."

He paused, while he fumbled for some glimmer of an idea. He needed to define this 'sticking to basics' thing. But he was talking off the top of his head, and he had no clue where this was leading. (If it was leading anywhere.)

Then, it came to him. Not a brilliant idea, but at least it was coherent. And if he chose the right words, he might be able to make it sound pretty good.

"We're going back to our core competencies," he said. "We're going to concentrate on the things that made *The Design* such a strong brand to begin with. We're going to approach and greet the customers. Listen to their needs, and take the time to actually *understand* those needs. We're going to properly qualify our customers, offer them useful suggestions, and we're going to *ask* for the sale."

Derrick paused again. The phone line was silent. He had their full attention.

He continued. "The number one complaint we hear is that we don't have enough help on the sales floor. Like all of you, my store is staffed according to budget, so I can't hire more associates. I have to use the people I've already got. My management team needs to be out on the floor, engaging customers, and *I* will be out there with them."

His panic was fading now, as the answers popped into his head. This basics thing was actually starting to sound like a decent idea.

"My store is also going to work on phone calls," Derrick said. "As store managers, we all hear complaints about how no one answers incoming calls, and no one returns phone messages. This is something so basic that we've almost forgotten how important it is. When the phone rings, we need to answer it. If a customer leaves a message, we need to call them back. Yes, it's time consuming. But if we don't have time to communicate with our customers, then we don't have time to be in business."

Hey... That sounded pretty good too.

"At store 1254, we're not going to reinvent customer service. There's no need for that. We already *know* what to do, we just haven't been doing *enough* of it."

He decided to finish with a zinger...

"If all I offer is *merchandise*, my customers can order just about anything in my store cheaper, if they buy it online. If I want to drive sales, I have to offer them something they can't get from an online retailer. And that something is guidance, help, and personal attention. In other words, basic customer service."

"That's my idea," he said. "It's not new, and it's not flashy. But I think it will work."

Judy could be heard clearing her throat. "That's very good, Derrick."

Her tone of voice reminded Derrick of an elementary school teacher praising a student.

"I think your assessment is dead on target," she said. "I agree with every word you said."

Derrick all but fell off his chair. "Ah... Thank you, Judy."

"Thank you all," Judy said. "Every one of you brought up good points, but as Derrick just pointed out, your plans were all essentially the same."

Wait a minute! He hadn't said that!

Judy continued. "That being the case, we should focus on Derrick's concern about our level of customer service."

Derrick threw up his arms in surrender. Great. Judy had just marked him as the teacher's pet, and turned his fellow managers into instant enemies.

Judy was still talking. "I want each of you to make sure that your salaried managers are walking the floor, to ensure that our people are engaging the customers. And when the sale is closed, you will follow up. That can only be accomplished by answering and returning phone calls, just as Derrick suggested."

Derrick wanted to bang his head on his desk. That bitch had taken his gung-ho double-talk, and used it to increase the daily workload of every store manager. He might as well shoot himself now.

"Memorial Day is next Monday," Judy said. "That's when the promotion starts. Let's all meet at Derrick's store for a preparatory meeting, and discuss final plans."

Derrick could practically hear the other managers rolling their eyes at the thought of another meeting.

Then, Judy threw a curve ball. "Derrick, I'd like to have a word with you after the call. Will you please stay on the line?"

Shit! What the hell had he done?

One by one, he listened to the other managers hang up and leave the call. For a half-second, Derrick thought about hanging up too.

Chapter 12

9:00 AM

"I want to be sure there's no misunderstanding," Judy said.

Derrick had no idea what to expect, so he kept his mouth shut and listened.

"I know I surprised you yesterday with your promotion," Judy said. "And I'm about to surprise you again."

Uh-oh. That didn't sound good.

"Are you there, Derrick?"

"Yes, Judy. I'm listening."

"You're not being called on the carpet," Judy said. "I didn't ask you to stay on the phone because you did something wrong. On the contrary, your contribution to the call was the best I've heard in a long time."

Derrick still didn't know where this call was going. "Thanks."

"I'm going to be very candid with you," Judy continued. "I *hate* these conference calls. I think the other DMs would all agree with me on that. Most of these calls are a waste of time, but we have to do them anyway. Do you know why?"

Derrick hesitated. "Why?"

"You've heard the old saying that *perception* is *reality*?"

"Of course."

"Well," Judy said, "these calls are mostly about managing perception. It's important that we do our due diligence, and look for ways to drive sales. But it's every bit as important that we *demonstrate* that we're doing our due diligence. These calls are one of the ways that we show the top company executives that we're actively seeking ways to drive sales."

Derrick suppressed a sigh. "So these conference calls are nothing but a dog and pony show?"

"No," Judy said. "Sometimes, we really *do* hear good ideas during these calls. Not often, but it *does* happen. And besides, they're not really optional. All the DMs are required to hold these calls, so that's what we do."

She paused. "Derrick, this may come as a shock to you, but gaining position and power in the company doesn't mean having total control. I have to play ball, just like you do."

Derrick rolled his eyes. Did she think he'd just joined the company yesterday? He knew about playing ball. And he knew what happened to managers who tried to avoid it.

"I understand," he said. "You have to play ball, and so do I. It's part of the business. So, what kind of ball do you want me to play? What is it that you need me to do?"

"What I need you to do," Judy said, "is make sure the Memorial Day promotion on Monday is your best sales day ever!"

Huh? That was *it*? *That* was the big message she wanted to give him? A glorified pep talk?

"I'll certainly give it my all," Derrick replied.

"No," Judy said. "You're not hearing me. This promotion is do-or-die for some of the stores in this district, and yours is one of them."

Derrick sat up straight in his chair. "Wait a second," he said. "Are you telling me that my store is operating in the *red*? I haven't been into the numbers in detail yet, but I have looked them over. As far as I can see, this store is in the *black*."

"Your store *is* in the black," Judy said. "Sales at your location have been down for the past couple of months, but overall, you're operating at a fairly good profit."

"Then why is my store on the chopping block?"

Judy cleared her throat. "What I'm about to tell you is strictly confidential. If this leaks out in any way, you will be subject to immediate termination." She paused for effect. "Is that clear?"

Derrick swallowed. "Yes."

"The company is not doing well," Judy said, "and the senior executives are looking to cut our losses. The stores in the red are obviously subject to closure. But some of the profitable stores may be closed as well."

Derrick winced. "And my store is on that list."

"Yes," Judy said. "Unfortunately, it is."

Derrick waited for her to continue.

"The company is restructuring every district," Judy said. "We... I mean the *company*... believes they made a mistake by oversaturating the market. They opened too many stores in each district."

Derrick caught Judy's accidental use of the word '*we*,' but he let it go without comment.

"Kearny Mesa was our first store in San Diego," Judy said. "They have more volume than Encinitas. Both stores are in the black, but we believe... I mean the *company* believes... that San Diego only needs one home improvement design store."

There was that 'we' again.

Derrick leaned back in his chair. A million thoughts raced through his head, and none were to his liking.

Why had they promoted him to manager of a store they were planning to close? Was it because the company considered him expendable? Would the company relocate him? Or would they just toss him out with the trash? Oh shit... How was Jen going to take this? Oh shit. Oh shit. Oh *shit*!

"Are you still with me, Derrick?"

He snapped out of the trance. "I'm still here," he said. "But for how *long*?"

Judy either failed to hear the question, or she ignored it.

"Here's the score," she said. "I've convinced SSC that Encinitas is holding its own, and that the store's profit ratio is going to get even better over time. But not everyone agrees with me. Several of the senior decision makers are ready to pull the plug on Encinitas right now. I've talked them into giving you a chance to turn the store around. I gave you Rob's position to show the doubters I mean business. I'm ready to shake things up, and show what store 1254 can do."

Derrick wasn't sure how to respond to that. Was he supposed to thank her? Judy had just thrown him into frying pan. Thanks did not seem to be in order.

"That's why you have to pull off a better-than-expected sales day on Monday," Judy said. "It will buy us time. We need to prove to SSC that we can maintain sales consistency, but that takes time. That's what I need you to do for me. Blow the lid off this sales promotion, and buy us some time. Do you understand me?"

Derrick understood perfectly, probably far more than Judy wanted him to understand. The store was operating in the black, but they had thrown Rob to the wolves anyway, to appease some company crony with his (or her) panties in a knot.

"I understand," Derrick said. "Do you think my leadership is enough to impress the top brass that store 1254 should remain open?"

"I'm counting on it, Derrick. You said you wanted a shot at running your own store, and your back-to-basics plan is the strongest idea I've seen in a long while. I don't know if you realize it, but you impressed your fellow store managers today."

Derrick wondered if that were true. "Do you have any other surprises for me, Judy?"

"No. Keep a cool head, and follow your game plan for the upcoming promotion. Make sure you're ready for our meeting on Friday. Call me if you need anything."

Derrick was about to hang up when Judy said, "Oh, and Derrick, one more thing"

"I'm all ears," he said, unenthusiastically.

"Congratulations on your promotion. You worked hard for it."

Judy hung up and when she did, he heard the phone beep twice, an indicator she was no longer on the call. Derrick was about to do the same, when he heard the phone beep twice again. Then, an automated voice said, "You are now the last person on the call. Goodbye." The line went dead.

Had someone else been on the call? Judy had clearly said that she wanted to speak to him alone, after the others got off the call. Had one of the other managers stuck around to eavesdrop on his conversation with Judy? Or could it have been someone else entirely? Maybe someone who wasn't authorized to be on the line at all?

Derrick was still thinking about the eavesdropper when he returned the handset of the phone to its cradle. Then, another thought struck him. Shit! He had forgotten to ask about his raise.

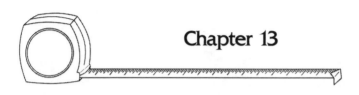

Chapter 13

9:15 AM

Tina Nodzak cursed herself for not being more careful. She should have waited until everyone was off the call before hanging up! What was she thinking?

Listening in on the store managers' call without permission was a ballsy move, but she had weighed the risks against the potential benefit and decided to go for it.

Getting onto the call had been no problem. She'd covered Robert Morrison's position when he'd gone on vacation. She had the phone number, the pass code, and the balls to use them.

She'd known something was wrong when Rob had been terminated without warning. She'd decided to sneak onto the call to find out what the hell was going on. Now, she was more confused than ever.

Despite Judy's half-assed explanation, firing Rob didn't make sense. Sure, they'd had a couple of months of slump, but the store was making sales plan, and the Profits and Loss monthly reports were good. Markdowns were below plan, merchandising initial markup was above plan, and average inventory turns were good too. If things continued as they'd been going, the store was on track for a bonus.

So why the fuck had they fired Rob? She didn't know, but she was damned well going to find out.

Tina had a reputation for being blunt, and she had earned it. A woman had to do whatever it took to get ahead, and Tina was more than willing to play rough.

She hadn't exactly hit pay dirt with the conference call, but there were a few nuggets in there that she could use. And she *would* use them. She was good at turning information into power. That was one of the ways she got ahead.

Anything for an advantage. Well... *Almost* anything... She had never used sex to further her agenda, but then again, she'd never really had the opportunity. Men were not exactly lining up to get her into bed.

She leaned back in her chair and tried to piece together the developments of the past 24 hours. Rob's dismissal was certainly a mystery, and why had Judy promoted this Derrick guy?

As the human resources manager, Tina had access to personnel files. She had read Mr. Derrick Payton's file from cover-to-cover. There was nothing special about him. So, why had they handed him the store on a silver platter?

Tina had been with the company for five years, and she was ready for a shot at running her own store. She knew that she could do it, even if she didn't have the formal experience to back up her self-confidence.

Her entire career had been in human resources, and there weren't many companies willing to put someone with no merchandising background in charge of a home improvement design center.

But that hadn't disqualified her from interviewing for the job twice before. She was smart, she knew how to lead, and she could manage the store better than Rob had. Certainly, she could run it better than this Derrick could.

So she was pissed off that Judy hadn't selected her as a candidate for Rob's position. The DM had completely disregarded Standard Operating Procedure, and hired this other idiot without following the process.

Okay... Maybe Judy had *technically* stayed within the SOP, because Derrick *had* interviewed for store manager within the last 90 days. But Tina had interviewed for store manager too, and so had a number of other assistant managers. That should count for something, right?

As far as Tina was concerned, Judy should have lined up all the recent interviewees, *including Tina*, and interview them all over again for this new position. Then, Judy should have notified all of the candidates who *didn't* get the job, before she announced the name of the new store manager.

But the bitch hadn't done that. She hadn't given Tina a chance.

Ordinarily, this would have been enough to put Judy at the top of the deadly Tina Nodzak shit-list. But Tina couldn't afford to make an enemy of Judy. If Tina was ever going to get her own store, she would need Judy's support. Which put Judy off-limits, for purposes of revenge. For the moment.

Right now, Tina needed to find a way to make the situation work for her. She remembered what Judy had said to Derrick on the call. Store 1254 needed to have better-than-usual sales during the Memorial Day promotion. Judy was trying to prove to the suits at store support that the Encinitas store should remain open, and she was counting on the holiday sales event to do that for her.

That meant the store would be on the radar between now and Monday. It would be an opportunity for someone to get noticed for their contributions in making the event a success.

Tina smiled. Someone could come out of this smelling like a rose. But the someone in question was going to be Ms. Tina Nodzak.

Derrick Payton's days as store manager were numbered. He just didn't know it yet.

Chapter 14

9:20 AM

There was nothing new about thieves scoping out retail stores. In fact, it happened all the time.

Fran spotted the man with the blue jeans and the baseball cap the moment he walked into the contractor department. She wasn't sure how she had recognized him as a thief. But she had a bad feeling about the man, and she had learned to trust her instincts.

Fran had a knack for nabbing shoplifters. Indeed, she had done such a good job of thwarting theft that she was the store's unofficial Loss Prevention Associate. The title was unofficial, because the position had been eliminated some months earlier, when the company had scaled back personnel.

"How may I help you?" Fran asked, when Jean-Man entered the office.

The man tipped the visor of his ball cap. "Just lookin'."

Fran glanced at the clock. "We're not open yet," she said.

"I thought you were open for contractors," Jean-Man replied.

He was right. Regular business hours were 10:00 a.m. to 8:00 p.m., seven days a week. But, Monday through Friday, the store's contractor department was open from 8:00 a.m. to 5:00 p.m., to accommodate the needs of professional installers.

The contractor department was also referred to as *'trade,'* in recognition of the tradesmen who usually shopped there. Each store had a separate entrance for contractors, usually located in front for convenience.

Fran gave the man a doubtful eye. "Are you a contractor?"

Jean-Man nodded. "Uh-huh."

"I don't believe I've dealt with you before," Fran said. "May I have the name of your business?"

Jean-Man paused before answering. "Walker Construction."

His hesitation was not lost on Fran. Neither was his lack of confidence. Contractors tended to be arrogant, and most of them acted as though their shit didn't stink. Time for them was money, and they expected better than average service, especially when they were dropping big bucks for home remodels.

The guy standing before Fran had none of the familiar mannerisms of a contractor.

Fran pulled a binder from the front desk and opened it, taking her time flipping through the pages.

She stopped at a page near the end, and looked up at Jean-Man. "Walker Construction? I don't see the name of your company in our register."

"That's weird," the man said "I've been here lots of times."

Fran doubted that, but she didn't say so. Instead, she pulled a blank registration form from the back of the binder. "Would you care to sign up?"

Jean-Man paused again, and scratched his head. "Well, I'm really in kind of a hurry. I know what I gotta get for my customer, and my boss is waiting at the jobsite."

"If you want contractor privileges and contractor rates, your company is going to have to be registered," Fran said. "And we'll need the licensing number of your company."

Jean-Man hesitated.

For a moment, Fran thought he was going to bolt out of the store. When he didn't, Fran decided to play along for kicks.

"Tell you what," she said. "I'll allow you to come in, on the condition you have your boss come in and register with us."

"I can live with that," Jean-Man said.

As he started walking into the store, Fran called out to him. "Hey! Where do you think you're going?"

Jean-Man stopped in his tracks. "I thought you said it was okay for me to come inside?"

"All customers have to be escorted until we open at 10:00 a.m."

"Why?"

The first thing that came to Fran's mind was, '*because I said so, Dip-shit*,' but she didn't say that.

"It's for safety reasons," she said. "Employees are operating forklifts at this time of morning, and we can't risk having a customer get injured."

Jean-Man frowned at this while Fran walked from around the front desk to take him into the store.

She led him down the aisles. "So, what are you looking for?"

The man shrugged. "I'm just browsing."

"I thought you said your boss was waiting for you at the jobsite?"

Jean-Man lost his composure, but only for a second. "Yeah, that's right. But he asked me to look and see what else you have for some other projects we're working on."

Fran nodded. "I see."

Jesus. This clown must think she'd been born yesterday.

She led him through the store, explaining how *The Design* operated, and how the install and design services worked. She noticed that he paid little attention to what she said. His focus was on the expensive cash-and-carry products on the shelves.

"See anything you like?" asked Fran. She was about a half-second away from calling security.

Jean-Man seemed to like everything he saw. He stopped in the middle of the aisle and reached for a kitchen faucet with a price tag of $400.

"Is that what you need?" Fran asked.

Jean-Man held the box in both hands and nodded. "Oh, yeah."

Then, a smile flashed across Jean-Man's face, and he bolted past Fran, knocking her to the floor as he ran for the emergency exit door.

"Hey! What the fuck do you think you're doing?" Fran screamed.

She scrambled to her feet and ran after the thief. Her voice was loud enough that employees on the other side of the store could hear her.

Jean-Man never looked back. He was nearly to the emergency door when he tripped over a pallet and tumbled across the floor.

Fran gained some ground on him, but the thief was on his feet in an instant and continued his dash for freedom, leaving his left shoe behind.

When he burst through the door, the alarm cut loose with a high-pitched wail that could be heard throughout the building.

Fran reached the door just in time to see Jean-Man jump the fence on the other side of the parking lot, the faucet box tucked under one arm like a football.

The guy had to hop on his right foot to keep his left foot off the rocks and thorns.

Fran snatched his abandoned shoe off the floor and shook it at the retreating thief like some strange kind of weapon. "YOU LITTLE PRICK!" she shouted. "I KNEW YOU WEREN'T A CONTRACTOR!"

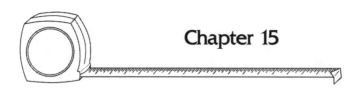

Chapter 15

9:25 AM

What the hell had he done to deserve this? Derrick had already asked himself that question a dozen times, but he couldn't get it out of his mind.

He left his office to walk the sales floor before the store opened, hoping to clear his head. The question wouldn't go away. What the hell had he done to deserve this?

He'd played the waiting game. He hadn't griped when he'd been passed over for promotions—even when the jobs had gone to people who were obviously less qualified. He'd stayed out of trouble, and he had done what he was told. So why the fuck had Judy put him in this situation?

Derrick wanted to know the answer. And he *didn't* want to know. He'd been around long enough to know that companies didn't flip a coin and decide to shut down a store. The CEO and senior suits had been discussing this for months. Maybe years.

So why had they picked him to run a store that was about to be closed?

Derrick wasn't buying Judy's little song and dance about her confidence in his abilities. There were others who were more capable and better prepared for the job, and he knew it.

He could only think of one reason, and he didn't like it. Judy had decided that he was expendable.

What the hell was he going to tell Jen? He'd forgotten to ask for a raise, and now his job was going down the toilet. She was going to *love* this. Especially if she had to go back to work.

"Stay positive," he said aloud. "You have until Monday."

He had until Monday. Big deal! No matter how he looked at the situation, the cards were not in his favor.

Suddenly, the alarm went off. Derrick shook his head and thought; someone probably tripped the emergency door by accident again.

"YOU LITTLE PRICK! I KNEW YOU WEREN'T A CONTRACTOR!"

The shout came from the customer will call pickup department.

Derrick saw a number of associates running in that direction, and he followed them. When he rounded the corner, he saw Fran from trade standing at the open door, spitting out a string of curses.

Fran's face was red with fury. "If I ever see that motherfucker again, I'll kill him! Nobody knocks me down! *Nobody*! Who the fuck does that moron think he is?"

"Are you okay?" asked John from plumbing department.

"Do you need an ambulance?" asked Brian, also from plumbing.

"I'm calling the cops," said Michael in trade.

Derrick immediately took control. "Everybody hold on a second..."

He pushed his way through the circle of associates and faced Fran. "What happened?"

She filled him in on the details, continuing to draw from her elaborate vocabulary of profanity.

When she finished, Derrick asked, "Do you need medical treatment?"

Fran rubbed her knee. "No."

Derrick turned to Michael. "*Now* you can call the police."

When everyone dispersed, Derrick walked Fran back to her department. "I didn't want the others to hear what I have to say," he said, looking over his shoulder to make sure no one was within earshot.

Fran gave him a wary look. "Oh?"

"You know safety SOP, don't you?"

He could tell from the look on her face that she knew where he was going with this. "The company doesn't want us chasing shoplifters."

He paused. "What would've happened if that guy had been armed? What if he had *hurt* you?"

Fran's face flushed. "You think that little prick could hurt me? I dare him to show his face here again! I'll—"

Derrick raised a hand to stop her. "I'll concede that you can probably kick his butt. But that's not the point. This kind of thing could cost you your job. Is that what you want?"

Fran shook her head.

"Well, I don't want you to lose your job either," Derrick said. He reached the door of the trade office and stopped.

Fran's face took on a worried expression. "You're not going to tell loss prevention about this, are you?"

"I have to tell them *something*," replied Derrick. He had no choice. As store manager, it was his responsibility to report the incident. If he didn't, he could be subject to disciplinary action for failing to follow the safety SOP.

Loss prevention was the department in charge of store security, and they'd give him hell, which was the last thing he needed now.

Derrick sighed. "Don't worry," he said. "I know Bob Jacobs, in charge of that department. I'll let him know no harm was done. He'll probably leave it up to me."

A look of relief swept over Fran's face. "Thanks! I can't afford to lose this job."

"Then don't go chasing shoplifters again," Derrick said.

"I won't."

Derrick smiled. "Fair enough."

He turned to go.

"Hey..." Fran said.

Derrick turned back. He saw Fran leaning against the doorway to the trade office. She had a solid athletic frame and an obvious abundance of self-confidence. He knew that she probably *could* have kicked that thief's ass.

"You're not as bad as Robert," she said. "He would have thrown me to the wolves, as sure as you're standing there."

Derrick hadn't been expecting that. "What do you mean?"

"I mean that asshole enjoyed firing people," Fran said. "He wouldn't have hesitated to boot me out the door."

Derrick raised an eyebrow. "Really?"

Fran nodded. "Really."

"Okay," Derrick said. "Then let's be glad he didn't get the chance."

Fran grinned.

Derrick checked his watch. "Looks like, it's almost time for the morning meeting."

"Yeah," Fran said. "See you there."

But Derrick didn't head for the flooring department, where the associates would be assembling for the meeting. Instead, he made a beeline for the human resources office.

Chapter 16

9:45 AM

Derrick closed the door to Tina's office behind himself. What the hell had Fran meant by that?

The voice of Steven Evans blared out of the overhead pager. *"Will everyone please come to the flooring showroom for the morning meeting."*

Derrick checked his watch again. Shit! He didn't have time for this. But maybe he needed to make the time.

He called Steve on his in-store mobile phone. "Steve, I have to take care of something. You hold the meeting, okay?"

Steve's voice was cheerful. "You got it, Boss."

Derrick looked through the drawers of the file cabinet until he found the tab marked *Associate Terminations*. He pulled the first file out and read it silently.

Jorge Mendez—terminated six months ago for failing to follow instructions. Derrick read the box labeled *Explain Extenuating Circumstances*. The entry was short, and clear:

> *'Jorge was asked to assist customers in plumbing and refused to do so. Jorge stated he was a trade associate and his job profile did not require him to work the sales floor. He was again asked to help customers, and again refused. Jorge was then told to clock out and go home.'*

Derrick shook his head. He could never understand why otherwise good workers steadfastly refused to do what they were told.

He thought back to his father's theories on the subject of employment...

'When it comes to work, you're on time or early,' his father had said. 'You are *never* late. It takes more effort to be late to work than it does to be on time.'

His dad had been equally blunt about doing what you were supposed to do. He'd heard his father say it a hundred times... 'You have a boss for a reason. The boss says, and you do. It's no more complicated than that.'

But his father had shared the work ethic of a bygone generation. These days, coming to work on time and following instructions was not as important as stopping by the *Cafecito* coffee stand at the Carlsbad Library, while texting friends and downloading the latest music on your phone.

Derrick wondered how long the current crop of workers would have remained employed in his father's day. But there was no point in dwelling on that.

He turned his attention back to the Jorge Mendez file. He scanned down the page until he spotted the name of the manager involved in the altercation. Robert Morrison.

Seriously? An associate had refused to do what the store manager asked him to do, and didn't think he'd lose his job over it? Was that balls? Or just plain stupidity?

Derrick pulled out another file. Kari Majors—a twenty-something designer who hadn't been making her sales goal. She'd been given three separate warnings over the course of six months. She had never improved her sales, so she had been let go. Derrick read the name of the manager who terminated the woman. Again, it was Rob Morrison. Derrick wondered why Debbie hadn't handled the termination. She was the project manager, so it should have been her responsibility, not Rob's.

Derrick opened a file belonging to a Michael Jackson—no relation to the deceased singer—fired for excessive tardiness and absences.

The next two files were more associates who'd been let go for the same reason. Again, Rob had handled the terminations, in place of the assistant managers.

That was odd... Most store managers preferred to give the okay to terminate, when there was sufficient cause and the human resources department concurred. But the actual terminations were deferred to assistant managers.

"Why would Rob do the firing himself?" Derrick asked aloud.

"Because he was the manager," said the voice from behind.

Derrick turned around so fast he nearly gave himself whiplash. "Tina... I didn't hear you come in."

Tina eyed Derrick and the files he was examining. "You seem surprised to see me," she said, calmly. "This is my office."

Derrick caught the air of superiority in her tone. This bitch really did think she was queen of the fucking palace.

"I'm aware that it's your office," he said in his most authoritative and self-confident tone. "I simply didn't hear you come in."

Tina's body language and expression showed quite clearly that she didn't like him coming into her office unannounced.

Her eyes narrowed a fraction. "Anything I can help you with?"

Derrick went back to flipping through the files. "No. I'm finding what I want."

The awkward silence between them held for about thirty seconds, then Tina spoke again. "Why don't you tell me what you're looking for? Maybe I can help."

Derrick was certain that Tina had no desire to help. She just wanted to know what he was up to.

He did a quick scan off a half-dozen more files, then he held the folders out to Tina.

"I notice from these files that Rob handled the actual terminations of associates, instead of the assistant managers. Do you know why?"

Tina took the offered folder's. "Rob was store manager," she said flatly. "He could do whatever he wanted."

Derrick wasn't buying that. "I haven't met a manager yet who didn't delegate that task to assistant managers."

And it was true. You handled more than enough job terminations as an assistant manager. When you made it to store manager, you were happy to delegate that chore to your subordinates.

Tina put the files back in the cabinet, and closed the drawer a little too forcefully. "Rob is gone, so I guess we'll never know why he didn't choose to delegate terminations. Of course, you can always call and *ask* him."

No, Derrick wasn't going to ask Rob. But he could ask Tina...

"The word on the floor is that Rob actually *enjoyed* firing people," Derrick said. He paused to gauge her reaction. "Did you ever get that impression?"

"I never pay much attention to rumors," Tina said. Her tone suggested that *real* managers did not engage in petty shop floor gossip.

Once again, she was trying to put Derrick on the defensive. He decided to turn the tables, by giving *her* something to think about for a change.

He raised an eyebrow. "I'm surprised to hear you say that. I learned a long time ago that smart managers pay attention to what their people say and do."

He flashed Tina a sly grin. "If you don't know what your people are talking about, you're not going to be ready for what happens *next*..."

Before Tina could respond, he walked out of her office, closing the door behind himself.

That should keep her busy for a while.

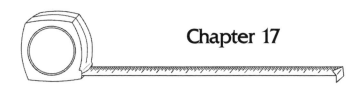

Chapter 17

10:00 AM

A score of customers rushed in, pushing carts and talking on cell phones. Some brought children, warning them to stay close and not to wander. Others talked with their new best friend, a designer paid by the hour. Most were women. (Sixty percent of home improvement customers were female.) And all were on a mission to get what they wanted, without paying through the nose.

Teresa had been with *The Design* since leaving the grocery business after twenty years of service. The 2003 employee union strike had soured her opinion of the grocery industry, so she'd gone looking for a career change.

She was an experienced cashier, and *The Design* had snapped her up without hesitation. In less than a year, she'd been promoted to front end supervisor (or FES, in the acronym-happy company).

As usual, she was the first person to arrive in her department. She looked around the registers and in the returns office, but she couldn't find anyone.

Where the hell were her cashiers? Why was it so damned hard to get people to show up on time?

Teresa generally enjoyed her position as FES, but keeping the registers fully staffed to customer demand was a nightmare. She honestly tried to accommodate the personal schedules of her cashiers, but it wasn't always possible to give everyone the exact shifts and hours that they wanted to work. And when she finally got a workable schedule hammered out, someone would call in sick because they wanted the day off.

But Teresa couldn't really blame her team for their lack of devotion. When you pay people shit, you can expect to get shit in return.

It didn't help that the company treated the cashiers differently from everyone else. SOP for cashiers was the strictest in the company. A sales associate or a designer could make an error that would cost the store thousands of dollars. Their punishment would be a verbal warning, or—at worst—an annotation in their personnel file. But let a cashier come up five lousy bucks short on the till, and it was *game over*.

Cashiers rarely got to take their breaks or go to lunch on time, because nobody cared enough about them to make sure they were relieved on schedule. Managers were slow to respond to calls for an approval at the register. When a cashier called for a price check, employees often pretended not to hear. And they *never* had enough help at the front end registers.

It was hard for Teresa to condemn her cashiers for not being enthusiastic. They didn't have much to be enthusiastic *about*.

Samantha was sipping her latte at the cash register, when she was approached by an elderly customer.

The company had an SOP prohibiting food and drink on the sales floor, but the associates could usually ignore the no-food rule with relative safety. As long as Samantha didn't wave her *Starbucks* cup in everyone's faces, she could get away with the occasional latte.

The old man dropped a large rectangular box on the counter. "I'm in a hurry. Can you ring me up now?" He was breathing heavily, from having dashed inside the store when the doors first opened so that he could get what he was looking for, and be on his way.

Samantha set her coffee cup next to her keyboard. She lifted the box, and saw that it was a kitchen faucet.

"Good morning, sir," she said, cheerfully. "Did you find everything you were looking for?"

"Yes," the customer said. "This is all I need, and I'm in a big hurry." He was still breathing heavily.

Samantha located the UPC tag on the box, and swept it over the barcode scanner in her counter top. "Got a big day ahead of you?"

"I've got to get back to the job site," the man said. "*Now*."

The scanner failed to produce its usual beep.

Samantha waved the box past the scanner three or four more times. Nothing.

She flipped the box over, and punched the UPC numbers into the register keyboard by hand. Still, nothing. The register did not acknowledge the item.

Samantha reached for the phone and dialed three numbers, allowing her access to the overhead pager. "Can I have a plumbing associate come to the front end for a price check, please? I need an associate in plumbing to the front end, please."

"I don't have time for this!" the customer growled. Beads of sweat rolled down his forehead, and his eyes were filled with desperation.

"I'm sorry, sir," Samantha said. "But the tag isn't working. I need an associate for a price check."

"How long is this going to take?"

Samantha smiled. "Just a couple of minutes, sir."

She knew that probably wasn't true. More than likely, the guys in plumbing had ignored her page. They usually did.

But the delay was much shorter than she expected. A few minutes later, a middle-aged man came ambling to the front. It was John from plumbing, who had helped the customer find the faucet he was looking for.

"The faucet you gave me isn't registering," the customer said. "And I need to leave, *now*."

John rubbed the back of his neck. "Is that right?"

John was a retired plumber, working part-time. He frequently told people that he needed to get out of the house a few days every week, to keep his nagging wife from driving him crazy. But his coworkers agreed that John's wife was the lucky one, having him out of the house those few days.

John picked up the box. "Let's have a look," he said.

He read the UPC numbers to Samantha, and she entered them on her keyboard. The register still did not recognize the code.

Samantha looked at him and shook her head.

John had Samantha enter an alternative set of numbers he had memorized, but the register failed to acknowledge the new code as well.

The customer pounded his fist on the station. "Do you people not understand that I'm in a hurry?"

John straightened. "We understand, sir, but there's no need for alarm. I'll go back and get you a different box."

"How long is this going to take?" the customer demanded.

"Not long," John replied. "I'll be back in a few minutes."

The customer snorted. "How many minutes is a *few*?"

John stopped in his tracks, and turned to face the customer. "Let me put it this way," he said. "It will take me longer to stand here and discuss this, than it will take me to actually go get the box."

He paused, to see if the man was going to respond. "Is that fair enough?"

The customer's face turned red, but he didn't say anything.

John returned inside of three minutes, with a new box for Samantha.

She ran it across the scanner, and the register sprang to life. She sighed with relief. "That'll be $353.76 with tax."

The customer held out a credit card.

As Samantha reached for the card, her sleeve brushed against the cup of latte. The cup tipped onto its side, its contents spilling into the keyboard and the register.

The machine made a series of violent popping noises, and sparks shot from the ventilation louvers at its back. A thin ribbon of blue smoke rose into the air, and the register went dark.

Chapter 18

10:15 AM

Derrick was walking through the appliance showroom when the overhead lights flickered.

Customers and associates stopped what they were doing and looked up toward the ceiling, anticipating a power failure. Then the lights steadied, and everyone went back to what they were doing.

Derrick wondered about the momentary power surge. He had enough problems. He didn't need the lights to go out, and he certainly didn't need the expense of electrical repairs.

Operating costs were death on the profits and loss reports, and store support questioned *every* expense, no matter how small. As long as you stayed within your operating budget, no one questioned your performance. But the budget was so low that you had nothing to work with, even for legitimate expenses.

Derrick's friend, Kevin Adams, had lost his job for approving a work request to upgrade the electrical breakers in the seasonal department. *The Design* in Monrovia had working waterfall displays on the seasonal showroom floor, and city building code required businesses to use ground breakers in all electrical outlets.

The bill was $600 over budget, and when the next quarterly audit came around, the company had terminated Kevin for not getting the district asset protection manager's approval.

Approving the work order was a city code requirement, and it fell clearly within the safety responsibilities of the ops manager. Kevin had protected the company from building code fines that would have cost a lot more than $600. That didn't matter.

Kevin might also have saved the company from a major lawsuit, if (heaven forbid) a customer had been injured by an unprotected outlet in close proximity to running water. That didn't matter either. What mattered was that Kevin had gone over budget without approval. End of story.

After he'd gotten the pink slip, Kevin had called Derrick to tell him about the entire mess, including his termination.

"That's ridiculous," Derrick had said. "If you had approached the asset manager, he wouldn't have had a choice. He'd *have* to approve the upgrade, to keep the company operating within the law."

Kevin had chuckled bitterly. "Yep," he said. "But they fired me anyway."

"That's ridiculous," Derrick had said again.

"No," Kevin had said. "That's *retail*."

And Kevin had been right. That was life in the world of retail.

When he entered the décor showroom floor, Derrick noticed a number of customers browsing through the displays. This area had vignettes of draperies and window shades, all of the latest design and fashion.

Where *was* everyone? Several of the customers were obviously looking around for assistance, but the associates for this department were nowhere to be seen.

Derrick pulled out his in-store mobile phone, to dial the number for overhead paging.

Before he could punch in the code, he saw Emily, the store's phone operator, hurrying toward him.

Her face was ashen and she was visibly trembling. "Derrick, I need to talk to you!"

"What's wrong?"

She opened her mouth to speak, but she seemed to be struggling to find words.

"Take your time," Derrick said. "No hurry."

Emily swallowed heavily, and tried again. "It's Keith... Or, rather, it's Keith's *wife*..."

Derrick waited for Emily to continue.

Emily swallowed again. "Keith's wife called the store, looking for him. And I told her Keith wasn't answering his phone, because he was helping customers."

Derrick nodded.

Emily grimaced. "Then, his wife started yelling at me..." Emily stopped in mid-sentence, unable to continue.

"It's okay," Derrick said. "What did Keith's wife say?"

Emily took a deep breath and exhaled. "She said she knows that Keith is fucking Hannah. And she's going to come to the store, and put a stop to it."

Whatever Derrick had been expecting, this was *not* it. How the hell was he supposed to respond to *this*?

Emily stood watching him, waiting for the all-powerful store manager to tell her what to do.

Derrick nodded to her. "Thanks, Emily. You can go back to the phone room. I'll take care of it."

Emily scurried away, obviously happy to be absolved of any responsibility for the train wreck that was about to happen.

Derrick looked around for one of the other managers. They'd been working with Keith and Hannah for a lot longer than Derrick had. Why hadn't one of them spotted this situation, and done something about it before it turned into a problem?

But none of the assistant managers were around, and it was too late to head off the problem now. The best Derrick could hope for was damage control.

Hannah was supposed to be here, in décor, but she obviously wasn't. Keith was supposed to be in flooring, the next department over. Derrick walked that way, in the hopes of finding Keith.

But when Derrick walked into the flooring department, no associates were in sight. He saw two female customers walking from vignette to vignette, glancing at tile displays hanging on the wall.

Shit! Keith's wife could be here any minute. Derrick had to find Keith, so that he could stop his wife from making a scene.

Derrick hurried toward the outdoor furniture department. Some of the associates liked to hang out there on breaks, because the illumination from the skylights and the ambience of the displays created a comfortable environment. It was a nice place to relax.

As he passed the supply closet between flooring and décor, Derrick heard a high-pitched whimper. He looked around, unable to pinpoint the source of the noise. Then, he heard it again. It was coming from the supply closet.

Derrick Jerked opened the door, and froze at the sight before him.

Keith and Hannah were locked in a bone-crushing embrace, kissing violently. Hannah's dress was hiked up above her waist, and Keith's hands were inside her panties, fondling her buttocks.

They were so wrapped up in their moment of passion that they didn't notice Derrick at all.

He cleared his throat loudly, and the two lovers jerked away from each other, as though they had both received a jolt from a cattle prod.

Hannah snatched the hem of her dress down, hiding her panty-clad butt.

Keith's eyes were bulging with shock. He wiped his hands over his apron. "Derrick! I was helping Hannah with—"

Derrick cut him off. "Never mind! I need to see you. *Now!*"

Hannah squeezed past Derrick, and out the door of the closet. "I'll... I'll be getting back to the desk..."

Her voice was shaky with fear and embarrassment. She completely avoided all eye contact with Derrick.

Keith stood there squirming. "I know what this looks like," he said, fumbling for words. "I promise, it won't happen again."

"You are one crazy mother f..." Derrick stopped himself from finishing the sentence.

He took a calming breath. "Do you have any idea how much shit you're in? Your wife is on her way to the store right now, to kick your ass!"

"I'm s-s-sorry," Keith stammered.

Derrick raised a hand to silence him. "Tell that to your wife. She'll be here any second. And if she's going to kill you, she had damned well better not do it in my store."

Keith stood motionless, as though his brain had just shut down. He looked like a kid who was told there is no such thing as Santa Claus.

Once upon a time, Derrick would've felt sorry for a guy like Keith. He understood male urges, because he had them himself. He also knew exactly what it felt like when you weren't getting enough at home. And it didn't help that Hannah was a flirtatious gal with a body meant for pole-dancing.

But none of those things excused Keith's behavior. Urges aside, when you put the little head in charge of your decision-making process, you were screwed. Literally.

Sure, Derrick had been tempted more than once. But he'd seen what happened to guys who gave in to the temptation. He'd seen guys with perfect wives throw everything away for a one-shot roll in the hay.

First, you got thrown out of your own house. Then, your wife hired some bloodthirsty lawyer to take away the kids, the car, the bank account, and the house that you were no longer welcome in. She got everything, and your only reward was the chance to pay alimony and child support.

No thanks! Derrick was *not* going down that road. Not for anything, and *definitely* not for a quick grope session in the supply closet.

If Keith was stupid enough to jeopardize his family and his entire quality of life, he deserved whatever he got.

"You'd better get outside to meet your wife," Derrick said. "I'm not kidding. If there's going to be an incident, it's *not* going to happen in this store. Is that clear?"

Keith nodded. He walked out the door, leaving Derrick alone in the closet.

Derrick whistled softly through his teeth. Damn! He shouldn't have to deal with shit like this.

And he hadn't even gotten a raise.

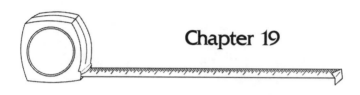

Chapter 19

10:30 AM

Derrick walked the sales floor to make sure his associates were engaging with the customers.

He remembered Judy's words from the conference call. "Be sure your people are approaching customers, and greeting them with a smile."

Yeah... Like *that* wasn't completely obvious.

But Judy had shared other pearls of wisdom... "When our associates are trying to close the sale, don't let them focus on price, because that's not what it's about. People come to us because they *want* to shop here. People visit our stores because they want to be trend-setters. Price shouldn't be the issue."

All of that sounded fine, but it was essentially bullshit. Derrick knew the score. Sure, people shopped *The Design* because they wanted better-than-average products, but that didn't mean they wanted to part with their money. The company went out of its way to advertise that it had the lowest prices in town. So naturally, people balked at high prices, even when the product was labeled with a high-end vendor name.

The Design was stocked with low, medium, and high-end kitchen and bath fixtures. It was necessary to carry the full price range, in order to be competitive. Unfortunately, customers wanted to buy *high*-end items at *low*-end prices. This attitude wasn't realistic, but it was common nevertheless.

Prices on the web were sometimes half of what you could find in a brick and mortar store. So it wasn't surprising that more and more potential customers were starting to do their shopping online.

The only saving grace for the industry was the level of customer service (or lack thereof) offered by many internet outlets. The early swing toward online shopping had slowed down somewhat when web customers began sharing horror stories about their experiences on the internet.

Apparently, companies selling online made it difficult for customers to return products. Many websites promised hassle-free returns, but those promises turned out to be mostly empty air when products arrived in damaged condition, or when the customer made a mistake in ordering. Which, as far as Derrick was concerned, proved the old saying that you get what you pay for.

Eventually, the industry had tried to rebalance itself by introducing MAPP pricing. Minimum Advertised Pricing Policy prevented online retailers from offering products at prices too low for brick and mortar retailers to compete with. Some vendors went so far as to void the warranty for any of their products that were purchased online.

The customers also returned to the stores to enjoy one-on-one relationships with employees. If a customer had a question, a store associate could usually answer it. If there was a problem, the associate could correct it.

Okay, that last part was a stretch. In reality, the associates rarely corrected the problems. Instead, they bumped the issue upstairs to Derrick, which meant that most problems automatically became *his* problems.

Not that he was complaining. He knew that was part of the store manager's job, and he had to accept the bad parts along with the good parts. Although, come to think of it, he hadn't actually *seen* any of the good yet. He was no longer fully convinced that there *were* any good parts to this job.

And there he was with the negative thoughts again. He really needed to concentrate on some positive thinking.

There was one good sign, at least. From the number of customers in the store, this was going to be a busy day. The people were here. Now, all his team had to do was close the sale.

Unfortunately, closing the sale was a major challenge for some associates. It was hard to make them understand that people shopping in their store actually *wanted* to spend their money here.

He remembered an orientation speech he'd given to a bunch of new hires at the Kearny Mesa store. He'd given the new employees an example, to illustrate the point. "Let's pretend that you've just taken a job as a salesperson at a high-end jewelry store," he'd said. "I mean the kind of place that carries sixty-thousand dollar engagement rings. You're the newest member of the sales force, drawing a starting salary, plus commission. Do you think you can afford to buy every item that your store carries?"

The newbies had shaken their heads in unison.

"Some of the jewelry in that store may be within your budget," Derrick had said. "But a lot of the merchandise will be well outside of your price range."

The new hires had nodded.

Derrick had nodded as well. "You won't be able to drop a half-million bucks on an emerald necklace. Don't feel too bad, because I can't do it either. My house costs less than that, and I had to take out a thirty year mortgage to buy it."

This had brought low-key laughter from the new employees.

Derrick had smiled in return. "But there are people who *can* afford to buy the high-end jewelry in our imaginary store. And those customers will come to that store, looking to buy things which you or I can't possibly afford."

Derrick had paused, to let the idea sink in.

"It's no different at *The Design*," he had said. "We can't afford to buy some of the high-end items we carry. But that doesn't mean our *customers* can't afford them. So, we can't let the price of an item prevent us from asking for the sale."

Derrick thought it had been a fairly good speech, and the jewelry store example had seemed to get the message across. He might need to use it here, to help some of his associates get over the price barrier, in closing the sale.

But the irony the associates felt was real. There was something strange about selling things you couldn't afford to buy for yourself. Strange, and sad…

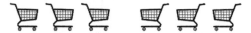

Derrick entered the appliance showroom and saw a short, stocky, fiftyish man, sitting at a desk and looking over paperwork.

Derrick approached the desk. "Morning."

The stocky man glanced up. "How ya doin'?" He didn't bother rising from his chair.

So much for manners.

Derrick stuck out his hand to be shaken. "Good to meet you. I'm Derrick Payton, the new store manager."

Stocky Man set down his ink pen with some reluctance, and shook the offered hand. "Walter," he said.

Apparently, it was too much effort to say his full name.

"I introduced myself to most of the associates at the morning meeting yesterday," Derrick said. "But I don't think I saw you there."

Walter picked up his pen. "I had prep work for an appointment with a client who was looking to buy an appliance package."

He looked down at the paperwork on his desk, as if it was so urgent that he could barely spare a few seconds to talk with the store manager. It was a not-too-subtle way of telling Derrick not to bother him.

Derrick had missed the morning meeting himself today, because of his exploration of the termination files in Tina's office. But he was ready to bet his last dollar that Walter had missed the meeting too.

Derrick decided to find out. "I don't think you were at the morning meeting today, either," he said. "Another meeting with a client?"

"Yes," Walter said. "I'm expecting him any minute now. I'm wrapping up the paperwork now."

Another not-too-subtle hint that Derrick was wasting his time.

When an associate repeatedly came up with reasons not to attend the morning meeting, it usually meant they didn't care much for team spirit, recognizing the efforts of others, and working together. Walter was beginning to look like a follower of the Lone Ranger-theory: sell as much as you can, any way you can, and grab all the entitlements you can lay your hands on. Lone Rangers figured that—as long as they met or exceeded their sales plan—the management team would leave them alone.

This was true to a point. The CEO, VPs, DMs, merchants, and shareholders all cared about one thing, and one thing only. *Sales!* Team spirit was lovely, but it didn't do them any good if the sales numbers weren't there.

Unfortunately, some of the most successful sales personnel were great at moving merchandise, but sucked when it came to building synergy. This made them good for the store's profit margin in the narrow sense, but bad for the overall culture and effectiveness of the store.

Walter's attention was buried in his paperwork again.

Derrick got the feeling that Walter might be one of those prima donnas who are more detrimental to positive change than they're worth. But he shouldn't be so quick to judge. He'd only just met Walter, and for all he knew, Walter could be one of the finest examples of professionalism in the entire company.

He decided to give Walter the benefit of the doubt. He sat in the chair on the opposite side of the desk. "What type of project is your client working on?"

Walter lifted his head, clearly irritated by Derrick's continued presence. "It's a trade customer," he said. He returned his attention to the spreadsheet on his desk.

Before Derrick could ask another question, an elderly lady and a young couple walked into the showroom and began looking at the appliances on display.

"We've got customers," Derrick said in a low tone. "You help the elderly woman and I'll help the couple."

Walter continued working on his spreadsheet, as though Derrick hadn't spoken.

Derrick cleared his throat and spoke more forcefully. "Walter, you have a *customer*. Go help her."

Walter paused with his pen still on the spreadsheet, and looked up at Derrick. "I told you, I have to finish this paperwork before my client arrives this morning."

"That was before you had a customer enter your department," Derrick said, speaking like a school master to a troublesome student. "Go and help her."

Walter huffed and dropped his hands on the desk loudly. "*Fine.*"

He stood up and stalked over to the customer.

'Glad to have you on the team,' Derrick said silently. 'I can tell you really love your job.'

Chapter 20

10:45 AM

Nancy was the supervisor over trade. When Derrick entered her department for the first time, she met him with her hand extended and a smile on her face "Hi. Welcome to our store."

Derrick shook her hand. "Thank you. It's nice to meet you." He was relieved to see someone appear genuinely happy to have him on the team.

Nancy took a few moments to introduce her staff. There was Dan, the hardware and plumbing specialist; Vanessa, who oversaw flooring clients; Michael, who handled the design customers; and Cassie, who expedited their orders.

Derrick was impressed by the professionalism of the associates in Nancy's department. At the wages the company offered, it wasn't always easy to hire qualified people, so this was refreshing. These people were actually smiling at him—a nice change from his first encounter with Lanky Man.

"I've heard a lot about you and your team," Derrick said. "You've enjoyed an exceptional rate of success with contractors and designers."

Nancy blushed.

"What's your secret?" Derrick asked.

Nancy reflected before answering. "Our biggest success has been reaching out to the business community, and explaining how we can help with their project needs. We don't wait for the business to come to us; we visit their shop to let them know who we are. We also work closely with the rest of the store and the operations staff, to ensure that we have their support to expedite projects."

She was about to say something else, but a thirtyish man walked into the office. He wore jeans, a T-shirt, and a very sour expression on his face.

Nancy recognized him as a regular trade customer, and excused herself to go speak to him.

As with Derrick, she approached the man with a smile. "Mr. Cooper, how are you?"

Mr. Cooper didn't return the smile. "Not too good."

Everyone looked up, to hear what else the man had to say.

"You didn't deliver my order this morning, and the delay is holding up my job. And I want you to know that this delay is costing me money."

Vanessa rose from her desk and walked over. "I scheduled the flooring to be delivered at 8:00 a.m. sharp. They didn't show up?"

Mr. Cooper answered irritably, "If they had, I wouldn't be here."

Derrick stood in the back, observing the situation.

Vanessa mumbled something and returned to her desk, where she quickly picked up the phone and dialed a number.

Nancy turned to the contractor, apologized and assured him they would do everything they could to find out what was going on with his delivery.

She flashed a pleasant smile. "I'm sure the delay is temporary, but we'll get down to the bottom of this."

Unfortunately, her charms were not going to work today. Mr. Cooper was out for blood.

"This is the umpteenth time you people have let me down," he said, loudly. "You people are killin' me! What's it going to take to get service around here? Every time you fail to make a delivery, it holds up the job and costs me money."

Derrick knew what was coming next...

"What are you going to do to make this right?"

Derrick stifled a laugh. He'd seen at least a hundred variations of this scenario. Whenever there was any sort of an issue, the customer would exaggerate the problem, to justify a fat discount.

Nancy took a deep breath. "Mr. Cooper, I'm sorry about the delay. But to my understanding, this is the first time we've failed to get a delivery to you on schedule."

'Good for you,' said Derrick, silently.

"Don't make me laugh," the contractor snapped. "I've had problems here since you opened this store. Deliveries don't show up, product arrives damaged, or you guys order the wrong produced entirely."

"And we always make it right by getting you what you need to complete the job," said Nancy.

The contractor shook his head. "That's not the point! I shouldn't be put through this inconvenience. Last night, I received a message from one of my customers. The exhaust on her range hood blower isn't working, so now I have to make a special trip to find out what the problem is. This costs me more time, and money. Is that so hard to understand?"

Derrick resisted the temptation to roll his eyes. This guy was a dick.

Nancy was beginning to show signs of losing her patience. "Mr. Cooper, you've been in the business for years."

"Damn right I have."

"Then you know that problems crop up," Nancy said. "They're an unavoidable part of the home improvement business. But you *also* know that we'll work with you to resolve them. That's what set us apart from the competition."

"Not when it costs me money," the contractor said. "I want to know what you're going to do to make this right."

Derrick was rapidly growing tired of this guy's abrasive personality. He was just about ready to toss this Mr. Cooper out on his ear.

Nancy sighed. "I can offer you a discount on your next purchase," she said.

The contractor gave a sarcastic laugh. "I don't *want* a discount on my next purchase. What I want is to be reimbursed for my crew's lost wages."

Nancy shook her head. "Mr. Cooper, we can't pay wages for your crew. Vanessa will find out how soon the delivery can be made for the flooring, and we'll contact the vendor for the range hood blower and ensure that they replace any defective parts. And I can offer you a discount on a future purchase. That's about all I can do."

"That's ridiculous!" the contractor snapped. "This is *your* mistake, but it's costing *me* money! I want to speak to the store manager!"

Nancy turned and pointed to Derrick. "He's standing right there."

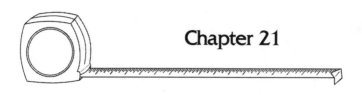

Chapter 21

11:00 AM

Derrick answered his in-store mobile phone, relieved to have an excuse to interrupt Mr. Cooper's ongoing tirade. "This is Derrick."

"Hi, Derrick, this is Sheila at special services," said the voice on the other end of the line. "We have a customer requesting to speak with the manager. Are you free to speak to her?"

Hell yes, he was free.

"Yes," Derrick said. "I'll be right there."

He hung up the phone and turned to face the contractor. "Sorry, but I have a scheduled appointment with another client." He lied with a straight face, an ability that drove his wife crazy.

He finished by saying, "Nancy and Vanessa will follow-up on your delivery issues." Then, he turned to leave.

Mr. Cooper flashed him an incredulous look. "You're leaving? What about *me*? I'm a customer too, *right*?"

"Of course you are," Derrick said. "And we value your business, Mr. Cooper. But Nancy and Vanessa were handling your situation perfectly before I got involved. They're tracking down your delivery, and making arrangements to take care of the defective range hood blower. Nancy has offered you a generous discount off your next order."

Derrick patted his shirt pocket. "I have your number here, and I'll call you to discuss this further if you like. But, frankly, I don't see what else there is to say on the matter. Nancy and Vanessa have listened carefully to your complaints, and they've taken every reasonable step to correct the problems."

Derrick nodded toward Nancy. "It was nice meeting you and your team," he said. He faced Mr. Cooper again. "And it was nice meeting you too, Mr. Cooper."

And then, Derrick made his exit from the trade department.

Mr. Cooper glared at Derrick's receding back, and sneered, "What the hell kind of manager is *that?*"

Nancy didn't say what was on her mind. He was *her* kind of manager.

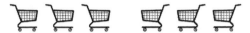

The special services desk was located in the center of the store. It was staffed by three associates, who processed special orders for sales associates and customers.

Derrick rounded the corner from bath showroom, and stopped dead in his tracks. Standing at the service desk was the most obscenely dressed, sixty-something woman he'd ever seen. Her skin was pale and her body was skeletal, with hardly any meat on her bones. She wore a blond afro-style wig twice the size of a basketball, and her oversized breast implants were nearly as large. They stood out like two mountains, her nipples practically poking through her blouse. And her too-short skirt was skin tight, revealing the outline of a G-string.

The woman spotted Derrick and locked eyes with him.

"I'm ba-a-a-a-a-ack," she said—in the same cheesy manner that late night TV hosts are so fond of.

Derrick had never seen the woman before, and he wondered what he had done to deserve an introduction now. Was she deliberately trying to look like a skank? Or did she actually think she was attractive?

He held out his hand to shake hers.

The Chihuahua in the crook of the woman's elbow nipped at the offered hand, narrowly missing Derrick's fingers.

Derrick snatched his hand away from the snapping teeth.

"Careful," the woman said. "You don't want to upset Chewy."

Derrick shook his head. "No. Of course not."

The dog was about the size of a rat, and she patted it affectionately. "I named him after my third hubby," she said in a scratchy voice. "He left me the most, when he died last year."

Derrick frowned in confusion. "The *most?*"

The woman gave Derrick a seductive smile. "Wouldn't *you* like to know?"

Oh God. This woman had trouble written all over her.

Derrick cleared his throat. "How can I help you?"

"I'm Rosalyn," the woman said, "and I am *not* a happy camper."

She rubbed her right eye with her free hand as she spoke, and when she looked back at Derrick, her blue contact lens was no longer covering her eye.

"Oh phooey," Rosalyn said. "My contact has rolled under my eyelid again."

She put Chewy on the special service desk counter, tilted her head back, and rolled the tip of one forefinger over her eyeball.

Derrick glanced around. Every associate and customer within earshot had apparently stopped to watch this little drama unfold.

Derrick made eye contact with Sheila, who shrugged.

He turned back to Rosalyn. "Do you need some help? Perhaps one of our ladies here can lead you to the women's restroom."

"Nope," Rosalyn said. "That won't be necessary."

She spent several more seconds groping for the errant lens. Then, she turned toward Derrick. Her left eye was still blue; her right eye—devoid of its contact lens—was brown.

"Do you have contact drops?" she asked.

"I'm sorry," answered Derrick. "I don't wear contact lenses."

Sheila came to the rescue. "Here's some," she said, handing over a tiny bottle she pulled out of her purse.

Rosalyn tilted her head back again, poured a few drops in her eye. She pulled back her eyelid with one hand, and rolled a forefinger over her eyeball again.

Everyone looked on in silence, as though a delicate surgery was taking place in the middle of the store.

A moment later Rosalyn held up her hand. "Success!," she shouted, in that same scratchy voice.

A few nearby customers clapped feebly.

Rosalyn took an exaggerated bow. "Thank you, my loyal subjects. Thank you all..."

She picked up Chewy, ignoring the fact that her insect of a dog had peed on a stack of papers.

"Now," Rosalyn said. "Let's get down to business."

Derrick gestured for her to continue.

"I purchased two under-counter glass bowls for my master bath," said Rosalyn, "and one of them has a crack in it. I know, because there was a puddle of water in my cabinet this morning."

Derrick pointed to the circle of dog urine on the papers. "Are you sure that Chewy didn't make the puddle? As a friendly surprise?"

Rosalyn glared at Derrick. "I'll have you know," she said, "that Chewy is perfectly housebroken."

Derrick didn't bother pointing out that the dog's perfect housebreaking didn't seem to extend to store counters.

"I'm glad to hear that," Derrick said. "If you'll follow me to one of our consultation rooms, we can sit down and discuss how to resolve this."

Rosalyn shook her head. "Oh, *no*. We'll discuss it out *here*, where everyone can see and hear us. That way, if you try to give me the brush-off, your other customers will all know."

The nearby customers applauded again, louder this time.

Great. He was dealing with a regular Zsa Zsa Gabor.

Derrick nodded. "Certainly, we can talk out here if you prefer. So, how may I be of assistance?"

"I told you," Rosalyn said. "One of the glass sink bowls in my master bath has a crack. And I want to know what you're going to do about it."

Derrick turned to Sheila. "Do you have a copy of her sales order?"

"Yep," answered Sheila, handing it over to him across the counter. "Don't worry," she said. "It's dry."

Derrick gave her an I-don't-have-time-for-jokes look, and accepted the paper. He read it carefully. Then, he read it again.

"I'm not sure I understand," he said. "You purchased these fixture more than two years ago?"

Rosalyn stiffened. "Yes. What does *that* have to do with anything?"

Derrick examined the sales order again. "Rosalyn, these fixtures have a one year warranty, to cover defects in manufacture. If your bowl was defective, it would have started leaking a few minutes after it was installed. Maybe a few days, at the most."

He looked into the woman's fake-blue eyes. "In any case, the warranty expired more than a year ago. There's no way the vendor is going to pay to replace this bowl."

"I'm not talking to the vendor," Rosalyn said. "I'm talking to *you*! I paid $1,500 for each of these glass bowls, as you can see."

She flicked at the edge of the work order with one of her long acrylic fingernails. "A bowl that costs $1,500 should last longer than two years, don't you think?"

What Derrick *thought*, was that the doctor had given this bony bimbo an overdose of valium.

He was absolutely positive that the vendor would wash its hands of this matter. For all the vendor knew, the customer dropped something in the bowl, and cracked it herself. In view of Rosalyn's general lack of physical (and emotional) stability, Derrick figured that she probably *had* broken the bowl.

But he didn't want the other customers to see him throw this back into her lap.

"Come on," he said. "Let's see if anything can be done."

Rosalyn's overdone face-lifted face cracked into a smile, and she moved too close to Derrick, as though she wanted to get cozy with him. "I knew we'd get along, right from the start."

She wrapped her free arm around Derrick's. "You know what they say... The customer is *always* right."

Derrick managed a half-hearted smile.

He would love to hire the idiot who had dreamed up that stupid saying, just so he could have the pleasure of *firing* the brainless bastard.

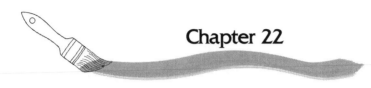

Chapter 22

11:30 AM

Where did these people come from? Derrick had no idea, but the more he considered the question, the more he realized that he was better off not knowing the answer. He really didn't *want* to know what hole these nutcases crawled out of.

Derrick went over the options in his head. Well, he didn't actually *have* any options. Rosalyn's cracked lavatory bowl was more than a year out of warranty. There was exactly zero chance that the vendor would step up to replace it.

Which meant that Derrick would have to eat the cost of ordering another bowl, along with the cost of removal and reinstallation. What choice did he have? If he wanted this has-been trophy wife out of his life, he was going to have to give her whatever she wanted.

So, he sat in the consultation room, made a few phone calls, and took care of the arrangements.

Ten minutes later, Rosalyn and Chewy the Wonder Dog were gone.

Derrick walked back to the service desk.

Sheila saw him coming, and made a face. "I am soooooooo sorry," she said. "I didn't know who else to call."

"What about the manager-on-duty?" Derrick asked. "Whose shift is it?"

"It's Steve's shift," Sheila said. "But it wouldn't have done any good to call."

Derrick frowned. "Why not?"

Sheila hesitated.

Derrick recognized that look immediately. She didn't want to say anything that would get her in trouble.

Derrick motioned for her to step away from the counter.

He lowered his voice. "Look," he said. "If something's wrong with the way the MOD shift has been handled, I need to know about it. I can't fix a problem, if I don't know what it *is*."

Sheila bit her lower lip, and glanced toward her two co-workers, Annabelle and Allison. They were at the counter, helping customers, but it was obvious that both of them were trying very hard to listen in on this conversation at the same time.

They turned their faces away when Derrick looked in their direction. They were not exactly discreet.

Derrick turned back to Sheila. "It's okay. You don't have to tell me if you don't want to."

He watched her, mentally begging her to grow some courage, and spit it out.

Sheila seemed to reach a decision. "Nobody answers the phone," she said.

The words came out in a rush.

"It's true," Sheila said. "The managers almost never answer their phones. And when they *do* answer, they get angry at us for calling them."

Derrick glanced over at Annabelle and Allison. Their body language confirmed what Sheila was saying.

Derrick opened his mouth to speak, but Sheila spoke first.

"And they're not the only ones..."

Sheila's hand flew to her mouth, as if she couldn't believe she was actually saying these things out loud. But she didn't stop. "The department heads don't pick up their phones either. It's useless to even try to call them."

Derrick couldn't believe what he was hearing.

"You can ask anyone," Sheila said. "They'll tell you the same thing. All of the cashiers, the returns desk, any of us. We can't get any of the management team to answer calls, and that does *not* look good in front of the customers."

"I guess not," Derrick said.

Derrick started to say, "Well, I certainly..."

But Sheila cut him off. "And, lately, the associates have been doing the same thing. When we call for a price check, or to answer a customer's question, the associates blow off our phone calls."

"Not only that," Sheila said, "but they don't even come to get their returns."

She pointed to the carts filled with merchandise that customers had returned for refund, or exchange.

Derrick waited, to see if Sheila had more to add, but she appeared to have run out of steam.

"Okay," he said. "That gives me something to work on."

He lowered his voice again. "Thank you, Sheila. Don't worry; I won't tell anyone about our conversation."

Sheila nodded.

Derrick smiled, and walked away.

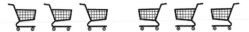

Something to work on? Something to *work* on? There were only five days left before the holiday promotion, and Derrick already had too many things on his plate. He definitely did not need *something to work on*.

He shook his head as he continued walking the sales floor, aimlessly following the linoleum squared aisles, crisscrossing between departments.

Complaints about managers not answering phones were nothing new. Store support had created the manager-on-duty shift as a resolution to the problem. It was one thing for associates to complain about managers not making themselves available, but when customer complaints about the lack of service began piling up on Yelp.com and other websites, someone in authority had decided that enough was enough.

Every manager was expected to carry the MOD in-store mobile phone for four hours every day. In addition to answering calls, they were required to be on the sales floor to ensure that associates engaged customers.

Derrick remembered how veteran managers had grumbled over this new expectation. Didn't the big dogs already have enough ways to micro-manage the store management teams?

When Derrick had been promoted to assistant manager, Christy, the phone operator at the Kearny Mesa store, had taken him aside. "Derrick, I'm happy for you. I've always liked you, because you come to work on time, and you put your best foot forward. Now that you're an ASM, I only ask one thing of you. Please, please, p-l-e-e-a-s-e answer your phone."

Derrick had been surprised by this simple but heartfelt request. "That's *it*? Just answer my phone?"

"That's it," Christy had said. "None of the other managers will answer calls, and our number-one customer complaint is that no one picks up the phone."

Derrick had agreed, and it hadn't take him long to earn a reputation as the only manager who answered his phone. His fellow managers had retaliated, by claiming that was the only thing Derrick did well. So much for synergy...

But the memory had given him idea for something that might help his current situation in the store. He was busy trying to think it through, when two female associates approached him in the aisle between flooring and the kitchen showroom.

The woman on the right spoke first. "Hi, Derrick. Can we have a word with you?"

It was phrased as a polite request, but her tone suggested that Derrick didn't really have a choice.

Derrick quickly scanned the two women's name badges.

He smiled. "Of course, Lindsey. What can I do for you and Felicia?"

"My sister is flying in from New York this weekend," Lindsey said. "And she'll be staying through the holiday."

"I've got family coming in too," Felicia said. "My husband and I are expecting our daughter to visit us this weekend. She's going to college in Austin, and she's taking the Memorial Day break to come home."

Derrick didn't have to be a mind reader to know what was coming next.

Lindsey shifted her weight from one foot to the other. "I need... I mean we *need* the weekend off."

Derrick put on his best sympathetic face. He needed a pay raise. But it didn't look like he was going to get one.

"Family time is important," he said. "But this holiday promotion has been planned months in advance. *The Design's* strategy for major holidays has *always* been to have all hands on deck to meet customer demand."

"That doesn't mean we should sacrifice all our family time," replied Lindsey.

"And my family is important to me," said Felicia.

"I understand how you feel," Derrick said. "My family is very important to me. But I'm going to be here this weekend, right alongside you. We're all scheduled to be here for this promotion. It's important for our store to have a successful sale."

"Not *everyone* is going to be here," said Lindsey.

"Yeah," said Felicia. "The designers have the weekend off."

Derrick held up his hands in a halting gesture. "Just a second. I gave clear instructions that everyone is to be here this weekend."

Felicia shrugged. "Well, I guess your instructions don't apply to the designers. Because *they're* not coming in."

Lindsey nodded in agreement. "The designers never work weekends or holidays. They're exempt."

Derrick suppressed a groan. Lindsey and Felicia were half right. Designers worked Monday through Friday, so their availability would coincide with the work hours of most contractors and installers. Associates on the sales floor grudgingly accepted this, but they resented the fact that they were required to work Saturdays and Sundays, while designers had every weekend off.

"I know designers don't ordinarily work weekends," Derrick said. "But company policy requires them to be on hand for major promotions. And they're each supposed to work at least one Saturday or Sunday per month, to help drive project sales."

Felicia shook her head. "Not at *this* store. The designers never contribute to these promotions. And I've never seen one here on a weekend."

"Neither have I," said Lindsey. "It's favoritism, pure and simple."

Derrick was puzzled. "Did you ever discuss this with Rob Morrison?"

Felicia and Lindsey exchanged glances.

"We couldn't," Lindsey said.

"Why not?"

The two female associates traded another glance.

"We didn't want to get slammed," Felicia said. "If we complained to Rob, he'd hold it against us."

Lindsey nodded. "He didn't like for people to make waves. If you asked about a problem, or a procedural issue, Rob would decide that you were a trouble maker. Next thing you knew, he was screwing with your schedule, making sure you worked closing shifts every day."

"It's true," Felicia said. "And he'd also make sure you didn't participate in the monthly weekend-off rotation."

Derrick found that hard to believe. The company was far from perfect, but it wasn't a cold-hearted bureaucracy. Operations had come up with a system to give each associate a scheduled weekend off every month. Not exactly generous, but it did allow everyone to enjoy a little family time.

If Rob Morrison had carried out personal vendettas against the associates—as Lindsey and Felicia were claiming—he would have left the company open to harassment complaints, or even lawsuits. Was *that* why Rob had been removed so suddenly?

Maybe, Judy had gotten so many HR complaints against Rob that it was easier (and safer) to pull the plug on him, before the problem escalated to a legal battle. Derrick had to admit that it was possible.

Whether it was true or not, Derrick didn't want to continue this conversation on the sales floor.

He nodded to the two female associates. "I understand your frustration," he said. "And I'm going to look into what you've said about the designers. But it's out of the question for anyone to take personal time this weekend."

The women started to protest, but Derrick held up his hand.

"If it was any other weekend, we might be able to work something out. But this is a major holiday, and you know how hard the company is pushing this promotional sale. We're all going to be here, doing our parts."

Okay, that was enough of the bad news. Now, to inject something positive...

"I'll coordinate with Tina," he said. "If there has been tampering with the weekend rotation schedule, I'll put a stop to it. Going forward, we'll make sure that everyone has a fair share of weekends off. For right now, I need you to focus on engaging your customers, okay?"

The women nodded, but they didn't look happy. They did seem to find some hope in Derrick's promise to correct the monkey-business with the weekend rotation. That would have to be enough, for now. Derrick couldn't fix everything at once.

When the ladies were gone, Derrick was left to wonder how much truth there might be in their comments about Robert Morrison. Had he really been that bad? Derrick remembered what Fran in the trade department had said about Rob—how the former manager would have enjoyed firing her for going after Jean-Man.

It didn't make sense. Rob had a solid reputation at store support, and Derrick had met the man several times. Rob had always struck Derrick as a mild-mannered guy. Derrick couldn't picture Rob going after employees, simply because he didn't like them. And he found it hard to believe that Rob actually enjoyed firing people.

The associates seemed to regard Rob as a heartless bastard. But that picture completely contradicted everything Derrick believed about the man. Could Derrick's assessment of Rob Morrison be that far off base? Or was something else going on here?

If Derrick was going to find out, he'd have to do some investigating. He needed answers. It was time to go dig up his two favorite people.

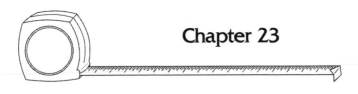

Chapter 23

12:00 PM

Mark Burkett had a smile on his face as he drove up to the loading dock of *The Design* store. He was excited! He'd gotten the call earlier today. His order had come in—a double wall oven that he'd bought as a surprise gift for his wife.

She was away for the week, visiting relatives. She'd be gone long enough for him to line up a cabinet modification specialist and appliance installer, to have the new oven ready to go when she returned. He and his son, Mark Jr., had driven to the store together, to bring the oven home.

Mark Sr. spotted the roll-up door to the will call department and drove toward it. "Finally, your mother will be able to make a home-cooked meal," he said.

"Come on, Dad," said Mark Jr. "It hasn't been all that bad. Mom's always been a great cook."

Mark Sr. decided to let it go at that. If he made any further comments about his wife's cooking, his remarks would undoubtedly reach her ears.

When father and son entered the store, there were two customers standing in line ahead of them.

"We've waited this long," Mark Sr. said. "A few more minutes won't matter more or less."

Under normal circumstances, that would've been true. But the few minutes stretched into half an hour as Sean, the lone will call associate, brought out two pallets of tile for the customer ahead of the Burketts.

The woman insisted on inspecting each twelve-by-twelve piece of tile, and that took time. A *lot* of time.

"My last shipment of tile was a nightmare," the female customer said in a nasal-tone. "A third of the pieces were either chipped, or outright broken."

She continued to scrutinize each piece of tile with the grudging precision of a jeweler grading precious diamonds. "I'm not taking any chances this time. I paid a lot of money for this tile, and I had to wait six weeks for it to arrive. I'm not leaving until I know that it's perfect."

She showed no signs of trying to hurry the process, and she clearly didn't care that others were waiting in line behind her.

By the time the woman had finally accepted the order, Mark Sr. had reached the end of his patience.

Sean had been with *The Design* for less than a year, and was a reliable associate who came to work on time, and did what was asked of him without complaining. He was twenty-two years old and a senior in college. He was looking forward to graduating, so that he could pursue a career in engineering.

Although this job was a part-time gig for him, his work ethic was appreciated, and he was paid a generous $15 per hour for a position that usually paid anywhere from $10 to $12 an hour.

When the Tile-Woman was safely out the door, he wiped the sweat off his brow with the back of a hand. It never hurt to remind an impatient customer that you've been working your ass off.

He stepped forward. "How can I help you, sir?"

"I'm here to pick up my oven," replied Mark. He held out his sales receipt.

Sean looked it over and nodded. "No problem. I'll have this outside in five minutes."

"I sure as hell hope so," Mark Sr. said. "Do you know how long we've been waiting here?"

Mark Jr. tugged at his father's shirt sleeve. "Come on, Dad. There's no need for that."

True to his word, Sean brought the oven out on a pallet with the Reach Lift, a compact forklift that had two forks capable of squeezing in tight areas, rising twelve feet in the air, and extending its forks to retrieve and bring down pallets from the overhead. He expertly drove the lift outside, and approached Mark Burkett's pickup truck.

When he raised the forks of the lift level with the bed of the truck, Mark Sr. stopped him.

"Hold it," he shouted, raising a hand. "I don't want that pallet in my truck. It'll scratch the bed."

Sean gave Mark Sr. a quizzical look. "It's a pickup truck, right?"

"What does it look like?" Mark Sr. snapped. "Of *course* it's a pickup truck. But that doesn't mean I want it scratched up."

"*Sir*, your oven is at least four feet tall. The pallet is for your safety, so the oven won't roll out of the bed of the truck. I have twine you can use to strap the pallet to your safety hooks."

Mark Sr. glared at him. "What do you mean, *I* can secure the pallet? That's what I'm paying *you* for."

Sean pointed to a sign on the wall outside of the building. "We're not allowed to secure any product to a customer's vehicle," he said. "It has something to do with liability issues."

"Well that's chicken-shit, if you ask me," replied Mark Sr.

'I didn't ask you!' Sean wanted to say.

But there was no point in arguing with the customer. Sean lowered the pallet, cut the shrink wrap, and helped the customer and his son load the oven in the truck.

Mark Jr. slid the oven to the front of the bed, so that it rested against the back window. Then he tried moving it from side to side with his hands.

"I guess it'll be secure enough," he said. "It's a bit top heavy, but I don't think it'll fall out."

Sean produced a clipboard with the release form, and Mark Sr. took his sweet time reading it.

"Come on, Dad," Mark Jr. said. "Sign the paper, and let's go home."

"Hold on, Son," said Mark Sr. "I want to make sure everything is in order."

He spent thirty more seconds reading the form. Then, he signed the paper and handed the clipboard back to Sean.

Sean tucked the clipboard under one arm. "Good luck, sir. And thank you for your business."

Mark stared at Sean, as the store worker climbed onto the Reach Lift and started it up.

Was that young punk being a smart-ass?

Mark Sr. started to say something, but Mark Jr. called for him to get in the truck.

"Come on, Dad, let's go."

Mark shrugged and climbed into the truck. He switched on the ignition and faced his son with a grin. "Let's get home so they can install this thing first thing in the morning. By this time tomorrow evening, we'll be enjoying one of your mom's home-cooked meals."

Mark Jr. nodded appreciatively.

Mark Burkett drove up the hill alongside the building and came to a stop at the intersection, looking in both directions for crossing traffic.

Mark Jr. turned around and looked at the oven. He was having second thoughts about not tying the oven down. He scratched the back of his head. "Dad? Maybe we should strap that thing down."

Mark Sr. shook his head. "Nah... It's heavy enough so that it won't move. Besides, I don't want to go back and ask that kid for help. He had a bad attitude."

"He seemed nice enough to me," Mark Jr. said. "I didn't see anything wrong with his attitude."

"That's because you haven't been around as long as I have," Mark Sr. said. "You can't let people push you around. You have to stand your ground and show them whose boss." He emphasized his point by slapping the steering wheel.

Mark Jr. didn't say anything. He'd heard his father talk like this before, and he knew better than to try and reason with someone who idolized Carroll O'Connor's character from *All In the Family.*

When he spotted an opening in traffic, Mark Sr. made a sharp left onto the main road.

The instant he began accelerating, the oven rolled out of the back of the truck and fell onto the street.

The sound of metal crashing against asphalt was deafening.

Mark Sr. stepped on the brake, and stared into his rear view mirror. It took two or three seconds for the reality of the situation to sink in.

Chapter 24

Derrick tapped twice on the door to Tina's office. There was no response, so he rapped again. Still no answer.

Derrick opened the door and stepped inside. Tina was seated at her desk, sucking on a popsicle. Debbie sat in the guest chair, nibbling at an ice cream cone. They pretended not to notice Derrick.

"Sorry to interrupt your lunch break," said Derrick. "But I need to ask you about Rob Morrison."

Neither of the Wicked Witches looked up to acknowledge his presence.

Derrick leaned forward, rested his palms on Tina's desk, and stared at her.

After several awkward minutes passed, she slowly lifted her eyes to meet his. "Rob no longer works for *The Design*," she said, flatly.

For a brief instant, Derrick imagined himself slapping the popsicle out of Tina's hand, to get her attention. He decided to stick to a more civil approach.

"Let's assume that I'm already aware of Rob Morrison's departure," Derrick said "In view of the fact that I have his job."

This brought no overt reaction from Tina, but her eyes narrowed a fraction.

"I want to know whether or not there were employee complaints lodged against Rob," Derrick said.

Tina slurped her popsicle, took a bite, and paused to swallow it. "How do you mean?"

She had obviously decided to play dumb. Fine.

"I'm hearing a lot of complaints about Rob," Derrick said. "And—based on what I know about the man—they don't add up. They certainly don't match his reputation at store support."

Now, it was Debbie's turn to slurp, as she devoured a melting glob of ice cream. "What about it?" she asked.

Derrick shot her a *who-the-fuck-asked-you?* look, and she turned her attention back to her ice cream cone.

Derrick repeated the stories he'd heard from Fran, Felicia, and Lindsey, but he left out their names. No sense giving the Wicked Witches a chance to retaliate, and he didn't put it past them to try.

Tina leaned back in her chair, in an obvious attempt to appear in control of the conversation. "Do you know what people said about me at the previous store where I worked?"

Yeah, thought Derrick. *They said you were a back-stabbing bitch.*

"I really don't care to speculate," he said. He was quite sure that Tina picked up on his tone of voice.

Tina sat up in her chair "The point is, you can't go by what people say."

"No," Derrick said. "That's not the point at all. The point is *this*... I'm asking you a direct question, and I want a direct answer. Did you receive any official complaints about Robert Morrison?"

Tina glanced in Debbie's direction, and Debbie cleared her throat. "Do you know what *I* think?"

It was obvious that they were going to try double-teaming him again. If these bitches wanted to play rough, Derrick could play rough too. For all of their little games, *he* was the store manager, and they could kiss his ass.

Derrick stared at Debbie. "No, Debbie, I *don't* know what you think. But if I have any questions about *design*, I'll be sure to ask for your opinion. Right now, I'm asking the human resources manager a question about HR."

Debbie dropped her gaze, and focused her attention on the remainder of the ice cream cone.

That was good. The Wicked Witches needed to understand that Daddy was here, and he wasn't in the mood for word games with naughty little girls.

Derrick turned his gaze back to Tina. "I'm still waiting for an answer," he said. Did you receive any official complaints about Robert Morrison's behavior toward the associates?"

Tina tossed her popsicle stick into the trash can, got up from her chair, and walked over to a file cabinet. She pulled out a file and handed it to Derrick.

He opened the folder, and began scanning the documents it contained. There were statements from a number of associates, accusing the store's former manager of favoritism, harassment, retaliation, and prejudice. In every case, the accusations has been corroborated in writing by Tina and Debbie. At the bottom of the uppermost page was Judy Polakoff's signature, verifying that she had accepted Robert Morrison's resignation.

Derrick closed the folder. He was about to speak when his phone rang.

He couldn't very well ignore it, not when he was about to read the riot act to his management staff for not answering phones.

So, he took the call.

"This is Derrick... What? When did this happen?"

He sighed. "Okay, I'll be right there."

He turned, hung up his phone and looked at Tina. "I have to go to will call, but we're not done talking about this."

He left the office quickly.

When he was gone, Tina flashed Debbie a look that said, quite plainly, '*I think the shit has hit the fan.*'

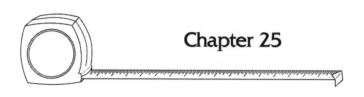

Chapter 25

When Derrick reached the will call department, he had no trouble spotting the unhappy customer, so he walked straight over to where the man was standing. "How can I help you, Mr. Burkett?"

Sean had spoken clearly on the phone, and Derrick hadn't had any trouble understanding his message. Even so, he was having trouble believing what the will call associate had just told him. Surely, this Burkett dude hadn't *really* been that stupid. Or *had* he? Either way, Derrick knew that he was in for a long and painful conversation.

"Well..." the man said. "My wife and I have been shopping here for years, and we've spent a lot of money in this store. In fact, we probably spent close to fifty-thousand dollars here last year alone."

Derrick was familiar with Mark Burkett's strategy. By starting out with a nice fat figure like that, the customer was announcing that he was a major client, and he deserved special attention. It was his way of saying, *'don't tell me anything I don't want to hear, because you owe me.'*

A lot of disgruntled customers liked to take that approach. It didn't work, but they never stopped trying.

Derrick flashed his happy/sympathetic smile. "Thank you for giving us the opportunity to serve your project needs," he said. "I'm sorry to hear about what happened on the road."

Burkett glanced at Sean, and then back to Derrick. "You can thank me by doing the right thing. You can replace my oven, since it's your fault that it got damaged."

Derrick knew what was coming next, but he needed to let this little drama follow its course. "I don't think I understand," he said. "The damage occurred *after* you left the store, while you were driving. You had already accepted custody of the oven. So, how does that make the accident our fault?"

Sean sighed heavily. "He says I didn't tell him to tie down the oven. And, he says that makes it our fault."

Derrick frowned, and rubbed the back of his neck. "I'm afraid I still don't understand."

Burkett's face was beginning to flush with anger. "Your employee didn't tell me I had to tie down my oven in the bed of the truck. If it had been strapped down, this wouldn't have happened."

Derrick had to fight the urge to laugh out loud. This clown had destroyed his own oven through sheer carelessness, and now he wanted the store to replace it. You gotta love the retail business...

"You need to make this right," Burkett said. "I *demand* a new oven."

Derrick didn't bother to respond. He spotted the oven in front of the rollup door. He was no appliance expert, but the appliance was obviously beyond repair. The top had been crushed; the glass door was smashed and bent; the handle had broken off; and the finish looked like it had been dragged behind a truck. Which, come to think of it, was pretty much what had happened.

Derrick looked over at Sean, who was watching the exchange with interest. Why the fuck had Sean taken the damned thing off the guy's truck? Now, this asshole would never let them load it back on.

Well, there was nothing they could do about it now.

Derrick walked over to the mangled oven and pretended to inspect the damage. He jotted down the model number and serial number, while he thought about how to respond.

He needed to play this right. There was no point in trying to reason with a guy who was determined to avoid any trace of responsibility for his own actions.

Finally, Derrick held up his notepad. "I have the information from your oven, and I'll contact the vendor to see if they'll replace it. I'll give you a call when I hear from our vendor rep. It will probably take a couple of days."

Burkett shook his head. "Uh-uh! No! This is *your* problem, not the vendor. It wasn't *their* job to tell me I should strap down the oven. They're not responsible for this, so they're not going to replace it."

Finally, the guy had said something that made sense.

Derrick pointed to the large sign next to the roll-up door. "Mr. Burkett, it's the responsibility of every driver to secure his vehicle's payload. That's store policy, and it says so on signs all over this loading area. It also happens to be state motor vehicle law. We can remind people until we're blue in the face, but—whether we remind them or not—the responsibility always rests with the driver of the vehicle."

Burkett's face had reached a shade of red approaching crimson.

"Are you telling me this is *my* fault?"

Derrick shook his head. "I'm telling you that I will not replace this oven. I'll check with the vendor, but—when they hear how the damage occurred—I don't think they're going to replace it either."

"I can't believe you're treating me this way!" Burkett said. "I spent close to a hundred-thousand dollars at your store, and this is how you show your gratitude?"

Suddenly, the mythical $50,000 had doubled. It was now $100,000. Derrick decided not to comment on that.

Instead, he took a different angle. "Mr. Burkett, is this the first time you've owned a truck?"

The customer looked confused. "What does that have to do with anything?"

"Please," Derrick said. "Humor me. Is this your first truck?"

Burkett shook his head. "No. I guess I've had four or five trucks, over the years. So *what?*"

Derrick nodded, as though this was rare and fascinating information. "Do you just like owning trucks? Or do you actually use them to carry loads?"

"I carry loads sometimes," the customer said.

Derrick nodded again. "Do you always leave stuff lying around loose in the bed of your truck? Or do you tie it down sometimes?"

"Sometimes I tie stuff down," Burkett said. "If it's heavy, or it looks like it might..."

He chopped himself off in mid-sentence, realizing that he had just painted himself into a corner."

"I see," Derrick said. "So, sometimes you tie down your payload, and sometimes you decide to take a chance that whatever you're hauling will stay put in your truck bed without being tied down."

Derrick looked toward the ruined oven. "That's what happened today, Mr. Burkett. You figured that your oven was probably heavy enough to stay put in your truck bed, and you decided to take a chance. Unfortunately, it didn't work out this time."

Burkett jabbed a finger in Sean's direction. "He didn't tell me to tie it down! That makes this whole thing your fault!"

Derrick shook his head. "I don't mean to be rude, Mr. Burkett, but I have to ask... Do you really need a kid who's half your age to tell you *when* to tie things down? You said you've had four or five trucks. Surely, you've figured out how trucks work by now..."

"Who's going to replace my oven?" Burkett shouted.

Derrick sighed. "Well, the store is not going to replace it. And the vendor probably isn't going to replace it, either. In all likelihood, you're going to have to replace it—since you're the one who dumped it in the street."

The irate customer took a half step toward Derrick, changed his mind, and stomped over to the truck. He snatched the door open, hurled himself into the driver's seat, and slammed the door.

He started the engine, and gunned it heavily. Then, he stuck his head out the window. "You haven't heard the last of this, you sonuvabitch!"

His foot came down hard on the accelerator, and his truck sped away in a frenzy of squealing tires.

When he was gone, Sean spoke up. "I didn't want to argue in front of the customer," he said. "But that guy was lying. He wanted me to tie down his oven. I showed him the sign, and told him that it's the customer's responsibility to secure whatever they purchase. He got all huffy about it, and said it was a chicken-shit policy. His *kid* even said he should tie it down. But the guy just wouldn't listen."

"He was too busy dodging personal responsibility," Derrick said. "He didn't have time to listen to anyone."

Derrick pointed toward the wrecked oven. "Take that piece of junk inside, secure it to a pallet, and put it in the overhead."

"What do you think he'll do?" asked Sean.

Derrick shrugged. "He'll probably call his credit card company, and try to have the charges reversed."

"Can he sue over this?"

Derrick laughed. "This is California! You can sue anybody for anything."

"Ah…" he said. "You've gotta love retail!"

Chapter 26

1:00 PM

Thank God it was lunch time. Derrick needed the break. He was only half-way through the day, and he'd already dealt with Jean-Man's grab-and-dash routine, that crazy bimbo's cracked lavatory bowl, and Mark Burkett's amazing flying oven act. Not to mention Hannah and Keith's love-fest in the supply closet. It was time to get out of the store and let his brain cool down.

Derrick had originally planned to slip over to one of the strip mall cafés for a sandwich and some relaxation. But he had changed his mind. The Rob Morrison thing was still bothering him, and Derrick was determined to get to the bottom of that little mystery.

He walked to his car, and punched Morrison's address into the GPS unit on his dash. The gadget wasted no time in plotting a course.

Derrick started the engine and pulled out of his parking spot.

The associates had made a lot of remarks about Rob Morrison, and none of them seemed to match the real man. The written records didn't seem right either, and neither the verbal comments nor the written complaints were consistent with Rob's professional reputation at store support.

Something was going on. Derrick was becoming increasingly convinced that someone had stabbed Rob Morrison in the back. And the poor bastard had never seen it coming.

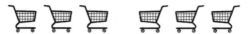

The GPS unit pinged quietly when Derrick pulled up in front of Rob Morrison's home in La Costa.

The disgraced manager had left the store in a hurry, because not all of his belongings had been cleared out of what was now Derrick's office. Rob had left several framed certificates of accomplishment behind, along with a photo of him posing with the CEO, and an award statue for successfully completing the company's leadership course. These items were gathered in a small white cardboard box, which now rode in the passenger seat of Derrick's car.

On top of the box was Rob's address book, which had proved helpful in locating his house. Derrick could have gotten the address from Tina, but he didn't want the Wicked Witches to know what he was up to.

Derrick climbed out of the car, tucked the box under one elbow, and walked up the sidewalk to the front door. He pressed the doorbell.

Rob lived in a house on Caringa Way, with a nice view of the Pacific. With the economy in shambles, it would be tough for him to find a job with a high enough salary to keep a place like this. Derrick hoped that Rob had a good network, and solid prospects for new employment.

Rob opened the door and greeted Derrick with a smile. "I didn't expect a house call from my replacement," he said.

His voice was unexpectedly cheerful. He was dressed in khaki shorts, tank top, and a 48 hour shadow on his face. He stepped back into the living room, and motioned for Derrick to follow him into the house.

Derrick handed him the box. "I thought you might want these."

Rob reached in and pulled out the black address book and accepted the box. "Thanks," he said. "This is really the only thing I cared about, but I appreciate you taking the time to bring me my stuff."

He dropped the box onto the carpet, and pushed it away with his toe.

"Sorry," said Derrick. "I wasn't trying to…"

Rob waved a hand. "Forget it."

He tossed the address book onto a side table, nearly knocking over a lamp. "I was sitting out back having a beer. Can I get you one? Or is it lunch only?"

Derrick was tempted. "Thanks, but I'd better stick to solids."

Rob led Derrick through the kitchen, and out the back door. He motioned for Derrick to have a seat on the outdoor patio furniture, shaded by a large umbrella.

The view of the ocean was amazing, and Derrick told him so. "Man, you must spend every free moment here."

"Well," Rob said. "I suddenly find that I have a lot more free time on my hands."

Derrick felt like an idiot, but Rob laughed it off.

"Don't worry about it," Rob said. "I've been trying to figure out what happened, but I'm discovering that I have a much bigger question…"

Derrick nodded. "What's that?"

Rob picked up his bottle of beer and took a hefty swig. "I'm wondering why the hell I stayed with *The Design* for so long in the first place. I *hated* that job."

That took Derrick by surprise. "You did?"

Rob inhaled deeply. "I was not happy there. I hadn't been for years. I guess I stayed because nobody fucked with me."

He chuckled. "At least not until *yesterday*, that is."

Derrick didn't know whether or not he was supposed to laugh. If things didn't work out, he could be sitting in this same position a week from now, minus the ocean view, of course.

Rob set his beer bottle on the table. "Okay, let's talk about what you *really* came for…"

He gave Derrick a strange smile that was equal parts anger and sadness. "You want to know *who* threw me under the bus," he said. "And how they did it."

Derrick watched the ocean. A white sailboat was moving up the coast, tacking against the wind. "I think I've figured out *who* did it," he said. "But I'm not sure how they pulled it off…"

Rob gave him a searching look. "You've had the job two days, and you already know who's out to screw you?"

"My prime suspects are Tina and Debbie," Derrick said. "They've been giving me problems since I walked in the door."

Rob lifted his bottle, and downed the last swallow of beer. He leaned forward and fished a bottle of *Sam Adams Light* from a stainless steel ice chest. He popped off the cap and took a drink.

"You've got the right suspects," he said. "But I'm surprised that they're letting you see their claws. They usually work very quietly, behind the scenes. They were as sweet as pie to me, while they were setting me up for the fall."

Derrick nodded. His suspicions about the Wicked Witches of the West were correct.

Ron took another swallow. "Getting me booted must have made those two lovely ladies a bit over-confident. Or else, they'd never let you know that you're on their hit-list."

He sighed, and took two more gulps of beer. "They took their time setting me up. And when they finally pulled the trigger, I didn't even see it coming."

"You can't just let them win," Derrick said. "What if I go to—?"

"Forget about Judy," said Rob. "She knows, but she can't do anything."

Derrick frowned. "How is that *possible*? Tina is only an HR, and Debbie is just a project manager."

"They lined up all the dominos," Rob said. "It was all there... The paperwork; written and verbal complaints; statements from my associates. More than enough to hand me my hat."

He took another drink, emptying half the bottle. When he lowered it, he stared at Derrick. "You'd better watch your back, my friend. They didn't just get rid of me for the hell of it. Those two have plans for good old store 1254. And—whatever they have in mind—they will happily cut your throat if you try to get in their way."

Derrick watched the sailboat, still moving into the wind. It didn't seem to be making any progress.

He had one week to prove he could turn things around. And the Wicked Witches would be doing everything in their power to make him fail. How the hell had he gotten into this spot?

Rob took a final swallow, draining the last of his newly-opened beer.

He regarded the empty bottle with a philosophical eye. "I don't know how the fuck they did it, but you'd better figure it out. Because you're next."

He opened the ice chest for another bottle. "Then again, maybe those bloodthirsty bitches did me a favor."

Derrick stared at him.

"I'm serious," Rob said. "Think of all the bullshit we have to go through."

He gave a slightly slurred imitation of Judy's voice. "*What are you doing to drive sales? What are you doing to improve customer service? Your numbers are lousy! What are you going to do about it?*"

He sighed. "The shit never ends, my friend. And life is too short. Waaaaaaay too short."

"Okay," Derrick. "I'll admit that the job can be a pain in the ass. So what are you going to do about it? Drink yourself to death?"

Rob set the bottle down and belched again. "Nope. I'm going on vacation. Yellowstone National Park!"

The answer took Derrick by surprise. "That's your answer? Go play Davy Crockett?"

"I don't have an answer yet," Rob said. "But I need to let off some steam before I jump back into the job market. And I've always wanted to go to Yellowstone."

He regarded Derrick. "I don't know if there *is* a big answer. Maybe we've been doing it wrong. Maybe Tina and Debbie are playing the game the way it's supposed to be played."

"Maybe..." said Derrick. "And maybe I'll have a beer after all. If the offer is still open."

Rob reached for the cooler. "You're a pretty decent guy," he said. "I think you'll make a good store manager. Right up until the point where Tina and Debbie stab you in the back."

Chapter 27

2:30 PM

Derrick replayed the conversation in his mind on the drive back to the store. Business shouldn't be so complicated. If you did your job properly, you should be left alone, or even rewarded. But Rob Morrison's reward had been a termination slip, and a cooler full of *Sam Adams* on the back patio. Speaking of which...

Derrick fumbled in the glove compartment for a box of mints. He chewed three or four, and then sucked on several more to get the smell of beer off of his breath.

Oddly, he wasn't worried about being caught for drinking alcohol at lunch. He was more concerned about what to do to make the upcoming promotion a success.

They were putting too much on his shoulders too soon. But that didn't really matter. He didn't have a choice. If he couldn't come out of this situation on top, he'd have to go buy a cooler full of beer.

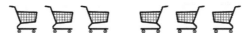

When he got to the store, Derrick took his time walking the sales floor, doing his best to remain unnoticed. He wanted to see how the associates behaved in the absence of the store manager.

The first group of associates he saw were less than impressive.

Florence and Tiffany were cashiers, standing at their registers texting on their cell phones, instead of focusing on the customers waiting to make a purchase.

There was a company SOP, forbidding the use of personal cell phones, pagers, and iPods at work. Apparently, the two cashiers hadn't gotten the memo.

He'd met Florence and Tiffany on his first day in the store. They seemed like nice enough girls, but the store didn't *need* nice girls. The front end registers needed to be manned by professional cashiers, with solid customer relations skills. Unfortunately, you couldn't hire employees of that caliber for $10.50 an hour.

At the old store, he'd had several conversations with Tom Ebert on this very subject. Derrick had pointed out that the company promised customers that it would deliver the best service in the industry. Then, it hired service personnel at the bottom end of the pay band.

Tom had responded that the company's position about pay scales wasn't likely to change. The problem was never going to go away. It was up to managers to learn to deal with it.

Derrick would have to add the texting issue to his growing list of things to fix.

He left Florence and Tiffany to their text messages.

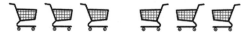

When Derrick walked into the flooring department, he brightened at the sight of three groups of customers looking over displays and take-home samples. That is until he saw Kelly sitting at his desk, texting.

Kelly didn't bother looking up when Derrick walked over to stand next to him.

Derrick leaned over, and spoke softly. "Kelly, why are you on your personal cell phone? There are customers in your department."

Kelly was startled by Derrick's voice. He blinked several times, rapidly. "I'm… ah… responding to a customer question."

Well, that was obviously bullshit, but Derrick let it pass.

"I'm not going to ask to see the messages," he said. "Because I'm sure that you're telling me the truth, Kelly. But in the future, if I see you texting at work, I may decide to read the message thread. Just as a quality control check, to be sure that whatever you're texting to our customers is in good alignment with our customer service guidelines."

Kelly nodded feebly, and put the phone back in his pocket.

"Thank you," Derrick said. "Now, please go attend to your customers."

Kelly jumped to his feet, and approached the customers with a smile on his face. "How may I help you this afternoon?"

After listening to the customer, he said, "And how many rooms do you have in your home?"

Then, he nodded. "Let me show you the samples we have over here. I think they may be what you're looking for. By the way, we offer free delivery with installation."

Derrick didn't wait around to hear the rest. Kelly was obviously hamming it up, with the new store manager watching, but he was actually doing a good job.

Even so, one thing was clear. The entire staff needed a reminder in the importance of customer service.

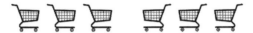

Derrick rounded the corner and stopped a few yards away from the special service desk.

Sheila must have been at lunch, because only Allison and Annabelle were present. They seemed busy with paperwork, and answering the never-ending stream of phone calls.

Derrick watched as an elderly couple approached the desk.

Allison glanced up, and smiled. "Hello, how may I help you?"

"I'd like to speak with the manager in charge," said the lady.

The man—who might have been a husband or boyfriend—stood to the side, looking aloof. He had that, *I'd-rather-be-golfing* expression.

Derrick could sympathize with that. He'd much rather be golfing.

Allison dialed the MOD phone, and waited. And waited. And waited some more.

She hung up and dialed again. "I'm sorry," she said. "I'm dialing the manager-on-duty again."

Her face flushed with embarrassment when the MOD failed to answer.

She made a third attempt, and that was all the customer allowed.

"Who is the manager in charge of this store?" asked the old woman.

"His name is Derrick, but I don't know if he's back from lunch."

Derrick breathed a sigh of relief. Good. She hadn't noticed him standing there.

The customer scowled. "This is ridiculous! I've been waiting for my outdoor furniture for six weeks, and now I'm told that my order won't arrive for another month. This is completely unacceptable! I want to talk to the store manager right now!"

Allison bobbed her head. "Yes ma'am. Let me try his phone."

Derrick's phone rang loudly, and everyone at the desk turned to face him.

"*There* he is," said Allison. The relief was clearly visible on her face.

Derrick stood up straight, and strode up to the desk. "Hello, I'm Derrick."

He flashed his *I-hope-I'm-not-in-deep-shit* smile, and asked his least favorite question in the world. "How may I help you?"

Chapter 28

3:00 PM

"I want you to deliver what you promised," Mrs. Jane Summers said, in her scratching old voice.

"I used to shop at *Expo Design Center* until they closed, so I thought I'd give you my business." She made an exasperated sound that was very much like a snort. "A friend of mine warned me about shopping here, and I should have listened."

Derrick wished he could thank the unnamed friend for her recommendation. And he wished even more that the old woman had heeded the advice.

Mrs. Summers was from his grandparents' generation, and long experience had taught Derrick that they were a hard group to satisfy. They didn't buy into the idea of paying in full up front for a special order product, and then waiting for it to be delivered. They came from an age in which you paid for something, and you walked out the store with it—then and there.

Derrick leaned forward on the consultation table, grateful that Mrs. Summers had allowed him to lead her into the room, out of sight of other customers.

"So if I understand you correctly," he said, "you purchased your outdoor furniture set six weeks ago... And today, you received a call from Wayne, telling you that your order will be delayed for another four weeks?"

Mrs. Summers sighed heavily, and her sagging breasts filled out momentarily beneath her faded blue blouse, before deflating as she exhaled. "That's what I said. And I am *very* disappointed."

Her eyes rolled behind the thick lenses of her glasses.

Derrick was reminded of the little old lady shooting at the rats in her kitchen in the movie *Ratatouille*. Mrs. Summers even had the same friggin' hairdo.

Derrick took out his in-store mobile phone and dialed Wayne's number. No answer.

"I know Wayne is in the store," Derrick said. "But he's not answering his phone. Let me try him again..."

"I'm not at all surprised," Mrs. Summers grumbled. "No one answers their phone in this store. That's why I had to come down here. I'm seventy-four years old, and I shouldn't have to put up with this kind of foolishness. Don't you people care about your customers?"

Derrick didn't want to go down that road. "Let me try to reach JC. He's the assistant manager over seasonal department."

"Whoop-Dee-Do," replied Mrs. Summers.

Derrick ignored her jibe, and dialed JC's number. Again, there was no answer.

"Surprise, surprise," said Mrs. Summers.

Jesus... Didn't *anyone* in this store answer their phones? Apparently not.

Derrick decided to cut to the chase. He reached for the computer, and typed in the old lady's phone number to call up her order. It appeared quickly on the screen. Derrick read the phone number of the vendor on the screen, and dialed.

"Hello, this is Derrick Payton, store manager of *The Design* in Encinitas."

It took an effort for him not to appear relieved that someone had actually answered the phone. "I'm trying to find the status of a special order, placed six weeks ago. Are you able to help?"

"Yes," came the reply. "My name is Barbara. What's the order number?"

Derrick read the digits off the screen. He could hear Barbara typing on a keyboard.

Hopefully, she would say something soon, before Derrick had to look at Bug-Eyes again.

"Okay," said Barbara. "I found your order."

Hallelujah!

"Excellent," Derrick said. "What's the status?"

"I'm afraid it's not good news," Barbara said. "It looks like that order is going to be delayed for another eight weeks."

Eight weeks? What had happened to *four*?

"Can you double-check that?" Derrick asked. "Mrs. Summers was notified this morning that the delay would be *four* weeks. She's already waited six weeks, and she wants her furniture set now, as I'm sure you can understand."

"I do understand," said Barbara. "But the shipment is coming out of China, and the manufacturer has some kind of a customs problem from previous shipments. All orders have been placed on hold, until the customs issue is resolved."

"But you must have received notice that the order didn't ship from China on schedule," Derrick said. "Someone should've notified us of the delay, so we could offer the customer an alternate choice."

Mrs. Summers interrupted. "I don't *want* an alternate choice. I want what I ordered."

Derrick covered the mouthpiece of the phone with a cupped hand. "That's what I'm working on, ma'am."

He removed his muting palm from the phone. "Barbara, this customer is understandably upset. There must be something you can do?"

"I'm sorry," Barbara said. "But the product comes from China, and the holdup is with U.S. Customs. All we can do is wait."

"This is precisely what Mrs. Summers doesn't *want* to do."

"Do what?" asked the old woman.

Derrick waved a hand for her to be patient, and let him handle this.

"Don't you dare shush me!" she hissed.

"I'm sorry," Derrick said. "I'm trying to figure out a way to get you your furniture."

"I don't want your apology. I want what I *paid* for. I want my outdoor furniture set."

Derrick turned his attention back to Barbara. "I'm going to have to get back to you," he said.

He hung up the phone, and leaned back in his chair. What the hell was he going to do now?

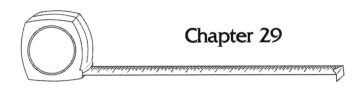

Chapter 29

3:30 PM

Derrick was more than pissed after his altercation with Mrs. Summers. He couldn't remember the last time he'd been so embarrassed. The MOD wasn't answering his phone, none of the ASMs answered their phones, and neither did the associates. What the hell was going on in this store?

He arrived in the seasonal department. It was deserted. No sign of Wayne, or JC Fuller.

He stopped in the nearby lighting department, and saw a pair of associates—one male, one female—leaning over the computer. The male associate sat at the desk, working the mouse, while the female associate watched over his shoulder.

"Have either of you seen Wayne in seasonal?" asked Derrick.

Neither associate responded. They didn't even bother to look up, to find out who was doing the asking.

Derrick walked around the desk to see what had their attention. His mouth dropped open. "Are you watching *Saturday Night Live* reruns?"

The man glanced up. "Who are *you*?"

Derrick read their name badges. Carlos and Claudia. What a pair...

He tried again. "Have either of you seen Wayne?" He could hear the impatience in his own voice.

Carlos stood up, with an uncertain expression, as if it was just occurring to him that this might be the new store manager. "Sorry, can't say that I have."

"Me neither," said Claudia, with a tone of complete indifference.

Derrick wanted to drag both of them into his office and scream at them for an hour or two, but he didn't have the time.

Instead, he headed for the break room, hoping to find Wayne or JC.

When he passed the phone room, his nostrils were assaulted by a horrific stench. He practically keeled over.

It must be some kind of chemical spill… They might have to evacuate the building, and call for a hazardous waste cleanup team…

He was about to stumble into the phone room and warn Emily, when he spotted her chatting happily over her head set.

She looked up and spotted him, and then muted her line. "Are you okay?"

Derrick coughed. "What the hell is that *smell*?"

Emily looked around the phone room, sniffing at the air like a bloodhound. "I don't smell anything."

That's when Derrick identified the source of the hideous odor. It was Emily's perfume.

Derrick had no idea what the offending fragrance was called, but it should have been outlawed by the international ban on chemical weapons.

He coughed again. "Sorry," he said. "Must have been my imagination."

As he was retreating quickly from the open door to the phone room, he heard Emily's voice. "Do you want to sit down for a while? You look sick."

"No," Derrick said over his shoulder. "I'll be fine."

He ducked into the expeditor's office down the hall, and closed the door behind him, breathing heavily as he inhaled fresh air. "What the hell is she wearing?"

"I see you've been in the phone room with Emily," said a woman's voice from one of the office cubicals.

Laughter broke out in the room, and three people stood up, their heads appearing above their cubical partitions.

This was the vendor-to-call, or VTC, room where associates followed up on customer orders by checking the status with vendors, and notifying associates to call customers regarding delays.

There were two women and one man. Derrick didn't think he'd met any of them before.

He smiled. "I'm Derrick, the new store manager."

One by one they introduced themselves. "I'm Mary," said the first.

"I'm Brandon," said the only male expediter.

"And I'm Jayne."

Derrick looked at the closed door. "I see why you had it shut," he said. "Emily's perfume nearly killed me."

All three laughed.

Derrick would have loved to stay longer; they seemed a pleasant group. But he was on a mission. "Have you seen Wayne or JC?"

"I think they're in the break room," said Brandon.

Derrick eyed the closed door and grimaced. Now, he'd have to open it again, and expose his tender nostrils to Emily's cologne-of-death.

"Thanks," he said. "I'll catch up with you later."

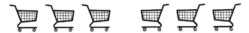

Wayne and JC were sitting in the break room, drinking sodas, eating chips, and watching a golf tournament.

"I sure wish we had cable," Wayne said.

JC shrugged. "Maybe the new SM will okay the expense."

"The *hell* I will," said Derrick. He entered the break room, making no attempt to mask the anger in his voice. "I've been calling you two for the past 20 minutes! Don't you answer your phones?"

JC and Wayne nervously rose from their chairs. "We're on break," they said in unison.

"There's no one in seasonal to help customers," Derrick said. "And Mrs. Summers wanted to know what's up with her order."

He could see from Wayne's expression that the associate knew all about the Bug-Eyed Mrs. Jane Summers.

"I called her about the delay," said Wayne. "I told her what was happening, and why it was happening, and how long it's going to take to fix it."

"That's good," Derrick said. "But she came in looking for alternatives. Neither of you were around, so I had to sell her the display set at fifty percent off suggested retail."

"You sold her the display?" JC and Wayne asked, again in unison.

"You're damned right I did," answered Derrick. "That woman was hopping mad, and threatened to cancel her order."

"You should've let her cancel," said Wayne. "I told her before she bought it that the vendor was having trouble shipping, because of some customs issue. I offered her an alternate set, but she insisted on having the one on display because it's the newest line."

"The seasonal merchant made it clear to all stores that we shouldn't sell the display sets," added JC. "Because we can't get a replacement unless we pay for it."

It was beginning to dawn on Derrick that he had been played by a customer. People often asked to speak with someone up the chain of command, to tell them a new (and carefully selective) version of their problem. One that would get them the results they wanted, regardless of whether or not their claim was actually legitimate.

"That's why I called both of you," Derrick said. "I wanted to know the full story before making a decision. But I couldn't leave a seventy-four year old woman sitting in a consultation room all afternoon. I had to come up with a resolution. And if either of you had taken a moment to answer your phones, you could've filled me in on the situation."

JC and Wayne exchanged a guilty look. Neither one of them spoke.

Derrick looked at his watch. "How much longer are you on break?"

"A few minutes," replied JC.

"Fine," Derrick said. "Finish your break. Then, call all the ASMs and DHs to the training room. I want to see them *all* in half an hour. No exceptions."

He stalked out of the break room shaking his head. When he approached the phone room, he held his breath and darted down the hallway.

Emily's voice followed him. "Are you feeling better?"

Derrick didn't answer. He concentrated on getting outside of the striking radius of Emily's perfume. By the time he had to breathe again, he wanted to be far enough away that his nostrils wouldn't implode.

Chapter 30

3:45 PM

The designer's office was empty, save for Susan and Marie. They sat at their desks facing each other, talking about life as single women. Marie painted her nails, while Susan fixed her hair.

Derrick looked at his watch. Their shift didn't end for another 45 minutes. Why were they just sitting around?

"You ladies through for the day?" he asked, casually.

"My client rescheduled for tomorrow," said Susan, not taking her eyes away from the mirror on the wall by her desk.

"I met with mine early this morning," answered Marie, blowing on her nails to dry them.

Derrick wondered if they had anything productive to do, other than touching up their looks. Lord knows, they need time for that, but not on the company clock.

"Either of you have anything else planned for the day?" He hoped they would say yes, but both women shook their heads.

"So what does Debbie want you to do when you've caught up on your appointments?"

He wasn't sure which bothered him more: the fact they were sitting on their butts doing nothing, or their lackadaisical behavior in front of the store manager.

"Whatever Debbie has in mind," Susan said, "I hope it doesn't involve leaving the building. It's so damned hot outside, I felt like I was on my period!"

Derrick was sure that he had misheard her.

Marie spotted his discomfort instantly. "Oh, come on, it's not *that* hot."

Susan laughed. "Wanna bet? It's so hot outside, I could feel the sweat rolling down my ass."

Derrick decided that this conversation was nearly as disgusting as Emily's perfume.

Both girls laughed over the face he made.

"Don't worry," said Susan. "We're not usually this candid."

She got up and walked over to Derrick, holding out a black binder.

Derrick accepted it. "What's this?"

"A client of mine," Susan said. "We're remodeling her kitchen, but things have been going south for a while. First, the cabinets arrived damaged, and the job was pushed back four weeks until replacements arrived. Then, the installer had to postpone because of a previous commitment with another client. All in all, we missed completion by five weeks."

Derrick opened the binder to skim through the pages. "That's not ideal," he said. "But it could have been a lot worse."

He wasn't trying to be facetious. A lot of things could come up during a major remodel. Delays were an expected part of the process.

"Agreed," Susan said. "I kept the client in the loop the whole time, and she knows that the delays were beyond our control. But, she won't sign off on the checklist to release us of further obligation."

Derrick looked up from the binder. "Why not?"

Susan made a face. "She wants a partial refund as compensation, for suffering and inconvenience."

Derrick flipped through a few more pages. "What does Debbie say?"

Susan made another face. "Debbie says no refund. The customer wants to speak with her, but Debbie won't call her."

"What do you mean, Debbie won't call her?"

Susan glanced in Marie's direction.

Marie shook her head. The expression on her face said, '*don't go there.*'

"Debbie is pretty busy," Susan said.

Derrick didn't push the matter. He looked at the total cost of the job. "She paid slightly over fifty-eight thousand. Has the customer given you a dollar amount that would satisfy her?"

"She wants ten percent. But I told her that wasn't possible, because we gave her that much off when she signed up for a retainer during our earlier project promo."

Derrick exhaled irritably. "Good call on your part. Ten percent is too much. From what I can see, these were just the ordinary delays that creep in when you tackle a big job."

He looked at Susan. "I'm in agreement with you. Ten percent is over the top. She's your client. What's your feel? What will it take to make her happy?"

The question appeared to surprise Susan. Derrick got the impression that she wasn't accustomed to being asked her opinion.

Susan's face brightened. "To be perfectly honest, I believe I could get her to accept five hundred dollars, plus our promise of ten percent off when she remodels her bathroom next year. She's a tough customer, but she's also smart. We did good work for her on this job, and she knows it."

Derrick liked what he was hearing. Maybe he had misjudged Susan and Marie.

He nodded. "Okay. Do it."

Susan and Marie stared at him in astonishment. "Huh?"

"Do it," Derrick said again. "You've convinced me. You've got a good plan. So, make it happen."

Susan gave him a disbelieving look. "Just like that?"

Derrick nodded. "Just like that."

"Wow!" said Susan. "You're the first manager I've met who can make a reasonable decision without second-guessing everything to death."

"Yeah," said Marie. "We're not used to that. And you don't just blow us off, like Debbie usually does."

The act of speaking Debbie's name must have summoned her like a demon. She was suddenly standing in the doorway of the designer's office, with a distinctly unhappy look on her face. She pointed long hard glances at Susan and Marie before turning her eyes toward her new store manager.

"Derrick, can I see you in my office?" Her tone was obviously meant to be intimidating.

Derrick knew that any sign of levity would piss her off, so he smiled broadly. "Of course," he said in his best cheerful voice. "I actually came here looking for you."

He followed Debbie out the door, flashing a last smile over his shoulder at the two designers as he left.

A few seconds later, Debbie closed the door of her office behind Derrick, and took a seat behind her desk.

Derrick dropped into the other chair. "You go first," he said. "We'll get to my stuff in a minute."

Debbie stared at him without speaking. She clearly didn't like his tone. Derrick, just as clearly, did not care.

Debbie still didn't speak.

Derrick looked at his watch. "If you've forgotten what you wanted to talk to me about, we can move on to *my* business."

"I haven't forgotten," Debbie said acidly.

"Good," Derrick said. "What's on your mind?"

"I overheard you just now," Debbie said.

Derrick nodded. "Yes..."

"You authorized a five-hundred dollar discount for a project client."

Derrick nodded again. "Yes."

"You can't *do* that," Debbie snapped.

Derrick spoke evenly. "Actually, I can. In fact, I just *did*."

Debbie's voice was perilously close to a sneer. "In case you haven't realized, *I* am the project manager in charge of design sales. I *never* offer more than a ten percent discount off projects. What gives you the right to go against my policy without consulting me first?"

This bitch couldn't be serious...

Derrick leaned back in the chair and assumed a more relaxed pose. "Debbie, you *do* remember that I've been promoted to manager of this store, right?"

The only answer was a cold, hard stare.

"I'm going to take that as a *yes*," Derrick said. "So we'll cut to the chase... As store manager, I'm in charge of every department in this store. Including yours. I just thought I'd say that, because it appears to have slipped your mind."

This time, it was his voice that was icy. "I report to Judy, not to you. In fact, I don't have to justify my decisions to you at all. *Ever*."

He stood up. "You work for me, Debbie. Not the other way around. You might want to remember that."

He looked at his watch again. "I'm calling a meeting of all managers and supervisors in about twenty-five minutes. Be in the training room at 4:15."

He opened the door and gave Debbie a frosty smile. "I'll see you there..."

He walked out the door, and closed it before Debbie could respond.

Chapter 31

4:15 PM

Derrick sat at the head of the horseshoe-shaped table while stragglers entered the training room. They sauntered in casually, as though they didn't have a care in the world.

Derrick looked around the table, trying to remember names. JC and Steve were present, as were Nancy from trade, Kent from receiving, and Jesus in appliances. Who was that sitting next to Nancy? Oh yeah, that was Martha, who ran décor.

He recognized the lighting department supervisor sitting between Kent and Jesus, but he couldn't recall the man's name. That was okay. He'd been here less than two days. He'd get them all sorted out before long.

He looked down the table to his right and spotted two empty seats. "Who's missing?"

Sarah looked around the table. "I think it's Tina and Debbie."

The small crowd fell silent.

The management team was obviously aware of the animosity between Derrick, Tina, and Debbie.

He was a half-second from sending for the Wicked Witches when they strolled into the room. They took their seats without looking at Derrick.

Derrick had decided to speak from a sitting position, to keep things informal. "Now that everyone is here," he said, "I want to go over some first impressions I have of the store.

He tried to make his voice sound friendly and non-judgmental. No sense in getting everyone all keyed up.

"Firstly, this store's location is excellent. It's only two miles from the highway, and surrounded by neighborhoods where the average income is one-fifty-plus. Because our target customers are those looking to be above the cookie-cutter trend, we couldn't ask for a better spot."

Derrick cleared his throat and continued. "We're staffed to customer demand, and the store's overall appearance is clean and ready for business."

He paused. He'd gotten things started on a positive note. Now, it was time for some not-so-positive comments. "Having said that, I want to share some interesting observations."

"Such as?" asked Tina.

The bitch just didn't know when to quit...

"How about associates texting on the sales floor, for starters? And when we're done kicking that around, we can talk about people not answering phone calls. Customer complaints not being resolved in a timely manner. Associates asking for the Memorial Day weekend off, when everyone knows that all hands are required to be here. Does any of this sound familiar?"

Silence.

"When a new store manager takes over, it's always a good idea for him or her to observe the store in operation for a while, before making changes."

Derrick saw that he had the attention of everyone at the table. Good. They needed to understand what was at stake.

"That was my intent when I first learned that I was being promoted to store manager of this facility," Derrick said. "But things aren't working out that way. I've already heard enough from the floor-level associates to know that they have no faith in the leadership team. And that happens to be everyone in this room."

"I don't think managers should pay attention to gossip," said Tina.

Derrick raised a hand. "What was that, Tina?"

She looked him coldly in the eye. "I said, I don't think managers should pay attention to gossip..."

It sounded like a challenge. Hell, it *was* a challenge.

Derrick nodded, as if weighing her words. "You mentioned something like that to me earlier," he said. "It struck me as an unusual comment then, and it still seems strange to me, coming from an HR manager."

Tina's cheeks reddened. "What do you mean?"

"I mean that a large part of the human resources job is about listening to the complaints and concerns of company personnel. And I don't understand how you can do that job effectively, if you assume that the complaints of the associates are nothing more than gossip."

"I know how to do my job!" Tina said.

"I'm sure you do," Derrick said. "Which is why I'm confident that you are every bit as concerned as I am about what's going on at the floor-level in this store."

The silence in the room was deafening.

"So, let's talk about that," Derrick said. "Let's talk about what we can do to restore confidence in our management team. And what we can do to improve our responses to customer complaints. Because, as far as I'm concerned, both problems have the exact same solution. Anyone want to take a stab at what that might be?"

Still, no one spoke.

"You already know the answer if you think about it," Derrick said. "Our people don't have faith in us, because we're not following the basics of customer service."

He looked out over the silent group. "What are the basics of customer service?" he asked. "Let's see some hands."

Sarah's hand went up. "Approach and greet the customer."

"Right! And the next? Let's see more hands."

Nancy raised her hand. "Ask questions to properly qualify the customer."

"Correct-a-mundo," said Derrick. The cliché made famous by Henry Winkler in *Happy Days* brought a few laughs from his generation, but the other, younger half of the table had no idea what he meant.

The lighting DS raised his hand next. Derrick still couldn't remember the man's name. "Make recommendations."

"So far, so good." Derrick then pointed to Jesus.

"Ask for the sale?" He sounded unsure.

Derrick smiled. "Are you *asking* us? Or *telling* us?"

Jesus cleared his throat. "I'm *telling* you. Ask for the sale."

The answers were coming more quickly now, and the faces at the table were beginning to brighten.

"Now, it's time for the hard question," Derrick said. "Who can tell me why our associates don't believe in these steps?"

The silence was back.

"I respect everyone in this room," Derrick said. "So I'm not going to sugar-coat this. The behaviors I witnessed today made me sick."

He saw the smiles at the table turn sour. Maybe that was a little *too* honest.

"Our people aren't doing their primary job, which is to help customers."

He waited a few seconds for that to sink in.

"Today, I've seen customers ignored in virtually every department in this store. I've had to personally deal with multiple complaints from customers, because no one else was bothering to engage with them. I don't mind having the worst problems dropped in my lap. That's one of the things I'm here for, to resolve issues that no one else can manage. But nearly every problem I handled today could have been dealt with by the manager of the department in question, or the manager-on-duty. Instead, those problems came to me, because no one—and I mean *no one*—bothered to answer their phones."

Derrick looked around the table. "When we ignore a customer's complaints, what do you suppose happens?"

"We lose business," said the guy from lighting. (Derrick still didn't know his name.)

Derrick nodded. "Right! A woman once told me, that when we lose a customer, we lose a neighborhood. I believe we lose more than that. I believe we lose an entire community."

"That sounds impressive," said Debbie. "But what's it supposed to *mean*?"

Derrick didn't bother looking in her direction.

"Most of the products in this store are not cheap," Derrick said. "To attract customers, we have to offer them something that justifies the expense. So, we promise professional advice, solid customer service, and excellent complaint resolution."

He looked around the table again. "Answer me honestly... Do you think we're making good on that promise?"

Nearly every head in the room shook. No.

"How do we look, when we don't answer our phones?" Derrick asked. "How do we look when we ignore a half-dozen customers in our department, because we're watching television? How do we look when we're more interested in taking the weekend off than we are in having the store succeed?"

"We look like a joke!" said Leonard from flooring, speaking for the first time. "We look like we don't care..."

Derrick nodded slowly. "Sounds harsh, doesn't it? But no one ever said that life in retail is easy."

"Okay," said Tina. "What's your magic solution? What's your big plan for fixing everything?"

Derrick started to answer, but stopped short. These people didn't need to be handed the answer. They need to be challenged.

"We have more than fifty years of experience in this room. Closer to seventy-five. Here's what we're going to do... Tomorrow, I want each of you to tell me what we can do differently to improve customer service."

"Does that go for you, too?" asked Tina.

Derrick looked directly at her. "If you don't want to be here, Tina, you can consider your presence optional."

He stared hard, letting his words hang there.

Tina lowered her eyes. "I just wanted to confirm that this is a group activity."

Derrick couldn't help rolling his eyes. "It's an activity for *all* of us. And I promise each of you—when I see you tomorrow, I will tell you what I'm going to do differently to improve how we serve the customer, and how we serve each other."

The meeting broke up, and Derrick could tell that he'd gotten through. Everyone either shook his hand, or nodded in respect before leaving the room.

He was sure that everyone would work hard to meet his challenge. Everyone except for the Wicked Witches of the West, anyway.

Chapter 32

5:30 PM

Derrick sat quietly in his office, listening to Debbie explain why it was in the best interest of her clients that she and her design team *not* work the Memorial Day weekend.

"We work Monday through Friday, to accommodate cabinet makers, installers, and clients," Debbie said. "We can't take days off during the week, because our clients expect us to be here to serve them. That only leaves the weekends."

Derrick forced himself not to shake his head. What a load of bullshit.

"None of the other stores are having their designers work this weekend," Debbie said. "So I don't think we should be forced to. It wouldn't be good for morale. Besides, many of my people have prearranged plans with family and friends. It wouldn't be fair to cancel at the last minute."

She paused before adding, "Isn't family important to you?"

Derrick had been waiting for her to play that card. So, he nodded. "My family is very important to me. That's why I work."

Debbie straightened in her chair. "This is a serious matter, and I don't think you should be cracking jokes."

"I wasn't joking," Derrick said. "I have a job in order to feed my family, and put a roof over their heads. Providing for their wellbeing is more important to me than having a weekend barbeque with friends, or taking out-of-town relatives to Sea World."

Debbie didn't have a good answer for that, so she shifted tracks. "Every designer was hired with the understanding that their work hours are Monday through Friday, from 8:00 a.m. to 4:30 p.m."

Derrick rubbed the back of his neck. "Is that in their employment contracts?"

That stopped Debbie cold. "What?"

"It's a simple question," Derrick said. "I keep hearing about this 'all-important' understanding that the designers don't have to work weekends. I'll make you a deal... Show me the section of their employment contracts where the company agrees to the hours you mentioned, and I'll never ask the designers to work another weekend."

"I don't think it's in writing," Debbie said.

"I don't either," Derrick said. "And I've *checked*."

Debbie's eyes narrowed. "I know what this is about," she said. "I hear the gripes from everyone on the floor. They bitch about having to work weekends, while the design room doesn't. You don't want to stand up to the complaints, so you're knuckling under, and my people get punished."

Derrick had heard just about enough of this shit.

"First," he said, "I don't think it's punishment to ask someone to do their job."

Debbie started to speak, but Derrick cut her off.

"I'm not finished yet," he said. "Second, this isn't about complaints from the floor-level associates, or anyone else. This holiday promotion was designed from the very beginning to be all-hands-on-deck. You chose to interpret that to mean that the design team is exempt. I'm telling you that your interpretation was wrong."

Debbie opened her mouth again.

"I'm still not finished," Derrick said. "Third, I've seen the orientation briefing that's given to designers when they're first hired. In fact, I've given that orientation myself, more than once. I can practically quote it verbatim. Designers are told that they will *generally* be scheduled to work on weekdays, and that they will have *most* weekends off. But they are also told that they *will* be required to work on certain weekends, when there are major promotions to drive project sales."

"That's what this is," Derrick said, "a major weekend promotion, to drive sales. It was announced that way, and structured that way from the very beginning. So, none of this should be a surprise to you, or your designers. This Memorial Day promotion is perfectly within the boundaries of the designers' employment contract, and it's perfectly supported by the orientation briefings given to all designers."

Derrick sat back in his chair.

"I have no intention of telling my team to cancel their weekend plans," Debbie said. She was trying for her usual air of defiance, but her voice had lost its cocky edge.

Derrick savored the moment. '*Who's your daddy, now?*' he asked, silently.

"YOU HAVE NO RIGHT," Debbie shouted.

Derrick suppressed a laugh. "I know that," he said, calmly. "I have no right... But *The Design* does."

Debbie rose from her chair. "You haven't heard the last of this," she sneered. And she stormed out of the office.

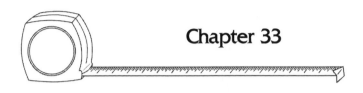

Chapter 33

8:30 PM

Derrick was glad to get home at a decent hour, but sorry that he missed saying goodnight to his son. When he came through the front door, he called out like he usually did. "Honey, I'm home." But he kept his voice low, for fear of waking Etienne.

He walked quietly upstairs and opened the door to Etienne's room, staying in the hallway and watching his sleeping boy. A feeling of pride swept over him. Etienne found magic in everything. He turned a simple walk through the park into an adventure. Every bird and every squirrel was a source of wonder to him. 'Wow, Dad!' he'd say. "Did you see *that*?"

A hand touched Derrick's shoulder. "Come on," Jennifer whispered, "before you wake him up."

Derrick closed the door carefully. "I just wanted to see him for a moment."

"If he wakes up, *you're* going to be the one to stay with him until he falls asleep."

They went to their bedroom, where Jen returned to bed. She sat up against the headboard, so she could continue reading. "How did it go today?"

Derrick sighed, and shook his head. "Not good. Pissed off customers, late orders, missing shipments, crazy internal politics, and associates trying to weasel out of working the holiday."

He began to undress for bed. "Oh, and one of my cashiers managed to melt her register. I still don't know how that happened."

Jennifer lowered her book. "Hmfff. Anything else?"

"Yeah," Derrick said. "Nobody answers their phones. The associates will let the phones ring, and ring, and ring. I practically have to break someone's arm to get them to answer a call. Of course, by then it's too late. The customer is irate, and wants to speak to the store manager."

"You're not the only manager in the store," Jen said.

Now it was Derrick's turn to "Hmfff!"

He reached for his pajama bottoms and pulled them on. "My management team is just as bad as the associates. Maybe worse. They avoid ringing telephones like the bubonic plague."

Jennifer rested her head against the backboard. "What are you going to do about it?"

Derrick slipped into his pajama shirt, and started to button it. "I'm going to bed. It's not worth losing sleep over."

A noise from the hallway caused them to turn and face the door. It was Etienne, and he was heading for their bedroom.

Derrick started to move, but Jennifer held up a hand. "I'll put him back to bed."

Derrick finished buttoning his shirt, listening to them talk.

"Why did Daddy take so long coming home?" Etienne asked.

"Daddy was scheduled to work late," Mommy replied.

"Why?"

"They needed his help at work."

"Does Daddy like working late?"

"He has to pull his weight, same as everyone."

"Doesn't he like being here with us?"

Derrick froze, waiting for her response.

"Of course he does," she answered, finally.

Derrick breathed a sigh of relief. He wondered... Had she paused on purpose?

Etienne shifted gears. "Do you think we can visit Daddy at work?"

"Yes, but now you have to go back to sleep. Remember why boys need to have a good night's sleep?"

Etienne nodded enthusiastically. "Yes! Boys need to get rest, so we can do well in school, and learn a lot of cool things that will help us when we grow up."

"That's right."

She hugged Etienne and laid him back to bed.

"Does the same go for girls?" Etienne asked.

"Yes, the same goes for girls. Now, promise me you'll go back to sleep."

"I promise, so long as you tell Daddy I love him."

"I will."

Jennifer returned to the bedroom and saw Derrick brushing his teeth. "Feeling better?" she asked.

"He's quite a boy," Derrick said.

"Oh, he's quite a boy," said Jennifer. She climbed back into bed. "And he's quite a handful."

"Want a glass of wine for bed?"

Jennifer made a face. "I already brushed my teeth, but…Yeah, why not?"

Derrick tip-toed downstairs and returned with two glasses of red wine.

Jen sipped at her glass, and made a face. "What is this?"

"Merlot. We've been stuck on Pinot and Shiraz for a while. I thought it might be nice to try something different."

Jennifer glared at the wine in her glass as though it had physically assaulted her. "Don't be ridiculous! No one drinks Merlot anymore."

Derrick sipped his wine, and raised his eyebrows approvingly. "Oh, I don't know," he said. "This brand isn't as dry as some of the others. Besides, you only feel that way because of that movie where the guy screams about how he's not drinking any fucking Merlot."

Jennifer laughed. "Well, that guy in the movie was right. Merlot sucks!"

Now it was Derrick laughing. "I love it when you talk dirty."

They tapped glasses in a toast, took another sip, and kissed.

Jennifer put down her glass and picked up the book she was trying to finish.

Derrick reached for his crossword puzzle.

"This one's got me stumped," he said, tapping on the line. "What do they call the person who assists someone driving?"

Without skipping a beat Jennifer replied, "A backseat driver."

Derrick turned to face her. "Don't be a wise gal."

"It's not a person," Jen said, snickering. "It's navigational assistance, sometimes referred to as group assistance. A lot of the expensive new cars come with that feature."

Derrick counted the blocks on the puzzle and deciphered the answer. "You're right! It's G-R-O-U-P-A-S-S-I-S-T-A-N-C-E."

Jennifer made a face. "Now, you can sleep well."

But Derrick did not sleep well.

He tossed and turned, and woke up repeatedly. His restless body accidentally kicked Jennifer in the legs a couple of times, until she elbowed him in the ribs.

What was wrong with his store? It had a terrific location, and the layout was consumer-friendly. They were price-competitive, provided free delivery, and offered finance options. When one sale ended, another began, so the problem couldn't be a lack of promotions.

He sat up in bed, trying to figure the answer.

Jennifer rolled over, showing him her backside. "Go to sleep."

"I can't sleep," he said. "I'm trying to figure out what I have to do."

He lay back down in bed, his eyes pointed toward the darkened ceiling.

"Well figure it out quietly," Jen said. "I need some sleep."

Derrick continued to stare at the ceiling. He remembered what Tim had said, about the store having no synergy. That was true, but synergy was the result of other things, like team spirit, motivation, and inspiration.

That last word stuck in Derrick's head. *Inspiration...*

He couldn't force his people to feel team spirit. He couldn't create true motivation, not in a week. But maybe he could become a source of inspiration...

His associates didn't care, because no one above them seemed to care. That was why they didn't help customers, or answer phones. They didn't see their managers taking the job seriously, so why should they bother?

Derrick sat up again. "That's it!"

Jennifer turned her head and opened one eye. "*What's* it?"

"I'll lead by example," Derrick said. "Everyone's biggest gripe is that the managers don't answer their phones, so why should anyone? I'll show them what happens when everyone from the store manager on down answers his phone every time it rings."

Jennifer yawned. "And you think that'll help turn things around?"

"Hell yes!" Derrick said. "If my people see me giving my best, it'll inspire them to do the same."

Jennifer closed her eye and snuggled deeper under the covers. "That sounds like an awfully simple solution for such a complex problem."

"Why shouldn't it be simple?" Derrick asked. "Customer service isn't complicated. It just takes attention to the basics. If I set a good enough example, I can help my people see that."

Jennifer yawned again, and nodded. "Good. Now, we can both get some sleep."

Chapter 34

Wednesday
9:45 AM

When everyone arrived in the rug department for the morning meeting, they found Derrick standing there, smiling broadly.

One associate whispered to another, "What's he got up his sleeve?"

The response was a shrug.

A few stragglers shuffled in, drinking coffee and munching bagels or croissants.

Derrick waited patiently, still wearing his happy-face. He was here to win them over, not hammer them.

At last, he stepped forward. "Good morning, everyone."

A few of them returned his greeting. The rest stood silent.

The Wicked Witches hovered at the edge of the small crowd like a pair of vultures. They were in for a surprise.

"Yesterday was an interesting day," Derrick said. "We didn't hit our sales goal, but our customer count was ten percent better than last year at the same time."

So far, so good. He'd made it clear that everything was not perfect, but he was keeping the tone positive.

"I've spoken to a lot of you," he said, "And it's clear that not everyone is excited about working this holiday weekend."

A few heads bobbed up and down.

"I want you all to know that I understand how you feel," Derrick said. "I have a family, and I'd like to be with them this weekend, but..."

He held out his arms with his palms facing upward, as if to say, '*it-is-what-it-is.*'

"Unfortunately," he said, "such is the nature of retail."

Before Derrick could continue, Jesus in appliances said, "Amen to that!"

All eyes turned in his direction, and Jesus nodded toward Derrick, slightly smiling.

Then Fran Silva added her own nod. "That's the way it's always been."

"Who doesn't know that?" asked someone in the back.

"We *all* need to be here," said another.

"I'd rather spend that time with my family," said Kelly in flooring.

Everyone stared at Kelly, shocked that he had the balls to be so blunt.

Kelly shrugged. "Hey, I'm just telling the truth..."

"I'd rather be drinking a beer," said Michael from trade, "but I have a family to support. That's why *I'll* be here."

The group rippled with laughter and applause.

Derrick's smile widened. This was precisely what he'd been hoping for. It was a long way from real team spirit, but laughing together was a start.

He looked at Tina and Debbie. They wore the only scowls in the group.

More than one person followed Derrick's gaze, and caught a glimpse of the negative energy between the two women and their new store manager.

Derrick raised his hands to quiet everyone down. "Okay folks, thanks for the support."

He loved the sound of that. "I don't want any of you to think I don't empathize with your view of quality family time. I appreciate it, the same as the person standing next to you. Having said that, we all know what we have to do. I'm asking each of you to put your best foot forward, to ensure that we have a successful sales event this holiday weekend. I promise you that my best foot will be right next to yours. I'll have to ask you not to make fun of my shoes."

This brought another round of laughter.

"We have some terrific ideas to help generate customer excitement," Derrick said. "A few of those ideas came from me, but most of them came from you and your leadership team." He pointed toward his assistant store managers and department supervisors standing to one side of the group.

"I've only been here a couple of days," Derrick said, "but I've already come to the conclusion that you have high expectations for our assistant managers, our supervisors, and me."

More than a few heads bobbed up and down.

"I *love* a challenge," Derrick said.

People smiled at this.

"Your management team has to meet a lot of expectations," Derrick said. "We have to meet the expectations of the company, the expectations of the stockholders, and—of course—the expectations of our customers.

But before we can do any of those things, we have to do something else. We have to meet *your* expectations."

He had their attention, now. Even the coffee and bagel bunch was listening to every word.

"Can anyone guess the number one complaint I heard yesterday?" Derrick asked.

More than a few hands were raised, and he called out Annabelle from the service desk.

"No one answers their phones," she said.

Heads nodded all over the crowd, followed by murmurs of assent.

The faces of the ASMs and DHs went rigid. They were obviously not happy about finding themselves at the center of the crosshairs.

Derrick nodded. "You're absolutely right, Annabelle. No one answers their phones. But before you start throwing rotten tomatoes at the management team, keep in mind that they're not the only ones. I've seen cashiers, support personnel, and sales associates ignore their phones too. So, let's just admit that we're all guilty."

There was no response from the group.

Derrick continued. "All of us know how important this Memorial Day promotion is. It's going to be one of the biggest sales days of the year. The company is sending out mailers and newspaper ads, announcing huge discounts. That's why we need everyone to be here, and playing at the top of their game."

Okay, that was enough of the pep-talk. He didn't want to overdo it, and lose them. Time to get to the meat of this little speech.

"In order to do your job, you need the leadership team to be here for you. Am I right?"

Again heads bobbed around the group.

Derrick pulled out his phone, and held it over his head. "I promise you that I will answer my phone *every* time it rings."

He paused, letting his words hang there.

"I will *be* there for you, and for the customer, as long as I'm in the store," he said. "And so will the rest of our leadership team."

Derrick glanced in their direction, and saw glum expressions. He didn't let it worry him. They'd get over it.

"Nothing is more disappointing than waiting endlessly for a manager to pick up their phone," he said. "So I stand before you to say I will answer my phone twenty-four-seven."

At that exact instant, the phone in Derrick's hand rang.

Derrick didn't hesitate. He pressed the talk button, and put the phone to his ear. "Thank you for calling *The Design*. This is Derrick. How may I help you?"

The caller hung up.

Derrick caught movement out of the corner of his eye. He glanced at Tina in time to see her phone slide back into her pocket.

"Guess we have a prankster," Derrick said.

This created a laugh from the group, and more than one person looked in Tina's direction.

Derrick checked his watch. "Okay everyone, it's time to open the doors. Let's have a million dollar day, and a million smiles!"

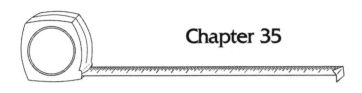

Chapter 35

10:00AM

Derrick's phone rang. Shit! They were putting him to the test already. The caller ID was from the front end cash registers. He answered the call in the most cheerful tone he could muster. "This is Derrick."

"Derrick, this is Florence, at the front end. Sam called; she's going to be late. Who's going to give me my break?"

Derrick shook his head. She's only been on the clock fifteen minutes and already she's asking for a break? "I'll have someone from the service desk relieve you when it's time. Call Teresa, if you have to. She's the head cashier, and will know who can give you your break."

"No one answers the phone," said Florence.

"That changes as of today," Derrick replied, flatly. He hung up and said to himself, "I hope."

Derrick walked to the center of the store and stopped at the crossroads of the sales floor. Which way should he go? To the north was the bath showroom. Designers loved this area, and often walked clients here for ideas.

To the south was the appliance department. He didn't feel like going there. Lighting was to the west. Too hot in there. To the east was kitchen showroom. Been there and done that.

He decided to check out the bath showroom.

When he arrived, he spotted two female customers browsing the selection of vanity cabinets.

It was time to inspire... Set the example... Engage the customer.

He stepped forward. "Hello, how may I help you today?"

Only one looked up to see who was talking. "Just looking."

Derrick knew better. No one just looks. "Is there anything in particular you're looking for?"

He beamed proudly, happy at the thought of following the steps of the sale by asking questions.

This time, the other woman spoke. "When we want help, we'll ask for it." Her glare was as curt as her tone.

Derrick maintained his polite demeanor. "Is this your first time visiting our store?"

The women ignored him, and went back to perusing the displays.

An awkward silence ensued before Derrick said, "Well, thank you for coming. Should you have any questions, I'll be happy to—"

One of the women silenced him with a glare.

Derrick nodded. "I'll leave you two alone then," he said.

He strolled away as casually as possible, but he knew that his ears must be bright red with embarrassment. He should have visited kitchens.

Naomi had been a certified kitchen designer for three years before joining *The Design* a year ago. Time management was not her strongpoint, which accounted for her jumping from three design firms in two years.

"If you can't meet clients on time, you're in the wrong business," her former-employers had said on more than one occasion.

Naomi was a skilled designer, but her close-ratio was below expectations. Every week, the PSM met with her team to discuss projected sales, timelines, and milestones for project orders. Every week, Naomi was late, unprepared, and unable to close her projects.

To Debbie's credit, she worked closely with Naomi to ensure she understood *The Design's* process.

Time and again Naomi had proven that she did understand the process, by explaining each stage of the client project on her plate. She completed the necessary paperwork. She turned in design drawings to installers, so they could submit a bid. She partnered with sales associates to assist in selling required fixtures, such as appliances, faucets, fixtures, lighting, flooring, and other products. She definitely understood the process.

Naomi's problem was tardiness. She simply couldn't make it to work on time, and clients do not appreciate being stood up.

Debbie had discussed the problem with Naomi multiple times.

Naomi's response was always the same. "I'm simply a late person."

"I've had it with Naomi," Debbie said to Tina in the HR office. "She's working the system, and playing us for fools."

Tina hated T&A issues. SOP stated that if a person was late to work 10 times in a single year, they were subject to job termination. But that was only if the manager had proper documentation showing that they had discussed the matter with the associate, and implemented a game plan for improvement.

The trouble was that most managers failed to document tardiness and excess absences, making it difficult to hold anyone accountable.

"You've got the necessary documentation to suspend her," said Tina. "What do you want to do?"

Debbie sighed. A suspension was the first step to termination, but that could take weeks, including an investigation. All of which added up to a ton of paperwork which Debbie had no intention of doing.

But Debbie had an idea...

"I think this is a decision for our new store manager," she said. Her tone was laced with contempt.

Tina brightened at the thought. "I think that's an *excellent* idea."

Chapter 36

10:45 AM

Gina Strasser was feeling the heat as she unloaded pallet after pallet from the trailer onto the receiving dock. Her supervisor had told everyone to expect a hard day, in anticipation of the upcoming sales event.

What an understatement.

In addition to the pressure of unloading 18-wheel trailers, checking in each pallet to verify inventory, and sending them to the floor to be stocked on the shelves, Gina believed that she constantly had to prove herself.

"This job is hard enough as it is," said the receiving supervisor, Kim Purcell. "I don't need slackers with no *cojones*. I need men!"

That statement had nearly cost Kim her job, and it had assured Gina the position in receiving when she threatened to sue the company.

In truth, Gina didn't really blame Kim for feeling that way. Gina was five feet tall and weighed less than a hundred pounds. She was so thin that many people wondered how she expected to heft product off pallets. To top it off, she was pretty. That shouldn't have mattered, but it did. She didn't look like she should be driving a forklift. She looked better suited to the sales floor, as a specialist or concierge.

But Gina needed to work in receiving, because the schedule allowed her to go to school on week nights and study during the weekend.

"She'll have to pull her weight, same as all of us," Kim had declared.

And that's precisely what Gina did.

She had learned how to drive the forklift, electric pallet jack, reach lift, and order picker. And she had remained accident-free for over a year. She flawlessly completed her paperwork when checking in inventory, something that none of the male veterans in receiving could boast. She even assisted the return-to-vendor associate in obtaining vendor credit for product damaged prior to receipt—something that no one wanted to do.

Gina was a model operations associate. She came to work on time, worked safely, assisted the operations manager in quarterly audits, and even served as a backup cashier for the returns desk.

None of this endeared her to Kim Purcell.

"Aren't you finished yet?" said Kim. It was more an accusation than question.

"This is the last pallet," said Gina, lowering the forks that dropped it right in front of Kim's feet.

"It's about time," Kim snapped. "Throw away the trash and go to lunch. I don't want anyone having late lunches in my department."

Gina switched off the propane-powered forklift and climbed down.

Marcos was checking in product on one of the pallets. When Kim was out of earshot, he looked at Gina. "Why do you let her talk to you that way?"

Gina laughed. "Why do you always wait until she's gone before you ask questions like that?"

Marcos snickered, and returned his limited attention span back to his work.

Gina knew he would have loved nothing better than to instigate an exchange between her and Kim, and Gina wasn't taking the bait.

Gina's revenge was to do her very best every day. So she kept her nose clean and stayed out of trouble.

When Gina went to throw the trash down the compactor, she saw the padlock was locked.

Shit. She checked her watch. 10:55 a.m. If she didn't empty this trash before she clocked out for lunch, Kim would give her hell. She hurried to find Kim for the key.

She caught up with Kim in the break room. "Kim, the compactor is locked."

Kim stared blankly. "You know I can't give you my key."

This was true. Only authorized key holders could use store keys.

"I'm not asking you to give it to me," Gina said. "I'm asking you to please open the compactor, so I can empty the trash."

Kim took a bite of her sandwich. "I'm at lunch. You know I can't work when I'm off the clock."

This was also true, but lame.

"Fine," Gina said. "Then I'll throw away the trash after lunch."

She walked toward the time clock.

"You'll do no such thing," declared Kim. "I told you before; everyone carries their weight."

Gina turned to face her. "Then I'll take a late lunch, and say it was because you refused to let me go to lunch until I threw out the trash."

Her tone caught Kim off guard.

Kim could feel the eyes of everyone in the room on her. Finally, she reached into her pocket and pulled out the key to the compactor. "Here. Bring it back to me when you're done."

Gina snatched the key from her hand and flashed a kiss-my-ass grin. "No problem."

She was out the door before Kim mouthed a single word. "Bitch."

The trash can weighed at least 20 pounds more than Gina did, but she wasn't about to ask Marcos or Darrell for help, despite their obvious stares as she unlocked the compactor and slid the trash can up against the wall.

"Where'd you get the key?" asked Darrell.

"What do you care?" Gina asked. That ended further inquiries.

Having practice at doing things on her own, Gina slid the trash can up against the compactor wall for leverage, making sure to bend at the knees to protect her lower back. With skill that never ceased to amaze others, she tilted the can over the ledge, and the trash emptied down the chute.

As she began to pull the can out of the chute, it slipped from her grasp, and slid down into the compactor.

Marcos laughed. "That sucks. Maybe you should've asked for help this time?"

"Go fuck yourself," said Gina.

She stared down the chute, and then looked at her watch. If she didn't clock out for lunch before her fifth hour, that cunt would write her up. Nothing would please Kim more than to have a reason to hold her accountable for an SOP violation.

"You could disconnect the trash bin outside," suggested Marcos. "But that will take at least 15 minutes."

Gina absent-mindedly chewed her nails, a habit that only manifested itself when she was nervous.

Finally she said, "I know a faster way." She lifted herself over the ledge, and slid down the compactor.

A few seconds later, she threw the trash can out of the compactor and climbed up the chute, pressing hands and feet against the walls to keep from sliding back down.

When she jumped to the floor, Marcos and Darrell stared at her in disbelief.

"Are you out of your fucking mind?" Darrell asked.

"Can't you read?" added Marcos. He pointed to the placard next to the compactor door: '**CLIMBING IN THE TRASH CONTRACTOR IS STRICTLY PROHIBITED. VIOLATORS ARE SUBJECT TO IMMEDIATE JOB TERMINATION.**'

Gina shrugged. "What the hell do you guys care? I've seen both of you do it before."

"*I* haven't," said a voice from the hall entrance.

Everyone turned and saw Kim. Her head was cocked to the side. A slight smile pulled up the corners of her mouth.

"I wondered why you were taking so long to bring back my keys," she said.

She looked at the warning sign, and then at Gina. "Now, I know."

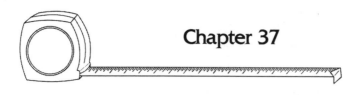

Chapter 37

11:15 AM

Sheila was ready to call it a day after two hours at the special service desk. And who could blame her? Every customer who called or came in to the store had a complaint that was beyond Sheila's ability to resolve.

"Where's my patio set?" asked the customer over the phone. "It was supposed to be delivered two weeks ago!"

"I apologize for the delay," said Sheila. "The sales associate who placed the order is here. I'll transfer you to him now, so he can look up the status of your order."

That was the only simple call she had taken, thus far.

"I checked with my credit company, and they said they have no record of the refund you processed last night," said another customer via phone call.

"It can take 24 to 48 hours before their system receives the refund information, ma'am," explained Sheila. *I told you this last night when I processed it. DUH!*

But the worst call was an appliance delivery and install gone wrong.

"Your delivery people brought my refrigerator, but they refuse to install it," the customer said. "They said I didn't pay an install fee. When I spoke with Gary, I specifically told him I wanted *The Design* to install it."

The customer was so angry that he had to pause to catch his breath. "If I was required to pay a fee, why didn't he bring it up when I was in the store? I would have gladly paid for it."

Sheila rolled her eyes. How the fuck would she know? She wasn't Gary.

"I apologize, sir," she said. "Let me see if I can get Gary on the phone."

"What good will that do?" the customer snarled. "He's going to say he doesn't remember, or that I declined an install. And you know where that'll leave me?"

Sheila waited for him to continue, but apparently he actually expected her to answer. Finally, she said, "Yes sir, with a refrigerator that needs to be installed."

"You're damned right!" He shouted loud enough that Sheila had to hold the phone away from her ear. "Now what are you going to do about it?"

Again, Sheila rolled her eyes. Like she was going to pull a rabbit out of her ass and get the damned thing installed for him.

"I'll have to get in touch with Gary so he can find an installer, sir."

"No you don't," the customer said. "I don't think you understand my situation. I came to you people because I was dissatisfied with the service I got at *Expo Design Center*. They remodeled my bathroom, and nothing went right. The salesperson ordered the wrong sized tub, pushing back my install two weeks. The toilet arrived damaged, and I had to pay an installer a trip charge that *Expo* refused to reimburse. The shower faucet leaked, and so did the bathroom sink. Like I said, nothing went right."

Life's a bitch, thought Sheila.

"When I went to *The Design*, I explained to Gary why I was willing to shop with you," continued the customer. "I didn't want any more problems. I believe if people do their job right the first time, problems will be avoided."

Sheila held back a laugh. If the world actually worked that way, she'd win the lottery, and steal Brad Pitt away from Angelina Jolie.

But the customer wasn't done venting yet...

"Now, I'm told by your delivery people that I have to call the store, which is why I'm talking with you now, to find out what happened and when I can get my fridge installed."

He paused again, to catch his breath. "What you don't seem to appreciate is that I took this day off from work to be here, and have my new fridge installed. I inconvenienced myself, because *The Design* doesn't do installs on the weekend. Not only did I lose a day's pay, but I *still* don't have my fridge installed. Are you hearing me?"

"Every word, sir," Sheila said. "So what you're saying, is that the install did not take place, and that you want to know what we will do to make this right. Is that about right, sir?"

The customer grunted. "Yeah."

"Okay, then," Sheila said, "I'm going to have Gary speak with you, so he can explain how this will be resolved to your satisfaction. I work at the special services desk, sir, not the appliance department."

The customer sighed. "Fine. Put me in touch with Gary."

But Gary wasn't available. He was out to lunch.

The last thing Sheila wanted to do was tell the customer he'd have to wait for a phone call. The bastard would probably keep her on the phone another half hour, going over the same thing again!

Then it came to her. She could ask Derrick to speak to the customer. After all, he said he'd be available twenty-four-seven.

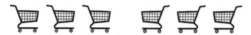

"Transfer the call to me," said Derrick, trying to sound upbeat. They were really putting him to the test.

"Wait," he said. "What's the customer's name?"

"PJ Nabors," replied Sheila.

Derrick stiffened. That wasn't possible. Life couldn't be that cruel. What were the odds that the same trouble-making asshole would haunt him at two different stores?

"Did you say his name is PJ Nabors?"

"Yes."

Derrick shook his head as he remembered his previous encounter with Mr. Nabors.

"Okay, Sheila. Transfer the call."

Chapter 38

12:00 PM

Derrick was about to leave his office for lunch when Debbie walked in. "Got a minute?" She wasn't asking a question.

"I'm done," Derrick said. "I'll be back in thirty minutes. I'm gonna grab a bite."

After his exchange with PJ Nabors, his appetite was anything but hearty.

Debbie blocked his path. "I've got something that can't wait."

Who the hell didn't?

"Fine," Derrick said. "Let's hear it."

Debbie took a seat in front of his desk, an indication that he should sit too.

"It's about a member of my team," Debbie said. "Her name is Naomi."

Derrick didn't need this. He sat listening, while Debbie launched into a detailed explanation of Naomi's continual tardiness.

Aside from a much-needed break—which he had yet to take—he had to find out if an alternate installer was available to handle the refrigerator install today, and then make a follow-up call to PJ Nabors.

And here was Debbie, handing him a problem she knew to be as delicate as nitro glycerin.

Time and Attendance issues should have been black and white. As far as Derrick was concerned, you came to work on time or you didn't. You took your lunch before your fifth hour of work, or you didn't. You clocked out when scheduled, so as not to acquire unauthorized overtime, or you didn't. It was no more complicated than that. Or at least it shouldn't have been.

In reality, terminating an employee for excessive tardiness was tricky, because the company's policies were not enforced consistently. Derrick knew that each store had a different view of what was considered excessive tardiness, and therein lay the problem. Was ten times in a year excessive? Or twenty? Or even thirty? Some stores had people on the books with close to fifty instances of tardiness in a single year!

"At what point do we terminate an associate for this violation?" Derrick asked on more than one occasion.

The answer was always the same. "Partner with human resources."

Of course, HR always threw it back in the lap of the store manager... And there the issue stayed.

It would be easy for an associate to sue the company for unfair treatment, when it was learned that other associates with more tardiness violations had not been fired. The last thing any manager wanted was a lawsuit for favoritism, and so the standard practice was to turn a blind eye.

Derrick didn't want to be seen as the type of SM who looked the other way. He was proud of his image as someone who addressed problems, rather than sweeping them under the rug. But he also didn't want to juggle hand grenades, and that's what this issue with Naomi could turn out to be.

"You're the project manager," he said to Debbie. "How do you want this handled?"

The question seemed to startle Debbie. She gave Derrick a *what-the-fuck* look. "You're the store manager," she said. "It's your call."

"Yes," Derrick said. "The final decision is mine. But I'm not going to make the call until I know that reasonable due diligence has been taken to protect the company from legal action."

"What do you mean?" asked Debbie.

"It's common knowledge this company has been inconsistent in holding people accountable for time and attendance issues," Derrick said.

Debbie looked puzzled. "So?"

"You've done a good job with the documentation," Derrick said. "You've clearly shown that she has a problem arriving to work on time, and that you've addressed it with her on numerous occasions."

"So you're going to terminate her?" demanded Debbie.

Derrick shook his head. "No. Or, at least, not yet. Before we go down that road, you need to run this by Tina to make sure that terminating Naomi won't create a liability issue for the company."

"Tina already knows about this," Debbie said. "She told me I should bring it to *your* attention."

"I understand that," Derrick said. "But to adequately protect the company's interests, we need to make sure that the T&A policies have been applied consistently across your entire department."

Debbie's voice took on a cautious tone. "What do you mean?"

Derrick could see by her expression that he'd stymied Debbie. Right about now, she was probably wishing she'd brought the other Wicked Witch along to this meeting.

Derrick smiled. "I mean—if the time records for all of the designers were examined—it would cause problems for the company if it turns out that tardiness problems have not been documented as carefully for other members of your department."

Debbie's cheeks turned red. "What are you insinuating?"

"I'm not insinuating anything," Derrick said. "I'm just pointing out that the T&A records for your department will probably be subpoenaed if Naomi decides to sue. And things could get ugly if her attorneys could demonstrate that the policies are selectively enforced."

"So, what are you saying?" Debbie snapped. "She breaks the rules and gets away with it?"

Derrick shook his head. "I didn't say that at *all*. I'm suggesting that you confer with our HR manager, and make sure that you've covered the bases. It might also be a good idea for you to have another one-on-one discussion with Naomi, and offer concrete suggestions for improving her attendance. Maybe she needs to be scheduled to work a later shift, or take longer lunches. You won't know, until you discuss it with Naomi."

"It won't work," Debbie said. "I've tried that."

"You may be right," Derrick said. "But giving it one more try is a win-win situation. If you counsel Naomi and her tardiness problem is corrected, you win. If her problem doesn't improve, you have documented proof that you've been more-than-generous in working with her. Then, if it becomes necessary to terminate her, you've done everything in your power to cover the company's back. You *still* win."

Derrick stood up, walked to the door, and opened it. "Either way it goes, I'm sure you'll handle it perfectly."

Debbie followed him reluctantly out of the office.

He closed the door behind her, and left for lunch. He was quite certain that she *wouldn't* handle it perfectly, but he had batted the ball back into her end of the court.

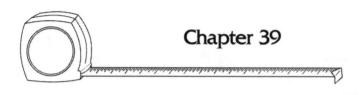

Chapter 39

12:30 PM

Tina rocked back and forth in her chair, carefully digesting Debbie's version of her conversation with Derrick. "So if I'm hearing you right, Derrick is *refusing* to hold Naomi accountable for excessive tardiness."

She looked to Debbie for a response.

Debbie had an uncertain expression on her face. She hadn't liked some of the things Derrick had said about company liability. He hadn't outright *said* that this could come back to bite her, but she didn't like the part about subpoenas.

Finally, she shrugged and nodded her head twice. "I guess so," she said feebly. "He said he wants me to consult with you, and handle it carefully."

Tina sat up straight. "But you asked *him* to handle it, because you've already written her up three times, right?" She was practically putting words in Debbie's mouth.

Debbie caught the drift of what Tina was hinting at, but she still wasn't completely sure that the two of them were in the clear. Then again, Tina was *very* good at making bad things stick to other people. She'd practically gotten Rob Morrison burned at the stake.

Debbie felt some of her confidence beginning to return. "Yeah," she said. "I guess that's about how it happened."

The smile on Tina's face held no joy, and no humor. "Well..." she said slowly. "This changes *everything*..."

At quarter to one, Derrick was mopping up a few stray crumbs of blue cheese with his last garlic fry. *Charlie's Bar & Grill* was just across the parking lot from the store, and he'd chosen the place pretty much at random. He had literally walked out the front door, and selected the first restaurant that caught his eye.

He'd been carefully avoiding junk food since making his ritual New Year's resolution to eat right, and set an example for his son. But the temptation of a buffalo burger with blue cheese and garlic fries had been too much for him.

Besides, he'd passed up a lap dance with a beautiful stripper the night before. It wasn't too much to treat himself to a burger and fries.

He downed the last of his ice tea and crunched on the ice.

The waitress appeared at his elbow. "Can I get you a refill?"

"I'd rather have a beer," Derrick said.

"We have about a dozen micro-brews, and four kinds of draft," she said.

Derrick smiled. "I've got to go back to work, so I'll take a rain check instead."

After paying his bill, he took his time walking across the parking lot. The sunshine felt good on his face. He needed to get out of the store more often.

Florence was taking her break in front of the store, near the entrance. She'd had a busy morning at the cash registers, and her hourly cigarette was most welcome.

"Careful," Derrick said. "Those things will give you cancer."

His phone rang, and he raised it to his ear.

"Those things will give you cancer *too*," said Florence, grinning.

"Hello," said Derrick into the phone. He walked past Florence, acknowledging her comeback with a nod.

The call was from Annabelle. "Derrick, are you back from lunch? I need you at the special service desk. I've been trying to get hold of a manager."

"What's up?"

"I have a customer who wants to pay for his special order in cash."

"Okay," Derrick said. "So what's the problem?"

"He doesn't want to fill out the IRS Form 8300," said Annabelle.

Derrick walked in the front door of the store. "What has he got against Form 8300?"

Annabelle sighed. "He said that's not a good way to do business."

That struck Derrick as odd. "How much money are we talking about?"

"He wants to pay thirty thousand dollars in twenty dollar bills."

Derrick stopped in the middle of the sales floor. "He has thirty thousand in twenty dollar bills with him?"

"Yep, in a brown paper bag."

Derrick whistled softly. "I'll be right there."

Miguel Martinez was a practical man, or so he said several times, as he repeated his story to Derrick. His only flaw was failing to play by the rules.

"We value your business, Mr. Martinez," said Derrick. "But the law doesn't give us any leeway on this. Any cash purchase over ten thousand dollars must be reported to the IRS."

Derrick was certain that Miguel had heard all this before, but the man was pretending that the whole IRS thing was news to him. He wasn't a very convincing actor.

"I make large cash purchases all the time," explained Miguel. "I *never* have to fill out some form. It's easy... I hand you my cash, and you place my order."

Yeah, right!

"Look, Mr. Martinez…"

"Call me Miguel."

"Okay, Miguel, I can't answer for what other stores do. If they let you skip IRS Form 8300, that's between you and them."

The customer opened his mouth to speak, but Derrick continued. "Legally, we have no option if you decide to pay cash. We *must* report cash payments over ten thousand dollars to the IRS, or we risk being fined."

"I've done this at your other stores," Miguel said. "They never made me fill out that stupid form."

"I heard you the first time," Derrick said. "But my store follows the law. As Annabelle explained, if you pay with a money order, check, or credit card, you don't have to complete the form. If you want to pay cash, the law requires a Form 8300."

Miguel shifted his weight from one foot to the other. "Why do you insist on making this complicated? All I want to do is give you my money, and you persist in giving me a hard time."

Derrick glanced over his shoulder. Annabelle, Sheila, and Allison were watching—clearly happy that he had kept his word about making himself available.

Miguel stuck his hands in his pockets. "So how are we going to do this?"

Derrick resisted the urge to raise his voice to this idiot. "You have two options," he said. "The same two options that Annabelle has already explained to you. Fill out the form, or use a different form of payment."

"I don't want to fill out the form," Miguel said.

Derrick nodded. "That's fine. Then we will be happy to accept a charge card, cashier's check, or money order."

"You don't understand," Miguel said. "I don't want to fill out that form."

Derrick looked down at his feet. He was getting tired of running in circles. Besides, who the hell carries thirty thousand dollars in cash?

Chapter 40

1:15 PM

"Derrick looked at his watch. Damn! That bonehead had taken up more time than he was worth.

Derrick hated to lose a sale, but the law was the law, and he wasn't about to violate an SOP that could cost the company a hefty fine, and kill his job.

In the end, Miguel Martinez had opened an account with *The Design*, and made his purchase on the *No Interest if Paid within 12 Months* plan.

Derrick had explained how Miguel could make monthly payments *under* ten thousand, and avoid the 8300 form altogether.

Miguel wasn't happy about it. He was accustomed to having his way. But he saw that Derrick wasn't willing to budge.

Miguel had grumbled the entire time he was filling out the credit application. "I'll never shop here again," he said.

The girls behind the service desk caught Derrick's eye. All of them mouthed the word '*Thanks.*'

Derrick felt a smile coming on, but he squelched it to avoid offending Miguel, who was clearly not in a smiling mood.

Derrick strolled away from the special services desk, and began to wander the sales floor. What to do now?

The supervisors from each department had submitted game plans for setting up displays and signage throughout the store. This might be a good time to see how that was coming along.

Rebecca, the supervisor over lighting, was working with Carlos and Claudia when Derrick walked into the department.

"How's it going?" asked Derrick, casually.

Rebecca looked relieved to see him. "Good, it's you. Maybe you can help us?"

Derrick gave her a mock frown. "I don't know... That's kind of an *unusual* request..."

Rebecca and her two associates laughed. Like everyone else in the store, they'd seen Derrick bouncing all over the place, helping people solve problems. It was common knowledge that his phone had been practically ringing off the hook.

Derrick smiled. "How can I be of assistance?"

"We need an extra person to help adjust the racks in the backroom for the inventory," explained Rebecca. "We had a truckload of product arrive this morning, and it's blocking the aisle in the back."

"I stocked as much as I could," said Carlos, "but we got busy with customers."

"And I can't climb up the racks," said Claudia. "I'm wearing a dress." She curtsied to prove her point.

Rebecca jumped in before Derrick could speak. "If I don't get this done fast, Kim is going to complain about the aisles being blocked."

Derrick understood her dilemma. The backroom aisles needed to be kept clear of freight, so that Kim and her crew could bring inventory from receiving to the sales floor. All supervisors were required to ensure that their freight was stocked on the racks assigned each department.

The problem was that they didn't have enough people on hand to get this done, so the aisles in back were typically clogged with pallets of freight.

"Let's have a look," said Derrick.

He led the way to the back of the store. True to their word, the aisle was blocked with pallet after pallet of lighting product, shrink-wrapped to the teeth.

"This looks familiar," Derrick said, walking between the pallets. "I take it you asked for help from the other DHs?"

They bobbed their heads.

"Alright," Derrick said. "Then I suppose we'll have to do this ourselves."

Derrick could not quite understand why people seemed to work with renewed enthusiasm alongside the store manager. He recalled his awkward, early years as an hourly associate assigned to the plumbing department.

After applying and reapplying for nearly two years Derrick, had been hired on as a plumbing associate. He had developed a fast friendship with his supervisor, Ronnie, who was excited to have someone on his team who actually worked. The other four associates were primarily concerned about doing as little as possible, and collecting a paycheck at the end of the week.

Upon reflection, Derrick recalled feeling punished for doing good work. Because Ronnie had continued to give him more to do, while never asking others to pull their own weight.

Eventually, Derrick had decided to speak up. "I only get paid for one job! I shouldn't have to do other peoples' work, simply because they choose to do as little as possible, and get away with it."

After this declaration, Derrick had expected some friction with his fellow associates. He was surprised to find that most of the resulting anger came from Ronnie. Apparently, Ronnie didn't appreciate being accused of looking the other way. He had begun hounding Derrick without mercy.

Derrick had endured two weeks of Ronnie's harassment. Then, he'd taken the matter to the store manager.

Maria Espinoza was one of the few female store managers in the company. She had a Bachelors Degree in Economics from SDSU, and took pride in having worked her way up through the ranks from associate to store manager.

She had one expectation from which she never waivered, and she repeated it often at the morning meetings. "Everyone needs to do their share. I expect an honest day's work from each of you, every time you're on the clock. If someone doesn't pull their share of the load, I wanna know about it."

So Derrick had approached Maria, and she had chosen to handle the problem in her own fashion. She had joined Ronnie and his team of associates, working side-by-side with them for a full week.

Derrick had been amazed by the results. The attitudes of his fellow associates had changed overnight, and the employees had retained their positive attitudes from then on.

Rebecca and her team held no such ill will toward each other, but with Derrick working alongside them, they seemed to become reenergized. Their task didn't feel so impossible after all.

Derrick mulled over this effect, while handing Carlos box after box of lighting merchandise to be stocked on the shelves.

They spent the next hour breaking down the pallets and stocking shelves with inventory. Derrick enjoyed this more than he had anticipated.

"It's fun to see the results of your hard work so quickly," he said.

Rebecca held her own by keeping pace with him. "You can work in my department any time."

If I only had the time, thought Derrick.

Annabelle from the service desk walked through the door. "Derrick, there you are!"

She sounded relieved and exhausted. "I've been searching all over the store for you."

Derrick brushed dust off his hands. "How can I help you?"

"I've been calling your phone for the last ten minutes," Annabelle said.

Derrick frowned. "Really? I haven't heard it ring."

He pulled the phone out and checked it. "The battery's dead."

"So much for your grand promises," said Rebecca.

Everyone froze. Rebecca's remark had clearly been intended as a joke, but it was perilously close to the line that no employee can ever cross safely. They were waiting to see if their new store manager would lash out in anger.

Derrick grinned. "Even Superman can be brought down by Kryptonite."

This brought a laugh from everyone present.

Derrick turned his attention back to Annabelle. "What's up?"

"I have a Mr. Michael Skelton at the service desk. He wants to speak with you." Her tone had a touch of apprehension, as though the mere mention of the man's name was somehow unpleasant, or dangerous.

Derrick slipped the dead phone back into his pocket. "What does he want to talk to me about?"

Annabelle took a deep breath. "Sarah in bath sold him a vanity cabinet, sink, faucet, bowl and countertop. We delivered it today, but he wants to know why we won't install it. Our delivery people said they were only supposed to drop it off. No install included."

"Did he pay for an installation?"

Annabelle shook her head. "Not a penny! I looked over his paperwork, and there's no install line."

Derrick nearly groaned. This kind of thing happened all too often. *The Design* offered free delivery, haul away of old product, and free *installation,* but exclusions applied. Naturally, no customer ever read the fine print to find out if their purchase actually qualified for the freebies. They just assumed that anything they bought would be covered, and then they got pissed off when things didn't work out that way.

The Design's Steps of the Sale procedure included an explanation of the full services offered, to prevent this kind of misunderstanding.

Derrick wasn't familiar enough with Sarah to know if she followed the Steps of the Sale. For that matter, he didn't know *anyone* in this store well enough to make such a judgment. But his gut feeling told him that Sarah wasn't one to leave loose ends dangling. No one in the company worked on commission, so there was little reason for anyone to be pushy with a customer.

"Have you spoken with Sarah about this?" asked Derrick.

Annabelle nodded. "Yes. She's with a customer, and can't break away to speak with Mr. Skelton. He doesn't want to talk with her anyway. He says we've got signs all over the store, promising free installation. He also says that Sarah didn't tell him he had to pay for an install."

"So *he* failed to read the fine print, but it's *our* fault," ventured Rebecca. She had her hands on her hips, shaking her head indignantly.

"I've dealt with this guy before," she said. "He makes a habit of pushing the envelope, because he knows if he complains high enough, he gets whatever he wants."

"You're damned right he does," added Carlos.

Derrick jumped in before the Skelton-bashing could continue. "Does Sarah consistently explain that certain installs require a bid, and therefore cannot be given free?"

The group was silent.

Derrick raised a hand. "Don't misunderstand me," he said. "I'm not asking you to dish dirt on a coworker. But I haven't been here long enough to know how a typical sales transaction works at this store. This customer sounds pretty difficult, and I want to make sure that I've crossed my T's dotted and my I's before I speak to him."

A look of relief swept over their faces.

"Yes," said Annabelle. "Sarah *always* explains what we install free, and what requires a bid. And we explain it to the customer again, when we ring them up at the service desk. We have a list of items requiring bids for appliances, kitchens, bath showroom, lighting, and flooring. When there's an install line, we tell them that a bid estimate will be required. Once the customer pays in full for the install, we schedule the work with our subcontractors."

Derrick nodded. Annabelle's explanation indicated that they were following the Steps of the Sale by the numbers.

Derrick pulled the dead cell phone out of his pocket, and held it out to Annabelle. "I'll make you a deal," he said. "If you'll take this phone to my office and plug it into the charger, I'll deal with your Mr. Skelton."

Annabelle accepted the phone without hesitation. "Deal."

"Okay," Derrick said. "Let me go and see how I can help this guy."

From the facial expressions of the associates, that would be easier said than done.

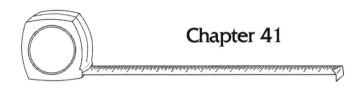

Chapter 41

3:15 PM

"Is this how you treat your customers?" whined Michael Skelton. "You're supposed to install my vanity for free, and that's what I *want!*"

Derrick was instantly glad that he'd steered Mr. Skelton to an empty consultation room. He definitely didn't want to have this conversation in front of other customers.

Listening to Michael Skelton was like playing a broken record. His nasal tone was irritating, and Derrick struggled not to make a face when the man spoke certain words in a piercing high-pitched tone.

Overweight, balding, and standing at six foot and two inches, Skelton apparently had the impression that he could go through life speaking to people like they were dirt, and still get what he wanted.

Skelton tapped a forefinger on the table. "I expect you to keep your promise. Don't you believe in keeping promises to your customers?"

Derrick started to speak, but Skelton cut him off. "Do you have any idea how much money I've spent here?"

It was all Derrick could do not to roll his eyes. He concentrated on following the steps to achieving customer satisfaction. Maintain eye contact. Let the customer finish without interruption. *Then*, offer a resolution.

The steps sounded easy enough, but Derrick knew he would be pushed to the limit with the person sitting across the table.

When the man seemed to have reached a stopping point, Derrick spoke. "Mr. Skelton, let me first apologize for the inconvenience."

"You're damned right this is an inconvenience," shouted Skelton. He looked through the window of the room at the customers nearby, trying to gauge whether or not his raised voice was enough to get their attention.

Derrick noticed the maneuver, and allowed the knowledge to show on his face. *Yes, Mr. Skelton, I know what you're trying to do.*

Mr. Skelton glared, as though he was about to reach over and tear out Derrick's throat.

Derrick looked on impassively. After an awkward moment of silence passed, Derrick spoke again. "Will you allow me to finish uninterrupted?"

Mr. Skelton sat in stony silence.

Derrick nodded. "As I started to say, I apologize for the inconvenience. We want to help you in all your project needs. In regard to the installation of your fixtures, your sales order clearly states that an inspection by our installer is required before we can give you an estimate for the installation cost. Every job is different, which is why we ask for our installers to inspect the job, so that we can provide the customer with the most competitive price on the market."

"I want you to install my cabinet," Mr. Skelton said, leaning forward. He spoke as though Derrick was a nine year old, trying to provoke him.

"I heard you the first time," Derrick said. "But as our service desk pointed out, you haven't paid for the install. Our installer needs to submit a bid first."

"This is unacceptable!"

"I can understand your frustration," Derrick said. "But your order clearly states that the price for installation is a separate charge."

Derrick held up the document, and pointed to the appropriate line of text. Then, he pointed to another section of the order. "This is your signature, acknowledging that you have read and understood the terms of the purchase."

Mr. Skelton didn't bother to glance at the document, an obvious sign that he was well aware of the verbiage.

"I can't believe the way I'm being treated," he said. "You're cheating me!"

Derrick mentally counted to ten before continuing. "No, Mr. Skelton, we're *not* cheating you. In fact, I'm trying to work with you to find a solution. I do have a proposal, if you want to hear it."

Skelton started to respond, but he stopped himself. "Go ahead…"

"What I have in mind is simple," Derrick said. "I propose to split the cost of the install price with you."

"That's ridiculous!" Mr. Skelton bellowed. "Why should I pay half? Do you take me for a fool?"

Derrick raised an eyebrow. "You don't really expect me to answer that, do you?"

He regretted the words instantly, but this guy was really starting to annoy him.

"How long have you been a store manager?" Skelton asked.

Derrick decided to dodge that particular curve ball. "I've been in the industry for nearly 20 years," he said. "But that's not really relevant to this situation."

"The hell you say!" Skelton snapped. "I'm in the real estate business. How would it look if I tell a buyer that a house costs a hundred thousand, then a week later, I come back and tell him he needs to pay a hundred and five?"

"Actually," Derrick said, "that's *exactly* what happens when you sell a house. You quote the buyer a sale price of a hundred thousand, but that's not what he pays. He also has to cover the escrow fees, appraisal fees, closing costs, and a number of other expenses. By the time transfer of ownership takes place, your buyer has shelled out a *lot* more than a hundred and five thousand. Does that mean *you're* cheating the buyer when he has to pay those additional costs?"

Skelton sat in stunned silence. He had no answer for that.

Derrick decided to keep up his momentum. "There are two ways this can end, sir. You can hire someone to do the install yourself, in which case you pay full price. Or, you can accept my proposal and split the difference."

"It's your choice," Derrick said. "Which will it be?"

The look on Skelton's face said it all. This had clearly not played out the way he had expected.

Finally, he shrugged. "I guess I've got no choice."

"Then we're agreed," Derrick said.

"Not by a long shot!" Skelton snapped. "I'm only accepting your offer because I want my install done before my family arrives for the holidays. But don't expect to ever see me again. This is the *last* time I'm ever going to shop here!"

For a split-second, Derrick thought about asking this knucklehead to put that promise in writing.

Chapter 42

4:00 PM

Derrick sat in Tina's office, reading the statement from Kim Purcell. Midway down the page, he shook his head. "Do we have signage posted by the compactor, prohibiting entry?"

"I put up the signs myself, when I helped open this store," Kim said. "They carry the standard verbiage required by the SOP: *Climbing in the trash contractor is strictly prohibited. Violators are subject to immediate job termination.*"

Derrick could feel Tina's eyes on him. She was watching for any sign of a mistake, waiting to pounce on him.

"What are you going to do?" she asked.

Derrick glanced up from the written statement. "The way I see it, Gina is not the only one in violation of the safety SOP."

Tina and Kim exchanged a puzzled look, and then their eyes flicked back to Derrick.

"What do you mean?" Kim asked.

"According to your statement, Kim, *you* gave an hourly associate your keys, to open the compactor."

The color drained from Kim's face, and Tina's jaw dropped open.

Derrick lowered the document. "You should know that only authorized personnel can be assigned store keys. Any manager supervisor handing over their keys to an unauthorized person is subject to, up to and including job termination."

"Now wait a minute!" exclaimed Kim.

Derrick nodded patiently. "I'm all ears."

Tina swallowed. "Let's all remain calm, shall we?"

"I'm perfectly calm," Derrick said.

"I only reported a safety violation," said Kim, defensively. "That's my job. I didn't expect retaliation for my actions."

Derrick felt the urge to smile, but he kept his expression bland. "Your own statement says that you gave Gina Strasser your keys to the trash compactor."

He held up the paper, as a reminder of what she had written. "In the event of a safety violation, I'm required to investigate, to determine the course of action needed to address the violation. This statement shows that there were at least *two* violations of the safety SOP. One on Gina's part, and one on *your* part."

Kim glared at Tina. "You didn't tell me I'd be *investigated*."

Tina began shaking her head. "We're simply covering all bases. There's no sense in blowing this thing out of proportion..."

She made eye contact with Kim and mouthed the words, *'don't say anything.'*

It was hard for Derrick to keep a straight face. Tina and Kim had concocted a fool-hardy plan to terminate an associate they didn't like. Now, their little scheme was blowing up in their faces.

It was about time to take Ms. Tina down off that pedestal of hers.

Derrick looked at Kim. "This is a serious matter," he said. "Your violation is no less serious than Gina's. Possibly more serious. As receiving supervisor, you're held to a higher standard than the associates who work for you."

He paused to let that sink in.

Derrick looked at Kim, then Tina, then back to Kim. "Is there something personal between you and Gina?"

Kim's silence showed that their clearly was something between her and Gina. But Kim shook her head no.

She looked at Tina. "My God," she said in a hushed voice. "You set me up."

"Don't say another word!" said Tina.

Derrick stared at her. "Excuse me? Did you just order a company employee to conceal information from the store manager during an investigation?"

Tina nearly cringed at the question.

"You're not an attorney," Derrick said, "and Kim is not your client. Your job is to assist me in uncovering the relevant facts. You can't very well do that when you're ordering one of the interested parties to keep her mouth shut."

Derrick was about to say something else, when his phone rang. He answered it.

"Two questions," the voice said. It was his wife, Jennifer. "What time are you coming home? And where are you taking us for dinner?"

Dinner? Shit! Derrick had forgotten that it was their family night out. He glanced at his watch. Where did the time go?

"I'll be out of here by six," he said.

"We'll be ready," Jen said. She blew him a kiss over the phone.

Usually Derrick responded in-kind, but not in front of associates. "Love you too," he said.

He hung up the phone, and slipped it back into his pocket. Then, he turned back to the matter at-hand.

Kim looked like she was about to wet her pants, while Tina glared evilly at him.

It was time to remind Wicked Witch #1 of who the daddy was around here.

"This can go two ways," Derrick said. "I can give each of you a counseling statement, with the understanding that any similar violations in the future will result in immediate termination."

He let the words hang there for several seconds.

"Or," he said, "I can terminate both of you right now."

Tina's face went bright red. "You can't terminate me!"

Derrick gave her a look. "I wasn't referring to you, Tina. I meant Gina and Kim."

He glanced around the office. "Where *is* Gina, by the way?"

"I sent her home, pending the outcome of our investigation," said Tina.

Derrick nodded, and turned to Kim. "Okay, you know the options. Which way do you want me to play this?"

Kim turned to Tina, who nodded ever so slightly.

"Fine," Kim said, looking like a deflated balloon. "Give each of us a write-up."

Derrick nodded to Tina. "Have the counseling statements completed, and on my desk first thing tomorrow."

Tina's eyebrows went up. "The HR *reviews* counseling statements. It's not my job to write them."

Derrick smiled. It was so easy to dislike this bitch.

"You are one-hundred percent correct," he said in a sweet voice. "I'll be happy to write them myself. I just thought you might want a little control over what they *say*..."

He could actually hear Tina grinding her teeth.

"Okay," Tina snapped. "I'll write them. Fine."

"Excellent," Derrick said. "Then, I guess we're all done here."

He was whistling when he walked out of Tina's office.

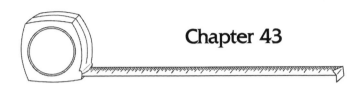

Chapter 43

5:45 PM

Derrick was ready to call it a day. After nearly two decades in the madhouse world of retail, he had seen and heard a lot of craziness. But this was his first go as store manager, and the pressure of having an excellent sales day on Memorial Day was unlike any other he'd experienced.

As an ASM, he'd always been able to lean on the store manager because the buck stopped with the guy in the big chair. Only now *he* was that guy.

Did he really want to deal with this shit? It wasn't going to stop. Hell, it probably wouldn't even slow down.

He remembered his conversation with Rob Morrison. Sure, the man was angry at what had happened to him. Who wouldn't be? But under Rob's anger, Derrick had seen a stronger emotion. Relief.

Derrick wondered if he had made a mistake in pushing for store manager. Maybe he should've stayed an ASM.

He shook his head. No use thinking like that. He was in it up to his neck, and his only choice was to make the best of the situation.

In the meantime, he was going to take his family out for dinner. Maybe he should leave early. What the hell, he was the manager.

He made it to the service desk when Sheila called out to him. "Derrick, do you have a moment to speak with this customer?"

Derrick saw a fashionably dressed woman in her sixties. She turned slowly turn to face him, like an old-school movie star, making a dramatic entrance.

Derrick fought hard to keep a straight face. "Certainly," he said. "How may I help you, ma'am?"

The lady held out her hand, as though expecting Derrick to kiss it. Who did she think she was? The fucking Queen of England?

Derrick took the offered hand in his, and gently shook it, bowing ever so slightly. "It's a pleasure meeting you, ma'am."

"I'm Barbara Roth," the woman said, holding her head high. Her cool voice suggested that she was accustomed to the red carpet treatment.

Well, they could certainly give her that.

"You wanted to speak with me?" Derrick asked.

"Yes," the woman said. "I want to tell you something about your store."

Derrick felt his smile narrow a fraction. "Is that so?"

"I've been living in this community for ten years," Ms. Roth said. "And we completed our kitchen remodel this week."

Derrick gave her the standard response. "Thank you for allowing us the opportunity to serve you. May I ask who your designer was?"

"It was Susan."

Derrick nodded. Then, he asked the question he dreaded most of all. "How did everything turn out?"

Barbara Roth sighed. "Well, let me tell you," she said. "When I decided to move forward with my remodel, I was reluctant to use *The Design*."

Uh-oh. Here it came! Why did this have to happen on his way out the door?

"But then I had dinner with my neighbor, and she said that your store had remodeled her kitchen, much to her satisfaction. So I decided to give you a chance after all..."

And they were back to the question Derrick hated. "How did we do?"

Ms. Roth smiled. "I'm pleased to say you did a terrific job!"

Thank the Lord!

"I'm glad to hear it!" Derrick said. "Thank you for telling me. Most customers don't bother to tell us when we're doing well. We only hear about it when there's a problem."

"I'm sure," Ms. Roth said. "That's why I came in-person, to tell you how satisfied I am."

"Thank you again," said Derrick.

Barbara Roth turned to leave, and then she stopped. "Although there was *one* thing I didn't like."

Derrick froze. Damn! He'd nearly been home-free.

"And what would that be?" he asked.

"The installers left their trash behind."

What the hell?

"I'm sorry," Derrick said. "Did you say our installers left their trash for you to clean up?"

Barbara Roth nodded. "You would think they'd have the grace to clean up after themselves."

"I don't believe it's part of the contract," Derrick said. "But it's certainly good business practice."

Barbara Roth didn't speak. She just stared at Derrick with an expectant look on her face.

Derrick cleared his throat. "Is there anything else, Ms. Roth?"

She frowned. "Isn't that *enough*?"

"I'm sorry," Derrick said. "I don't follow you?"

"Shouldn't I be compensated?" the woman asked. "I shouldn't have to clean up after the people you hired to remodel my kitchen."

Okay, so much for the compliments. This old gal hadn't come to the store to applaud good performance. She was angling for some freebies.

Derrick decided to put the ball on her side of the court. "What do you think is reasonable?"

She threw the ball back to him, without batting an eyelash. "That's not up to me," she said. "What do *you* believe is fair compensation?"

Derrick shrugged. "Do you have any other purchases you'd like to make? If so, I can accommodate you with a free delivery, or a discount for the inconvenience."

"Well..." she said slowly. "I suppose that will do for starters."

For *starters*? What the hell was she talking about? The installers hadn't damaged this woman's walls, or broken her windows. They'd left a little trash on the floor, and she was acting like tossing it in the garbage can was some kind of major inconvenience.

But Derrick didn't want to deal with this right now. He wanted to get out of this store, and take his family to dinner.

"Fine," he said, reaching into his pocket and pulling out a business card. "Here is my direct number, should you need anything."

Ms. Roth took the card and read it. "This card belongs to a Robert Morrison," she said.

Derrick shook his head. "Mr. Morrison was the previous manager of this store. As you see, his name has been scratched off, and replaced with mine. My new business cards haven't arrived yet. When they do, I'll be sure to give you one."

Barbara Roth tucked the card into her purse. "Very well," she said, "I'll be in touch."

When she looked up, Derrick was already some distance away, walking quickly toward the exit.

Chapter 44

Thursday
7:00 AM

Traffic was unusually light on his way to work, and that suited Derrick just fine. He had a lot of shit to do. *That* was an understatement. The District Manager meeting was scheduled to be held at his store tomorrow. Every store manager in the district would be present, and they would all have something to say about the store's appearance. Derrick wasn't looking forward to that. The sons of bitches would shoot him down, just to take the heat off their own stores.

Derrick was so wired up that he failed to realize he was doing 80 MPH, passing up cars and changing lanes as though his life depended on it.

His smart-phone rang, and he looked at the screen. It was a text from Judy Polakoff. *'I'll be down in your area this morning for a private meeting. Need to talk with you ASAP!'*

He tossed the phone on the car seat. "As if I don't have enough on my plate as it is."

Derrick arrived in the parking lot and was surprised to see Judy getting out of her car. Fuck! This day was getting off to a great start.

Judy nodded a greeting as she approached. "It's not unusual for a DM to make a surprise visit before a manager meeting."

"I know," Derrick said. "I just have a lot to do this morning."

He realized that he had just implied that he didn't have time to waste on the District Manager.

Judy looked at him with sharp eyes. "I'll keep this as short as possible," she said.

When they entered the store, Judy headed for the bath showroom.

Derrick followed her, trying hard not to look like a puppy bumbling along after its mother.

Judy looked over the bathroom fixture displays. "What have you done differently here?"

Derrick cleared his throat. "We've updated signage," he said, and pulled one of the 4x3 cards out of the sign holder to show her.

"These new signs display a description and price of each item, and a total price for the entire set at the bottom. This will give project clients a better idea of what a remodel will cost them."

Judy took her time studying the signage. "Are you sure this is a good idea? The last thing we want is to scare clients away with sticker-shock."

"I don't think that will be too much of a problem," Derrick said. "According to my associates, we've gotten a lot of feedback from customers who prefer to see the prices on display while they're browsing. Also, it helps us move more quickly into the sale, if the associate doesn't have to stop to check a price every time a customer expresses an interest in something. Sarah has wanted to do this for some time, and we're already getting positive responses from the customers."

Judy nodded absently.

Derrick got the impression that she hadn't come here to discuss signage. She had something else on her mind.

Before he could speak again, Judy wandered into the kitchen showroom, where she asked the same question. "What have you done differently here?"

Derrick pointed to the display signage. "Our countertop vendor has these colors of granite and CeasarStone on sale." He showed her a tower with 12x12 samples of the product.

"How are countertop sales this quarter?" Judy asked.

Derrick was certain that she already knew the answer. She was testing him. "Down ten percent month-to-date; up three percent for the year."

Judy nodded thoughtfully. "Why do you suppose month-to-date sales are down?"

Derrick smiled. "I've only had this store for three days. Do you really expect me to know that?"

Judy returned his smile. "You're the store manager."

"Yes," Derrick said. "But Rome wasn't built in a day."

"You've had three days," Judy said.

"That's true," Derrick said. "But I'm pretty sure Rome wasn't built in three days, either."

Judy's smile faded. "Walk with me," she said quietly.

When they reached the appliance showroom, she glanced around carefully, obviously making sure that no one was present. She motioned for Derrick to sit at the table with her. Then, she dropped the bombshell.

"There's been a harassment complaint filed against you."

Derrick blinked twice. "A *harassment* complaint?"

He watched to see if she was joking. She wasn't. "By whom?"

"You know I can't tell you that," Judy said.

Derrick raised his hands in surrender. "I've only been here three days. That's not long enough to create that kind of animosity."

Judy shrugged. "Apparently, you work fast."

Derrick absent-mindedly massaged his temples. "This is insane! Is the complaint from *this* store? Or the Kearny Mesa store?" He hoped it was the latter.

"This store," Judy said.

"Then I know who it is," Derrick said. "Tina and Debbie."

The look on Judy's face told him that he had guessed correctly. Not that it was much of a guess.

"What makes you think so?" she asked, curiously.

"Not because they have any legitimate gripe," Derrick said. "But from day-one they've had attitude towards me, like I didn't deserve this position. Or maybe they wanted the promotion for themselves."

"The complaint is serious," Judy said. "And it comes at a bad time."

Derrick laughed.

"You think this is funny?"

"I don't think it's funny at all," Derrick said. "I was just wondering when any complaint comes at a *good* time."

Judy made a calming gesture with her hands. "Look, Derrick, I know you were thrust into this position without warning."

That was an understatement.

"I also want you to know that I support you a hundred percent," Judy said. "I'm fairly certain that Tina and Debbie concocted these complaints, as a way of putting you on the radar."

"Those two make quite a team," said Derrick. "After what they did to Rob Morrison, I guess I should have been expecting this."

"What makes you say that?" asked Judy. "*I* made the decision to terminate Rob."

"I know you did," Derrick said. "But you did it based on his record, and I'm willing to bet that every negative thing in Rob's file can be traced back to Tina and Debbie."

"I feel like a lamb being led to the slaughter," he said. "I think this whole thing is a setup, to determine who's really in charge here."

Judy looked confused. "What do you mean?"

"Tina and Debbie want to establish that they have the know-how to remove anyone in this store who gets in their way. Making a harassment complaint is the fastest way to do that."

Derrick paused to let his words sink in. "They know the ropes! When a female makes a complaint against a male manager, everything stops. My hands are now tied."

He held out his hands as though he'd been handcuffed. "All of this, right before a major promotional sale. The timing is too good to be an accident. With me gone, the door will be wide open for one of them to slide in as manager."

Judy's voice went hard. "*I* decide who's going to be manager in my district."

Derrick shrugged. "I don't mean to be disrespectful, Judy, but you're telling that to the wrong person."

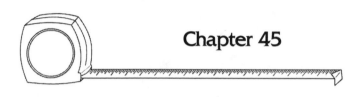

Chapter 45

8:00 AM

Derrick read the printed statements in silence. The jargon was common; he had read similar phrases many times. Only they'd never been pointed at him before. He was careful not to display emotion while Judy looked on.

"Anything to say?" she asked.

Derrick shook his head while continuing to read the statements.

> *To Whom It May Concern:*
>
> *On the date mentioned above, I Debbie Banks had a conversation with Derrick Payton about designers working weekends. I informed him it is not protocol for designers to work weekends, so we can be available for clients and installers during the business week. Derrick refused to listen. He made no attempt to fairly evaluate my words, or to understand a long-running standard for the design team. I felt as though I was being bullied and targeted by a man who is unwilling to take input from a member of the leadership team.*
>
> *Derrick stated repeatedly that HE was the store manager, and he would decide who worked what schedule. He refused to listen to reason, and he spoke to me in a condescending manner, as though he were speaking to a child.*

Derrick laid the first page on his desk. "Sounds vague," he said.

"How do you figure?" Judy asked.

Derrick met her eyes. "Do you really need me to explain? Or are you testing me?"

Judy didn't speak. When Derrick refused to lower his stare, a smile tugged at the corners of her mouth. "I only want to hear your thoughts," she said.

"Let me finish reading," Derrick said. "Then, I'll tell you what actually happened."

The next statement was from Tina.

> *On Wednesday of this week, I, Tina Nodzak informed Derrick Payton of an incident involving an associate from receiving, who climbed into the trash compactor. This is a clear violation of Safety SOP, and cause for immediate job termination. Derrick refused to take direct action, instead passing the responsibility on to me. As store manager, Derrick should have terminated Gina Strasser for this serious safety violation. Not only did he refuse to take action against Gina, but he threatened to terminate Kim Purcell, the supervisor of receiving.*

Derrick finished, and dropped the statement on the desk.

Judy looked at him. "Well?"

And so, he explained his version.

When Derrick finished, he asked, "What do you want to do?"

Judy tapped the desk with her fingernails. "This is the last thing we need, right before a major promotion."

"You'll get no argument from me," said Derrick, flatly.

Judy shook her head. "I always knew Tina and Debbie had aspirations to grow with the company, but this..."

Derrick liked the sound of that. Maybe Judy was on his side after all.

"It's obvious that Tina is rallying associates to take sides," he said. "Kim's version is off the mark, too. I didn't threaten to terminate her for allowing Gina to climb into the compactor. I pointed out that Kim's own written statement showed that she had surrendered her keys to an unauthorized person, which is *also* a violation of the safety SOP."

"I could have terminated her on the spot," Derrick said. "But I didn't. Instead, I gave her two options, both of which were clearly within the boundaries of my authority as store manager."

Judy looked unhappy. "Kim Purcell has a reputation with Ops as one of the best receiving supervisors we've got."

Derrick raised his hands in surrender. "Then, by all means, lets give her the run of the store," he said.

Judy ignored his comment. "Are you going to turn this store around-or not? I need to hear it from your own mouth."

Derrick sat back in his chair. "I want to be manager," he said. "And I know I can do the job properly. But you shoved me into this position after you tossed Rob Morrison out like a potato peel. And the two people who stabbed Rob in the back are already coming at me with their knives."

Judy stiffened.

"I'm not criticizing," Derrick said. "I have no doubt that you did the right thing, according to the available evidence."

He tapped the written statements on the desk. "The problem is, that evidence was almost certainly manufactured by Ms. Nodzak and Ms. Banks."

"I'm not talking about them," Judy said. "I'm talking about *you*. I want you to tell me straight out... Did I give this promotion to the right person?"

Derrick smiled sardonically. "If you have to ask that question, you should go ahead and replace me now. I'm sure that Tina and Debbie will make terrific candidates."

He and Judy stared at each other for several long seconds. Finally, Judy nodded. "Fair enough. I withdraw the question. Let's move on to a more immediate matter. How are you going to handle the differences within your team?"

By firing them, and hiring qualified replacements. But he couldn't really say that.

"First thing's first," Derrick said. "The holiday promotion is my top priority. That's where my focus is, and that's where it will remain through Memorial Day."

"Agreed," said Judy. "If we want to keep this store alive, we've got to build up your sales."

"I will," Derrick said.

"Sounds good," Judy said. "Show me what you've got."

'I could take that the wrong way,' Derrick said silently. He decided not to go there.

Chapter 46

8:30 AM

Derrick began Judy's tour in the lighting showroom. The department had five sections, with displays for living room, family room, den, kitchen, and bath.

"Our biggest sales come from kitchen and bath fixtures," he said. "Rebecca suggested that we merchandise more in the den section, because we haven't had a strong market for den and study room lighting."

"How did she come to that conclusion?" asked Judy.

Derrick shot Judy a glance. "The Store Walk report shows that Rebecca is right on the mark."

"I'm not challenging you," Judy said defensively. "I only want to be sure that our people know where and how to find answers."

"Oh, they know," Derrick replied, rolling his eyes. "A little too well, if you ask me."

Judy stopped in her tracks. "What's that supposed to mean?"

Derrick looked at her. Did she really want to know?

As if reading his mind Judy said, "I want to know."

Here goes... "You've got my people so busy scrambling for information that they can barely do their jobs."

Judy said nothing, so Derrick continued. "You, and everyone else at store support, randomly call stores asking what we did in sales, what our markdowns were the previous day, month-to-date, and—of course—what we're going to do to drive sales. I understand that it's important to take a pulse-check once in a while. But you're not doing it once in a while. You're doing it *all the time*."

Judy appeared to be genuinely offended. "We want to make sure that people understand our expectations."

"They understand your expectations," Derrick said. "The associates spend hours at a time in front of computers, working the numbers so they'll be ready in case SSC calls. The good news is, you're getting lots of nice data points for your spreadsheets. The bad news is, those numbers aren't very positive, because my people aren't out there selling product. They're too busy crunching numbers. If you want to see better sales figures, ease up on the phone call spot checks, and help my people with what matters most."

"And what matters *most*?" Judy asked.

Was she insulting his intelligence? Derrick reminded himself to stay calm, and keep it professional. "The customer shopping experience," he said.

"The customer shopping experience?" she repeated, in the form of a question.

"Yes," Derrick said. "Our priority is helping customers."

"Of course," Judy said. "Obviously."

"It can't be *too* obvious," Derrick said. "Because store support keeps loading us down with tasks which do nothing to support sales. If we're focusing on *you*, then we're *not* focusing on customer issues, like answering and returning calls, approaching customers, or following up on customer orders."

Judy motioned for Derrick to continue. "Give me some specifics. What kind of tasks are keeping the associates from helping customers?"

It was more of a challenge than a question. One that Derrick was ready to take on.

"Everyday, supervisors spend up to two hours going over whole store sales reports," he said. "That's one quarter of their work day spent, not selling product, not helping customers, and not providing leadership to associates. The supervisors also have to check markdowns, markups, place orders, call vendors, turn in safety reports, write associate action plans, and fill out touch-point scorecards to verify that every associate is following the steps of the sale."

Derrick made a show of catching his breath, to emphasize his point. "Associates are given aisle assignments, and expected to down-stock shelves with product, and put up signs and displays. They're graded on how they do this, so that's where they tend to concentrate most of their effort. Half the time, the customers are ignored, because everyone is too busy jumping through hoops to actually serve them."

"What's wrong with setting expectations?" Judy asked.

"Setting expectations is one thing," explained Derrick. "It's quite another thing to overwhelm our people with extraneous tasks."

He chose his words carefully. That was the only way to make his point stick. "Watch them out there," he said. "When you walk the floor, you're not watching the associates in action with customers. Instead, you review the checklist, to verify that they're completing all of the required tasks. And you ask them, over-and-over-and-over again, what they're doing to drive sales."

"Well, that's understandable," Judy said, clearly somewhat offended. "We can't expect to succeed without sales."

"I get that," Derrick said. "But sales don't happen magically. If we want to promote sales, we have to interact with the customers, and deliver quality customer service. Unfortunately, that's *not* on the checklist of tasks. And if it's not on the checklist, it's not a priority."

Judy started to speak, but Derrick continued. "On Monday, SSC asks what we're doing to drive sales. On Tuesday, SSC asks what we're doing to drive sales. See if you can guess what SSC asks us on Wednesday..."

"It's a legitimate question," Judy said.

Derrick stared at her. "Is it? Is it *really*? Because you never want to hear the same answer twice. SSC expects the store managers and associates to come up with a shiny new answer, every day of the week. And next week, we get to reinvent the wheel all over again."

"That's not our intention," Judy said.

"Maybe not," said Derrick, "but that's the result."

He softened his voice. "What if there isn't a new answer every day? What if we find a good method, and then stick with it long enough to actually see some results?"

"Give me an example," Judy said.

"Here's an easy one," Derrick said, "and I guarantee that it works. Ask our people on the sales floor how *they* would like to do things, rather than shoving a new batch of directives down their throats. People want to feel valued. They want to know that their ideas *matter*."

"Is that what you're doing throughout the store?" Judy asked. "Allowing associates to put their own ideas into action?"

"I'm not giving them carte blanch to do whatever they want," Derrick said. "But, yes, I'm listening to them. I'm trying to give my associates a chance to show what they know, and what they can do."

Derrick shrugged. "It's not fancy, and it doesn't come with flashy Power Point slides, but it works. I'm already seeing improvements in morale, and enthusiasm."

At that very moment, Derrick caught sight of Tina and Debbie, walking down one of the aisles. "And we're going to need all the enthusiasm we can get," he said. "Because we're swimming with *sharks*."

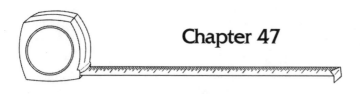

Chapter 47

9:00 AM

Derrick walked Judy to her car. "Did you find out what you wanted to know?"

Judy's cheeks flushed. "I hope you don't think I was trying to undermine you."

Derrick shook his head. "No. You had a couple of harassment statements dropped on your desk, and you had to check them out. I understand."

Judy opened her car door, and tossed her briefcase and jacket inside. "The store looks great," she said. "The manager meeting will take place as scheduled. From what I can see, you look as though you're ready."

"What about these harassment issues?" Derrick asked. He didn't want to keep opening the wound, but he didn't want that hanging over his head either.

"I'll speak with Tasha Holguin," Judy said. "And let her know I think these complaints have no basis."

Tasha was the district human resources manager. She was also Tina's official direct supervisor.

"Will Tasha be satisfied with that?" Derrick asked. He knew how tight the HR department was. They stuck together like flies on shit.

"I run this district," Judy said. She nodded goodbye, and started the engine.

Derrick watched as she drove away. You run this district... Yeah, right.

He returned to the store, not knowing where to begin. Tomorrow, the store managers would be here, and they would be looking for any excuse to hammer him. Anything wrong, no matter how small. Derrick didn't intend to give them the chance, but it was difficult to think straight with the Wicked Witches on his back.

Judy's support meant something, but a harassment complaint was serious business. During Derrick's years in the business, he'd seen women scream sexual discrimination as a way of escaping accountability, and men claim racial discrimination for the exact same reason. In every case, the situation had gotten ugly.

The company was understandably skittish about lawsuits, and the negative publicity that came along with them. No matter what the actual facts were, public opinion tended to side with the accusers.

Derrick had no doubt that Tina and Debbie would use the public's automatic presumption of guilt to make him look like an abusive manager. But he would be damned if he'd let them take over his store without a fight.

When he walked through the décor showroom, Martha, the department supervisor, stopped him. "Well," she said, "how did it go?"

"What do you mean?" Derrick asked.

Martha tilted her head and smiled. "Come on," she said. "I've got eyes."

Derrick shrugged. "She likes what we've done so far, but—"

Martha stepped closer and lowered her voice. "I know exactly what you mean."

Derrick was uncomfortable with the woman's close proximity, but her conspiratorial tone bothered him even more. "Go on," he said cautiously.

"I've wanted a moment with you all week," Martha said.

Derrick didn't like the sound of that. "Okaaaaaaaay..." he drawled.

Martha grinned and shook her head. "I don't mean it like that."

Derrick was relieved. "Then how *did* you mean it? Cut to the chase."

"I've been watching what we're doing all over the store," Martha said, "and I think we still have some room for improvement."

She waited for Derrick's reaction, but he gave none.

"Don't get me wrong," she said. "Everything we're doing is for the right reason. But we need to tone it down some."

She saw that she had Derrick's full attention.

"Come with me," she said, and she walked toward the lighting showroom. Derrick followed her, and they stopped at the entrance to the lighting display area.

Martha waved a hand in the air. "Look at the signage, and tell me what you see."

Derrick wasn't in the mood for games, but he couldn't resist her challenge. He looked at the displays in silence. Everything seemed to be in place. The displays were well positioned in front of the product, the shelves were stocked in neat rows, and signage was everywhere.

"Looks like they put in a lot of effort here," he said.

Martha said nothing. She was obviously waiting for him to notice something particular.

Derrick sighed, and looked again at the displays. It took him nearly a minute to spot what she was talking about. Holy shit! There were signs *everywhere*!

"Sign pollution," said Derrick.

"Bingo!" replied Martha. "Ever since I came to this store, I've complained about having too many signs. It takes away from the professional appearance of the store, and makes us look like a cheap-goods retailer."

Derrick followed Martha through the showroom, as she continued to make her point. He was amazed to find the problem not only in lighting, but all over the store.

He rubbed his temples. "How could I have missed this?"

"It creeps up on you," said Martha. "It's been the norm in this company for so long, that we've stopped noticing it. But now it's getting out of hand."

"We can fix that," Derrick said.

"I need all associates to come to the rug department at this time," Derrick's voice said through the overhead page system. *"We're going to have an early morning meeting."*

The associates caught the excitement in his tone, and hurried to the department.

Derrick stood before them, pacing like a caged lion, waiting for the stragglers to arrive. When all were present, he cleared his throat.

"I walked the floor this morning with Martha," he said. "And I was reminded of the importance of looking at things through other people's eyes."

He smiled at the assembled group. "Why do you suppose that's important?"

No one answered.

"It's not a trick question," Derrick said. "Anyone want to take a stab at an answer?"

Martha nodded. "To see what others see."

Every face turned in her direction.

"Right!" replied Derrick. "When we stop trying to see things through the eyes of our customers, we begin to get tunnel vision. We start to lose sight of how things look to people who don't work here every day."

There were murmurs among the associates, but no sign of comprehension.

"It's alright if you don't get it right away," Derrick said. "I didn't get it right away either. But when Martha asked me to walk the store with her, she helped me see something I've been missing."

Derrick gestured for everyone to take a look around themselves. "We've got a *lot* of signs up," he said. "And I don't just mean a *lot* of signage, I mean a *LOT* of signage."

"A metric *shitload* of signage," said an anonymous voice from the crowd.

Everyone laughed, including Derrick.

"That's a pretty fair assessment," Derrick said. "I don't know if it's a *metric* shitload, but it's definitely a shitload."

Everyone laughed again. They were enjoying this.

"What do we have going on Monday?" Derrick asked.

"*Memorial Day sale!*" they replied in a chorus.

Derrick grinned. "You've been paying attention."

This was good. He could feel the positive energy in the group.

He nodded toward them. "Okay," he said. "Here's what I want you to do... Get with you supervisor, and walk every vignette and display in the store. If you think you need to make a change, I want you to *do* it."

Another murmur went through the crowd. They hadn't been expecting that. It was one thing to *talk* about trusting the judgment of your employees. Nearly every manager did that. But their new store manager was actually trusting them to implement their own suggestions.

"You're all pros here!" Derrick said. "We've all been in the business long enough to know what needs to be done, so let's get out there and *do* it."

"I'm not giving you permission to paint zebra stripes on the ceiling, or put lava lamps on the cash registers," he said.

Another laugh from the team.

"Challenge each other, to ensure that your changes make sense," Derrick said. "And if someone disagrees with your idea, don't take it personally. Remember to look from the viewpoint of someone else's eyes, and try to understand what *they* see."

He paused. They were clearly liking this.

Derrick continued. "Our goal is not to criticize what we've already done. It's to learn what we need to do *next*, to make sure that we're ready for the big sale, and for the future."

"Getting rid of too many signs is only one thing," he said. "Maybe we have displays that don't make sense. Maybe we have to change out some of our displays, to generate excitement, or to create clarity."

More than a few heads bobbed.

"But don't tackle anything today that we can't finish by close of business this evening. If you've got an idea that can't be wrapped up today, I want you to save it until next week, after the big sale. Let's be smart, not bite off more than we can chew, and—above all—let's ensure that our changes make sense. And don't forget to keep your supervisors in the loop."

Murmured comments rippled through the group. "Yeah..." and "now we're talking."

"Be smart," Derrick said. "Be safe. And let's have some fun!"

The group broke into applause so loud that it took Derrick by surprise. He looked in Martha's direction. She was clapping louder than everyone.

Derrick caught her eye, and silently mouthed the words 'thank you.'

Martha silently replied, 'you're welcome.'

The group dispersed, the associates chattering happily among themselves as they ambled away.

Derrick watched until they were all gone. All, that is, except for two standing at the center of the rug department.

Low and behold, it was the Wicked Witches of the West. They locked eyes with his, standing with their arms folded across their chests, their expressions as cold as stone.

What the fuck was their problem? As if he didn't already know.

Chapter 48

10:00 AM

The store opened with a modest flow of customers, eager to get their shopping done before the afternoon rush. They looked like your typical stay-at-home wives, with family incomes running in the six-plus figures. Lean and fit, wearing over-priced body-hugging gym clothes with not a hair out of place and their makeup intact, they walked through the store like they owned the place.

"So long as they spend their money, I'm good with it," Derrick told Sheila.

She was working at the front registers, because Florence was running late to work.

"Thanks again for helping in the front end," Derrick said

"No problem," she replied. "I'm used to it."

Derrick caught the note of sarcasm in her voice. "Happen a lot?"

"Wouldn't be retail if we didn't have sick calls and people late to work," Sheila replied gloomily.

Derrick nodded sympathetically as he turned away and began his morning walk of the store. Sheila was right. The industry had changed in recent years, and not necessarily for the better. Companies were increasingly reluctant to offer good pay, making it difficult to hire quality people. With an average hourly wage of $10.20 per hour, the best applicants Derrick could expect to hire were kids working their way through college, or people waiting for something better to come along.

No wonder he felt like an old man. Only in his late thirties, Derrick was one of the oldest people in the store. But he wasn't about to allow himself to have a bad day, not with so much positive energy flowing through the store.

As he strolled through the aisles, he saw associates remerchandising their departments with high spirits. He'd only been at the store a few days, but the change in the attitudes of the employees was already clearly visible.

Martha was a genius. When he passed her department, she was busily discussing with her team how to reset vignettes in her area of the store.

Martha spotted Derrick, and he nodded respectfully in her direction.

She nodded in return, and gave him a slight smile. The signal was clear: she was glad to have helped.

Derrick continued walking through the store, and he was greeted with enthusiasm from every associate he came across.

As he passed the kitchen showroom, Vanessa waved for his attention. She was with a client, but she beckoned him over. She smiled as he approached. "Hi, Derrick. This is Ms. Easton, a client of ours."

"Pleased to meet you," said Derrick, shaking hands with the woman.

Ms. Easton looked to be in her early thirties, attractive, smartly dressed, and full of confidence. "Nice to meet you," she said. "I represent *Clyde Builders*, and want to tell you that we're very pleased to be working with Vanessa."

Vanessa beamed. "I'm glad to hear that too," she said.

"I've only been here a week," Derrick said, "but I can already tell how lucky we are to have her on our team."

They exchanged a few more pleasantries, and then Derrick moved on.

As he continued his store walk, a feeling of pride came over him. Associates were actively engaging customers, taking the time to offer help and suggestions, even if they happened to be busy when customers appeared. Between customers, the associates were making time to complete their daily tasks, down-stocking product, re-signing displays, and remerchandising vignettes. They worked smartly and efficiently, and— more importantly—they worked *together*.

Derrick felt a lump forming in his throat. His people were doing it. They were bringing the store to life.

Of course, it couldn't all be sweetness and light. Derrick had been in the business too long to assume that *everything* was running smoothly *everywhere*. Somewhere in this store, a problem was brewing. He decided to go looking for it, rather than waiting for it to find him.

The problem turned out to be in receiving. As soon as Derrick entered the area, he was greeted by Darrell.

"Derrick, I'm glad to see you!" Darrell looked as relieved as he sounded.

"Everything okay?" asked Derrick.

"Not by a long shot," conceded Darrell. "Gina called out sick, and Kim took an early lunch. That leaves only Marcos and me to receive deliveries."

Derrick knew this was a problem. Thursday's were heavy delivery days. The trucks rolling in would be loaded to the teeth with merchandise, so the store would be properly stocked for the weekend.

"What time is Kim coming back from lunch?"

Darrell hesitated.

"What is it?" Derrick asked.

"Kim likes to take an hour," Darrell confessed. "Usually, that's okay. Only, today is not usual. Gina *never* calls out sick."

That might be true, but she probably never got written up for safety violations either.

"I understand," Derrick said. "Do we have any receiving backups in the store?"

Darrell glanced at Marcos, who nodded his head slightly, as if giving his coworker permission to continue.

Darrell sighed. "No. Kim doesn't like to have anyone working back here who's not assigned to receiving."

That was understandable. The company tended to underrate the importance of the operations department. In truth, without operations, everything in the store would come grinding to a halt. Receiving was the heart that pumped product to the sales floor. Associates on the receiving dock had to work safely, check in product, fill out required paperwork, and be on time to work every day. Excuses were not tolerated. You had to be ultra-reliable to cut it here.

Which made most receiving supervisors skeptical about allowing other store personnel to work in the department. It wouldn't take much for some hotshot from another area to screw things up.

But that was not an excuse for not having a backup plan.

"Let me get this straight," Derrick said. "You're telling me that there is no one in the entire building who is able to help here?"

After an uneasy silence Marcos mumbled, "Dave Walker knows how to drive a forklift."

Darrell flashed Marcos a shut-your-mouth glance. "Forget it!"

"Who's Dave Walker?" asked Derrick.

Darrell turned his attention back to his work, apparently pretending not to have heard the question.

"I asked you a question," Derrick said.

Darrell sighed. "He works in the flooring department."

Dave Walker was working the sales floor.

Derrick recognized the man's face. He had seen Dave in-passing, but they hadn't been introduced yet.

Derrick stuck out his hand. "I understand you have experience in operations?"

Dave accepted the hand and shook it. "Yes," he said. "I was receiving supervisor at *Expo Design & Remodel* up until the company closed its doors, about six months into the recession."

"I remember that," said Derrick. "I was sad to hear about it."

Derrick wasn't being condescending. The closing of a competitor was nothing to cheer over. It left everyone wondering if their own stores would be next.

"A lot of people don't understand that competition is good," Derrick continued. "It keeps us on our toes, and helps us prove to customers why we're the best."

"So long as we *inspect* what we *expect*," replied Dave, without skipping a beat.

Derrick smiled. He liked this guy!

"I'm going to get right to the point," Derrick said. "We have a situation in receiving, and I need your help. Gina called out sick, and Kim's out to lunch. Don't know when she'll be back, and the receiving team needs a hand. Think you can do it?"

"I can do it," Dave said. "But if I go back there, you'll have problems with Kim. She doesn't want me on her turf."

"Why?"

Dave shrugged. "Maybe she's just territorial. Or maybe she's worried that I'll do too good a job, and make her look bad in front of the boss."

It was too late for that. Kim was already looking bad to Derrick.

"You let me worry about Kim," Derrick said. "I know how to handle this."

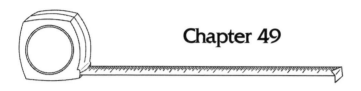

Chapter 49

11:30 AM

Kim strolled through the double receiving doors, fully satisfied with the meal riding comfortably in her tummy. *Magdalena's Mexican Restaurant* was just two blocks away from the store on El Camino Real. Easy walking distance. She had ordered her usual: huevos rancheros topped with salsa, two cups of coffee, and large glass of orange juice. For no reason in particular, the food had seemed tastier than ordinary. She must've been especially hungry this morning.

A forklift rolled across her path, headed toward the open rear doors of a trailer. When she caught sight of the driver's face, Kim stopped dead in her tracks. Was that Dave Walker, from flooring?

Darrell and Marcos stopped what they were doing when they spotted her. She glared in their direction, and they quickly went back to work.

Kim marched over to a spot near the trailer, and stood with her hands on her hips. "What the hell are you doing in my receiving dock?" she demanded.

Dave hooked onto another pallet and backed the forklift away from the trailer. He didn't even glance toward Kim.

The idiot was ignoring her! Or, maybe not... The propane-fueled engine of the forklift was pretty loud, and the radio next to Kim's desk was blaring music. Maybe he hadn't heard her.

"I told him to lend a hand," said a voice from behind her. The voice was vaguely familiar.

Kim spun around to confront the owner of the voice, but her eyes practically popped from the sockets when she saw Derrick walking toward her.

"*You* told him?" said Kim.

Derrick nodded. "I am the store manager."

Kim opened her mouth to speak, but Derrick beat her to it. "And as such, it's up to me to ensure that things get done. With Gina out sick, we're short-handed here."

He nodded in Dave's direction. "Mr. Walker has experience in ops, and he's forklift certified."

Derrick watched her reaction. "Can you think of a better candidate?"

Kim's face flushed with anger. She trembled furiously, but said nothing. Instead, she walked out of the department and headed straight for Tina's office.

Dave observed the exchange, shut down the forklift, and walked over to Derrick.

He stopped a few feet away, and scratched the back of his head. "I wish someone would tell me why she has a wild hair up her ass about me working here."

"She's on a power-trip," replied Derrick. He spoke loudly enough for the others to hear. "This is Kim's way of telling everyone that nothing goes on back here without her stamp of approval."

He shook his head. "That's a sure sign of inexperienced leadership."

"Listen," Dave started uneasily, "I don't wanna make trouble. This is your first week here, and I know the importance of getting started on the right foot. Maybe I should get back to flooring?"

Derrick shook his head. "Not a chance! This is where you're needed. I'm not letting anyone's ego get in the way of getting things done."

He took another look at all of the pallets that needed to be checked in. "With Kim whining to Tina over this, we're going to need some more help here. Is there anyone else in the store who can do what you do?"

Dave nodded. "Yeah. Mary Hines in kitchens worked with me in receiving at *Expo*."

"Good. Is she working today?"

"Yes, but—"

That didn't sound good. "But *what*?"

Dave inhaled deeply. "She doesn't like... ah... helping in other departments." He let his words hang in the air.

Derrick frowned. "I'm sorry. Did you say she *doesn't like helping other departments*?"

The tone in Dave's voice was sorrowful. "She's sort of a stubborn one."

Derrick sighed. "Then I guess I'll have to implore her."

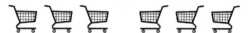

Mary Hines was alone in the kitchen showroom when Derrick approached her about helping in receiving

"My job profile clearly states I'm a *kitchen specialist*," she declared loudly.

"I understand that," Derrick replied in a softer tone. "But your name badge clearly states, *I work in all departments*."

Mary gave him a dismissive wave. "That's just the company's PR crap. I didn't come to this store to work in receiving!"

Derrick was tempted to point out that she had come to this store because her previous store had gone belly-up. But he decided to take a more diplomatic approach.

He spoke evenly. "It's *not* PR crap. It happens to be a core part of this company's philosophy. We hire people based on their adaptability, to give our personnel the broadest possible range of skills for coping with unexpected situations. That's what this is... An unexpected situation."

Mary said nothing.

"I'm only asking you to help for an hour or two," Derrick said.

Her response was barely short of a shout. "You have no *right*!"

Derrick stared at her. Was this woman for real?

"I wouldn't count on that," he said calmly.

Mary's eyes welled with tears. "This isn't fair," she said.

Great! Now she was going to start crying...

Derrick shifted into his best fatherly tone. "Mary, I wouldn't be asking this of you if it wasn't important. Why is this a problem for you?"

Mary fought back her tears. "I have a degree in design," she sniffed. "I'm certified in kitchen and bath designs with the State of California. I worked in receiving at *Expo Design & Remodel* to put myself through school. When I graduated, I asked for a chance at being a designer and do you know what they told me?"

Derrick shook his head.

Mary's voice was heavy with resentment. "They said I wasn't a good *fit*."

"I don't think I understand," Derrick said. "What does this have to do with helping in receiving for a couple of hours?"

"They didn't think I was pretty enough!" Mary blurted. "They thought I was too fat."

And then Derrick understood. Most designers were female, and they tended to form cliques as tightly-controlled as any squad of high school cheerleaders. They knew how to snub outsiders who failed to measure up to their lofty standards.

The image of a successful designer was to have a body like Beyonce Knowles and a voice like Jennifer Lopez. Or was it the other way around?

Derrick envisioned the difficulties that Mary Hines must have experienced when applying for a design position. She was in her mid-twenties, but looked at least ten years older. She was twenty-five pounds overweight, and her voice was strong and forceful.

Mary had come from receiving, and a woman had to be a tough character to survive in operations. That raw edge had probably caused the design team to shun Mary as an undesirable applicant for their clique.

"It's not that I don't *want* to help," Mary said. "I've been working hard for people to see me as a successful sales specialist. To do that, I have to erase the image people have of me in receiving. If Debbie catches me driving a forklift, how is she going to see me as a candidate for her design room?"

Derrick nodded. "I can't argue with that."

His words seemed to take Mary by surprise. "What?"

"You're right," Derrick said. "If you spend a couple of hours in receiving, you'd be helping me, but you'd be risking your own career prospects."

Mary stared at him. "So, I'm off the hook?"

"You're off the hook," Derrick said. "I agree with your reasoning, and I'm withdrawing my request."

He turned, and started to walk away.

"Just a second," Mary said. "Who will you get to help in receiving?"

Derrick smiled again. "I have no idea."

Chapter 50

Mary Hines was feeling good. The new store manager had actually listened to her. And when it had come down to the crunch, he hadn't strong armed her.

She was grateful for that. All of her efforts since joining *The Design* had been to wipe clean the image of her operations background.

The next time she filled out a resume, she'd spend less time detailing her work history in ops. It was solid job experience, but it didn't do anything to enhance her image as a prospective designer.

She rubbed her bulging stomach. *That* wasn't helping her career plans either. Hence, her recent emphasis on salads and exercise, both of which she hated.

She was bothered that her motivation to lose weight was completely external. She wasn't trying to get into shape because she *wanted* to. She was trying to match the accepted image of a designer. *Welcome to the wonderful world of design, where beauty is valued over brains...*

But, that was the world they were living in. No sense in pretending otherwise. She wanted to be a designer. If that meant that she had to lose a few pounds, so be it. Maybe she'd nab a man along the way.

When Sophia arrived for the closing shift, Mary excused herself. "Think I'll start my lunch a bit early," she said, reaching for her purse at the desk.

"How goes the diet?" asked Sophia. They both encouraged each other to eat right and exercise, so the subject was open for discussion.

"Still have a ways to go," replied Mary. "But I see the light at the end of the tunnel."

"You go girl!" Sophia said. She was losing weight faster than Mary, and continued to be an inspiration for her. "Before long, we'll both have pole-dancing bodies."

Mary laughed at the thought, and headed for the break room. Bringing her lunch to work helped her to stay on her diet, so she made a beeline for the salad she had stashed in the break room refrigerator.

Along the way, Mary spotted Debbie coming out of the design room. She made a deliberate effort to make her voice sound more feminine. "Hi, Debbie! How are you today?"

Debbie looked up from the sheaf of papers she was reading. "Oh fine," she said curtly. She made no attempt to hide how busy she was.

Mary knew that the only way to get into the design room was to win Debbie's approval, so she never passed up a chance to strike up a conversation with the woman.

"How are things in the design room?" Mary asked.

Debbie reluctantly stopped walking, and turned to face Mary. "Fine. Things are coming along fine. Thanks for asking."

Mary decided to ignore the hint. "That's great! Anything I can do to help?"

Debbie took a deep breath and shrugged. "Keep qualifying customers, and signing them up for retainers," she said. She started walking again, eyes refocused on the papers she held.

"I still work as a design consultant on my own time," said Mary, still pushing for conversation.

Debbie lowered the papers and slowly turned to face her. "...And?"

Mary's smile faltered slightly. "Well... I know you're taking interviews for design assistants..."

Debbie stared without speaking, almost daring Mary to continue.

Mary decided it was time to take the plunge. "I want to be a designer in your project room," she said.

Debbie gave her a chilly smile. "Let's have a word in private," she said. She motioned for Mary to follow.

To Mary, walking through the project room felt like walking through Disneyland. This was where she wanted to be. Her heart was in design. All she needed was a chance.

Some of the designers looked up from their desks as she followed Debbie to her office.

Mary smiled radiantly, but each of the designers looked on curiously, inspecting her body with disapproving eyes.

Mary told herself not to be paranoid. If she wanted to work here, she'd have to get along with everyone.

Still, their disdain for her presence couldn't be ignored.

Debbie closed the door behind them, and took a seat behind her desk, dropping her papers on the desktop. She motioned for Mary to sit down.

Mary took the offered chair.

Debbie reached into a desk drawer and pulled out a stack of folders. "Know what these are?"

"I'm guessing that they're resumes," Mary said.

"That's right," said Debbie. "And every one is from a person who wants to join my design team."

Mary glanced at the folders. "I'm sure they are. But how many of those applicants have a degree in design? And how many have CKD and CBD certifications with the State of California?"

Certified Kitchen Designer and Certified Bath Designer were the highest qualifications in the field of design. Mary would have bet a year's salary that not one of those folders held qualifications as high as hers.

"Qualifications are nice," Debbie said, "but they're not enough. I need to hire someone with *experience*."

Mary felt her cheeks go warm. "I've *got* experience," she said. "I told you, I've been consulting as a design specialist on the side. I'll be happy to show you some of the work I've done. And I can get you references from clients I've worked for."

Debbie said nothing.

"I don't believe this," Mary declared. "You're sandbagging me."

A flicker in Debbie's eyes was enough to tell Mary that she'd hit home.

"You've seen my portfolio," Mary said. "You know my capabilities. My qualifications are as high as any designer on your team. So why aren't you giving me a fair chance?"

"I don't think you're a good *fit* for my design team," Debbie said slowly.

From the expression on Mary's face, Debbie could see instantly that she had just said the wrong thing.

She nearly stumbled in her attempt to change the direction of the conversation. "I only have so many desks available," she said. "Only so many opportunities—"

"No," Mary snarled. "That's not what you said. You just made it clear that it isn't a matter of opportunities. I'm not a good *fit* for your team. *That's* what you said."

Mary's voice was rising now, her forceful operations-trained nature coming to the forefront. She stood up. "So, *tell* me how I'm not a food fit. It's not lack of experience, because I've got that. It's not lack of talent, because I've got that. And it damned well isn't lack of *qualifications*."

Debbie started to stand up, and then checked herself. Perhaps deciding that she didn't want to be face-to-face with Mary at this particular moment.

"What I meant was—"

Mary cut her off. "What you meant was that I'm not pretty! I'm not glamorous enough to work for you." Her words were as hard as steel.

"I was doing you a favor by speaking plainly," Debbie said. "That doesn't give you the right to insult me."

Mary laughed derisively. "You're not speaking plainly! You're saying everything but the truth! And I'm not insulting you! You're insulting yourself with your dishonest little games!"

Mary's raised voice had grown loud enough to be clearly audible in the design room. Every designer was staring into the PSM's office through the glass partition.

When Debbie flashed them a disapproving glance they pretended to return to their work.

Mary snatched the door open, and stood facing into the design room. "All of you think you're so much better than everyone," she bellowed. "You judge your team members by how *pretty* they are. Some of you don't even have design degrees, and less than half of you are CKD or CBD certified!"

Debbie practically fell out of her chair. She had gone to great lengths to hide her team's lack of qualifications. But now, the cat was out of the bag.

She rose from her seat, nervously staring at Mary's back.

"Everyone on my team is a good closer," she said feebly.

Mary whirled to face her. "Not according to the project sales numbers. And make no mistake, Debbie. Everyone on the sales floor *knows* that your team uses their looks to close most sales. It's not about skill; it's about sex appeal! And some of your designers even date customers! How much of a conflict of interest do you think *that* is?"

Debbie was shocked into total immobility.

"I don't need this bullshit," Mary said. "And I certainly don't need to be a part of your so-called *team*."

That said, she stormed out of Debbie's office and right down the middle of the design room with her head held high.

The designers watched her in stunned silence. The Mary they knew had always been friendly, and quick to offer help. They'd always turned her down, of course. They had standards to maintain, after all. Now, they saw a woman behaving like *she* was too good for *them*.

Mary didn't look back. Screw those bimbos. She didn't need them.

She walked straight toward the entrance to receiving. Through the Plexiglas windows in the door, she saw Marcos, Darrell, and Dave working feverishly to unload the trailers and check in product. Kim was nowhere in sight.

The scene was familiar to Mary. Truck drivers waited in line, to hand over their list of deliveries. The receiving crew worked with deliberation, and there seemed to be no relief in sight.

"To hell with it!" Mary said. Then she pushed open the double doors, and walked into receiving.

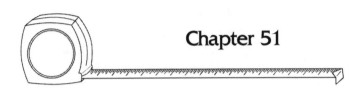

Chapter 51

Kim Purcell exploded. "I want that sonuvabitch's head on a platter! Who does he think he *is*, undermining me like that?" It was more an accusation than question.

Tina motioned for Kim to lower her voice. "These walls are paper-thin," she said. "And Derrick is the *store manager*, as you may have noticed."

Kim's face turned red at the mention of Derrick's name. "I don't give a damn about his title!" she hissed. "Nobody undermines me!"

"I get that," Tina said quickly. "Now, sit down, and tell me exactly what happened."

When Kim finished explaining her version, Tina leaned back in her chair, hands folded with the tips of her forefingers touching her lips. She sat in silence for an interminable time, causing Kim to stir uneasily.

Kim could take no more of this strange behavior. "Well?" she demanded.

Tina sat like a statue, unmoved. Finally a smile cracked the curves of her stone-cold expression. "I need you to write a statement precisely as you described it happened."

The two women exchanged a look that expressed volumes of information.

Kim smiled and said, "Got a pen and paper?"

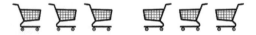

Derrick answered his phone after the first ring. "Hello."

The voice was young. "Derrick, this is Samantha."

Samantha? Had he met her? He couldn't remember. "What's up?"

"I need an approval for a markdown at the front registers," she said.

"Okay. I'll be right there."

When Derrick rounded the corner, he saw Samantha leaning over the check stand to scan the customer's product. Now he remembered her! The tattoo on the small of her back was a dead give-away. Why did people still get those?

He couldn't help noticing that her skin-tight slacks had slipped far enough down her hips to reveal the crack of her ass.

Derrick shook his head. Too bad all they could afford to hire were kids.

He walked around the register and unloaded the product in the customer's cart onto the check stand.

"Here, let's make this easy for all of us," he said, smiling at the customer.

"Thanks," replied Samantha. She sounded like a teenager.

Derrick reminded himself that she *was* a teenager. He needed to be patient.

He pointed toward the scanner. "You know that scan gun is cordless, right? You can move from behind the register, so you don't have to strain yourself leaning over."

Samantha stared at the gun, and then back to Derrick. "Yeah, I guess so," she said.

Suddenly, Derrick was reminded of the incident that had occurred his first day. *This* was the girl who had spilled her coffee on the register.

When she finished ringing up the customer's order, Derrick punched in his code, authorizing a ten percent discount for the items on sale.

"Thank you, Ma'am! Please, visit us again soon," said Derrick, cheerfully.

When the customer was out the door, Derrick turned to face Samantha. "I take it the drug test results came back negative?"

SOP required all associates involved in damaging company property in excess of $100 to be drug-tested. Samantha's damage to the cash register had come to considerably more than $100.

Samantha nodded absently. "Yes. Sorry for the trouble."

She did a cute little crinkly thing with her nose. If she hadn't been so young, Derrick would've thought she was flirting with him.

"Please be careful in the future," he said. "That mistake cost us $600 in store repair."

Samantha's eyes went wide. *"Really?"*

Derrick nodded. "Really."

When Derrick walked away, Samantha reached for the cup of latte next to her register, thankful he hadn't seen it. She took a sip, and set it on the floor next to the trash bin. No sense tempting fate.

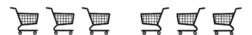

Derrick dialed Teresa's phone once he was out of sight of the front end registers. "Teresa, can you visit Samantha and explain food and drink policy for the last time?" The little bitch probably thought he hadn't seen it.

"*I told that idiot not to have food and drink at the register!*" Teresa blurted.

"I'm sure you did," Derrick said. "But kids will be kids."

Derrick rounded the corner by the main entrance when a woman wearing a uniform from the Sheriff's Department approached him.

"Excuse me," said the deputy sheriff, "can you take me to the manager?"

Shit!

"That's me," said Derrick. "How can I help you?"

The deputy sheriff glanced over her shoulder to make sure no onlookers were nearby. "I have a small claims summons to deliver to you."

She handed him an envelope. "No sense in others seeing this."

Derrick accepted the envelope. "Thanks. This is all I need to make my day complete," he said with a smile.

The deputy sheriff tipped her hat and bade farewell.

Short and sweet, with no drama. Just the way Derrick liked it.

He opened the envelope and read the header of the single page document.

SUPERIOR COURT OF THE STATE OF CALIFORNIA, COUNTY OF SAN DIEGO

SMALL CLAIMS SUMMONS
FOR PERSONAL APPEARANCE AND PRODUCTION OF DOCUMENTS

The words stood out in bold capital letters. What the hell was this? Derrick's brow narrowed as he read farther.

YOU ARE BEING SUED. YOU MUST GO TO COURT ON THE TRIAL DATE LISTED BELOW.

Derrick's eyes darted to the bottom of the page. The trial date was six weeks away.

BRING WITNESSES, RECEIPTS, AND ANY EVIDENCE YOU NEED TO PROVE YOUR CASE.

What case?

Then he spotted the name of the plaintiff: Mark Burkett. Derrick didn't have any trouble recognizing the name. Burkett was the idiot who'd dumped his oven on the street because he'd been too lazy to tie it down in the bed of his truck. The son of a bitch hadn't wasted any time in running to court.

He was suing *The Design* for $4,000. The oven was only worth about $3,700. The other three-hundred bucks must be compensation for the pain and suffering of having his stupidity revealed in public.

Derrick folded the paper and stuffed it back in the envelope. He didn't need this distraction. Not with the promo only a few days away.

He knew that the store didn't have any actual culpability in this matter at all. The fault was entirely with the customer, and Derrick could prove it. But that probably wouldn't matter. In cases like this, the cards were stacked against *The Design*. Regardless of facts, Mark Burkett was an upset customer against a multi-billion dollar company that surely could afford replacing his damaged appliance.

Derrick shook his head. *Welcome to California, where you don't have to be right to sue, and you don't have to be wrong to lose...*

His thoughts were interrupted by the ringing of his phone. He fished it out of his pocket and answered it. "This is Derrick."

"Hi Derrick, this is Allison from the service desk. I have a customer wanting to speak with the store manager."

"Can you tell me what it's about?" It paid to know how deep the water was before taking a dive.

Allison paused. "I'm afraid not," she said.

Derrick recognized the reluctant tone. Allison didn't want to talk about the problem with the customer standing three feet away.

Great! Another angry customer.

"I'll be right there," Derrick said. He hung up the phone and started walking.

When he rounded the corner near the lighting department, he nearly walked into Sylvia Sanchez.

"GEEZ! You scared the—" He didn't finish his sentence. He needed to keep it professional.

"Sorry," he said in a softer tone. "I didn't see you coming."

Sylvia gave him a smile that seemed almost flirtatious. "I didn't mean to scare you," she said. "I was on my way to the ladies room."

Derrick's eyes lowered slightly, just enough to glimpse her tits. He jerked his gaze back up to her face.

"I'm on my way to meet a customer at the service desk," he said. Why was he explaining himself to her?

"See ya later," Sylvia said in a playful tone. She waved her hand theatrically, like a cartoon princess among a flock of admirers.

Derrick nodded, and resumed his walk toward the service desk.

When Sylvia was safely out of earshot, Derrick spoke softly to himself. "Come on, Derrick... What the hell are you doing?"

Chapter 52

12:30 PM

Derrick arrived at the special services desk with his happy face on. He looked at Allison, and she motioned with a nod at the gentleman leaning against the counter at one end of the desk.

Showtime! "How can I help you, sir?"

The customer straightened his five foot-nine inch frame. "Are you the store manager?" He spoke in heavily-accented, but clear English.

Derrick extended his hand. "Yes, I'm Derrick."

The man shook Derrick's hand and said, "I'm Hugo Torres. I'd like you to match this price I found from a competitor."

Unfolding a piece of paper, Hugo handed it somewhat cautiously to Derrick.

Derrick took the paper and examined it. It was a picture of a Victorian-era cast iron, claw foot bathtub. Derrick was familiar with the model. In the late 90's, the store hadn't been able to keep enough on-hand to meet the demand. They had sold like hotcakes to people living in Point Loma and La Jolla. Then, sales had plummeted when the fad petered out.

Lately, claw foot tubs were making a modest comeback, but not to the point that vendors kept a steady supply available. Buyers had to wait four to six weeks for their made-to-order product, which did not sit well with customers.

Derrick scanned down to the bottom of the page. "Eleven hundred dollars. Wow!"

"That includes free shipping," said Hugo.

Derrick looked at Hugo, sizing him up without being obvious about it. The man was slightly overweight, but his stocky frame carried the extra pounds well. His face was adorned with an offset goatee, badly in need of a trim.

Derrick figured that the guy was probably trying to hide the scar on his cheek. It looked like an old knife wound, but Derrick couldn't imagine Hugo in a knife fight. Then again, you never could tell about people.

Hugo maintained good eye contact. He was obviously attempting to radiate sincerity, but Derrick's instincts told him that this guy had an agenda.

Customers today behaved as though they had the upper hand. Times were tough, and the recession was forcing business to close all over the country. The brick and mortar stores were scrambling to compete with online retailers, which was patently impossible, at least in terms of price.

Sure, the major web-based companies—like Amazon.com—had employees, and infrastructure, and all of the associated expenses. They had overhead. But a lot of people were operating internet businesses out of their garages. No payroll to meet, no employee benefits to pay, no worker's comp claims, no OSHA audits, and none of the other costs and complications of operating a real store.

Garage-based sellers could slash prices, because they had practically no overhead expenses at all. And if the seller's website was professional-looking, it was difficult for buyers to tell a major retailer from two guys working out of a mobile home.

Customers making online purchases could save up to fifty percent off the store price of a item, but there was a catch. To get that kind of discount, they had to do their research carefully—both to avoid outright scams on the web, and to make sure that they were ordering exactly the right item.

If the bathtub you bought at *The Design* was an inch too long for your bathroom, you could take it back. If you bought it online, you might be out of luck. A lot of internet sellers had shaky return policies, or no return policies at all. The same was true if the product you received was the wrong color, or if it turned out to be defective. You could easily be screwed.

Derrick understood this, and he wanted to make sure that Hugo knew it too. He held up the paper and smiled. *"The Design* is committed to our customers, and we pride ourselves on being price-competitive. Having said that, online retailers aren't true competitors."

Hugo feigned surprise. "What do you mean? It states on that paper I can buy this tub for *half* of what you're asking for it."

"I see that," Derrick said. "But this seller is out of state. Online retailers aren't permitted to sell products thirty miles outside their location."

Derrick watched Hugo's reaction. He could see that the customer was aware of the rule. The bastard had been hoping that Derrick didn't know.

Hugo shook his head. "I've spent thousands in this place, and I don't appreciate being treated this way."

He was doing his best to act as though he'd been insulted, but acting was not his forte, and he lacked conviction in his behavior. "I just wanna buy this tub. I wanna give you my business. Do you want my money or not?"

Derrick waited for more. He didn't want to respond if Hugo was going to interrupt him.

"I can't match that price," Derrick said flatly. "Online retailers aren't true competitors of brick and mortar businesses."

Again, Hugo's facial expression shows that he was fully aware of this, so Derrick pressed on. "We have overhead and employees to pay. The seller offering this tub is from..." He read the location of the shipper. "...Tucson, Arizona. For all I know, this is one guy, selling junk out of his garage."

Hugo said nothing, so Derrick continued. "If you buy from us, you get peace of mind with your purchase. You get expert advice. We explain features and benefits and sell you everything you need to complete your project."

"So will *this* guy," Hugo said defensively.

"I don't think so," Derrick retorted. "Not at *this* price."

He pointed to the paper. "I don't see the special drain required for claw foot tubs. I also don't see the faucet, and supply lines, and angle stops."

He paused to gauge Hugo's reaction. "When you buy from *The Design*, we go over everything, to make sure you're satisfied. And—more importantly—if any issues arise, we'll help you through them."

Hugo shook his head. "Issues? What issues can arise? I only want to buy a tub!"

Derrick refolded the paper quote and held it out for the customer to take. "If you're not worried about service, or quality, or technical support, you may want to go ahead and buy your tub from this online retailer. I think you'll be taking a chance, but that's entirely your choice."

Hugo grew red in the face. "I can't believe you're treating me this way! I spend *thousands* here!"

Derrick managed to keep from rolling his eyes. Why did they *always* say that?

"We appreciate your business," Derrick said. "If you've been spending that kind of money in our store, then you already know what kind of value we offer. You already know about our service, our support, and our quality guarantees. And I'm sure you're smart enough to know that you don't get that kind of follow-through from an out-of-state seller who might be operating out of his back yard.

"What kind of person loses a sale to an online competitor?" Hugo asked. "*How* did you get to be a manager?"

Derrick grinned as he reflected on the last question.

"I don't mean to state the obvious," he said, "but this store is in business to make money."

"I *know* that," Hugo blurted.

"Good," Derrick said. "Then you understand that we can't sell a big-ticket item at a loss. If we lose money on every sale, we won't last a week."

Hugo glared at him. "So, you don't care if I shop here?"

"Of *course*, I care," Derrick said. "But I'm not matching that online retailer's price. I'll tell you what I *will* do... I can give you the builder's price, and save you ten percent."

"That's what you give *everybody*," replied Hugo. He spat the words venomously.

"It's the standard contractor discount," Derrick said. "And I'll throw in a free delivery, which is another $135 savings."

Hugo stared blankly.

Derrick didn't want to continue this song and dance, so he broke the silence and asked, "What do you say? Wanna make medicine?" It was a favorite John Wayne line he liked to use whenever he found it appropriate. This was one of those times. But would the customer take the bait?

Hugo sighed. "Okay," he said. "Let's do this. It's still the best deal I'm going to find in town, and you're the only place that's got the damned thing on-hand anyway."

Derrick smiled. "Let me guess... Your online seller doesn't have it in-stock?"

"Ten week lead-time," Hugo said. "And that's just an estimated time of arrival."

He sighed. "I just want the tub, so I can finish this job. My customer is a lawyer, and she's threatening to sue if she has to stay another week in a hotel. The job got pushed back while we were waiting for permits, and—like an idiot—I promised her I'd be done two weeks ago."

He shook his head. "I'll be lucky if I walk away from this job with my shirt."

At the mention of lawsuits, Derrick felt an instant softening in his attitude toward Hugo. Derrick knew what it was to be tied up in legal wrangling over bullshit.

Aw, what the hell? It wasn't his money anyway.

His smile widened. "Tell you what, Hugo," he said. "I'll give you another ten percent off."

Hugo looked startled at the news. "Why? We already agreed on a price."

"I know," Derrick said. "But I *hate* lawyers."

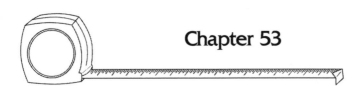

Chapter 53

Mary Hines finished checking in the last pallet of merchandise, and filed the paperwork in the cabinet drawer.

Darrell climbed off the forklift and marched over to stand next to her. "I wish we had more like you," he said with conviction. "Without your help, we'd have been stuck between a rock and a hard place."

Dave Walker nodded. "I *told* you she was worth her weight in gold." He caught the irony in his statement, and immediately wished he'd kept his mouth shut.

But Mary was feeling too good to let her weight issues spoil the mood. She grinned. "It feels great to help out in an area where I'm appreciated."

Derrick was walking toward his office when he spotted everyone huddled by the receiving desk. He looked around. The pallets of freight were staged for the afternoon crew to take to the floor, the trash had been thrown away, nothing blocked the RTV cage, and everyone was in good spirits.

"This place looks good," he said. "Thanks for helping out, Mary. I didn't think you were going to be able to make it."

Mary shrugged. "I had a discussion with the PSM, and I realized I don't want to be part of a team that doesn't want me. I'd much rather help in an area that appreciates what I do."

"And *we* sure do," said Darrell and Marcos in unison.

Kim Purcell appeared in the doorway. "What's going on here?"

All heads turned to face her.

"Just a little teamwork," Derrick said. "Darrell and Marcos were swamped, and you weren't around, so I called in some help. Doesn't this place look great?"

Kim looked around the receiving dock. The place hadn't looked this good since inventory six months ago. Her face flushed red with anger and humiliation. Her eyes locked on Derrick.

"Tina wants to see you," she said in a monotone.

Derrick cocked an eyebrow. "Is that so? Well she knows my phone number, and she knows where my office is."

Kim clearly didn't like his response, and that was enough to tell Derrick something was brewing.

He thanked Mary and the others, and left to walk the sales floor.

He was gonna make that bitch, Tina, wait until he was good and ready to see her.

When he walked through plumbing. he saw John and Brian talking with Katie, whom they referred to as Katie the *plumbette*. She'd been with *The Design* for four years, and she was a likable person.

Brian didn't like working with Katie, because he was old school, and he felt that plumbing was a man's trade. "At least it was when *I* worked in the field," he would say. That had been near thirty years ago, but old habits died hard for Brian.

On Derrick's first day, he'd seen Brian arguing with Katie because he wouldn't help her load a toilet and pedestal onto a flat cart.

"If you're not strong enough to pick up a toilet," Brian had grumbled, "you're not strong enough to do this job."

John had ended up helping Katie, but that hadn't stopped her from complaining to Tina, who had logged an official complaint for harassment and discrimination.

"There will be an investigation into your behavior," Tina had told Brian, much to his dismay.

"It's a free country," Brian had said, but he clearly sensed that he'd gotten himself into deep trouble.

"Yes, it *is* a free country," Tina had said. "But that doesn't prevent you from being held accountable for what you say. Next time, I suggest that you *think* before speaking."

Things had gotten a bit tense for a couple of days, so Derrick was mildly surprised to see that the trouble had apparently blown over. Today, the three plumbing associates were laughing like the best of friends.

John saw Derrick approaching, and gave him a friendly nod. "How goes the man of the store?"

"Doing fine, thank you," Derrick said. "You all seem to be in good spirits."

"*Everyone* is," Brian said.

Katie nodded agreement. "Most of us have wanted to reset our departments for some time, but were always told that we had to follow the company format."

"Technically that's what we're supposed to do," Derrick said. "SSC doesn't want every store doing things its own way. They feel like they need to measure our performance, and one way to do that is to gauge our compliance with a given set of layout standards."

"That's all well and good," said John, "but we know what our customers want to see. If we can set up proper displays, we can better explain the features and benefits of our products. Do you have a minute for me to show you what I mean?"

Derrick smiled. "Sure."

John led them around the corner to the vanity aisle and stopped in front of a 36 inch two-door, three-drawer cabinet display.

"Store support didn't want us to set up a display here," John said. "They wanted to max out freight stocking in this area. But customers want to look, touch, and feel the product before they buy it. So, we setup this display with a countertop, faucet, and toilet—to show the customer how this unit would look in their bathroom."

"We've already sold two this morning," said Katie.

"And I helped Katie load them onto flat carts," added Brian. He was smiling like a kid.

Derrick was loving the positive vibes. "Nothing better than teamwork, right?"

Derrick's next stop was bath showroom. Sarah was giving a product knowledge training class to her associates during the lull in customer traffic. Her team listened as she explained how to qualify a project client.

"Who knows the difference between a client and a customer?" she asked her group of five. Hands raised and she pointed to Leonard.

"A customer is someone making a purchase," Leonard said. "A client is someone looking for a relationship, for us to handle their remodel."

"Correct," said Sarah. She noticed Derrick enter the department and acknowledged him with a nod.

Everyone turned to see who it was.

Derrick motioned for Sarah to continue. "Please, don't let me interrupt."

Sarah continued. "How do we identify project clients?" she asked her group.

Everyone raised their hands. It paid to stand out with the store manager looking on.

Sarah asked Barbara to answer.

"By asking open-ended questions," Barbara said.

Sarah smiled from ear to ear. "You're all batting a thousand!"

"Next question," she said. "What questions indicate that the person we're helping is a client, versus a customer?"

She chose Andrew to answer.

"If the customer says they're remodeling their bath or kitchen, that indicates they're a project client."

"Correct! And what do we do *then*?"

"Explain the features and benefits of our design and install services," the group said in unison.

Derrick liked what he was seeing. Everyone was eager and participating. This was a sharp contrast to the behavior he'd seen on his first day in the store.

Things were starting to look up.

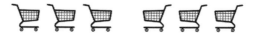

Derrick's next stop was in appliances, where Jesus was giving a demonstration. A small number of customers huddled in one of the vignettes where the associates had recently installed a 48" Professional-Grade convection range. The customers looked on as Jesus gave a demonstration.

"This all-gas range is made in America!" Jesus said proudly. "It has six 18,000 BTU high-powered burners, and a griddle."

One of the customers raised a hand. "What does BTU stand for?" she asked.

Jesus welcomed the question, a sure sign they were interested. "British Thermal Units," he answered. "It's the amount of heat energy needed to raise the temperature of one pound of water one degree."

He grinned. "That sounds like something you'd only hear on a science test, but the principle has practical application in your kitchen. It means that you have the ability to cook dishes faster, and more efficiently with this range."

He pointed to the burners. "The burners are sealed and easy to clean. The grates are made of cast-iron, and they're small enough to be cleaned in a standard-sized kitchen sink. And all six have the ability to drop to a low simmer for sauces."

He opened the oven door. "The oven has a convection fan that rotates the heat, so you have even cooking. It also sucks out odor. This means you can cook multiple dishes at the same time, without contaminating the flavors of whatever you happen to be making."

Jesus spotted Derrick standing in the back, but Derrick waved for him to continue.

"Convection cooking is twenty-five percent faster," Jesus said. "It utilizes twenty degrees less temperature than older models, making it far more efficient. And each range is calibrated, so that the actual temperature never varies more than plus or minus five degrees from the desired temperature, making this one of the best ranges on the market."

He decided to challenge his group. "Do any of you know what the ratio is for older models?"

No one raised their hand.

"To be frank," Jesus said, "they were off the charts!"

Confident that Jesus had things well under control, Derrick left and continued walking the sales floor.

"Can we have a cooking demonstration?" asked one of the customers.

"Of course," answered Jesus, eager to show off his pride and joy.

He placed a frying pan on the top right burner and switched on the auto-ignition. The burner made a clicking noise, but nothing happened. Jesus turned the knob to the OFF position and switched it on again. Once more, nothing happened.

What the fuck is going on? This was the last thing he needed during a presentation. He heard the group of onlookers mumble and snicker, and looked up to face them. "To be expected, right?"

They laughed.

"Let me take a quick look at this," Jesus said.

He removed the frying pan, and switched on the ignition again. The clicking sound went on and on, but no flame ignited.

Jesus leaned his head over the burner for a closer look. A spark caught and a flame sprouted from the burner, making a WHOOSHING sound.

The customers gasped, as Jesus jumped back.

Chapter 54

Derrick couldn't stop beaming. His store was looking good across the board. Displays were being reset in an inviting way, and the attitude of his associates couldn't have been more energetic if he'd wanted it to be. He was sure that the managers visiting his store tomorrow would be impressed. *Bring 'em on.*

His reverie was interrupted by a loud WHOOSH sound, coming from the direction of the appliance showroom. What the hell?

Before Derrick could investigate, a familiar voice called out to him. "Hey Mister, wanna take me out to lunch?"

Derrick turned and saw his wife standing before him. "Jennifer! What are you doing here?"

She was dressed in casual, tight-fitting jeans that showed off her athletic build and a green, front-buttoned blouse. It tugged her frame just enough to hint that her breasts were real, and not silicone-implants.

"I know you're going to work every day this week to get ready for your promotion on Monday," she said, "so I decided to take you out to lunch, to make sure you still eat right. Knowing you as I do, you'll probably skip lunch, and I know how grumpy you get when you don't eat."

Derrick couldn't argue. He had the tendency to get so caught up at work that he'd blow off lunch and come home late, missing dinner too.

He wrapped his arms around Jennifer's waist and pulled her to him. "I don't deserve you," he said, giving her a kiss and hug. He had to be quick about it. It wouldn't set a good example being overly passionate at work, even with his wife.

"Where do you want to eat?" he asked.

Jennifer flashed a sultry smile. "Where do you want to *take* me?"

Derrick opened his mouth to speak, but he stopped short when he saw Jesus walking toward him. The man's eyebrows were gone, and the front of his scalp was singed clean.

"What happened?" Derrick asked.

"My demonstration is over for the day," Jesus said. "I'm taking the rest of the day off." And he marched right out of the building.

Jennifer turned toward Derrick, a look of utter bewilderment on her face.

Derrick shrugged and smiled. "Just another day at the office."

Jennifer drove to a hole-in-the-wall Mexican restaurant called *Chico's Bar & Grill*, located a mile from the store along El Camino Real Boulevard.

At first sight of the store, Derrick thought Jennifer was playing games. "This isn't exactly what I had in mind," he said. "Are you *sure* you want to eat here?"

"Haven't I taught you how to recognize a good restaurant when you see one?" Jennifer asked.

She pulled her Toyota Prius into a parking spot, and pressed the 'stop' button to shut down the hybrid drive. Jen insisted on driving, because it drove her crazy when Derrick obeyed the speed limit and came to a complete stop at every light.

Derrick surveyed the surroundings. An overflowing dumpster was in plain view, and two homeless men were munching on leftovers handed to them by customers. The parking lot was littered with trash, and the walls of the restaurant could have used a fresh coat of paint.

Derrick climbed out of the car and closed the door, but he made no move to walk toward the sketchy-looking restaurant.

"I'd rather eat there," he said, pointing at a *McDonald's* across the street.

Jennifer made a face at him. "*You* would."

She pointed to the cars in the lot. "Tell me what you see."

Derrick looked around. "I see cars," he said mechanically.

Jennifer pointed toward the *McDonald's* lot. "*There* are cars." Her finger swung to point at the lot in front of *Chico's*. "And *here* are cars. But are they the same *kind* of cars?"

Derrick looked more closely. The cars in front of *Chico's* were expensive compared to the ones in the *McDonald's* lot.

"It means the owners of Chico's pay good money for an excellent cook, instead of wasting money on window-dressing," Jennifer explained.

She began walking toward the restaurant, without waiting to see if Derrick was following her. "Come on," she said. "I'm hungry."

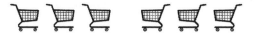

Fran Silva returned from lunch at the nearby grocery store's deli department. Usually, she brown-bagged her lunch, but the coupons she got in the mail had been a good incentive to buy her lunch. Besides, it was good to change things up every once in a while.

She drove toward her usual parking spot, a space under the shade of a tree. What the hell? Someone else's car was parked in *her* favorite spot.

Fran didn't recognize the car, so it probably didn't belong to a store associate. That was good for them, because—if it *had* been an associate—she'd be ripping somebody a new asshole right about now.

On her way to the trade department entrance, she walked past the returns office and saw Karen working behind the counter, helping a male customer. Fran could only see the man's back, but there was something familiar about him.

Where had she seen him before? Was he a contractor? She wasn't sure.

She was about to walk through the returns entrance when the man turned his head, and she recognized his profile. Fran's eyes practically popped from their sockets.

"Fuck me running!" she blurted.

Before the customer or Karen could get a glimpse of her, Fran trotted to trade department and reached for a bag under her desk.

Michael and Nancy were sitting at their desks. They both looked up, wondering what the commotion was about.

"What's wrong?" Nancy asked.

Fran gave her a malicious grin. "My prayers have been answered," she said.

"Without a receipt I can only issue you a store credit," Karen said. The company returns policy was to decline a cash refund if the customer had no receipt. It was a common practice in the industry.

The customer scratched his chin. "I'd really prefer cash," he said.

Karen was ill-fitted for the returns desk. When customers got balky, as they frequently did, she lacked the backbone to face up to them. She tended to call a manager to handle even the simplest of issues.

"Our system won't authorize me to refund you in cash, unless I have a receipt," she said nervously.

She prayed that this wouldn't escalate into an argument, and she was already reaching for the phone to call a manager.

The customer saw her hand grasp the phone and said quickly, "That'll be fine!"

Karen was relieved. She was starting to process the store credit when Fran walked up.

"Hi Karen," Fran said cheerfully. "Anything I can do to help?"

The customer and Karen looked at Fran.

Karen shook her head. "No, thank you. He's just returning a faucet."

She was surprised by the offer. Usually, the returns desk associates had to pull teeth to get people to help with a return.

Karen turned her attention back to the customer. She handed him a returns slip. "Please sign here," she said. "And I'll need to see your driver's license."

The customer grew nervous.

"Anything *wrong*, sir?" Fran asked.

There was something strange about her tone.

The customer glanced at Fran, then back to the returns slip. "I don't have my driver's license," he said. "I forgot my wallet at home."

Karen explained that she needed a form of ID before she could process the return.

"Can't you make an exception?" the man asked.

"We don't make the rules, sir," Fran said. Her voice was nearly a growl. "We just *follow* them."

The customer stared at Fran, annoyed with her intrusion.

Fran could hardly believe it. This ass-wipe didn't remember her.

She looked down at the man's feet. "Nice shoes. What *size* do you wear?"

The man's shoes weren't actually very nice at all, and he was clearly taken aback by Fran's question.

"It's none of your business what size my shoes are," he snapped. "I just want to return a faucet and get my money back!"

"You look like a size ten to me," Fran said.

She placed the bag on the counter and pulled out a shoe, holding it in both hands.

The customer's expression shifted instantly from agitation to fear.

"Care to try it on?" Fran asked in a sweet voice.

She could see it in the man's eyes now. He had finally recognized her.

"That's right, asshole," Fran snarled. "I'm the bitch you ran from when you *stole* this faucet."

Karen gasped and stepped back from the counter.

Jean-Man didn't hesitate. He bolted through the door, leaving the faucet on the counter.

Fran calmly walked through the door after him. "Don't forget this!" she shouted.

She threw Jean-Man's shoe after him, striking the fleeing thief squarely in the back.

Fran laughed. "Bull's-eye!"

Jean-Man didn't stop running to pick up his shoe. Instead, he made a dash for his car. He clearly wanted to get the hell out of dodge.

When he reached his, car he fumbled for the keys in his pocket.

Fran watched his frenzied performance, and relished the moment. "This is classic!"

Karen stood just inside the entrance. "So that was the guy who got away this past Monday?"

Fran nodded, still laughing. "Yeah. Ain't it sweet?"

Jean-Man finally pulled the keys from his pocket, unlocked the car door and climbed in. Inserting the key, he turned the ignition, but the engine sputtered.

He swore, and attempted to start the car again. Once more the engine sputtered.

"Hey Beavis," Fran shouted. "Maybe you should call Butthead, to give you a jump-start!"

Jean-Man flipped her the bird.

Fran was un-phased, still laughing over the idiot's frantic attempts to escape.

On Jean-Man's third attempt, the engine came to life and he pulled out of the parking lot, tires screeching on the blacktop.

Fran stood at the entrance of the store, applauding enthusiastically.

As Jean-Man screeched out of the parking lot, he flipped her off again.

Fran walked back into the store, still chuckling. "The little prick still managed to pull a fast one on me," she said.

Karen walked back to the returns counter. "How do you mean? You got the faucet back, and you hit the guy with his own shoe. I'd call that a clear victory."

"Maybe so," Fran said. "But the asshole had his car in *my* parking spot!"

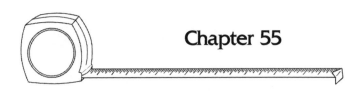

Chapter 55

"So, how are things at work?" Jennifer asked. She thrust her fork into her machaca burrito, and cut a slice off with her knife. The burrito was too big to be easily picked up by hand and eaten.

"About as good as can be expected," replied Derrick with a shrug.

His chorizo burrito was equally large, but he decided to skip the knife and pick it up. He bit off a chunk and chewed. Delicious. As usual, Jen had known what she was doing when she selected the restaurant.

Derrick swallowed, and was about to compliment his wife on her choice of eating establishments, when he caught sight of her expression. The look on her face clearly said, '*how-dare-you-embarrass-me-by-eating-that-way.*'

Derrick was too familiar with that look, but he decided to ignore it and enjoy his burrito.

"Take your elbows off the table," Jen commanded.

Derrick rolled his eyes. "Lighten up, Honey," he said. "First, this is how burritos are meant to be eaten. And second, I'm not wasting elegant table manners on a place that has an overflowing dumpster out front. We don't want people thinking we're snobs in a place like this, do we?"

Jennifer shifted gears. "What time will you be home tonight?"

Derrick shrugged. "Probably late. We're gearing up for Monday's promotion."

"How much do you have to do for that?" she asked.

Derrick shook his head. "Too much. Waaaaaaaay too much."

He swallowed a gulp of tea from his glass. He could sure use a beer right about now.

"You can have a beer when you get home," Jen said.

Derrick set down his tea glass. "Are you reading my *mind*? Is that how you do that?"

Jen smiled. "I don't *have* to read your mind. I'm your wife. I know how you think."

Derrick smiled and took another bite of his burrito.

"So what all do you have to do?" Jennifer asked.

Derrick sighed, and began rattling off the list. There were ads to be distributed throughout the store, signage to be posted denoting special buys, schedules to be adjusted, stock to be shelved, and the store needed to be cleaned from top to bottom.

When he finished, Jennifer waited to swallow a mouthful of food before speaking. Unlike her husband, she never talked with her mouth full of food.

"That sounds like a lot of work," she said. "But most of it seems like the responsibility of the people who work for you."

"That's true," Derrick said. "But I'm asking my associates to pour their hearts into this holiday sale. If I want them to have that level of dedication, I have to demonstrate that kind of dedication myself. I have to show that I'm the right man for the job."

"What does that mean?" Jennifer asked. "Are you saying that a woman can't do the job as store manager?"

Derrick lowered his burrito. "Did I say that? Have you *ever* heard me say anything like that?"

"You implied—"

"I didn't imply any such thing!" Derrick said. "I said the right *man* for the job, because I happen to *be* a man. Since I'm the store manager, and I am a man, it doesn't make much sense for me to talk about the right woman for the job, *does* it?"

Jennifer set down her fork. "What are you getting so steamed up about? I didn't say you were being sexist."

"No," Derrick said. "You didn't say it. You *implied* it. And I don't mind telling you that I resent the implication."

"Okay," Jennifer said in a calming voice. "I apologize. I'm sorry for even suggesting it."

Derrick left the half-eaten burrito on his plate, and reached for a napkin. 'Do you remember Maria Espinoza?" he asked.

Jennifer frowned in concentration. "From the Kearny Mesa store?"

"Yeah," Derrick said. "She was the store manager when I first went to work in the plumbing department."

Jennifer reached for her own napkin. "What's your point?"

"My point is," Derrick said, "she was one of the best store managers I ever worked under. And you've heard me say so fifty times."

Jennifer sighed. "I said I was sorry, and I meant it. Can we drop this, now? *Please?*"

Derrick reached for his burrito. "Consider it dropped."

"Good," Jennifer said. "Let's change the subject. Did your boss say anything about a pay raise?"

"Not yet," Derrick said. "I'm fairly sure that Judy is waiting to see how I do with this big sale event."

Jennifer frowned. "It sounds like she's giving you a week to prove yourself."

"Or *hang* myself," Derrick said.

Jen nodded. "You could be right..."

Derrick took a bite of burrito, and then tried to talk around it. "It's not Judy I'm worried about."

His wife glared at him. "Don't talk with food in your mouth," she said. "And who exactly is it that you *are* worried about?"

Derrick swallowed, took a sip of iced tea, and then told Jennifer about the harassment complaints.

Before she'd become a stay-at-home-Mom, Jen had worked as a paralegal in a downtown law firm. She had seen dozens of harassment claims. Many of the cases that had crossed her desk had been genuine, but a significant percentage of the claims had been frivolous, or completely trumped up.

It was a relatively simple matter for a female employee to evade responsibility by accusing her supervisor of harassment. It made no difference whether or not there was any basis for the complaint. Once the accusation was made, most companies went into damage control mode, willing to do nearly anything to avoid a lawsuit. Usually, the manager would be instructed to back off, and the employee who made the complaint would be free to do whatever she wanted.

Jennifer was all too familiar with this tactic, and she knew how effective it could be.

"Their complaints don't have any merit," she said. "Your so-called '*ladies*' are trying to keep your head down. They want you so busy dodging bullets that you won't be able to keep an eye on whatever they're up to."

"That's exactly what I told Judy," Derrick said. "Luckily, she knows that I'm telling the truth. She's backing me up on this."

"Do your troublemakers know that?" Jen asked.

"No," Derrick said. "They think I'm digging my own grave."

He exhaled heavily. "You've got to love the retail business."

Jen placed her hand on top of his and smiled. "Don't worry, Honey. It'll all work out in the end."

Derrick smiled back. "It always does," he said.

Chapter 56

2:30 PM

Jennifer kissed Derrick, and dropped him off in front of the store.

Derrick waved goodbye, and waited until Jen's car was out of sight before going inside. Her unexpected visit was exactly what he had needed. He was glad she had come by. How had he ever gotten lucky enough to deserve her?

He walked through the front end register entrance and was caught off guard by a familiar voice.

"Have a nice lunch?"

Derrick looked over his shoulder and saw Sylvia leaning against the entrance to trade. "Sylvia," he said with surprise.

"You remembered my name," Sylvia said.

What had gotten into this girl? Derrick wasn't the only one who was noticing it, either. Samantha and Teresa were watching the exchange with obvious interest.

Sylvia glanced at the clock on the wall. "Looks like you took a long lunch."

Derrick studied her carefully. She was up to something, and—whatever it was—it would probably add up to trouble.

"I plan on working late anyway," he said. "Lots to do before Monday. Speaking of which, how are things in seasonal? Coming along okay?"

"They're coming along *great*," Sylvia said. "Would you like me to show you?" She stepped closer.

Derrick halted her with a raised hand, careful not to touch her. "No," he said quickly. "I'll walk the floor with the department heads before closing."

As he backed away, he saw Samantha and Teresa still looking on curiously. All Derrick needed was for someone to start a rumor about him and an hourly employee.

The fun around this place just never stopped.

Stephan Young was a veteran sales associate, but new to *The Design*. After twenty years working commission sales in the flooring industry, he was relieved to be working as an hourly-paid associate. The back-stabbing, and one-upmanship of the commission game had taken its toll, and this was a welcome change. He actually felt as though he could make friends with his fellow associates, and not worry about losing his shirt.

"How may I help you?" he said to the man and woman looking at tile samples in the flooring showroom. Stephan's experience made him a shoe-in candidate for this department, and Leonard felt lucky to have someone who knew what they were talking about.

"Just looking," answered the man. He didn't make eye contact, instead continuing to peruse the samples with the woman Stephan assumed to be his wife.

Ever the true specialist of his trade, Stephan pressed on. He had greeted the customers; now, he was supposed to ask questions, to qualify their needs. "Is this your first time visiting *The Design*?"

"We've been here before," the woman replied mechanically.

"Thank you for coming back," Stephan said cheerfully. "I see you're looking at ceramic tile samples. What room are you looking to replace flooring in?"

He was good at asking open-ended questions.

The man looked Stephan in the eyes for the first time. "We're just looking," he repeated.

Still undaunted, Stephan was determined to have this couple warm to him. "If you're looking for specific tile samples, I'd be happy to show them to you."

The woman turned abruptly to face him. "When we need help, we'll ask for it!" she snapped.

Stephan stepped back. "Of course. When you're ready, I'll be right over there." He pointed to a desk with a computer on it.

The man and woman continued perusing displays, hovering closely to Stephan as he worked on customer orders. He couldn't help wonder if they were intentionally trying to make him uneasy, so he busied himself with everyday tasks. He'd be damned if he was going to let them ruin his day.

He spent the next twenty minutes calling vendors for estimated delivery dates, then calling customers to keep them up to date on when their orders were due to arrive. Things went smoothly until he called Mr. Jason Haggard, to inform him his flooring order was back-ordered, and delivery would be delayed another two weeks.

"What the hell kind of business are you running?" Jason Haggard screamed into the phone. "You promised my shit would be ready in four weeks. Now you're telling me I'm going to have to wait another two weeks!"

Stephan shook his head. Here we go again... "Jason, we never promised you a specific date," he said calmly. "We don't have the ability to make such promises, that's why we provide you with an ETA."

"What the hell's an ETA?" Jason shouted.

Stephan wondered if this guy was feigning ignorance. "Estimated time of arrival," answered Stephan. He pronounced each word slowly, so there would be no misunderstanding.

"So why can't I have my order delivered tomorrow, like you promised?"

"I *didn't* promise," Stephan said. "We just went over that. You were given an *estimated* time of arrival. And now, the vendor who manufactures the tile is telling us that they had a problem with the die-lot, and your tile didn't come out in the color you chose. They need another two weeks to get it right."

"Why couldn't you tell me this sooner?" Jason snarled. "I scheduled installers to be here tomorrow, and now I'm going to have to pay them $250 to cancel and reschedule. Who's going to reimburse me for my time and trouble?"

Stephan didn't appreciate being yelled at, but he did understand the man's frustration. Jason was right. The vendor had known that they would miss the estimated shipping date. So, why hadn't they contacted the store, so that Stephan could warn the customer? If they had performed that simple task, the customer would have had time to reschedule his installers.

"I'm sorry," Stephan said. "But we can't reimburse your $250. As I've already told you, the delivery date is an *estimate*. With made-to-order items, the vendor can't always support the estimated date."

In fact, Stephan had only learned of the problem when he called the vendor to confirm the ETA for the customer's tile. When he'd learned of the delay, he'd asked the obvious question. "Why didn't you notify the store *sooner*? You've known for at least a week that you've got a problem on your production line."

"I'm just the expediter," the woman on the other end of line had said. "I pass along the information as it comes to me." There had been no trace of empathy in her voice.

Stephan was trying hard not to show the same lack of empathy to this customer.

"I apologize for the delay," he said. "When you deal with special-order products, sometimes the vendors have problems."

"That still doesn't make up for the two-fifty I'm out of pocket," Jason shouted. "Are you going to cover that?"

Stephan knew *The Design's* policy on this backwards and forwards...

ALL SPECIAL ORDERS ARE ESTIMATED TIME OF ARRIVAL ONLY. WE DO NOT COVER LABOR AND INSTALLATION CHARGES DUE TO BACK ORDERS.

Short, and to the point. But there were exceptions. All an angry customer had to do was bark up the tree until he got the answer he wanted. If he complained long enough and loud enough, eventually one of the senior company officers would issue the standard company line... *'Take care of the customer.'*

Stephan had informed Jason at time of sale not to schedule an install date until delivery of his order had been made. This was *The Design's* way of protecting its interests against unforeseen issues.

"I can't refund your out-of-pocket expenses," Stephan said. "We've already been over this—"

"Fine," the customer snapped. "How about I throw a monkey in the wrench, and cancel my order? How would you like *that*?"

Stephan struggled not to sigh over the phone. "Jason, you know you need this order. If our vendor can deliver it in two weeks or less, that will still be faster than you can get from anywhere else."

He was comforted by the fact he was telling the truth. The ceramic tile Jason had chosen was made-to-order. No one else had it in-stock.

"Canceling at this point would only compound your problems," Stephan said.

"And yours," Jason said quickly.

This was true. *The Design's* policy was clear...

SPECIAL ORDERS ARE NON-REFUNDABLE, AND UNCANCELABLE.

Again, short and to the point. It was also completely unhelpful.

Stephan was about to reply, when he looked up and saw the couple who had spurned his offer to help. They were standing in front of a nearby wall, and they had obviously been listening in on his conversation with Jason Haggard. The man and woman both had condescending smiles on their faces.

Their smirk, combined with Jason's badgering, got Stephan's temper going. For the first time during this conversation, he felt himself start to lose his cool.

"Jason, I can't go down to the plant and make the tile myself," he said. "The vendor knows that they screwed up, and they want to deliver this order as quickly as possible."

"How come *you* don't want to deliver this as quickly as possible?" Jason asked maliciously.

Stephan looked up, and saw the couple staring in his direction. They were clearly enjoying his situation.

Stephan stared back at them as he spoke into the phone. "I'm working with the vendor," he said. "At the moment, that's all I can really do."

"You know something, Stephan?" Jason shouted. "You're a weak son-of-a-bitch! I went to you, because a friend told me that you could make things happen. So far, you haven't shown me *dick*!"

Stephan felt his knuckles tightening on the phone, but Jason wasn't through hurling insults yet.

"You're a lying bastard!" Jason screamed. "You falsely represented your company! You took my money, and now you're holding me hostage. You know what I'm going to do?"

"By all means," Stephan said, "tell me."

The loitering couple was making no attempt to disguise their enjoyment at watching Stephan have his ears ripped off by this irate customer.

"I'm going to sue you!" Jason shouted. "I'm going to cancel this order, and then I'm going to sue your sorry ass. And that piece-of-shit company you work for."

Stephan was just about fed up with this crap. "You go ahead and do what you have to do," he said. "I'm cancelling your order right now, and I'm authorizing a full refund of your money. I wish you the best of luck in finding another provider who can deliver your order in two weeks."

Jason's voice was shriek. "*What*? You can't cancel my order! You can't leave me flapping in the breeze? Where the hell am I going to get the tile, *now*? How long have you been a salesperson, you son of a bitch?"

"I'm sorry we couldn't meet your expectations," Stephan said. "You have a nice day."

He slammed down the receiver of the phone so hard that it sounded like a hammer striking an anvil. Then, he stood up and walked toward the eavesdropping couple. Their condescending smiles vanished, as he approached.

Stephan stopped a few feet away. "You folks having a good time?" The anger in his voice was palpable.

The couple's eyes practically popped out of their sockets.

"All I did was offer to help you," Stephan continued. "I showed you courtesy, and respect. You responded with rudeness."

He jerked his finger toward the phone. "Then, you stood around and made rude faces while I tried my very best to help a customer whose order had been delayed."

Stephan brought the accusing finger back around to point toward the couple. "Do you people not have friends? Are your lives so miserable that you get your kicks from laughing at people who are having a difficult time? What do you do for fun? Stomp on kittens?"

The man took a step forward. His chest came up short against Stephan's outstretched finger. "You... You can't talk to us that way..." he stammered.

Stephan lowered the finger. "You know what?" he said. "You're right. I *can't* talk to you that way. Because I'm too good a person for that, even if you *aren't.*"

He gave the couple a chilly smile. "You folks have a nice afternoon, okay?"

The eavesdroppers did an abrupt about-face, and practically sprinted down the aisle. In a couple of seconds, they were out of sight around the corner.

Stephan turned back toward his desk, and found Derrick standing there, watching him.

Stephan sighed. "Did you hear that?"

Derrick nodded. "Some of it."

The anger was gone from Stephan, now. He shook his head. "I'm sorry. I'm having a bad day."

"I can understand that," Derrick said. "We all have bad days sometimes."

He beckoned to Stephan. "Come walk with me."

Derrick led the associate through the main aisles of each department, but away from earshot of customers and associates.

"Dealing with people is tough," Derrick said. "Customers don't want relationships any more. They want quality product, for the lowest price."

Stephan was a bit surprised that his new store manager was coming to the point so quickly.

Derrick continued. "We want our customers to be happy with their shopping experience. We offer competitive prices, financing, delivery, and installation. We also offer professional assistance, on a non-commission basis. And when you put all of those things together, it should create a positive impression with most customers. Unfortunately, despite our best efforts, things don't always work out that way."

Stephan nodded. He thought he could see where this was going.

"Some of our customers can be reasonable when things go wrong," Derrick said. "But some of them seem to completely lose their minds, even their basic human decency, when things don't go according to plan."

"I know all about that," Stephan said. "And I know I shouldn't have let that couple get under my skin. I won't let it happen again."

Derrick smiled. "Fair enough," he said. "If you'll promise to stick to that, we'll let this little incident end right here, between you and me."

Stephan looked at him. "Really? That's *it*?"

"That's it," Derrick said. "You've been in this business a long time, and you know how to do your job. I don't see any reason to push this any further. I trust you to do the right thing in the future."

"Thanks!" Stephan said.

"No problem," Derrick said. He patted Stephan on the shoulder. "You can get back to work now."

Stephan grinned, and walked away, whistling as he went.

When the associate was out of sight, Derrick took out his notepad and jotted down their discussion in a few brief sentences. He didn't expect any more problems out of Stephan, but it never hurt to cover one's ass.

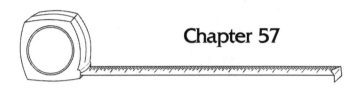

Chapter 57

3:00 PM

Tim Lyons wasn't looking forward to his next task. He had a ton of prep work for the upcoming promotion, and now they wanted him to conduct job interviews.

He raised his hands in surrender. "What the hell? Does he want us to be ready for the promotion? Or to waste time interviewing applicants?"

The question was directed to Steve Evans, but a different voice answered it. "Both!"

Steve and Tim turned quickly, and saw Derrick standing behind them. They glanced nervously at each other.

"Derrick, I didn't mean anything by it," Tim stuttered, his face turning red.

"I gathered that," replied Derrick. "How many interviews do you have?"

Tim counted the folders in hand. "Three."

"Any women among them?"

Tim nodded. "Yes. Two."

"Good," Derrick said. "Sixty percent of our customers are female, and most prefer a woman's point of view. It stands to reason that we should look to hire female specialists in kitchen, bath, appliances, décor, and lighting."

Steve nodded. "Yeah, that makes sense, but we don't understand the point of interviewing applicants so close to the promotion."

"That's right," Tim said. "Even if we hire them today, we'll have to wait two weeks for the drug tests and background checks to come through."

"And by then, the promo will be over," interjected Steve.

"True," Derrick said. "We've got three days before our sale begins, to demonstrate we have the right people in place to turn this store around. When Judy asks what we're doing to drive sales, we're gonna look her in the eye and say, 'in addition to resetting displays, putting up promotional signs, distributing flyers, and inviting builders, contractors, and designers to visit our store, we're interviewing people to ensure that we have a pipeline of talent available to serve our customers.'"

Steve and Tim shared a doubtful expression.

"You're talking as though we're walking the plank," Steve said.

"Yeah," agreed Tim, "It sounds like you're saying that this store is in serious trouble."

Derrick realized instantly that he had given too much away. He had to back-pedal fast. "Not at all," he said. "But the more we do to keep store support off our backs, the simpler our lives will be. The last thing we need is a deep-dive, to show what we're *not* doing."

A 'deep-dive' was a store audit, and everyone hated them. It meant a visit by the district manager and a team of operations specialists, who checked to ensure that the store followed the ordering, hiring, firing, receiving, and operational and safety processes required by the company. A deep-dive always took up a whole day, and they seldom achieved anything beyond creating headaches for the store personnel.

"Everything is about the process," Derrick said. "We're going above and beyond expectations, because we want Judy and the rest of store support team to leave us alone to do our jobs. Does that make sense?"

Tim and Steve nodded slowly.

Derrick wasn't sure they were buying it, but he'd been specifically forbidden to tell the truth on this matter. Judy had threatened his job if he let slip that the store was on the chopping block.

Steve started to say something, but was cut short by Derrick's phone.

Derrick was grateful for the interruption. He fished out his phone and answered it. "This is Derrick."

He listened for several seconds, and then said, "okay, I'll be right there."

He glanced back to Steve and Tim. "I have to go talk to a customer at the front registers. I'll see you two later. Let me know how the interviews go."

Both associates nodded, and Derrick walked away.

He hoped he'd managed to divert their attention away from his slip of the tongue. He didn't need any doom-and-gloom rumors floating around about the future of the store. Or, rather, its possible *lack* of a future...

Chapter 58

Tim entered the consultation room located in bath showroom, where a perky-looking, twenty-something girl sat munching on a muffin. The room was filled with the aroma of strong coffee she had purchased at the coffee cart located in the parking lot. Tim recognized the signature cup with the *Cafecito* name on it.

"How's the muffin?" he asked. He glanced pointedly at the snack and coffee cup, but the girl failed to read his hint about how inappropriate it was for her to be eating and drinking during a job interview.

"Not bad," the girl replied, taking a sip of coffee. "Want some?" She held up the muffin.

Tim shook his head and dropped her application heavily on the table. "No thanks."

He sat in the chair across from her, opened the folder, and began reading her application. "Your name is Millicent Dreyfus."

"Everyone calls me Millie," she blurted.

Tim lifted his eyes to hers. "Millie," he repeated. He frowned and said, "I suppose it's catchy."

He continued reading in silence, while she sat eating and drinking. Millie's chewing echoed loudly in the small consultation room, and Tim found it difficult to concentrate. He looked up at her.

"Change your mind?" Millie asked, holding out her muffin.

Tim wasn't sure if she was purposely trying to blow the interview, or if she was truly naïve. He decided that it was probably the latter.

He put down the folder. "So, Millie, tell me about yourself."

Millie wolfed down the last piece of muffin, and chased it with a sip of coffee. She wiped her hands clean of crumbs, scattering them carelessly on the table.

"I'm twenty-two," she said. "I graduated from SDSU last December. My dad said I should get a job, so I applied here."

Tim waited for her to continue, but that was apparently all she had to say on the matter. "What was your major?"

"Chemical engineering," Millie said.

"The position you're applying for is bath specialist," Tim said. "That's quite a difference from a chemical engineer. Why aren't you seeking work in the field you studied?"

Millie laughed. "I don't wanna be a chemical engineer."

Tim was puzzled. "Then why did you study chemical engineering?"

"Well," Millie said, "I'm interested in chemical engineering. I like the science part. But I don't like the people. So it's not turning out to be a good career path for me."

Tim motioned for her to continue.

"I like being around people," Millie said. "But I interned for an industrial lab, and the people weren't friendly or talkative. I don't want to spend my whole life sitting in a cubicle, staring at a computer."

"That sounds reasonable," Tim said. "Are you looking for a career with *The Design*, or something part-time?"

"To tell the truth," Mille said. "I need something to hold me over until I figure out what I want to do with myself."

Her answer didn't surprise Tim. The low wages offered for most retail positions didn't inspire many applicants to pursue long-term employment in retail.

Tim tapped a finger on the girl's application. "I see you have experience in sales and remodeling, but I'm not familiar with the names of businesses you worked for."

Millie gave him an embarrassed grin. "Uh... I made those places up. I don't actually have any sales experience."

Before Tim could speak, she continued. "I need a job. My dad says if I don't find work, he's going to cut my allowance."

Tim was becoming annoyed. "I'm not sure I follow..."

"I needed an interview," explained Millie, "and I knew I wouldn't get one if I admitted that I don't have any experience. So I padded my application, to get my foot in the door."

Tim closed her application folder. "I see."

"Look," Millie said quickly, "I know I shouldn't have done that. But I didn't try to hide it from you. I told you the truth right away. And I can *do* this job. I *know* I can."

She was talking even faster, now. "I've seen how you people work. You greet customers. Listen to what they have to say. You tell them what they need, and you close the sale. It's not exactly rocket science, is it?"

Tim was caught off guard. Millie's tone and demeanor had gone from lackadaisical indifference, to logic and confidence. Still...

He shook his head. "You lied on your application."

"Just to get in the door," Millie said. "And I'm not asking for a lot of money. How many applicants understand the requirements of this job, and are okay with low pay?"

She had a point there.

Tim shook his head again. "Even if we hire you, the background check will reveal that you lied about your previous employment. That's cause for immediate termination."

Millie was ready for that. "I'll rewrite my application."

She smiled. "With the turnover you've already got in this company, what have you got to lose?"

Tim thought about it for several seconds. What the hell? Why not?

"Okay," he said. "We'll give it a try. You'll have to pass the drug test, and I'll start you off at $10.50 an hour. Then, we'll see."

Millie cocked her head. "Yes, you *will*."

As they rose to shake hands, Tim asked, "Do you have any other surprises for me?"

She gripped his hand. "Well, there is *one* thing I should tell you." There was a trace of reluctance in her tone.

"Let's hear it," Tim said, pulling his hand free of hers.

Millie sighed heavily. "I have a twin sister. She likes playing games with me."

"You mean the world is blessed with *two* Millie's?"

"You could say that, but—"

"But *what*?"

"My sister likes to pretend to be me, and she's always doing silly things to embarrass me."

Tim took a moment to digest this. "You're kidding, right?"

Millie shook her head emphatically. "No, and frankly, it can be downright humiliating. Once, she flirted with a geek, making him think I was completely into him. When he saw me the next day, it was all I could do to keep him from coming on to me."

Tim nodded thoughtfully. "Well, one thing's for sure," he said. "This is *not* going to be dull."

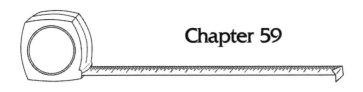

Chapter 59

3:20 PM

The customer stood by the front end registers, waiting for the general manager. He was Hispanic, looked to be in his late sixties, and dressed as though he had never broken free from the fashions of the '70s. His jeans were faded blue, the type you only found in thrift shops nowadays, and he wore a safari-style buttoned down shirt. His head was adorned with a baseball cap, embroidered with the words AIR FORCE RETIRED.

Florence observed the customer from her register, while waiting for Derrick to arrive. There was something about the old man that made her nervous, so when Derrick walked around the corner, Florence anxiously pointed to the customer.

Derrick nodded acknowledgement and walked up to the customer offering his hand. "Hello. How may I help you?"

The customer ignored his handshake and grunted. "You the manager?"

"Yes I am," answered Derrick.

The customer lowered his folded arms and said, "Come with me."

It was *not* a request.

Derrick glanced quizzically at Florence, who shrugged.

Derrick shrugged in return, and followed the customer into the parking lot. "What's this about?" he asked.

"That's what I'm going to show you," the customer said dryly.

He stopped in front of a 1970 blue and white Nova, and turned to face Derrick. "This is my car."

Derrick waited for more, but the customer stared without continuing.

"I'm not in the market for a car," Derrick said. "But, if you're looking to buy home improvement products, you've come to the right place."

The customer was not amused. He pointed to the driver's door. "Look what happened!"

Derrick gave the door a quick once-over. The sheet metal had a fist-sized dent, and the paint had been scratched.

Derrick straightened up. "Did you see the person responsible?"

"They drove off before I could write down the license plate," the customer said. "What are you gonna do about it?"

Do about it? Why in the hell should Derrick do *anything* about it?

"I'm sorry," he said, "but I didn't get your name."

"That's because I didn't give it!" the customer snapped.

"If you want my help," Derrick said, "then I'm going to have to know your name. Mine is Derrick."

The customer mumbled, "Jose Rodriguez."

"Okay, Jose, this incident falls under the property management's responsibility. I can give—"

Jose cut him off. "This happened in *your* parking lot!"

"I understand that, Jose," Derrick said. "But you have to—"

The man cut him off again. "Don't call me Jose! I'm not your buddy!"

He was right about *that*.

Derrick smiled politely. "Fine, Mr. Rodriguez. As I've been trying to tell you, this parking lot is not owned by *The Design*. And since your car was not damaged by an employee of ours, I'll have to direct you to the property management office."

He fumbled in his pockets for the phone number and address, knowing perfectly well that he didn't have it on him. "I'll have to get the number from my office," he said.

Jose leaned against his car, arms folded across his chest. "That's great!" he said. "I'll wait here, since I have nothing better to do with my time."

Derrick walked back toward the store. "Another satisfied customer," he said. "You've gotta love retail."

Chapter 60

4:00 PM

Tina was on a mission! The day was nearly over, and she was determined to make it one the new manager would never forget.

She thumbed through the file on her desk. That bastard thought he was pretty smart. Getting everyone to like him... Sucking up to Judy... Letting people do whatever they wanted... All in the name of prepping for the sale promo... She was gonna shove that idiot's balls right down his throat, and make him swallow hard!

Tina had spent the majority of her career in human resources, but that didn't mean she wanted to stay there. Her performance reviews were exemplary. She excelled in following the process, training, completing performance reviews on time, and recruiting talent. Everyone—from the vice president of HR, down to the district manager—praised her. But that wasn't enough for her.

She wanted to be *The Man*. She deserved it. And she was determined to get what she wanted. She didn't much care what happened to Mr. Derrick Payton in the process.

She closed the file, stood up, and shut and locked the door to her office. Then, she headed for the sales floor to find him.

On the way through seasonal, she saw Sylvia and Wayne putting together an outdoor furniture set. Tina recognized the set from the new advertisement flier the company was mailing out to customers.

"Sylvia..." Tina called out in a frosty tone, "isn't this table set supposed to be in the corner of the department?"

Sylvia glanced up at Tina and said, "She's ba-a-a-ack."

Wayne laughed so hard that he dropped his end of the lounge chair they were carrying.

Tina stiffened. "Excuse me?"

Sylvia smiled sweetly. "It *was* supposed to be in the corner," she said. "But I told Derrick that it would get more attention *here*, because it's a mid-priced set that won't scare customers away like the higher priced sets. Derrick agreed."

Tina felt the blood rush to her cheeks. Moving the furniture set made sense, but she didn't like the fact that Derrick was buying popularity with the associates by making them feel valuable.

"Not even the store manager can deviate from the showroom layout," she said angrily. "What kind of example is the manager setting if he disregards company policy?"

Wayne stopped laughing, and Sylvia said, "We have to get back to work. We want to be ready for the walk tomorrow."

"Yeah," added Wayne. "We want the new boss to look good in front of the brass."

Tina hesitated. This was not the time, or the place.

She walked away, shaking her head. "That guy's ass will be mine," she mumbled.

Tina walked through the bath showroom, but *The Man* was nowhere in sight. "Where is that motherfucker?" she asked.

"Can I help you?" asked a voice from behind.

Tina turned abruptly, and was startled to see Stephan Young standing there with a box of tile samples.

Tina glared at him. "Did you say something?"

Stephan set the box of samples on a nearby desk. "I believe you're looking for someone—" he said. "I think you said his name was *motherfucker?*"

"It's rude to eavesdrop," Tina snapped.

Stephan grinned. "Not as rude as referring to the store manager as a motherfucker."

Tina's back went rigid. What the hell was happening? No one had ever challenged her before. Why was everyone suddenly acting like they had authority?

"I'm looking for Derrick," she said icily.

Stephan nodded. "I gathered that. Sorry. I haven't seen him."

"Then why are you wasting my time?" Tina growled. She turned and began walking away.

She'd only gone a few steps when Stephan called out to her. "Would you like me to help you look for Derrick?"

"Mind your business," Tina said dryly.

It was the same throughout the store. Associates treated Tina as though they had nothing to fear from her. They were either slow to answer, or they ignored her altogether.

But that wasn't what was *really* bothering her. Why were they all so damned happy?

Throughout the store, associates were engaging with customers, and working together cheerfully. They actually looked like they wanted to be here. How had that bastard Derrick *done* this? What had he promised them?

Tina didn't know, but she was going to put a stop to this nonsense.

When she finally found Derrick, he was joking with a number of associates and customers at the service desk.

A couple paying a retainer for a kitchen remodel listened to Derrick talk about how happy he and his wife were with their own remodel, which had been completed the previous year. Derrick assured the couple that they could count on *The Design* to handle any issues that arose.

"A remodel is an exciting event," he said, "but it will definitely shake up your life for a while. When the real work starts, you'll suddenly find yourselves without a kitchen."

He smiled. "That's the bad news. The good news is—when your remodel is done—you'll be glad you went through the effort. Your new cabinets and fixtures will make your home stand out in the neighborhood like no other."

The husband chuckled. "For sixty-five thousand bucks, it *better*!"

The group laughed together, and the customer's wife had tears of joy in her eyes.

Tina was completely befuddled by the scene. She pushed her way through the little crowd to Derrick's side.

"I've been looking for you," she said.

"And you *found* me," replied Derrick, still smiling.

He thanked the customers again, shook hands with them both, and politely excused himself.

Taking Tina aside by the arm, he led her to a bathroom vignette where no one was present.

When he was certain they were alone, Derrick said, "What the hell do you mean, barging in like that?"

"I need to see you."

"Those customers are paying sixty-five thousand bucks for a kitchen remodel," Derrick said. "Don't you think we owe them at least a couple of minutes to enjoy their purchase?"

Tina could see that her timing was fucked up, but she was determined to stick to her plan.

"I need you to handle this," she said, handing Derrick the file.

Derrick sighed. "And this is so urgent that you had to interrupt me when I was with customers?"

"This associate needs to be terminated before the end of the day," Tina said.

Derrick opened the file and read the top document. "This is ridiculous!" he said. "We're days away from a major sales promotion, and you want to terminate an associate for tardiness?"

"I don't see how you can avoid the issue," Tina said. "SOP clearly states—"

Derrick cut her off. "Don't talk to me about SOP! Do you take me for an idiot?"

Tina recoiled. She hadn't anticipated this type of response. "I'm only doing my job," she said feebly.

Derrick stepped closer, causing Tina to back away. She dropped onto a toilet display, sitting on it unexpectedly.

Derrick looked down at her. "Don't think for one moment that I don't know what you're up to," he said. "I know exactly what you did to Rob Morrison, and I know what you're trying to do to me. I can tell you right now, Tina, it's *not* going to work..."

Tina stared up at him. She was speechless.

"I'm not going to let you stand in the way of this store's success," Derrick said. "If you want to continue being a part of this team, you'd better dance to the same tune as everyone else."

He gave her a smile that was closer to a leer. "And if you don't, you're gonna have to find somewhere else to dance."

Derrick turned, and strolled away, leaving Tina sitting on the toilet like a lost little girl.

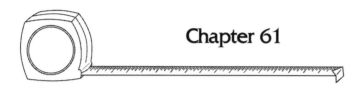

Chapter 61

Derrick was close to laughter as he returned to his office. The image of Tina sitting on the toilet was almost too much for him. From his first day, she'd gone to great lengths to thwart his every move. It was gratifying to see her humbled.

Derrick's elation began to fade when he sat at his desk and began to read Helen Silverman's file. Helen was a five-year veteran, with experience in décor and lighting. Her performance review scores were above average, and Helen's supervisors had praised her several times in writing for her genuine friendliness, and willingness to help.

Why was Tina gunning for this woman? Derrick knew that Wicked Witch #1 had a secret agenda with this case, as with everything else she did.

Still... The issue of tardiness had to be dealt with.

Why couldn't this Helen come to work on time?

Derrick wasn't about to terminate anyone on his first week. It would destroy his attempt to rebuild the store's morale. But he couldn't sit back and do nothing.

Helen Silverman knocked on Derrick's office door, and then opened it a crack and stuck her head in. "You want to see me about something?"

Derrick rose from his seat. "Yes. Please come in, and sit down."

They shook hands and Derrick closed the door part-way, leaving it a crack several inches wide. One had to be careful sitting alone in a closed office with a female, and Derrick left nothing to chance.

Derrick returned to his chair. "I don't believe I've met you yet."

Helen nodded. "I saw you in the morning meeting, but I haven't had the pleasure. How do you like your new store?"

"I couldn't be happier," Derrick said. He hoped he didn't sound sarcastic.

Helen was an attractive woman, and smartly dressed. Her makeup was impeccable, and she clearly took pains to look professional. Her appearance was a sharp contrast to the younger generation of associates, who didn't seem to care how they looked in public.

After spending a few minutes listening to her background—married with two kids, pushing forty and grateful to have a job in this economy—Derrick got down to the business at-hand.

"I hate to bring this up in my first meeting with you, Helen," he said. "But we need to discuss your time and attendance issues."

Helen stiffened. "What do you mean?"

Derrick could tell that she knew perfectly well what he meant.

"According to the timesheet," he said, "you've been late to work twelve times in the past two months. Is there something going on that's preventing you from coming to work on time?"

Helen took a deep breath. "What exactly do you mean, *late*?"

Derrick suppressed a sigh. There went his chance of getting home at a decent hour.

He went over the five minute rule, which stated that an employee could clock in five minutes before or after their shift, and not be considered in violation. He handed Helen the timesheet in her file, which clearly outlined her pattern of tardiness.

Helen read the sheet for much longer than necessary. She didn't speak.

"Once again," Derrick said, "if there's something preventing you from coming to work on time, now is a good time to talk about it."

Helen met his eyes. "I can't believe I'm being called out for ten minutes," she said. "It's not like I don't do my job, you know."

"Actually," Derrick said, "I *do* know. I've read the comments from your supervisors, and they're clearly pleased with your work performance."

"Well there you go," Helen said. "I do my job, just like I said."

Derrick nodded. "But coming to work on time is *part* of your job. And, while you're obviously very good at other parts of your job, you seem to be having some problems with the company's standards for punctuality."

"I'm not hammering you," Derrick continued. "Far *from* it. I'm pleased with your performance in other areas. I just want to know if there's something we can do to help you with *this* part of your job."

Helen's eyes filled with tears. "I don't know why you're singling me out!" she wailed.

Derrick was surprised. Why was she getting so worked up? He wasn't being critical. He hadn't even raised his voice.

"There's nothing to get upset about," Derrick said in a calming voice. "I'm just trying to help you come up with a plan for improving in the future."

"You want to *fire* me!" Helen sobbed. "You just want to document a counseling session, so you can *fire* me!"

Derrick saw a couple of associates stop in the hallway, to stare through the partially-open door.

With Helen crying all over his desk, Derrick could only imagine how this looked.

"Nobody wants to fire you," Derrick said.

Then, he realized that wasn't quite true. Tina wanted to fire this woman. Tina wanted her fired today.

And suddenly, he knew what this was about. That sneaky bitch, Tina, had done it to him again.

Chapter 62

6:00 PM

Derrick stood outside his office mulling over the day's events. There had been a few wrinkles, but overall morale was visibly climbing. The associates were clearly enjoying their taste of ownership.

But it was too early to celebrate. Derrick's efforts could still backfire. He had deviated from the approved store layout, and the company wouldn't like that part. The big dogs wanted customers to feel familiar with the arrangement of every store, whether they shopped in San Diego, Encinitas, or Los Angeles. Consistency was highly valued, even when it made no sense.

Derrick was taking a risk, but it was a calculated risk. He was counting on Judy to be more interested in the things that were really important. He was building enthusiasm, and his people were dedicating themselves to improving the customer experience, and taking the store's performance to a new level. Hopefully, when the sales figures were tallied, results would count for more than blind adherence to the store layout plan.

Besides, it was a done deal. It would either work, or it wouldn't. It was too late to change now.

Derrick went down a mental checklist. Receiving looked great. All promotional signs were up. Displays were in place, signed, and highly visible. Vendor reps were scheduled to come for product knowledge (PK) training before the store opened in the morning. Advertising flyers would go out with tomorrow's mail. The work schedules were approved. Everything was going good. Except...

He had a bad taste in his mouth about his meeting with Helen Silverman. He had finally gotten the woman to stop crying, but her flawless makeup had been wrecked by her tears. Anyone who saw her would know that she'd been balling. And then, there were the associates who'd walked past Derrick's office.

But maybe they wouldn't gossip.

Yeah, right. And maybe the Tooth Fairy would leave the keys to a Ferrari under Derrick's pillow.

Derrick sighed, and walked toward the exit. If anything was going to come of the Helen Silverman thing, it wouldn't happen until tomorrow.

Derrick arrived home at 7:30 p.m. The traffic had been heavier than usual. Then again, when had traffic ever been on his side?

The family dog, Gnarly, was first to greet him at the door.

"Get down," Derrick said as the dog jumped on him.

"If you don't like him jumping up on you, you should've trained him when he was a puppy," said Jennifer.

She came out of the kitchen wiping her hands on a cloth, and kissed him. "How was your day?"

Derrick made a face. "Do I have to answer that?"

Etienne was next to come running. "Hi Daddy, I missed you!" He jumped on Derrick as hard as the dog had.

"Hey," Derrick said, "you're getting as bad as Gnarly."

He reached down and picked up his son, holding the boy high above his head. "And how was your day, big fella?"

"Come on you two," said Jennifer. "Dinner's ready."

Dinner was Derrick's favorite—meatloaf, with mashed potatoes and salad on the side. Like most boys his age, Etienne would have preferred a hamburger and fries, but he was not in charge of the menu.

Derrick helped set the table while Etienne entertained himself with a toy airplane.

"Ready for your big day tomorrow?" Jen asked. She was referring to the manager walk.

"I'd rather not think about it," Derrick said.

He knew he'd done everything possible to prepare. But he also knew that a walk could go south quickly. He'd seen managers get the axe after an unfavorable store walk. If you fell out of favor with the DM (or someone else at SSC), they'd arrange a walk to see how your store was performing.

A walk could be as simple as the DM checking the store layout, to make sure you were following the approved sales strategy. Or it might mean an asset protection audit, to evaluate your store's alignment to the company's operational process; or a human resources audit, to verify that you interviewed, hired, terminated, and delivered performance reviews in accordance with SOP.

It was easy for a manager to fail a store walk, especially if someone at SSC wanted him gone. One bad walk was all it took.

"It can't be that bad," Jennifer said.

Derrick shrugged. "I've done all I could in four days' time. If they're not happy with it, they can send me back to Kearny Mesa."

"Oh no they can't!" Jennifer blurted. "My husband is *store manager*, and I'll be damned if you let them walk all over you."

There she went with the cursing again. What was getting into Jen these days? Derrick was grateful that she had such confidence in him. But he wondered if her confidence was misplaced.

Jennifer caught him thinking and said, "Guess I'll have to give you something to keep your mind off work."

Derrick practically dropped the plates on the table. "You've been busy in the kitchen," he said with a sly grin.

"Don't go counting your chickens," Jen challenged. "I'm not *that* easy."

For the first time all week, Derrick found himself thinking of something other than work.

The next two hours were as smooth as silk. Dinner, dessert, kitchen cleanup, walking the dog, and then a shower.

As a rule, Derrick only showered before bed if he worked out that evening, or—he grinned at the thought—if he was going to have sex.

Jennifer bathed Etienne, and put him to bed.

Derrick said good night to his son, kissing Etienne on the forehead, and telling him how proud he was of his little boy.

"He must've had a busy day in school," Derrick said. "He's exhausted."

"Don't you remember? Today they went on a field trip to the USS *Midway*. That's where he got the toy plane."

"I'm glad he had fun," Derrick said. He paused, checking out his wife's body. "Now it's time for *us* to have a little fun."

Jennifer rolled her eyes and held back laughter. "You're about as romantic as a tree stump."

Derrick came up behind Jennifer, and grabbed her butt cheeks. "Nice!"

She whipped around and pushed him away. "Not so fast. At least wait 'til we're in our own room."

Etienne yawned. "What are you gonna do in your room, Mommy?"

Jennifer flashed Derrick a disapproving look. "Daddy and Mommy are going to change the sheets," she said. "And then, they're going to go to sleep."

Derrick stifled a sigh. She didn't sound like she was joking.

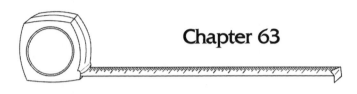

Chapter 63

10:00 PM

Derrick rolled onto his side, facing Jennifer's back. He lifted a hand, and touched her gently on the arm. No movement. Was she really asleep?

He snuggled up behind her, pressing his body firmly against hers, and slid his hand under her arm, resting the palm on her breast. Then he gave a gentle squeeze.

"Don't even think about it!" Jennifer said.

Derrick withdrew his hand and lifted his body on his elbow. "Okay, what have I done wrong now?"

"You know very *well* what you did," Jennifer said.

Derrick dropped heavily onto his back, and stared at the ceiling. "Fine," he said. "I'm sexually attracted to my wife. I didn't realize that was a crime."

Jen rolled over to face him. "It's not a crime," she said. "But you know I don't like to do anything like that in front of Etienne."

Derrick sighed. "You're right. I shouldn't have done it."

Jennifer inched a little closer. "What did you just say?"

"I said *you're right*," Derrick said.

Jen sat up in bed. "Those are very sexy words," she said. "If you want to turn a woman on, those are the exact words you should say..."

Derrick laughed.

Jennifer climbed on top of Derrick, straddling his hips in cowgirl fashion. She leaned down and kissed him gently. "Promise to be good?"

Derrick answered by sliding his hands under her shirt, and fondling her breasts.

"*Promise?*" she repeated.

Derrick squeezed her nipples. "I promise," he whispered.

Jen let out a sigh of mock exasperation. "The things a woman must do for her man."

Then, she raised her hips, and slowly slid him inside her.

Chapter 64

Friday
6:00 AM

Derrick was at the store bright and early. Judy Polakoff and the store managers were due to arrive at 7:00 a.m., and he wanted to be ready well before they showed up.

He grabbed the sales binder from his office, and headed straight for the showroom floor. Walking through each department, he looked for anything out of place. He checked signs, display settings, work stations and desks for cleanliness and organization.

He found nothing wrong. The store looked great. Everyone had done a fantastic job!

Derrick went to the computer room to print up the previous day's sales. Judy was bound to go over the numbers, and Derrick wanted to have everything on hand and memorized.

Victoria was the computer room/vault associate. She worked Monday through Friday, beginning 6:00 a.m. It was her job to print out store reports for the managers and supervisors, and to balance the tills and the vault.

"Morning," Derrick said. He went straight for the papers stacked in neat rows on a table.

"I haven't finished printing all the reports," replied Victoria. She was sitting in front of a computer typing away.

"I'll take what you've got," Derrick said.

Victoria stopped typing and swiveled in her chair to face him. "I could take that the wrong way, you know?"

Derrick gathered up the available reports. "I have to get ready for the walk. They'll be here any minute."

"You know where to find me," said Victoria.

Derrick was grateful that he didn't have to spend much time in the computer room. Victoria could easily turn out to be bad news for him.

She was a middle-aged woman, twice divorced, and happy with her reputation as a cougar. If the rumors were true, most of the men she went out with were about half her age.

Derrick figured Victoria to be in her early fifties, not much older than him. She was attractive, and her body showed that she definitely took care of herself.

Derrick didn't approve of what she wore to work, tight jeans and body-hugging blouses that displayed her curves. He probably wasn't the only guy who wondered if her bosom was real, but the biggest distraction was her habit of bending over her desk when she was reading reports. It was an obvious attempt to show off her butt.

Derrick walked out of the computer room with the reports in-hand, reminding himself for the seventh time to avoid going in there. Victoria was definitely trouble.

Everyone arrived at 7:00 sharp. Judy and the other store managers climbed out of their cars and trooped across the parking lot toward the entrance to the store.

Derrick knew most of the store managers by reputation, but he hadn't worked with any of them.

He felt slightly awkward. His promotion had been sudden and unannounced. The bastards probably thought he was wet behind the ears.

He reached for Judy's briefcase. "Nice to see you."

"I can manage," the DM replied.

The store managers, seven in all, greeted Derrick and congratulated him for his promotion. He could feel their eyes boring into him. Probably wondering if he had a cousin in a high place at store support, or—worse—that he had done Judy to get the job.

Not that *doing* the district manager wouldn't have been fun. Judy was a good-looking woman, and Derrick was certain that he wasn't the only person in this crowd who wondered what she was like in bed.

They gathered in the training room, everyone dropping their briefcases on the floor with loud *thumps*.

Derrick wondered if most of the briefcases were even necessary. Probably for show, he figured.

Coffee and bagels were prepared and waiting at the table. Judy allowed her team to help themselves before settling down to business.

During this time, each of the managers made a point of greeting Derrick individually.

"How does it feel to have your own store?" asked Tyra. She ran the Redondo Beach store.

"Good," replied Derrick lamely. He'd seen pictures of Tyra before, and he had the impression that she was stuck on herself. But that was only because he knew people who worked with her, and talked shit about her.

Dillon from Imperial Beach was next. "This is a great opportunity for you," he said with a mouth full of bagel. He tried an attempt at humor by following up with, "Don't blow it."

Derrick bobbed his head once. "Good advice," he said.

David from Oakland invited Derrick to visit his location for a look at how a store *should* be run. He behaved as though he were God's greatest gift to retail.

Beth from Phoenix said she'd heard good things about Derrick from people they both knew at the Kearny Mesa store.

"They say you're reliable, and you can be trusted," she said. She took a sip of coffee, and made a face. "With a recommendation like that, I'll give you less than six months."

Everyone laughed, and Derrick was compelled to do same.

Emerito from Huntington Beach patted Derrick on the back, and invited him for a couple of beers whenever Derrick was in his neck of the woods.

Derrick liked Emerito, and it sounded like a genuine offer. "I'm thirsty already," Derrick said.

Alex from Anaheim took a long drink of coffee, and bit into a bagel, chewing it slowly. When he swallowed, he nodded toward Derrick. "I knew Rob Morrison," he said. "I hoped that he'd do better."

"We all did," said Nick from Monrovia. "But, let's face it... Rob wasn't cut out for this." He turned to face Derrick squarely. "I'm sure this guy will do much better."

He didn't sound convinced.

Judy poured herself coffee, and avoided the bagels. She took a seat. "Knock it off, everyone. We've got work to do." Her tone indicated that she was not amused by their exchanges.

Everyone took their seats around the U-shaped tables in the room.

"We all liked Rob," Judy said. "And I'm sure we'll like Derrick even more."

She looked in his direction, winking encouragement. "Lord knows, he's up for a challenge. And we're going to show our support, by sharing ideas that will ensure his success."

Everyone nodded and glanced in Derrick's direction.

Derrick stared blankly at Judy. *Success*? This store wasn't failing to begin with. He was tempted to remind Judy that this store was *already* making gross margin, and that it had also been making gross margin under Rob Morrison's leadership. This store was already succeeding.

But there wasn't much point in fighting that battle. To the knuckleheads at SSC, perception was more important than facts.

Judy conducted the meeting in textbook fashion. Sales, markdowns, staffing, and gross margin return on investment were at the top of her agenda. She went around the table from one manager to the other. "How're you doing in sales month-to-date?"

Derrick struggled not to roll his eyes. It was a silly question. The DM received the exact same reports as the managers, and she probably got them sooner. So why go through this charade? There were more important things to do. But he knew the answer to that too. Judy wanted to be sure that her managers were on top of their game, and doing whatever it took to meet or exceed their individual sales plans.

Of course, the better the stores in Judy's district performed, the higher her bonus would be. So, Derrick couldn't really blame her.

When it was Derrick's turn to dance to the music, he was ready. His sales binder was already opened and he rolled the numbers off his tongue without skipping a beat. "Week-to-date, we're at $185,000 versus $135,000 budget. The design room is expected to close two projects tomorrow, totaling $150,000. This should put us around $75,000 over plan for the week, and $45,000 over month-to-date plan."

"Nice!" said Judy. She held her pencil close to her mouth, like she was sucking on a Popsicle. "How about markdowns?"

"We're 0.9%, versus a 1.5% plan."

Judy smiled broadly. "I like it!"

The enthusiasm of her response puzzled Derrick. Why was Judy so happy? She hadn't acted that way with the other SMs.

He wondered if her praise was more from surprise at how well his store was doing. That was silly too. After all, how much could he fuck up in four days?

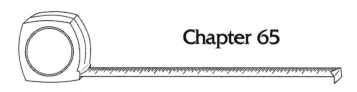

Chapter 65

7:45 AM

Showtime! Judy was ready to walk the sales floor.

Derrick knew that he could take credit for morale, store preparation, and for not fucking up the things that had already been working. With that in mind, he led his group of VIPs to the service desk, feeling good that his store's numbers exceeded plan.

Clasping his hands and standing before the DM and store managers, Derrick explained what they were doing to make the Memorial Day sale successful.

"Like the rest of you," Derrick said, "we've scheduled all hands to be on deck. Our visual team has reset the front end and showroom floors with new product, and we've made sure that all displays are signed to show customers value and price competitiveness."

Derrick led the group down the main aisle to the store front, where the glass windows had full-sized vignettes of bath and kitchens.

Nick raised a hand, which surprised Derrick. He didn't strike Derrick as the courteous type.

Derrick nodded toward him. "Yes, Nick?"

"These vignettes don't follow the floor strategy Olivia Tyler forwarded last week." Nick held up a folder with a store layout sheet. "Did Olivia send a change I don't know about?"

Everyone's head swiveled from Nick to Derrick, in the same mechanical movement common to spectators at a tennis match.

Derrick laughed. "This company talks a *lot* about ownership and entrepreneurship. We give training courses and seminars about innovation and buy-in."

He pointed to the vignette that Nick had questioned. "We're not just *talking* about ownership and entrepreneurship at this store. We're *doing* it. We're not just talking about innovation. We're *innovating*."

The entire group looked like they had collectively shit their pants. Even Judy was stunned.

Nick turned his head toward Judy, as though he was waiting for her to slap Derrick down for stepping outside of his expected role. The assembled SMs had close to 60 years of combined experience. As the new kid on the block, Derrick was expected to speak softly, and mind his manners.

Well, they could kiss his ass.

Derrick could see that Judy was about to say something, so he decided to speak first. "I look at it like this," he said. "Judy put me here to make a difference in the way this store operates. But I can't possibly hope to make a difference, if I'm doing the same old things."

Judy held up a mollifying hand. "I don't think the company's intention is to deprive our associates of ownership. The store layouts are standardized, to create consistency."

"I understand that," Derrick said. "But *The Design* values performance above consistency. I know this, because every manager standing here right now gets regular calls from SSC, wanting to know what they're planning to do *differently*, in order to drive sales and improve the company's bottom line."

Nearly every head present nodded. They all knew that Derrick was speaking the truth. It was a paradox. The company wanted to get different results (*better* results). But it was impossible to get different results, by doing the same crap they'd always done.

"If Olivia's got a problem with our layout," Derrick said, "she can see me about it." He spoke in an even and respectful tone, but he was clearly not backing down from his position.

Judy cleared her throat. "Okay. Good. Why don't we continue with the walk?"

Derrick smiled. "That's an excellent idea. Let's do that..."

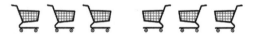

Derrick led the DM and SMs into the kitchen showroom, where associates were gathered for a product knowledge training class being conducted by the vendor rep for countertops.

When Derrick and his troupe rounded the corner, the associates were listening with every sign of rapt attention, as the rep—who identified himself as Roger from *Tops-R-Us*—explained the differences between granite and Caesarstone countertops.

Much of what Roger said was common knowledge. No two granite stones were alike, making each countertop unique. Caesarstone was man-made, composed of 93% quartz and 7% resin.

"The benefits of Caesarstone outweigh granite," said Roger.

A female associate raised her hand. "Such as?"

Roger launched into a description of the features of Caesarstone, as though he had invented the stuff himself. "It's maintenance-free, scratch-resistant, heat-resistant, and stain-resistant."

He raised a cautionary finger. "Notice that I said *resistant*. Scratch-resistant and heat-resistant does not mean scratch-*proof* and heat-*proof*."

Roger held up a trivet provided by his manufacturer. "Whether we're talking Caesarstone or granite, countertops are not cheap. That's why we offer a variety of accessories, designed to protect your customer's investment. Of course, we recommend that you offer these accessories when the customer is making the initial purchase of the countertops."

One of the associates snickered.

Derrick stepped forward and spoke up. "What's so funny?"

No one answered.

"I'm not looking to hammer anyone," Derrick said. "And I don't want to embarrass anyone. But if there's something funny about offering our customers advice on how to protect their investment, I'd like to know what it is..."

A female voice from the middle of the group spoke. "It always goes back to the money, doesn't it? It always comes back to sell-sell-*sell*..."

A couple of the associates laughed nervously.

Derrick made no attempt to single out the associate who had spoken. He really didn't want to embarrass anyone.

"That's a legitimate question," he said. "And I can understand how you might come to feel that way. But we're in business to sell things. And we provide an honorable and necessary service. More importantly, it's a service that our customers want, and *need*."

Derrick walked over to stand next to the countertop representative. "Let me ask you a hypothetical situation," he said. "Not something outlandish, that takes a wild stretch of the imagination. Something simple. Something that happens every day..."

He saw that he had the undivided attention of the associates. He also had the attention of the DM, and the other SMs.

"Let's say you need to buy a set of tires for your car. You drive down to the Firestone outlet, or Michelin, or whatever kind of tires you like. What happens if the guy working behind the counter doesn't want to sell you tires?"

No one spoke.

"That's not a rhetorical question," Derrick said. "I'd like someone to answer. What happens if the Firestone guy doesn't want to sell you a set of tires?"

"I'd get pissed off," someone said.

"I'd go to another tire store," another voice said.

"I'd sue the bastard for discrimination," said a third voice.

Everyone laughed.

Derrick smiled. "Those are all excellent answers," he said. "And they all illustrate an important point. Our customers *want* us to sell them things. That's what they come here for. And they get upset—understandably so— if we don't make the effort to sell them what they need. They get angry. Or they go somewhere else to buy. Or both."

He could see heads nodding among the associates. They were getting it.

"But that's still only part of the equation," Derrick said. "Keep thinking about that tire store for a minute... What happens if the guy behind the counter sells you a set of radials, but he doesn't sell you the balancing service? Or he doesn't offer you a front-end alignment for your car?"

"Your tires go to hell," said a woman in the front row.

"They certainly do," Derrick said. "You just plunked out several hundred bucks for a set of Bridgestones, and your new tires get chewed up within a few hundred miles. Why?"

An associate at the back of the group said, "because the idiot didn't sell you what you needed."

Derrick grinned. "Bingo! When the guy at the tire store sells you a balancing job, he's not lining his pockets. He's protecting your investment."

Derrick gestured toward Roger, the Caesarstone rep. "So, when we offer a customer the accessories needed to protect her new countertop, are we doing her a disservice?"

The associates shook their heads in unison.

"It's our job to sell customers what they need for their projects," Derrick said. "And the simple fact is, they don't always *know* what they need. If we're not telling customers about our full product lines, and our design and install services, *then* we're doing them a disservice."

This time, the associates all nodded in unison.

Judy walked to the front of the group. "Come on, people. I know you have the knowledge and experience to sell."

She gave them a confident smile. "What are the related items for a countertop?"

The associates remained silent.

When the answer came, it was from the group of managers. Alex, SM of the Anaheim store, spoke up. "A sink and faucet."

Judy nodded.

"And appliances," said Beth White, manager of the Phoenix store.

Judy nodded again.

"Flooring and cabinets," said Emerito from Huntington Beach.

"All good answers," said Judy. "And these are all things we should be offering when a customer is shopping for countertops."

"Why don't we do a roleplay?" asked Nick. The question was directed toward Judy, but Nick's eyes were locked on Derrick.

Derrick started to speak, but Judy beat him to the punch. "That's a great idea!" she said.

Derrick could see from the looks on the associates' faces, that they didn't want to partake in such an exercise. Roleplays were designed to help associates gain selling confidence when dealing with customers. But roleplaying made some people feel like they were being put on the spot, which pretty much defeated the purpose.

Given a choice, Derrick would have avoided the roleplay. But that bastard, Nick, had thrown him under the bus.

"Okay," Derrick said. "Before I choose a lucky volunteer, is there anyone who'd like to step up to the plate?"

The associates didn't exactly trip over each other in their eagerness to answer.

Right then, Joel entered the showroom carrying a personalized coffee mug that read *Me Boss, You Not* in bold letters. He was munching on an egg and bagel sandwich. "Hey everyone," he said gleefully. "What's going on?"

Judy turned to Derrick. "I think you have your volunteer."

Derrick looked at Joel. Great. Wonderful. This ought to be good.

Chapter 66

Susan sat at her desk in the design room, dreading the call she had to make. Ms. Justine Hildeman had paid fifty-eight thousand dollars for her kitchen remodel, and she was *not* happy. *The Design* had missed her estimated completion date by five weeks, causing Ms. Hildeman extreme pain and suffering. Or so she claimed.

Susan had been confident that she could resolve the issue with an offer of $500 and a promise of ten percent off the client's next remodel, but Ms. Hildeman hadn't gone for the offer at all.

"I want ten percent off my entire project, or I'm going to sue!" Ms. Hildeman had declared.

Susan was sure that the woman meant it. Ms. Hildeman was a retired lawyer, accustomed to having her way. At 62 years old, with a hefty retirement savings and several friends still practicing law, she was capable of raising hell with one phone call. Susan knew that the woman would do it, if only to prove that she could.

The irony was, Ms. Hildeman had started out as a nice client, serving coffee and biscuits at her home to go over design plans. Hell, she'd even invited Susan over for a 'before' soiree, to show friends how her kitchen looked before the remodel. There had also been an 'after' soiree, when the job had been completed. Susan had *not* been invited to that one.

Ms. Hildeman's Jekyll-and-Hyde behavior hadn't emerged until the project had gotten underway. And then, suddenly, she'd gone crazy with questions, most of which couldn't be answered.

"When are you going to finish?" she'd asked over and over again. They hadn't even begun building her cabinets, and she wanted to know when the job would be done. An estimated completion date was unacceptable.

"I demand to know the *precise* date my kitchen will be completed," snapped Ms. Hildeman. As if there was any possibility that Susan could give a rational answer.

Susan sighed, shaking her head. Why did she get all the good ones? Not only had her client refused the $500, but the woman had threatened to contact the CEO via her lawyer if she wasn't given the ten percent.

The thought made Susan queasy. She knew there was no way in hell store support was going to authorize a check for $5,800. But she also knew that Ms. Hildeman wasn't going to take no for an answer.

She looked across the room to Debbie's office. The PSM sat behind her desk, casually reviewing paperwork.

Susan wanted to hand over Ms. Hildeman's complaint to Debbie, but she knew from experience that Debbie would throw it right back at her.

She'd heard Debbie say it at least a dozen times. "Everyone takes care of their own clients, from beginning to end. Don't expect me to fix your problems. If you can't handle your clients, you don't need to be on my team."

Susan wanted to strangle the bitch. It was the project manager's *job* to resolve client issues, but Debbie refused to do it. What was the point in having a project manager, if you couldn't go to her for help?

That question led to another question. Why *shouldn't* Debbie call Ms. Hildeman? She wouldn't *want* to call the client, but hell, Susan didn't *want* to call the client *either*.

What gave Debbie the right to avoid a responsibility that clearly went with the position of project manager?

Susan jumped from her chair and marched straight to Debbie's office. The chit chat from designers in the room stopped, as they watched the scene unfold.

Susan didn't bother knocking. She opened the door and said, "Justine Hildeman wants $5,800 reimbursement, for pain and suffering."

Debbie lifted her head, clearly shocked by Susan's outburst. She opened her mouth to speak, but Susan cut her off.

"Ms. Hildeman says if she *doesn't* get it, she's going to sue."

She paused before adding, "What do you want to do?"

Debbie glanced out her office window, and saw her team looking on. This was the last thing she needed. She leaned forward, resting her elbows on her desk. "You know that I expect my designers to handle problems with their clients."

"How am I supposed to do that?" Susan asked furiously. "I can't stop the client from suing, and I can't authorize that type of compensation. So, how do you suggest I *handle the problem*?"

Debbie looked annoyed, but she held out her hand. "Let me see the file."

Susan handed her the folder.

Debbie examined the papers in silence.

Susan wondered what the hell Debbie was looking for. She already know the cost of the job, the start and stop dates, the delays, and what the client was demanding. What magical piece of information was she hoping to glean from the folder?

Finally, Debbie dropped the folder on her desk. "Okay," she said. "Tell me your version."

"You already know my version," Susan said. "I've kept you in the loop for every step of this project."

Debbie was unaccustomed to having a member of her team speak so abruptly to her. She kept a tight rein on her designers, and this unexpected display of courage had caught her off guard.

She shook her head. "The amount the client wants is beyond my limit too."

"I *know* that," Susan said. "Hell, everyone knows that!"

She swept her arm toward the window, where the rest of the design team was still watching. "You're the PSM. I need you to take this to the store manager."

Debbie flushed at the mention of Derrick. "I'll take care of it from here," she said in a flat tone.

Susan nodded. "And you'll call Ms. Hildeman?"

"I'll take care of it," Debbie repeated.

Susan turned to leave. "It's about time," she mumbled.

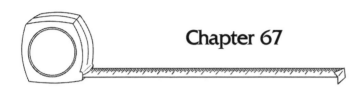

Chapter 67

Joel was a sixty-something semi-retired plumber, assigned to kitchen showroom part-time. He had been hired six months earlier, to fill in scheduling gaps for peak customer service hours.

"I'll work any shift you want," he had declared during his interview. "Just give me Thursdays off."

Steve Evans had conducted the interview. "What's so special about having Thursdays off?"

"That's my golf day," Joel had announced proudly.

And so, they gave him every Thursday off.

Joel stood about five feet nine inches, slightly bent from age, and he wore clothes a size too big for his meager frame. He wasn't exactly a super hero, but he was about the best you could get for a whopping $10.70 an hour.

Derrick could see that this was going to be a train wreck, but there wasn't really any way to get out of it. He gave the associate a hopeful smile. "What do you say, Joel? Are you up for a little roleplay?"

Joel nodded enthusiastically. "Roleplay is what I live for."

The other associates applauded.

Derrick played the part of the customer. Joel would be the sales associate.

To kick off the roleplay, Derrick walked around the corner, and then returned, as though he was a customer just entering the showroom.

Joel met him with a smile. "Hello, how may I help you?"

Perfect! He'd started with an open-ended question.

"Just lookin'," replied Derrick, casually.

"Fine," Joel said. "If you have any questions, I'll be right over here." He reached for his coffee mug and a donut.

The associates snickered quietly. Judy and the store managers watched in silence.

Derrick pretended to browse for several seconds, hoping that Joel would put down the damned coffee cup and re-engage. No such luck. Joel was chomping happily on his donut, spilling crumbs down the front of his black shirt.

Derrick was going to have to restart the conversation himself. He pointed to the 4 x 4 granite samples on the table.

Joel finished off the donut, and set down his coffee mug. "Those are granite samples," he said.

Derrick struggled to keep the impatience out of his voice. "I can see that. What other type of countertops do you sell?"

Joel froze. His eyes darted to the samples, and then back to Derrick. Then to the samples again, and finally back to Derrick.

Finally Joel blurted, "Do you have drawings for your kitchen?"

At last he speaks!

"I didn't bring them with me," Derrick said. "How can I get a quote?"

There! He'd just given Joel a perfect opening to offer the store's measuring and design services.

Joel shook his head. "Without a drawing of your kitchen, we won't be able to help you," he said. "You need to go home, get precise measurements, and then come back. Then, we might be able to do something for you."

Everyone but Derrick chuckled.

Derrick wanted to shoot himself. No… He wanted to shoot Joel.

Nick saw this as his opening. He stepped to the front of the group. "Come on, Alex. Let's show them how this is done."

Without asking permission, the two managers from Monrovia and Anaheim took their positions and started their own roleplay. Alex was the customer; Nick was the associate.

Nick walked up to Alex. "Good morning sir. How may I help you today?"

"I'm looking for countertops," replied Alex nonchalantly.

"We've got plenty of countertops to offer," said Nick. "Is this your first time visiting *The Design*?"

Alex nodded. "Yes."

"Thanks for coming. I'm Nick. Before I show you countertops, I'd like to ask if you require anything else for your home. *The Design* is a one-stop shop, with multiple departments offering a wide range of products. Are you doing a kitchen remodel, or replacing only your countertop?"

Alex got into his customer role, scratching his chin instead of quickly answering. "I guess you could say I'm doing a full blown remodel. I never looked at it that way before. I thought I was merely replacing my fixtures."

"You came to the right place," Nick said. "So, you'll need appliances, flooring, kitchen sink and faucet, and lighting, right?"

Alex bobbed his head twice.

"We'll fix you up," said Nick. "Are you familiar with our finance options?"

Alex shook his head.

Nick repeated the ad slogan verbatim. "We offer *12 Months, No Interest, if Paid in Full within 12 Months from date of purchase*. We also offer free delivery. We have installation services available too, but that will require a pre-measure to determine the scope of labor before I can quote you a price."

"I'm good with that," interjected Alex.

"Good," Nick said. "Not only are we price-competitive, but we offer rebates for applicable appliances, as well as service protection plans. I'll go over that after we've discussed countertops."

He moved over to the tower displays of 12x12 samples. "These samples are granite, and those samples are Ceasarstone."

"What's the difference?" asked Alex.

Nick smiled. "Granite is natural stone, and no two stones are alike, so whichever sample you select will make your countertop unique. Granite comes pre-sealed, but it requires maintenance. If you leave spilled orange or tomato juice on it for longer than 24 hours, you risk permanent stains. After 10 years it's advisable to have the granite re-sealed, to protect it from sun discoloration and stains."

Alex pointed to the second tower of samples. "What about the Ceasarstone?"

Nick darted a quick gloating expression in Derrick's direction, before he turned his attention back to the make-believe customer. "The features and benefits of Ceasarstone outweigh granite in many ways. First, it's man-made of 93% quartz and 7% resin. It's stain-resistant, and scratch-resistant, but not scratch-*proof*. It's heat-resistant up to 525 degrees Fahrenheit, but I always suggest using trivets when needed. No sense tempting fate."

"What about colors?" Alex asked.

Nick pointed to the tower of samples. "Ceasarstone is available in all natural stone colors, and in many designer colors to match the décor of your kitchen."

Alex nodded. "I don't have measurements with me."

"No problem," Nick said. "We can sign you up for a measure fee of $50, that will be applied to your total purchase. Our price for countertops includes fabrication and installation."

"Sounds great," Alex said with a smile. "Sign me up now."

Everyone applauded. Derrick clapped as well, to show good sportsmanship. He would have preferred to whack Joel over the head with his stupid coffee mug, and kick that smug asshole, Nick, right in the teeth.

Chapter 68

Tina looked up from her desk at Debbie, and smiled coldly. "We have the bastard now!"

The PSM started to say something, but Tina raised a hand. "You're going to have to trust me on this."

The two shared a common desire to be in charge. They conspired together, connived together, and worked together to crush anyone who tried to cross them. But the concept of trust was not high on their list of priorities.

Debbie fidgeted nervously. "You need to tell me what's going on."

Tina considered this for a moment. Then, she shrugged, and slid the folder on her desk toward the PSM.

"This is the report I'll be submitting to Judy."

Debbie looked at the folder. It had the numbers 666 labeled in white tape on its front. She knew the HR liked to do this to people on her shit list. Debbie failed to see the humor in it.

"Go ahead," urged Tina. "It won't bite you."

Debbie sat down and opened the folder. The first page was a statement from Helen Silverman, and Debbie's curiosity went from medium to high in a flash. With each passing sentence, her eyes grew larger.

When she was finished reading, she looked up at Tina.

The HR bobbed her head, flashing that familiar cold smile of hers.

"Is this legit?" Debbie asked cautiously.

"It's Helen's word against the store manager's," Tina replied. "We take accusations of this nature seriously."

Debbie had a vision of the store manager being marched, hands tied behind his back, to meet the hangman. A tall figure dressed in a black robe and hooded mask greeted him, and placed a noose around Derrick's neck.

Debbie shook her head to clear the vision from her mind. "How did you manage to get this?"

The HR displayed the same cold smile again. "It's my job to ensure the wellbeing of everyone in the store," she replied. "What kind of HR would I be, if I did anything less?"

Debbie was about to close the folder, when Tina pointed toward the file. "Turn to the next page. You didn't read the best part..."

Debbie flipped the top sheet and began reading the one below it. Holy shit! History was repeating itself!

She felt a strange intermingling of excitement and nausea. On the one hand, this could put the final nail in Derrick Payton's coffin. On the other hand—if something went wrong...

The HR seemed to read her thoughts. "Don't worry; it's legitimate."

Debbie shook her head doubtfully. "I'm not sure if this is the right way to go about this."

Tina's brow furrowed. "Not getting cold feet, are you?"

Debbie had no love for the new SM either, but she wasn't sure that he could be gotten rid of so easily. Tina had lined up some very powerful accusations, but they were of the he-said/she-said variety. Extremely difficult to prove.

"I didn't go look for either one of these," Tina said. "They came to me. I have a responsibility as HR to take this to the top."

She held out her hand, and Debbie gave her back the folder.

Tina's smile had no trace of humor or mercy in it. "The die is cast," she said. And then, she laughed uncontrollably.

Debbie left the HR office a few seconds later, feeling distinctly sick to her stomach.

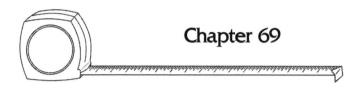

Chapter 69

10:00 AM

Derrick opened the doors and greeted customers as they filed past him. As usual, some acknowledged him with a smile or nod of the head, and some were too busy talking on their cell phones or to each other to pay him any mind.

Retail... You've gotta love it.

After the roleplay between Nick and Alex, Judy had emphasized the importance of following the basic selling steps. "Never forget the AURA principle," she'd said. "*Acknowledge* the customer with a smile. Listen to *understand* their needs, so you properly qualify them. Make *recommendations* based on what they tell you. And..."

She'd paused there, waiting for the associates to respond.

In unison, the associates had chanted, "ASK FOR THE SALE."

At least they'd gotten *that* right.

Derrick was still fuming over the roleplay with Joel. He was never going to live that down. That old fart had made Derrick look like an idiot.

A quarter before ten, Judy had sent the store managers back to their stores, which couldn't have made Derrick happier. No one enjoyed being put on the spot, especially in front of peers who would never let him live down a sour experience.

Derrick forced himself to take a deep breath and release it slowly. Let it go... It was water under the bridge. The only way to undo it, was to perform better in the future.

He checked his watch. Where the hell was Judy?

Tina had asked to speak with her in private, and the two women had disappeared shortly after the manager's meeting ended.

Derrick had checked his to-do list a hundred times. He knew that every item had been crossed off, but he decided to check the list again anyway.

He pulled out his notepad and flipped it open. The column of completed tasks was reassuring...

~~Promotional signage~~
~~Displays set~~
~~Scheduled to customer demand~~
~~Mailers and postcards sent to Post Office~~
~~Flyers on hand for customers~~
~~Balloons up in designated areas of the store~~
~~Bottled water available for customers~~
~~Cooking demonstrations underway~~
~~Toilet paper stocked in bathrooms~~

Derrick read the last item on the list with a rueful smile. Running out of toilet paper during business hours would be a disaster. He remembered when it had happened at the Kearny Mesa store. That had *not* been pretty.

When he looked up, he saw JC running toward him.

"What's up?" Derrick asked.

JC had to catch his breath.

Whatever was on his mind, it must be important.

JC panted heavily. "You really don't know?"

"If I knew," Derrick said, "I wouldn't be asking."

JC looked over his shoulder, and pulled Derrick aside. "Tina's bringing a harassment case against you."

The words didn't sink in at first. "Tina's bringing a harassment case against me?" repeated Derrick.

"Yeah," JC said. "On behalf of Helen Silverman, and another person whose name I didn't get."

Helen Silverman? The woman who couldn't come to work on time? Sure, she'd gotten a bit upset during their meeting, but *harassment*?

"That's not all," JC said. "Word is getting around about how you yelled at Helen for her T&A issues."

"How I *yelled* at Helen?"

"That's what Helen says," explained JC. "She says you bullied her, and threatened to fire her."

Derrick stared at him. "You're kidding, right?"

JC shook his head. "Nope. The store is rallying behind Helen, to keep her from being fired."

Derrick took a few seconds to replay the meeting with Helen in his mind. Had he said anything at all that could be interpreted as a threat to fire her? No. He was certain he hadn't.

This harassment thing was pure bullshit. Then again, around this store, *everything* seemed to be bullshit.

Although the promo didn't officially start until Monday, *The Design* was honoring the sales promotion on Friday, Saturday, and Sunday. "We're going to milk it for all it's worth," the CEO has announced via conference call.

With the DM sequestered somewhere in the store with Tina, Derrick took advantage of the free time to walk the aisles, ensuring that his associates were helping customers.

He was a bit rattled by what JC had told him, but he couldn't allow that to divert his attention from the job at hand. He'd come too far to be knocked down for the count by rumors.

Still, this new issue with Helen Silverman could be bad for morale. If everyone thought the new guy was firing a solid performer like Helen for time and attendance issues, it wouldn't take much for others to wonder who would be next to get the axe.

An overhead page caught Derrick's attention. *"Derrick, please dial 402. Derrick, dial 402."*

That was *his* office, and the voice was Tina's. Judy and Tina must have chosen his office for their little conference.

Derrick did an about-face and made a beeline for his own office. He had no idea what kind of shit Tina was up to now, but he was about to find out.

Chapter 70

Susan didn't believe Debbie one bit. She knew her too well. She wasn't not going to *handle it*. Long experience with the PSM taught her well, and she planned to hold her accountable for her short-comings. Payback is a bitch she said silently and this is your comeuppance.

Susan saw Derrick in the outdoor seasonal showroom and called out to him. "Derrick, I need to talk to you," she said urgently.

"Can it wait? I have a meeting with Judy."

"I won't be long," she pleaded.

He glanced at his watch, irritated. I suppose this comes with the territory, he reasoned. "What's up?"

She stopped in front of him, inches away from his face. "It's about that client of mine we talked about."

Derrick listened, very much alert as Susan explained her plight. When she finished he folded his arms across his chest, rubbing his chin with his right hand. He focused on Susan, causing her to feel slightly uncomfortable and curious at the same time.

After a few moments of silence Derrick said finally, "What do you think?"

The question caught Susan off guard. She was unaccustomed to a manager asking her opinion. Debbie usually gave orders, asking advice from no one, and the answer was not easy. Her previous suggestion was turned down flat, and Susan flushed embarrassingly upon reflection. He probably thinks I'm an idiot, she thought.

Sensing her hesitation, Derrick urged her to speak her mind. "I really have to go," he said flatly. "So let's hear it."

Susan took a deep breath, and then said what she thought would be the best strategy to resolve her client's issue.

Judy sat behind Derrick's desk in his office, her eyes glancing back and forth at the clock on the wall. What's taking him, she wondered. She looked over at Tina, who sat perched in the corner, tapping the folder on her lap in a way that made Judy uneasy.

Also in the room was Bob Jacobs, the district asset protection manager, or DAPM as he commonly was referred. His surprise visit caught even the DM off her guard, but not as much as his reason for showing up at the store.

All three sat silently in Derrick's office waiting patiently. When they heard hurried footsteps approach they straightened in their seats. "Sorry for the delay," Derrick said, breathing heavily from rushing to his office. The look on his face was as surprised as Judy's was at the sight of the DAPM. "Bob what a surprise."

The DAPM rose to shake hands with Derrick. "Congratulations on your promotion," he said enthusiastically. "It's always good to see the good ones take over a store."

Derrick's eyes darted in Tina's direction, then back to the DAPM. "Thanks! It's been a long time coming, but worth the wait."

Bob nodded agreeably. "You're going to rock this place," he declared, grinning.

Once the pleasantries subsided Judy motioned for Derrick to have a seat. She stayed put in the SM's chair, a sign that she was in charge of this get-together.

"What's this about?" asked Derrick. He noticed the condescending smile on Tina's face, and wondered what she knew that he didn't know.

"Bob's got something you need to see," replied Judy. Her tone was tinged with disgust.

The DAPM opened his laptop and turned it on. "The DVD you're about to see was provided by a client of this store. The client is remodeling his master bath, and we're handling everything: design, product, and installation."

So far that sounded good, thought Derrick. "But there's a problem you need to discuss with me?" he interjected.

"That's putting it mildly," blurted Tina. A slight smile pursed the corners of her mouth in a way that irritated Derrick.

Bob worked the mouse to the laptop, switching on the video display. "This is inside the customer's home." He stopped to look Derrick squarely eye to eye. "What you're about to see is highly confidential."

"I understand," said Derrick, anxiously.

The quality of the DVD was good as was the light from which the room was filmed. Derrick saw a team of three construction workers removing plumbing fixtures and flooring from the master bath. Audio was available on the disk and a voice could be heard in the back instructing the team to take a break. The three men left the room and a full minute passed before another figure entered the room. He wasn't one of the three first seen on the DVD.

Derrick glanced at Bob, who watched his reaction intently. Judy and Tina also watched him keenly. What the hell was their problem?

He turned his attention back to the laptop screen. He was not at all ready for what he saw.

The figure on the screen was that of a man in his late teens or early twenties, obviously a laborer on the construction crew from the clothes he wore. His shirt had the company name embroidered on its back, but too small to read. The young man walked over to the dresser in the room, and opened the drawers, rummaging through the contents. In the top left drawer, he found what appeared to be woman's underwear. The man looked over his shoulder as if to see that he was alone. When he was confident no one looked on he put the panties to his nose, inhaling deeply.

Derrick looked at Judy. His face turned red from embarrassment and he squirmed in his chair as he continued watching the scene on the laptop. He felt like vomiting when next the young man on screen slid one hand in the crotch of his jeans and began masturbating, all the while holding the panties to his face. Derrick couldn't decide what made him feel worse; the act itself or the look of pure ecstasy on the worker's face.

Bob clicked the mouse and the screen went blank. He observed Derrick with interest. As DAPM, he had seen it all, or at least he thought he had. But *this*? Nothing could have prepared him for this.

Derrick cleared his throat. "What's the installer's name?"

"The guy on the DVD works for Davidson Builders, Inc.," answered Bob. "His name is Luke, and he's on suspension, or so I'm told."

Derrick made a face. You think? He could guess what the customer had said over the matter, but had to ask. "...And the client?"

Bob lifted his eyebrows. "A settlement was reached between the client and our legal department. I'm bringing this to your attention now, because the payout is going to hit your P&L report this month."

Derrick felt his stomach tighten. "How much of a settlement are we talking about?"

The DAPM glanced at Judy, who nodded approval to answer. "Twenty grand."

Derrick turned to face Judy, who sat silently. She knew what he was thinking. This would devastate the P&L.

"Why now?" asked Derrick. "You can report this loss a couple of months out, so that it hits in July. That's one of our stronger months in sales, and the damage won't be as bad."

Judy anticipated his logic and agreed, but "We feel since we're going all out to drive sales this Memorial Day you'll have a stronger than usual month. The extra sales you make will soften the punch."

Derrick wasn't buying it. "You made me manager with the responsibility of turning the store's numbers around. You said if we don't have a better-than-normal holiday sale, store support would be in favor of shutting us down. The flip side of that double-headed penny is that if we have a good month of sales, store support would leave us alone." He sounded as though he was accusing the DM of back-stabbing.

"What can I say?" replied Judy defensively. "Shit rolls downhill..."

Derrick looked at Bob, who lowered his eyes.

Tina, on the other hand, made no attempt at suppressing the smirk on her face.

Derrick entertained a brief fantasy about tearing out her fucking throat. Instead, he turned to Judy. "Thanks."

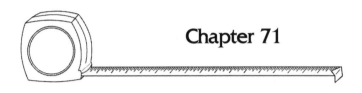

Chapter 71

Derrick walked the sales floor feeling like all he had worked for and hoped for was flushed down the toilet. He found himself wishing he had never been made store manager. Life was simpler as ASM, he reflected. As assistant manager he could lean on someone when the going got rough. But now he was *the man*.

I sure as hell don't feel like it, he said silently while walking the sales floor. Not only was a false rumor spreading like wildfire throughout the store, but their numbers on the P & L would be in the red, making it a hard sell to explain why SSC should keep the store open. I'm beginning to know the feeling of captaining a sinking ship.

When he entered the lighting showroom he saw Claudia and Carlos helping customers. They were busy explaining features and benefits of products, but could not help notice the store manager stopping to observe them in action. The color drained from their faces when their eyes met, and they quickly turned away.

What the hell is that about, wondered Derrick. He moved on to the flooring department and got the same treatment from Leonard, and again from Martha in décor. It's happening, he knew. They've chosen sides and see me as a tyrant. He felt his sudden popularity had come rather easy when morale took a positive turn, but didn't think he'd be on everyone's watch-out-for-him list so soon. His father used to tell him, "You've gotta take the bad with the good," and right now it took on a whole new meaning.

His phone rang and he answered it. "This is Derrick," he said in a monotone.

"Derrick," it was Susan from the design room, "Ms. Hildeman is here, and I'm taking her to the consultation room. Can you meet us there?"

"Yeah, I'll be right there." No one else seems to want anything to do with me, so why not explain to a customer why she's not going to get a $5,800 refund?

Tina asked to speak with Judy once Bob Jacobs left. "What the hell is Derrick talking about closing the store?"

Judy looked like she pissed her pants. She flashed a shut-the-hell-up look and closed the door to the office. "I don't want this getting out," she said in a stern voice.

Tina was unphased. "You don't want *what* getting out?" she demanded. Although she could guess, she wanted to hear it straight from the horse's mouth.

Judy sighed. What the hell, tell her. "Sit down," she said, motioning to a chair. Judy sat across from her and explained the situation. When she finished she sat silently, gauging the HR's reaction. This was the first time she knew Tina to have a loss for words and it made her equally uncomfortable. Tina looked as though she were about to go into cardiac arrest, and the DM said, "Don't worry; I still have a place for you in the company."

Tina stared back, shocked. "You sound as if you've already decided."

That wasn't the response I'd hoped for, thought Judy. "Derrick has til Monday to prove this store can hold its own and I have to be prepared for the worst. I want you and key people here not to worry." She paused for effect. "The odds are against this store remaining open."

"Why?"

Judy grew angry. "Stop acting like you don't know." Her words stung like a slap across the face, which was precisely the effect the DM wanted to deliver. "We know Encinitas has promise, but we're cannibalizing the Kearny Mesa store."

Tina looked as though she were about to burst into tears and Judy went on explaining how impractical it was to have so many project-driven stores in close proximity. "Even the L.A. stores are under scrutiny despite good numbers. We erred in opening stores as though this were a fast-food chain, or a big-box retailer. Those business formats can open on the corner of every street and would be successful because they have what people need versus what *The Design* offers." Judy decided to back off a bit. She didn't want to disclose too much. After all, she was on the team that laid out the vision of *The Design* and thought it to be a fantastic idea blanketing the market with their design and install stores.

Tina looked reflective. Everything she worked for appeared to be one step away from being flushed down the toilet. Her main goal of course was to have her own store, but she didn't want to switch to an ASM role to prove she was up for the challenge. She wanted to jump straight from HR to store manager, and she planned on doing that by building a strong network within the company hierarchy.

But that doesn't look like it's going to happen now, she told herself, grimly.

Judy read her face and tried to smooth things over once more. "There's always the chance you'll pull it off. As I said, if you have a strong Memorial Day sale we may consider keeping open the Encinitas store versus the Kearny Mesa store. It all depends who has the best numbers."

You might as well throw in the towel, Tina wanted to say. It was no secret that the Kearny Mesa store was number one in the company. If SSC made their decision solely on sales they would win hands down.

Judy gathered her things and opened the door to leave. She glanced one last time over her shoulder at the HR and said, "Good luck!"

Tina made a face like she bit into sour grapes. You might as well have told me to *get fucked*.

Derrick sat at the table across from Susan and Ms. Hildeman in the design consultation room located in the bath showroom. "Can I get you anything, Ms. Hildeman?" He offered. "Water, coffee, or tea perhaps?"

The old woman shook her head no. She was dressed in a smart looking outfit that looked straight out of a *Coldwater Creek* catalog; designer jeans, buttoned-down red blouse with collar, and a light yellow scarf. She topped off the outfit with equestrian-style boots that added flair.

Derrick studied her hard, gauging her personality. He wanted to get the meeting off on the right foot, but didn't see the opening he hoped for. I'll get her to open up soon enough, he told himself reassuringly.

"Susan tells me you aren't satisfied with the way we handled your project," Derrick said evenly. "You want ten percent back for pain and discomfort."

Ms. Hildeman looked him in the eye for the second time since he entered the room, but quickly lowered them to the table. Derrick thought she looked to be embarrassed, but wasn't sure. That certainly wouldn't fit the profile Susan told me of her. He pressed on.

"Except for the issue of your reimbursement request, the job is done, right?" He waited for the old woman to reply, but she gave none. Instead she continued staring at the table. Derrick's eyes darted at Susan, and she shrugged in a not too obvious way with the expression, I-don't-know-what's-wrong-with-her. Derrick motioned at the folder on the table. "Are those photos of your remodel? May I see them?"

Susan slid them across the table and Derrick opened the folder, thumbing through the pictures. He whistled his approval at the first few photographs of Ms. Hildeman's home. "This looks very nice, Ma'am! Very nice indeed."

He looked up at Ms. Hildeman and asked, "Was this design your idea, or Susan's?"

Susan appeared offended and opened her mouth to speak, but Ms. Hildeman beat her to it. "I told her what I wanted," she said, glancing at Susan, "and she designed it based on my vision." She paused as if to think before continuing. "I suppose in a way that makes it as much my design as hers."

Susan didn't like Ms. Hildeman's interpretation one bit, but was not about to argue. Instead she chose to do what most designers found difficult; say nothing!

"Well if you're ever in the market for a job, please let me know. I'm sure I'll have a place for someone with your talents." Derrick noticed the corners of Ms. Hildeman's mouth purse into a slight smile. Gotcha! He put down the pictures and folded his hands, resting them on the table. "How did the installers treat you, Ms. Hildeman? Anything you want to tell me?"

The old woman settled into her chair, appearing more relaxed than when Derrick first saw her. "I found them to be competent and efficient. Not like the usual people in the trade who show up to work with coffee stains on their shirts and oversized pants that fall to their knees when they bend at the waist."

Derrick thought her cheeks flushed with embarrassment, and laughed along with her. So she does have a sense of humor. That could prove useful. "The cabinets you selected in the pictures look great! Have you had a house-warming party to celebrate?"

Ms. Hildeman glanced at Susan, then back to Derrick. "Yes," she answered with a single nod.

"My wife and I remodeled our kitchen last August and couldn't be happier. We ordered the product as early as February, but our project manager couldn't begin work until July because he was so busy with clients wanting their homes done during good weather."

"How long were you without a kitchen?" asked Ms. Hildeman. She sounded more like she was fishing than curious, and Derrick caught that same as Susan.

Don't bite the bait. "About a month," replied Derrick, casually. "It took about six weeks for my product to arrive and I stored it at the company warehouse until June."

"How did you manage?"

Now she sounded more curious, thought Derrick. This old bag is good. "Jennifer made a temporary kitchen in our garage out of the laundry sink." He laughed reflectively. "She was so proud of her ingenuity I joked about leaving the house like that instead so we could use the money to buy an *Airstream* trailer in place of the remodel."

Ms. Hildeman laughed along with Derrick. "What did she say to that?"

"She told me I could make my own dinner if I felt that way about it."

Susan observed Derrick carefully. His attempt to get the client to lower her guard was working. She hadn't seen Ms. Hildeman this relaxed in all the time since working with her. This guy's good, she said silently. She wished Debbie had been more involved on client-designer issues instead of looking the other way.

Derrick pressed on with small talk about how he and Jennifer had all the holiday, birthday, and family get-togethers at their house, which was why they decided to go all out on their remodel. "The last time we did our kitchen was 15 years ago, so we decided to do this one more time before we retire."

Ms. Hildeman cocked an eyebrow. "You're going to retire soon?"

Derrick let out a laugh. "I wish! No, but we do want to save up for that *Airstream* trailer so we can visit the National Parks. That's why we didn't cut corners on the remodel. I don't want to go through this again."

"What problems did you come across?"

Hook! Derrick managed to suppress a smile. "Nothing out of ordinary. Our range hood came in the wrong size and had to be reordered. One of the flooring installers had a death in the family that pushed the job back by a week." He rolled his eyes as if to over-dramatize. Don't get carried away. Take it slow. "The flooring measurer was off by three square feet, leaving us to sweat it out while waiting to see if the vendor had enough tiles in the same die-lot to make up the difference."

Derrick knew he had Ms. Hildeman's full attention when she leaned forward and asked, "Did they?"

Line! He wiped imaginary sweat from his forehead. "Thank God! I don't think we could've stood another day of delays, let alone another week."

Ms. Hildeman sat back relieved. Derrick thought she looked as though a load of bricks had been lifted off her shoulders. "I know the feeling," she said, thinking back.

And sinker! Derrick leaned forward, elbows on table with hands folded. "I'm not going to pretend to know what you've been through, Ms. Hildeman." He paused for effect. "...But I know what my wife and I experienced during our remodel." That was good. Keep good eye contact.

She's listening. "You made a HUGE investment with us," continued Derrick. "You trusted us with your dream kitchen." He paused again. "I know we made mistakes." He glanced in Susan's direction. "Susan and I discussed your project at length."

Ms. Hildeman stared back in silence. She looked over at her designer sitting beside her. She started to say something, but Derrick motioned with a hand for her to wait. "Please let me apologize again. There's no excuse for what you've been through."

Ms. Hildeman lowered her eyes embarrassingly. "Susan did what she could, I know. It's just that the delays kept coming and coming."

"You don't have to say anything to convince me," said an empathetic Derrick. "Like I said, there's no excuse."

Ms. Hildeman squirmed uneasily in her seat. "I suppose things happen," she blurted. The look on her face indicated she was as surprised to say that as much as they were to hear it.

Susan's heart skipped a beat and Derrick flashed her a control-yourself look. "Believe me, we want to help," he said sincerely, "but what you're asking is beyond our ability to grant. Managers today don't have the kind of wand-wielding authority of yesterday."

He made a face expressing disappointment. "Today we're expected to follow SOP. Thinking outside the box is little more than a decadent phenomenon. When something like this happens we're expected to contact our customer care department."

Ms. Hildeman straightened. "I know you're authorized to resolve customer issues," she said assuredly.

Yes, but "When a client asks for $5,800 I think it's safe to say that's a bit higher than a store manager's authority to approve. I'd like to help, but if you persist in your request for such an amount I'm going to have to pass this on to my district manager."

Ms. Hildeman looked at Susan and then back to Derrick. "When can I meet him?"

Derrick smiled. "Our DM is a her."

"Well, when can I meet *her*?"

"I can call her as soon as our meeting is concluded." Derrick shrugged. "Of course, she's a busy person. I don't know when she'll be down to look this over."

"Can't you press her to?"

Derrick threw up his hands in surrender. "On the other hand, if you agree to let me resolve your issue within the confines of my authority I won't need to involve the DM. You and I can handle this together." Derrick held her gaze evenly while waiting for her response.

Susan thought she saw Ms. Hildeman's eyes twinkle. This was confirmed when Ms. Hildeman smiled and said to Derrick, "Why don't you call me Justine?"

Chapter 72

"You were amazing!" Susan said. She waited for Derrick by the front entrance as he returned from walking Ms. Hildeman, or was it Justine?, to her car. "How did you ever get her to agree to that?"

Derrick looked embarrassed. He shrugged and said, "Just lucky, I guess." He gestured for Susan to precede him back into the store.

"A gentleman to the last," she said appreciatively. She went over how things played out in the closing events with her client.

"I can't authorize a reimbursement for five thousand and change," Derrick told Justine flatly. "And to be frank no one would."

Susan observed Justine keenly, as if waiting for her to explode. Then she shocked her by asking, "How much can you authorize?"

Derrick arched an eyebrow. "As I said," Derrick began, "I know what Jennifer and I went through during our remodel, so I can only imagine how you feel." A look of relief came over Justine's face. "I know this is not about money," continued Derrick. "Your time, inconvenience, your very home have been affected by delays common in the industry." Uh-oh! Don't blow it by being blunt! "And we have no excuse." Now you're back on track. "I'd like to ask you, Justine" He saw a slight smile crack the corners of her mouth as he called her by name. The strategy is working. "What do you think would be fair to resolve this?"

He saw Susan in his peripheral vision turn to stone and prayed she kept quiet. Don't blow it by opening that hole in your face.

Justine Hildeman leaned back and thought about that. Her eyes remained affixed on Derrick while Susan's eyes darted from Justine to Derrick, and back to Justine and again to Derrick. She wanted to say, "Somebody say something," and it was all she could do to remain silent.

Finally Justine said, "I suppose Susan's offer will do."

Derrick saw firecrackers exploding in the sky, and Susan sat tall, beaming. He started to say something, but Justine raised a halting hand. "I only ask one alteration," she said suddenly.

Susan's heart fluttered and Derrick glanced in her direction as if to say, now what?

After an awkward pause Justine said, "I want you to personally oversee the handling of my bath remodel when I begin in June."

Derrick wasn't as surprised as Susan. He was after all flirting as a means of breaking down her barrier. "I'd be delighted," he replied, nodding thanks.

Justine's cheeks blushed and she glanced embarrassingly at Susan before looking away. Susan shook her head, still amazed over the results.

"That was one for the books," she said, reflectively. "I've never seen a store manager flirt so obvious with a customer to get them to agree to a resolution on our own terms."

Derrick halted in the middle of the aisle. "Hold on," he said, staring back stoically. "I wasn't flirting." It sounded as feeble to him as to Susan. Then he added, "I was merely appealing to her sense of practical compromise by sharing my own experiences."

Susan let out a laugh. "And I'm sure she'd like to share experiences with you."

A couple of associates walking past turned their heads curiously. Derrick stared back and they quickly moved along. That's all I need, he told himself. Rumors! He decided best to stay mellow.

"Don't go making a big deal about this," he said calmly. "We lucked out, that's all. A person with her money and influence could've bent us over at will." Susan was shocked by his bluntness. "I banked on her being lonely and would enjoy a harmless flirtation. I'm sure you've done similar to help a client decide on a design, right?"

Susan made a face. No way was she going there, but the SM had a point and she knew it. "In any case, thanks for being there." She's genuinely thankful, thought Derrick. Susan started to leave, then turned and said, "If only our project manager was as helpful and professional as our new store manager."

Derrick smiled. "I like what I hear, but a comparison with one of the Wicked Witches of the West isn't exactly hard to best."

Susan looked like she was going to drop, and Derrick laughed as he walked away.

The balls he has! Susan couldn't believe the store manager's display of audacity. In a way she felt privileged he was comfortable enough to speak plainly, and even more grateful she and the SM were on the same page when it came to Debbie.

She guessed the other Wicked Witch of the West, as he called them, was Tina. No one likes that bitch either, she reflected. *How I would love to throw that in their faces.* Of course she knew she'd have to keep that to herself. Spreading a rumor about the store manager's comment would do him more harm than good. On her way to the design room she heard voices in the HR's office and stopped short of the door.

"They're going to shut down this store!" Tina declared.

Debbie stared back shocked. She didn't want to believe it. "What are you talking about?" she asked, sounding scared.

Tina swept the office with her arm. "All this is gone! I got it straight from the horse's mouth." She went over her conversation with the DM while Debbie listened in stone silence. When she finished she sat down with a sinking heart.

"How did it come to this?" asked Debbie, mechanically.

Tina shook her head dismissively. "Those people are wired differently." She referred to the CEO and company, Debbie knew. "Doesn't matter our store is making money. We no longer fit their *vision*."

Another awkward moment passed before Debbie asked, "What's going to happen to us?"

Tina shook her head and looked disgusted. "Our fate is in the hands of our great store manager Derrick Payton!" She could speak plainly because she knew the PSM had as much contempt for him as she did.

Debbie wondered what else there was to say. *Ball game over!* "So what now? Do we all go home and call it quits?"

Tina mulled over the question. She leaned forward, consulting notes she wrote after her meeting with the DM. "No, we don't quit... *Yet.*" Then she said, "We have 'til Monday to demonstrate how well our store can do."

Debbie laughed with intentional sarcasm. "You don't believe we can have enough of a great sales day to make store support change their mind do you? They had to have made their decision to close us at least a year ago!"

"Ssshhh! Lower your voice." Tina got up and went to close the door. She peaked in the hallway and was relieved no one was there, and then closed the door behind her. She went back to the notes on her desk. "Let's see," she said, slowly turning page after page.

Debbie observed her silently. This was too much for her to handle and she couldn't think straight. She found herself grateful to have a woman as determined as Tina to lead them through this. She never considered Tina a friend in the sense of hanging out with her after work, but she liked her determination and take-charge style. She was sure she was a person going places, which was why she made a point of working close with her.

When Tina finished reading her notes she looked up and smiled coldly. "Judy is relying on Derrick. If we succeed *he* gets the credit." She keenly observed Debbie's reaction. "And if we fail..."

"If we *fail*, Derrick gets the blame."

Tina nodded, still smiling menacingly. Debbie made a face as though having second thoughts and Tina asked, "What's wrong?"

"Are you sure this is the right path? Making sure Derrick fails is no different than shooting ourselves in the foot."

Tina, true to form, already had an answer. "Not if we document our steps to make this Memorial Day Sale a success. When the sale is over store support is going to want a record of what we did. All we have to do is make sure the report they read states how Derrick failed to inspire and motivate our associates enough to ensure success. Putting up signs, displays, and handing out flyers that's a given. But maintaining high morale is the responsibility of the manager."

Debbie still seemed to be rethinking the strategy. Then she said, "But everyone seems to like Derrick."

Tina shook her head twice. "Not after they learn what's at stake."

Debbie suddenly realized what Tina had in mind and nodded compliance. Tina ended their little chit-chat by declaring, "By Monday Derrick won't have a single supporter in this store. And if our store does manage to have a better-than-good sales day, I'll make sure the credit goes to the person deserving it most."

Debbie had no illusion who Tina would think that person was. She followed Tina out of her office and down the hall to the sales floor. Both of them seemed relieved to have a strategy they could control.

When they were gone the door to the supply room next to the HR's office opened and Susan stepped outside. She looked up and down the hall, making sure the coast was clear before heading to the design room. Like the HR and the PSM, she was now on a mission.

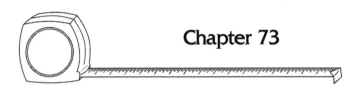

Chapter 73

12:00 PM

"This is Derrick," he said over the phone. He had hoped to step out for lunch, but the call had interrupted his plans.

"Derrick, this is Karen," said the voice on the other end. "I have a customer who'd like to speak with you."

Derrick rubbed the back of his neck. Was he going to have to handle every customer complaint for the rest of his life?

"Have you called the manager-on-duty?"

"I can't get them to answer."

That figured.

"Okay," Derrick said. "I'll be right there."

At one point in his career, Derrick had hoped that his habit of answering the phone would rub off on others. After all, how hard was it to answer a telephone?

Halfway to the returns office, he was stopped by Brian in plumbing. "You're just the man I was looking for," said Brian.

That didn't sound good. "Can it wait? I have to meet with a customer in returns."

Brian frowned. "Well... Okay, but don't forget me. What I have to say is important."

Derrick gave him a tired smile. "I won't forget."

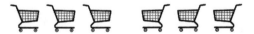

Derrick entered the returns office, and saw Karen behind the counter. On the opposite side of the counter stood a tall, middle-aged man, with curly brown hair, slightly greying on the sides. He had a bushy beard and mustache that covered his beefy face. He wore a *Charger* jersey, running shorts, and tennis shoes. His belly stuck out, giving him a pear-shaped appearance, and his thick-lens glasses magnified his eyes to twice their actual size.

Derrick forced himself to smile. "How can I help you, sir?"

"You the manager?" the man asked.

Derrick nodded. "Yes, at least until I can trick someone else into taking the job."

The pear-shaped customer was not amused. He thrust a piece of paper toward Derrick. "I was charged $75 dollars for a waterline hookup, and I want you to reimburse me."

Derrick took the paper and read it. It was a receipt from a sub-contractor *The Design* used to handle installations. He saw the normal charge for a toilet install, and an additional charge of $75 for an angle stop valve and supply line.

After reading the receipt Derrick looked up. "I'm sorry, sir, but this charge isn't covered in our basic installation."

Pear-Man stared back at him. "Why not?"

Derrick pointed to the receipt. "As it states on the back of the receipt, 'Final price is subject to change, based upon additional work required to complete the install.' If the installer put in a new angle valve, it was because he determined that the existing valve was inadequate."

"Inadequate?" Pear-Man was indignant. "There was nothing wrong with that valve."

Derrick examined the receipt again. "What did the installer tell you?"

Pear-man scowled. "He told me he needed to replace my valve and supply line. He said they were old, and they could leak."

"Well, there's your answer," Derrick said. "I'm afraid this is a legitimate charge."

The customer's scowl deepened. "When I bought that toilet, your salesman told me it would cost $135 to install. He didn't say anything about additional charges."

Derrick held up the receipt. "Your signature is right here, sir. You acknowledged, in writing, that you'd been notified that the installation cost could change if additional work was required."

Pear-Man's face turned red. "I don't ever read that junk. It's up to you and your people to quote me an accurate price."

Derrick read the customer's name from the receipt. "Mr. Macy, my associates can only give you an average estimate, based on what a typical installation costs. Without actually going to your house and examining the condition of your plumbing, it's impossible for us to know whether or not your installation will require additional work. Our salesperson gave you the best possible estimate, based on the information we had at the time."

"Oh that's just fine!" Macy said. "Your installer holds me hostage by refusing to install my toilet unless I fork over $75. And you're okay with that?"

Derrick decided to shift the direction of the conversation. "How long had it been since your previous toilet was installed?"

"I don't know," replied Mr. Macy.

"Just give me a ballpark estimate," Derrick said. "One year? Five years? Ten?"

Macy shrugged. "Maybe seven or eight years. I didn't exactly engrave the date on my heart."

Derrick nodded. "If it was five years, your angle valve was due for replacement. If it was more than five years, the valve was *overdue*. In other words, the installer did exactly what he should have done. And he probably saved you a lot of trouble, because your old valve could have failed at any time, causing flooding and water damage to your bathroom, and whichever rooms happen to adjoin it."

Karen nodded. She had seen variations of this scenario many times, and she knew that Derrick was right. But Mr. Macy was having none of it.

"I just want my money back," Macy snapped. "Can you handle that? Or do I need to speak with *your* boss?"

Derrick was unmoved by the threat. This was one case where the store was completely in the right, and the customer was completely full of shit.

Mr. Macy apparently decided that one threat was not enough. "I knew I shouldn't have shopped here after reading those online complaints about this store," he said. "Maybe I should write something to warn other customers about how you guys ripped me off. In fact, maybe I should write *seventy-five* online reviews. One online slam for every dollar you owe me."

Derrick was tired of this bozo. It would be worth $75 just to get this guy out of the store.

He nodded to Karen. "Give him a refund."

As Derrick was walking away, Macy called after him. "You're doing the right thing."

It was all Derrick could do not to stop, and tell Mr. Macy to shove his seventy-five bucks up his ass. Instead, he pretended that he hadn't heard, and kept walking.

Chapter 74

When Brian came out of the men's restroom, he practically ran smack into Tina.

"Sorry about that," he said quickly.

Like many store associates, Brian didn't like Tina, with her standoffish and uppity manner. He held up his hands, signifying a retreat as he moved out of her way.

Tina was about to enter the ladies' restroom, when she turned and called out to Brian. "How are you doing?"

Brian stopped. He'd never heard the HR express the slightest interest in his wellbeing. He looked around, to see if she might be talking to someone else. No... He was the only person here.

Brian shrugged "Well... I'm waiting to see Derrick."

Tina's curiosity was piqued to say the least. "Anything I can do to help?"

Brian shoved his hands in his pockets. What the hell? Why not tell her?

"I want Derrick to do something about the condition of the men's restroom. There's piss all over the floor at the urinals. Why can't people do a simple thing like taking a piss, without making a mess?"

He stopped himself. "Sorry... I hope I didn't offend you."

Tina's face warped into something that might have been a smile. "No offense taken," she said.

She looked around, as if to make sure no one else could hear what she was about to say. "I only hope we have a place to go after Monday."

Brian stared at her. "What do you mean?"

Tina's eyebrows went up. "Haven't you heard? The company might shut us down after Monday."

She waited for Brian to say something, but he continued staring at her with an uncomprehending expression on his face.

"It boils down to this," Tina said. "If we have a good sales day on Monday, we *may* survive. If we beat the Kearny Mesa store, we stand a chance. If not..."

She let her words trail off.

Before Brian could respond, Tina pushed open the door to the ladies' restroom, and disappeared from sight.

When the door closed behind her, the fake smile on her face transformed itself into an evil grin.

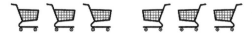

Derrick found Tim Lyon in the bath showroom and pulled him aside. "Why the hell aren't you answering your phone?"

Derrick kept his voice low, but he allowed his anger to show through. "You're MOD," he said. "And I just got reamed in returns, because you're not doing your job."

Tim lowered his eyes, but didn't speak.

"I can't do this all on my own," said Derrick, toning it down a notch. "You and the others have got to step up to the plate."

"Does it really matter?" asked Tim.

The question caught Derrick off guard. "What do you mean?"

Tim shrugged. "The rumor on the floor is that we're going to be shut down."

Derrick stared at him. "Where did you hear that?"

Tim shook his head. "I'm not saying. I don't rat out my coworkers."

"That's fine," Derrick said. "But let me give you two things to think about..."

He held one finger up in the air. "One, if the rumors are *false*, then you're screwing yourself and you're screwing the store by not doing your job to the best of your ability. Remember all that stuff you said about this store not having any synergy? About people not *caring*? When the manager-on-duty doesn't carry out his responsibilities, do you think that makes the situation *better*? Or *worse*?"

Tim started to respond, but Derrick raised a second finger into the air.

"Two, if the rumors happen to be *true*, then we have only *one* chance to save this store. We have to blow SSC away, with the best performance this store has ever had. If we all pull together and work our asses off, we just *might* be able to do that. But what are our chances of winning if you give up *now*?"

Tim looked at the floor. "Zero," he said.

"That's exactly right," Derrick said. "Whether the rumors are true or not, this store *needs* to do well on this promotion. We need to serve our customers. We need to support and guide our personnel. And we need to answer our goddamned *phones!*"

He said the last line forcefully, but with a smile on his face.

Tim looked up, caught the smile, and returned it with one of his own.

"Can you do that for me?" Derrick asked.

Tim gave him a thumbs-up. "Can-do, Boss."

Before Derrick could wrap up this little impromptu counseling session, a customer approached them. "You the manager?"

Derrick nodded. "How may I help you, sir?"

The customer looked over his left shoulder, then his right. What he wanted to say was obviously private.

"I don't know if you're aware of this," he said, "but the men's bathroom is out of toilet paper. Also, there's piss all over the floor by the urinals."

The customer glanced at Tim, and then back to Derrick. "I think a few guys had trouble aiming, if you get my meaning."

Derrick gave him a weary smile. Yes, I actually do.

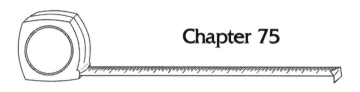

Chapter 75

2:00 PM

Derrick mulled over the day's events while having a late lunch at *Panera* in Carlsbad. He needed to clear his head, and there was no way he could do that at the store. Sitting at a table near the front of the café, he asked himself the same question multiple times.

What the hell happened?

He had a pretty good idea of how the rumor had gotten started... The number one Wicked Witch of the West.

Tina had been in the office when the DAPM had showed him the DVD of the installer's apprentice jacking-off in a client's home. That's when Derrick had let it slip. He had said something about how taking a hit on the P&L would kill the store's chance of being profitable for the month, giving store support the justification they needed to shut the store down.

And that bitch Tina had been sitting in the corner the whole time. *Damn!*

Derrick cursed himself for not having self-control. When was he going to learn to keep his mouth shut?

Well, there was nothing he could do about it now.

He might as well concentrate on something he *could* do. He reached for his cell phone, and logged onto the internet. He'd been thinking about Mr. Macy's nasty little hint about negative online reviews. It was time to check out that situation.

It didn't take him long to find mentions of his store on Yelp.com. Most of the reviews were not good.

> '*Worst customer service ever! Took forever to find someone to help and when I did, they couldn't because they worked in a different department. Don't go here. Waste of time.*'

> '*The Design doesn't deliver on promises! I ordered an air bath, and they promised to deliver it in three weeks. HA! THEY LIED!*

It took six weeks, and they didn't even offer a discount for the delay. I had to drive to the store and ask the manager, who didn't want to give me a penny. He didn't even apologize for my time and inconvenience! What poor service is that? Don't shop here. They'll take your money fast enough, and hang you out to dry.'

The next review was clearly from Mr. Macy.

'*Manager sucks! I paid $135 for a toilet install and they charged $75 more. Manager argued with me before giving me the $75 back, only after I twisted his arm! I'll never shop here again and am telling all my friends and family to keep away from The Design!'*

Derrick shook his head. The little bastard! So much for his pseudo-gratitude. ("*You're doing the right thing...*")

The store had a customer rating of two out of five stars, so Derrick logged on as Cynthia G, and wrote a review of his own.

'*I hired The Design to remodel my kitchen, and love it! My husband and I have dreamed of having a new kitchen for years, and their designers are courteous, professional. I saved 10% off labor and product. Most importantly, they gave me peace of mind. They kept me up to date on the progress of my remodel, and they finished my project on the target date. Shop here for your remodeling needs! You'll love them!'*

When Derrick submitted his bogus review, the rating jumped to three stars. He decided to ask JC, Steve, Tim, and the department supervisors to write a phony reviews of their own, to improve the overall rating of the store.

Why not? Companies write negative reviews on the internet all the time, to kill the competition. What was Derrick supposed to do? Lay there and take it?

He logged off and returned the phone to his pocket.

What else could go wrong? Derrick stopped himself before he went down that road. Once he started focusing on the negative, he'd never get his head back on a positive track. It was better to focus on what he'd done right.

Let's see. What *had* he done right?

He had shifted people to other departments to improve efficiency. True, Kim had pitched a fit over it, but she could kiss his ass. The move had been good for morale, and the work had gotten done on time.

He had allowed people to exercise their own ideas in setting up their displays, and in managing the arrangements of their aisles. And why not? The associates know their clientele better than Derrick did, and a *hell* of a lot better than SSC did. The associates knew how to arrange the store to be attractive to the community they served.

He had showed the associates that he was willing to listen to their complaints, and—most importantly—their ideas. That had improved morale considerably, especially considering how the Wicked Witches of the West treated everyone.

Debbie's designers came to Derrick with problems, because she was too busy to help. In fact, Debbie was so busy, that her door was usually closed to everyone. Except Tina.

The mental image of Wicked Witch #1 made Derrick's coffee taste sour. Still, she and Debbie deserved each other.

Let's see... What else was on the positive list?

The store was ready for business, and sales were looking good.

Were they good *enough*? He didn't know. All he could do was to try his best in the time he had been given.

Derrick chewed the last bite of his egg sandwich and stood up. Time to get back to the store.

He had work to do.

Chapter 76

3:00 PM

The rumor was spreading like wildfire.

"Did you hear they're closing the store?"
"What are you talking about?"
"The company is shutting us down!"
"Bullshit!"
"I heard it straight from the horse's mouth."
"Who?"

And that's where the finger-pointing stopped. People were willing to spread gossip, especially if the news was unwelcome. But no names! Revealing a source was taboo.

Mary Hines was returning to the kitchen showroom when Jesus in appliances told her the news.

He gave her a desultory wave. "Hi, Mary. How're you holding up?"

Mary looked at him curiously. She and Jesus had never gotten along, so she was a bit surprised by his greeting. They usually ignored each other.

"I'm fine," Mary said. "Why do you ask?"

Jesus scratched behind one ear. "Have you started looking for a new job yet?"

Mary felt her muscles tighten. "What are you talking about, Jesus?"

"This is our last week," Jesus said. "Sales are dragging, and our new leader isn't up to the job, so the company is shutting us down."

Mary caught the hint of contempt in the man's tone at the reference to Derrick.

She shook her head. "Nonsense."

"I wish it was nonsense," Jesus said. "No such luck. We're on the way down."

"Who told you that?"

Jesus shrugged. "Oh... *someone.*"

Mary brushed past him, shaking her head. "That's just more shop floor bullshit," she said dismissively.

She entered kitchens, and saw Sophia weeping behind the desk. Barbara from bath stood next to the woman, consoling her.

Mary hurried over. "What's wrong?"

Sophia kept her head down, wiping tears from her eyes and sobbing.

Barbara turned to Mary. "They're closing us down," she said.

Mary stared at Barbara. "Who told you that?"

Carlos ran across the sales floor to find Claudia, who was busy replacing burned-out bulbs on displays in lighting showroom.

"Claudia, did you hear?" He was huffing and puffing, trying to catch his breath.

"Hear what?" She didn't bother to look at him while screwing in a bulb.

When Carlos dropped the bombshell, Claudia froze. Her thoughts went instantly to her father. He'd worked as a computer salesman for twenty years, until his company had pink-slipped him without warning.

The computer industry was on the decline, and jobs were getting scarcer by the week. Claudia's father was pushing sixty, and he knew the odds of a person his age being hired at another company.

That had been two years ago, and her father still hadn't been able to find steady work. The family savings was almost gone now, and Claudia's parents were inches from bankruptcy.

Was the same thing about to happen to Claudia?

She shook her head, and looked at Carlos. "Have you seen Derrick?"

Carlos shook his head. "Not sure I *want* to," he said. "Word is that he's the reason they're shutting us down. The company doesn't believe he's up to the job."

Claudia made a face. "That makes no sense!" she said. "If the manager isn't up to speed, you don't shut down the store. You hire a new manager."

"I'm just telling you what I heard," Carlos said. "I hope they stick it to the bastard, for letting us down!"

Claudia shook her head again. It really didn't make sense. From the day Derrick had walked through the doors, things had seemed to turn for the better.

"He's the only manager we've ever had who actually listens to the associates," Claudia said.

Carlos made a palms-up gesture. "If I have to choose between being listened to, and having a job, I'll take the job every time."

"I still don't believe this," Claudia said.

"Why do you think so highly of this asshole?" Carlos asked with distaste. "How much good do you think he could do in only five days?"

And that was precisely the problem for Claudia. What could *anyone* do in five days that would make that much of a difference?

She didn't know, but she was determined to find out.

Naomi sat at her desk in the design office. "I knew the moment I saw him that he would be the ruin of us all." She lifted a compact mirror to her face, to check her makeup. "I'm thinking of suing the company for the way he treated me," she said.

Seated at the next desk, Marie gave Naomi a curious look. "I didn't know Derrick had spoken to you about your tardiness."

Naomi lowered her mirror and stared back icily. She didn't like for people to speak so casually about her time and attendance issues.

"Well, he didn't actually *speak* with me," she admitted. "But Debbie told me he wanted to fire me. She had to go to Tina, to get Derrick to back down."

Marie was no fan of the new manager, but she knew Debbie pretty well.

"First of all," Marie said, "Debbie doesn't go to bat for *anyone* but Debbie. And second of all, Debbie's been on your ass for months about your tardiness. If *anybody* wants to fire you, it's probably Debbie."

Her words stung Naomi like a slap across the face. Naomi snapped her compact mirror shut, stood up, and stormed out of the office.

Bill, another designer, sat at his desk across the room and watched the scene with cool interest. After Naomi disappeared, he turned to look at Marie.

She shrugged. "Have *you* ever seen Debbie go to bat for anyone else?"

A smile formed at the corners of Bill's mouth. "I'm sure we're going to hear a *lot* of things that don't make sense over the course of the next few days," he said.

Then he returned his attention to the papers on his desk.

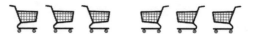

Gina drove the forklift carefully. The last thing she needed was an accident. One wrong move and she'd be terminated, or so Tina had told her.

Gina knew she'd been given a free pass with the counseling statement.

She'd thought for sure she was going to be axed. So why hadn't they fired her?

The question nagged Gina, and she desperately wanted to know. And the counseling session in Tina's office hadn't made any sense either.

"I believe in giving people second chances," Tina had told her.

Gina *knew* that was bullshit. Tina loved to snatch the rug out from under people.

"Derrick wanted to handle this by the book," Tina had said. "He was all set to terminate you. It took me a long time to talk him down. I reminded him several times that you are a deserving associate, and we can count on you not to make the same mistake." She paused. "Right?"

Of course Gina had agreed. "You bet!"

But then, Tina had threw a curveball. "Kim appreciates you too, and she fought hard to keep from *firing* you."

She had emphasized the word *firing*.

Now, driving her forklift in receiving, Gina still couldn't make sense of any of it. She knew that Kim hated her, and that Tina didn't think highly of her either. So why were they pretending to have saved her job?

When she drove under the rollup door, she brought the forklift to a screeching halt as Darrell came running in her direction.

"Have you lost your mind!" she shouted, angrily.

"Gina, did you hear the news?" Darrell was oblivious to the fact that he had nearly been run over.

"What news?"

Darrell spilled the rumor, practically stuttering as he struggled to get the words out quickly.

"Who told you that?" Gina asked.

"I heard it from Leonard," Darrell said.

"You heard it from *Leonard*? Well, who told him?"

Darrell shrugged.

Gina waved him off. "You know better than to believe bullshit rumors," she said. "Besides, how many times have we heard that before?"

Her question caused Darrell to frown. The rumor of the company closing stores was nothing new.

"I can't say if it's true or not," admitted Darrell, "but the whole store's talking about it."

"It's just gossip," replied Gina.

After parking the forklift, she headed for the break room. Halfway down the hall, she heard Emily in the phone room speaking with someone on the telephone.

"It's true," Emily said with conviction. She wore a headset with microphone. "The company is shutting down our store. I don't know all the details, but it has something to do with our new manager not being up to the job. I don't know, but that's what I heard. I'd rather not say who told me."

Gina shook her head and continued making her way toward the break room. As she approached Tina's office, Tina walked out into the hall, followed closely by Debbie. The two women were smiling and talking happily until they caught sight of Gina. They both went instantly silent, and the smiles on their faces vanished.

Gina nodded hello, and continued into the break room.

What was their problem? And why were they in such a good mood when everyone else was panicking about the possible closure of the store?

Gina opened the door to the fridge and pulled out her lunch.

She was taking the first bite of her sandwich, when two associates entered the break room, both talking at the same time.

"When do you think they'll close the store?" said one.

"I got it from a reliable source," said the other. "It's definitely happening."

"And all because our manager isn't up to the job," said the first associate.

"What's going to happen to us?" asked the second.

"Do you think they'll give us a severance paycheck?"

"I hope they get rid of Derrick first! If he's the reason our store is being closed why should he be last to go?"

Gina took a long drink of water, and shook her head. Could people really be that stupid?

It was happening. From the moment Derrick returned to the store, he was met by a throng of associates, all with the same question. "Why are they closing the store?"

Someone in the back shouted, "Is it because you're not up to the challenge?"

Derrick raised his hands in a calming manner. "People, please, let's keep it down."

He motioned toward the customers coming and going. "This is not the time or place."

"Well, when are you going to tell us what the hell is going on?" The question came from another courageous, unseen associate in back of the group.

"We'll talk about this at the morning meeting," Derrick said in a calm voice. "Right now, let's concentrate on finishing the day strong, and not listening to rumors."

No one moved.

"We have customers in the store," Derrick said. "Let's all get out there and do our jobs. I promise you, we'll talk in the morning.

The associates murmured, but they began to breakup and disperse.

Derrick saw a female customer staring curiously at him.

He put on his best smile. "I *love* the home improvement business!"

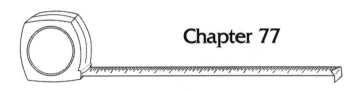

Chapter 77

8:00 PM

Derrick waited for Jennifer in the living room while she put Etienne to bed. He fixed them both a glass of rum and coke before sitting heavily on the sofa, glad to be off his feet after an absolutely brutal day.

Gnarly jumped up on Derrick's lap, nearly causing him to spill his drink.

Derrick scratched behind the dog's ears. "Take it easy, boy. It's okay. Everything's going to be fine."

Jen came downstairs and reached for her drink. "Long day?" she asked, taking a sip after giving him a quick kiss.

"Longer than most," said Derrick.

He spent the next several minutes telling his wife everything that had happened.

When he finished speaking, Jen took another drink, this time a big one.

Derrick knew that look.

"I don't want you to worry about a thing," he said. And then, he found himself repeating the exact same words he had just spoken to the dog. "It's okay. Everything's going to be fine."

Derrick could see the thoughts swirling around in Jen's head. They had spent close to forty thousand on a remodel the previous year, and their savings would only hold them over for a few months if Derrick got the axe.

"I'm not getting fired," Derrick said quietly.

"I don't know," Jen said. "From what you're telling me, it doesn't look good."

She put down her drink on the coffee table. "This promotion was a bad move," she said. "Maybe you can request a transfer back to Kearny Mesa."

The fear was visible on her face.

"I wouldn't have accepted this position if I didn't think I could succeed," Derrick said. It was a lie, but Jen needed to hear it.

She stared into his eyes. "How can you be sure, considering what's at stake?"

"Companies don't shut down stores on a whim," Derrick said.

He touched her cheek gently. "They know I've wanted to be a store manager for years," he said. "Setting me up for failure isn't in the company's best interest."

"You don't know that," Jennifer said.

Derrick leaned forward and kissed her, long and deeply. When he pulled back, he looked into her eyes. "You're going to have to trust me."

Jennifer managed to chuckle. "Like I haven't heard *that* one before..."

Chapter 78

Saturday 7:00AM

Derrick was at the store at 7:00 a.m. sharp.

Albert, a.k.a. Lanky Man, was sitting in the returns office when he walked through the door. "Morning, Derrick! How are you today?"

He was actually smiling, leaving Derrick to wonder if he was in the right building, or in the *Twilight Zone*.

"I'm fine, Albert. Thank you for asking."

"There's coffee ready in the trade office if you like."

Now Derrick knew he was in the wrong building.

He held up the mug he had brought with him. "Thanks, but I have some."

"I guess you're going to fill us all in at the morning meeting, right?"

Word traveled fast.

"That's right," Derrick said. "And I don't want anyone to worry about a thing. This store's got a lot of promise, and we're going to be here for a long time."

"I couldn't agree more," said Albert. He was smiling as he spoke.

Derrick smiled, and continued toward his office

From over his shoulder, he heard Albert's voice again. "Of course, if the company *does* shut us down, I imagine a number of us will be transferred to other stores?"

Derrick turned and looked the associate in the eye. "The company is *not* shutting us down," he said.

Albert nodded. "I never doubted it."

At 9:30, Derrick watched his associates assemble in the rug department for the morning meeting. The looks on their faces were a mixture of

weariness and apprehension. Except for an occasional flash of anger, their eyes showed no spark at all.

Derrick stood before them, smartly dressed and trying his best to appear supremely confident and in control. If he pulled this off, he should win the Best Actor Award for Biggest Bullshitter.

"Good morning everyone," he said eagerly.

The associates stood silently, waiting for him to get on with it.

Derrick wasn't going to let them off that easily.

"I didn't hear you," he said. "Let's try it again... GOOD MORNING!"

A few voices in the back responded feebly.

"We're still not there yet," Derrick said. One more time... GOOD MORNING EVERYONE!"

"Good morning," the associates replied in a solemn chorus.

Not exactly enthusiastic, but good enough. At least he had their attention.

"I've heard the same rumors you're hearing," Derrick said. "And I know how worried some of you are right now."

He saw a few genuine looks of interest. They were clearly surprised that he wasn't beating around the bush.

Derrick held up a closed fist. "Let's see if we can cover them all," he said.

He raised one finger. "One—The store is closing, and you'll all be looking for work next week."

He raised a second finger. "Two—This disaster was caused by the gross incompetence of a certain store manager, whose name I will not mention, but he happens to be wearing my clothes."

This brought a low ripple of laughter from the group, and the first sign of easing tension. After all, if the boss was joking about it, how bad could things be?

Derrick raised a third finger. "Three—The earth has been invaded by extraterrestrial life forms, who look exactly like Lady Gaga."

This time, the laughter was louder.

"Okay," Derrick said. "Maybe *I'm* the only one who's heard that third rumor."

He lowered his hand. "I guess we can scratch the Lady Gaga thing off our list, so let's talk about the other two rumors that have been running through this store like wildfire."

"But before we get to the rumors themselves," he said. "Let me say that I don't know how they got started. But I can tell you that whoever lit the fuse was either a liar, an idiot, or *both*."

He was looking directly at Tina when he spoke that last sentence.

She glared at him with contempt.

Derrick's hand went back up into the air, with one finger extended. "Rumor number one—this store is closing. I can tell you without hesitation that this is one hundred percent false. I hope you'll excuse my French, if I say that it is utter bullshit."

"I didn't know that word was French," someone from the back shouted.

This triggered another laugh.

Derrick sought out Victoria's face in the crowd. "Let's ask Victoria," he said. "Is this store making gross margin?"

Victoria nodded. "Yes," she said in a breathy voice.

"A little louder, please," Derrick said. "I'm not sure the folks in the back can hear you. Is this store making gross margin?"

This time, Victoria's voice carried clearly. "Yes!"

"Is this store operating in the black?" Derrick asked.

Victoria nodded vigorously. "Yes!"

"How are we doing on our plan for the week?" Derrick asked.

"We're about $75,000 over our plan," Victoria said.

Derrick nodded. "That's right. And how are we doing with our month-to-date plan?"

"We're about $45,000 over," Victoria said.

Derrick could see the glances being traded around the group. This was *working*...

"Excellent!" he said. "And I'm only going to tax your memory one more time. How are we doing for markdowns?"

Victoria brushed her hair back from her eyes. "We're under 1%, nearly a half percent below plan."

Derrick grinned toward Victoria and bowed. "Thank you very much!"

Victoria smiled in return. "You're welcome!"

Derrick turned his attention back to the group. "Let's see... Our long-term sales are in the black; our weekly sales are above goal; our monthly sales are above goal; and we've kept our markdowns below our target threshold. Now, does that sound like a store in danger of closing?"

Many of the associates shook their heads.

"You're right about that," Derrick said. "The people at corporate would have to be *crazy* to close a store that's doing this well."

One of the associates shouted, "the people at corporate *are* crazy!"

Again, the entire group laughed.

Derrick laughed too. "I can't argue with that," he said. "The people at corporate are crazy. But they also like money. They like money a *lot*! And this store happens to be *making* money!"

Almost the entire group was nodding now.

Derrick moved in for the kill. "Are those profit-hungry people at SSC going to shut down a store that's bringing in *money*?"

The response was a shouted, "NO!"

Derrick nodded. "So much for rumor number one."

He lifted the second finger. "Let's move on to rumor number two..."

The crowd was buzzing with positive energy now.

"Your new store manager, that would be *me*, is so grossly incompetent that he's putting your very jobs in danger."

Derrick dropped the fingers, and made a broad sweeping gesture that encompassed the entire store.

"Look around you," he said. "This store looks amazing! The displays are incredible. The signage is perfect. And a little birdie told me that receiving looks better than it has in *years*."

"It does!" a female voice shouted. (Definitely not Kim's.)

"How are we doing with teamwork?" Derrick asked. "Better? Or worse?"

"BETTER!"

"I'm glad to hear it," Derrick said. "And how about engaging with customers? Are we doing better? Or worse?"

"BETTER!"

"Okay," Derrick said. "Does that sound like the work of an incompetent store manager?"

"NO!"

Derrick grinned. "I appreciate that," he said. "Although, come to think of it... I might actually *be* incompetent. But—if I *am*—I've got such a great team that nobody will ever notice."

The group erupted into laughter and applause.

"Hey!" someone yelled. "At least you answer your damned phone!"

Another round of laughter.

Derrick clasped his hands in the air and shook them above his head like a victorious prize fighter.

When the laughter had died down, he lowered his hands. "Let's be serious for a moment," he said. "As much as I'd like to take credit for all the good things that are happening, the real credit belongs to all of you."

The associates broke into thunderous applause. Derrick had to shout to be heard over the tumult.

"I didn't do this," he yelled. "*You* did!"

The applause grew even louder.

Derrick's eyes swept the group. Of all the assembled personnel, only Tina and Debbie weren't clapping. And Derrick saw that he wasn't the only person to notice.

He motioned with raised arms for everyone to quiet down.

"We're doing well," he said. "But we're going to do even better. I want to make this coming promotion the biggest event in the history of this store! Are you *with* me?"

"YES!"

"Fantastic!" Derrick said. "Then let's open the store, and do what we love doing!"

It was the signal that the meeting was over.

As the group began to disperse, Derrick raised his voice again. "Just one more thing," he said.

He paused, to be certain they were paying attention. "Thank you," he said. "Thank you for everything you do..."

Steve Evans was so excited that he looked like he was going to pee his pants. "I don't know *how* you did it, but you *did* it!"

"I thought for sure you were buried," said Tim Lyon. He was smiling, and looking every bit as elated as the associates.

"Thanks for the vote of confidence," Derrick said in a teasing voice.

"Don't get me wrong," replied Tim quickly. "I was rooting for you all the way."

"Unlike some others I won't mention," said JC. He flicked his eyes toward Tina and Debbie, who were standing off at a distance.

Derrick waved for the two women to come over and join the discussion.

"What are you *doing*?" asked JC.

"I want a little powwow with the managers," Derrick said. "To go over a few loose ends."

JC's mouth practically dropped open. "You don't expect *them* to help, do you? Hell, they're probably the ones who started all the nasty rumors to begin with."

Derrick had no doubt at all that Tina and Debbie had started the rumors, but he wasn't going to say so out loud. "We still have to work together," he said.

The HR and PSM took their time walking over.

Derrick had chosen to have this little gathering right on the sales floor, amidst customers and associates. It was an unusual choice, but he wanted to demonstrate clearly that he had nothing to hide. (This was especially important, because he *did* have something to hide. Despite his gung-ho speech to the associates, this store was in imminent danger of closing its doors.)

"Okay people," he said "it's time to get down and dirty. We've still got work to do. If we're going to have a successful sales day, it has to be BIG!"

JC looked puzzled. "What more can we do?"

"We've followed the company strategy," said Steve, quickly. "Signage, scheduling, displays, inventory... What else *is* there?"

"Yeah," said Tim. "Unless you want us to go door-to-door, stuffing flyers in mailboxes, I don't see what else we can do."

Derrick looked toward Tina and Debbie. "Do either of you have anything helpful to offer?"

Debbie stiffened, as though she'd been insulted.

Tina gave Derrick a condescending smile. "I agree with everyone else," she said. "We've done all we can. If you've got some brilliant strategy up your sleeve, now is the time to share it."

"I'm not going to pull a rabbit out of my hat," Derrick said. "But I don't kid myself that I have a monopoly on good ideas. That's what this meeting is about: to see if any of you can think of anything I've missed."

Everyone shook their heads.

"Okay," Derrick said. "I guess all that's left to do is make sure we have all hands on deck for the sale."

"Well, *that's* not going to happen," Tim said. "The designers aren't going to be here."

Debbie shot a glare at Tim that could have turned him to stone.

Derrick looked at Debbie. "What is he talking about?"

The PSM said quietly, "My team is scheduled to have Memorial Day off."

"No they aren't," Derrick said. "We talked about this on Tuesday afternoon, Debbie. I told you that the designers are absolutely required to be here. I'll have to check my notes, but it was about 5:00 p.m."

Debbie looked startled at the news that Derrick had documented the conversation, but she kept her voice cool. "That's not what the work schedule says."

"Who approved that schedule?" Derrick snapped.

Tina squared her shoulders. "*I* did."

"Then you can un-approve it," Derrick said. "You and Debbie will have to get in touch with every designer, and let them know that they have to be here on Monday."

Tina shook her head. "That's not possible. Once I've approved the schedules, we follow them."

"Why didn't you check with me first?" Derrick asked.

"It's not that big a deal," Debbie said. "My team isn't really necessary."

Derrick could see the look in Debbie's eyes as she realized what she'd just said. Instead of pointing out that the presence of her designers wasn't necessary for the holiday sale, she'd just stated that her team wasn't necessary *at all*.

Debbie opened her mouth to correct her mistake, but Derrick didn't give her the chance.

"Did I just hear you correctly?" he asked. "Are you saying that this store doesn't actually *need* your design team?"

Debbie's face went white. Her stammered response was nearly incoherent. "That's... that's not... that's... not..."

Derrick raised his eyebrows. "Are you suggesting that we should out-source our design services? Or that we can do without designers *entirely*?"

"No!" Debbie said. It was practically a shout. "That's not what I meant!"

"I'm glad to hear that," Derrick said. "Because I happen to believe that the designers are an important part of this store. Would you agree with that?"

Debbie nodded vigorously. "Yes! Of course! My designers are *vital* to this store!"

"I think you're absolutely right," Derrick said. "And since we agree that the designers are a vital part of this store, can you *please* explain why you arranged for them not to be here during one of the most important sales promotions this store had ever done?"

Debbie said nothing.

"That doesn't matter," Tina said. "What matters is that the schedules are already approved. According to SOP, we can't change an approved schedule without the consent of the associates whose work hours will be affected."

Derrick stared at Tina and Debbie. "Then you'd better go *get* the designers to consent," he said. "Every person in this store has heard me say repeatedly that we *all* need to be here for the sale. The two of you caused this problem. It's up to the two of you to fix it."

Tina started to speak, but Derrick cut her off.

"Fix it!" he said. "I'm telling you right now, in front of witnesses. It's not a suggestion, and it's not a recommendation. You will *fix* this! Do I make myself clear?"

Tina glared at him, and Debbie looked at the floor. After a few seconds, they both nodded.

As the meeting broke up, the Wicked Witches stalked away, whispering furiously back and forth.

JC nodded toward their receding backs. "Talk about a Class-A fuck up..."

The other ASMs laughed.

"Yeah," Derrick said. "But they got what they deserved."

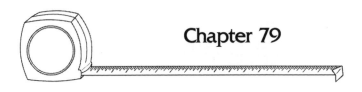

Chapter 79

11:00 AM

Tina headed straight for the solitude of her office with Debbie in tow.

When the door was safely closed behind them, Tina dropped into her desk chair and closed her eyes.

"What are we going to do?" asked Debbie. She sounded as desperate as she was irritated.

"Shut up," Tina growled. "I have to think."

Debbie didn't appreciate being put in her place, but if there was anyone who could get away with it, that person was Tina.

After a few silent moments Debbie sat down.

Tina's eyes popped open, as if she had been struck by a revelation. "We can't let him get away with this," she said.

"You don't say," Debbie replied with sarcasm.

Tina ignored the jibe. She opened the drawer to her desk and pulled out her *666* binder. "It's time to unleash the big guns," she said.

Debbie squirmed with discomfort. She remembered the document she'd read in that very folder on Friday morning. Not the complaint from Helen Silverman. The *other* document. The one with bad news stamped all over it.

"I think this is a mistake," she said slowly. "If this goes wrong, it could get us in no end of shit."

Tina wasn't listening. "That bastard isn't going to tell *me* what to do," she hissed.

"I'm not kidding," Debbie said. "If your little bombshell misses the target..."

"I told you not to worry about that," Tina said. "Emily from the phone room was a witness. She clearly saw Derrick touching a female associate in an inappropriate manner."

Debbie frowned. "I still think you're crazy! There's no *way* Derrick did that. Either Emily is mistaken about what she saw, or she's completely full of shit. Tina, the woman *lives* in gossip land. I don't believe *half* the crap that comes out of Emily's mouth."

Debbie had no desire to stand up for the SM. She despised Derrick as deeply as Tina did. But she couldn't believe (didn't believe) he would jeopardize his career by having a fling with an associate.

"You're going to have to trust me on this," Tina said. "I know what I'm doing."

But Debbie still wasn't buying it. "Look," she said. "There's an easier way to do this. Why don't you go to Judy and explain how Derrick is violating SOP? Once the work schedules have been approved by the leadership team—"

"You should stop while you're ahead!" snapped Tina. "Every other design team in the district will be working on the holiday. Do *you* want to explain to Judy how *we* created the schedule that gave the designers Memorial Day off?"

Tina shook her head. "Have you completely lost it?"

Debbie flushed with embarrassment, but she didn't respond.

Tina lifted her phone and made an overhead page for one of the associates in outdoor seasonal to call her office.

The two women sat in silence, staring at each other until the phone rang.

When it did, Debbie jumped, but Tina let it ring three times before lifting the receiver.

"Yes...thanks for calling," she said. "Are you with a customer? Good. Can you come to my office? I'd like to go over something with you."

When Tina replaced the receiver in its cradle Debbie looked at her with curiosity. "What's this all about?"

"Patience, my friend" said Tina. "Patience..."

A few minutes later, there was a knock at the door.

Tina smiled. "Come in."

When the door opened Sylvia Sanchez stepped inside.

Tina motioned the associate to a seat. "Thanks for coming," she said. "There's something I'd like to discuss with you."

Sylvia looked nervous. "Is anything wrong?"

Tina leaned back in her chair. "Well, that depends... It's about an incident that occurred in Derrick's office this past Monday..."

The color drained from Sylvia's face.

Chapter 80

"This is the last thing we need," declared Derrick.

JC and Steve sat silently while the store manager finished reading the three written statements from three associates.

Derrick rubbed the back of his neck. "Are these true?"

The ASMs exchanged nervous glances.

JC shrugged. "You have it in writing," he said. "I guess so."

Derrick looked over the statements quickly one more time. "So these women have an official complaint against..." He searched for the name of the associate in question.

"His name is Grant," said Steve.

"He's been a pain-in-the-ass from day-one," added JC.

"This is the last thing we need," Derrick said again.

He didn't need to explain his meaning.

"How come I haven't met this Grant?"

JC and Steve exchanged glances again. "He's the kind of guy who makes himself invisible more often than not," answered Steve with a chuckle.

Derrick smiled. "I know the type," he said. "Where can I find him?"

"Grant's in hardware," replied JC.

"Okay, I'll go have a word with him about this. In the meantime, I want you two to stay busy on the floor, where the associates can see you. They need to know that we're down there in the trenches, working alongside them."

They nodded mechanically. "If you say so, Boss."

"I say so," Derrick said. "I'll be back to touch base with you in a few minutes, after I talk to this *Grant* person."

Grant was quite a character. He stood close to six foot tall, with close-cropped blonde hair, and eyes as blue as the sky. Apparently, many women found him attractive, at least at first. But most members of the opposite sex quickly tired of his attitude, and he was vane about his own appearance, to the point of being obnoxious.

Derrick didn't want to discuss the issue in front of customers, so he led Grant to the outdoor break area where the smokers among the associates went for their periodic cigarettes.

When they were seated, Derrick told Grant about the complaints.

"I don't know what you're talking about," exclaimed Grant. "Who's complaining about me?"

Derrick shook his head. "You know I can't tell you that. But I can tell you the substance of the complaints."

He pulled out the three sheets and read them aloud, one at a time:

Grant whistles at me when I walk by, and he calls me baby.

Grant asks me out on dates, after I've told him repeatedly to stop asking.

Grant follows me to my car after work.

"I don't do *any* of that stuff," said Grant, flatly. "It's all a bunch of lies."

"These are serious charges," Derrick said. "And these associates want action against you. That means HR will have to conduct an investigation."

Grant's air of confidence disappeared. "You're taking sides just like *that?*"

"I'm not taking sides," Derrick said. "I don't know if there is any truth to these accusations or not. But I can tell you this, if you *have* been doing any of those things, it has to stop *immediately.*"

"Everyone's against me!" Grant said. "They don't like me, because I'm good-looking. I have so many women after me that it makes the girls in this store jealous."

It took Derrick several seconds to realize that Grant wasn't kidding.

Finally he said, "Let me see if I've got this right... You think these complaints are from women who are upset because you're *not* paying attention to them?"

Grant nodded. "Fucking-A right!"

Derrick laughed out loud. Now, he really *had* heard everything.

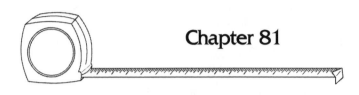

Chapter 81

Mary Hines went to receiving pushing a cart of returns. She saw Darrell walking through the doors munching on a sandwich.

"Hey Mary, how ya doin'?" he said, with a mouthful of food.

She turned away, disgusted. "Fine."

"Have you heard what Derrick did?" Her expression told him no, and he enthusiastically told him about the SM confronting Grant about the sexual harassment complaints against him. He grinned ear to ear when her eyes practically popped out of the sockets. "How about that, huh?" he said, stuffing the last piece of his sandwich in his beefy face.

Complaints were kept confidential, but in retail very little if anything was kept secret long. It's about time that bastard got his due, thought Mary. Then a sense of admiration for her store manager swept her over. And disgust for her HR quickly followed! Why didn't that bitch, Tina, handle this, she wanted to know.

"What did Grant say?" asked Mary, curious.

Darrell chuckled. "Suspended." He checked to make sure no one heard him talking about a subject no one was supposed to know, yet did. "You shoulda seen him," he went on. "Derrick escorted him to his locker and out the building. Grant was madder than a wet hen and I swear he looked like he was crying as he drove off in that convertible mustang of his."

Mary thought she would have enjoyed seeing that. Oh well, in another life.

"That's not all," added Darrell, still grinning. "Sylvia put in a sexual harassment complaint against Derrick too."

"What?"

Darrell told her what he heard about Sylvia's encounter in the manager's office on his first day and Mary shook her head in disbelief. "Did Sylvia tell you that?"

Darrell shook his head no. "Emily in phones saw the whole thing, and went to Tina about it."

Mary looked away trying to put two and two together. Her female intuition told her this was bullshit. "I can't believe it," she said adamantly.

Darrell shrugged. "Seems like Derrick is in for quite a week. Not only does he have to contend with the rumor about the store closing; now he has to deal with a sexual harassment suit."

He shook his head, chuckling. "You've gotta love retail."

Mary turned to face him. "You don't believe they're going to shut down the store, do you?"

Darrell let out a laugh. "Nah... I don't even believe this sexual complaint from Sylvia," he said. "You stick around long enough, and you'll hear *everything*."

Mary left receiving confused. She liked Derrick. He seemed to want to do the right thing. She grew embarrassed as she reflected on her first encounter with him. Why the hell did I act like such a baby? All he asked me to do was help out in receiving, she reasoned. It wasn't like he asked me to stand on my head.

When she entered the break room she saw a group of associates sitting at the table, laughing together. "Good for him," said one. "It's about time someone made them work!"

"They've been getting a free ride long enough," said another.

Mary walked up to them and asked, "What's going on?"

Barbara from bath department looked up and said, "The design room is up in arms about having to work Memorial Day."

The girls giggled like schoolgirls spreading gossip on campus. Claudia from lighting said, "They were hoping to have a three-day weekend, but Derrick is making them come in."

"He's even having Debbie bring them in tomorrow whether they were scheduled off or not," added Allison from special service desk. "And they're not happy about it one bit!"

Mary couldn't understand why this was an issue. Major holidays were always big sales day events at *The Design*, so for the designers to have been given the day off by the PSM in the first place was unusual.

The girls at the table noticed Mary deep in thought. "What's wrong?" asked Allison.

Mary stared at her. "Doesn't it seem odd that Debbie would schedule her designers off on a major holiday? Why would she do that unless she wanted the new manager to fail?"

The girls exchanged confused glances and shrugged. "Who knows what goes through Debbie's mind?" said Claudia.

Barbara agreed and added, "Yeah! A thought going through her mind would be a quick trip considering she has nothing between her ears."

"These fucking mystery shoppers," muttered Derrick. After reading the reports sent to him from Judy on his email he felt like putting his fist through a wall.

A mystery shopper was nothing new to Derrick. He understood why companies hired people pretending to be customers for feedback about their shopping experience. This allowed *The Design* to gauge strengths and weaknesses so they could set guidelines for associates.

But I don't need this shit now, said Derrick silently. On his way to the design service desk he ran into JC and Nancy in the outdoor seasonal department.

"What's up?" asked JC.

"Hi Derrick," said Nancy. She seemed to make an effort at smiling. "I thought your speech was good."

Derrick ignored the compliment and thrust the papers at JC. "Have you seen these?" Of course he hadn't, but Derrick was too angry to think clearly. "It's the latest mystery shopper scores, and they suck!"

Nancy appeared shocked and JC was at a loss for words.

Derrick took a moment to regain composure. Be calm and easy, easy and calm, he told himself. "This is the last thing we need right before the holiday sale," he explained in a calm tone. "If you read the bullet points you'll find our associates missed every major step of the sale." He paused for effect. "I mean, how hard is it to help customers?"

JC read the mystery shopper scores line by line and grew sick.

Were you greeted within three minutes after entering the store? No.

Did the associate introduce him/herself? No.

Did the associate ask questions about your project? No.

Did the associate appear interested in your shopping needs? No.

After explaining what you were looking for did the associate make recommendations? Yes.

At least we did something right, thought JC.

Did the associate talk about sales promotions, rebates, financing, and design and install services? No.

Did the associate recommend other products from all departments? Yes.

Did the associate ask for the sale? No.

JC didn't see the point in continuing. He understood the point Derrick made. "I'll have a word with the associates in question," said JC. He looked sick to the stomach.

"This is not something we can take lightly," continued Derrick. "Our line of work requires each of us to engage customers. If our associates don't do that, we have no chance in hell of—"

He stopped short, not wanting to say anything he would regret in front of Nancy. You're working to squash rumors, he reminded himself, not start them.

"I understand, Derrick, and I'll take care of this."

"We'll try harder in trade, too," offered Nancy. She saw Derrick brighten at the idea and continued. "We can talk about selling skills we use in trade when dealing with contractors. Sharing experiences has always been a good way to improve selling confidence."

This was precisely what Derrick needed to hear and he was already grinning ear to ear. "I like it!" he confessed. "Tell the associates they have to try harder if they tell you they're doing all they can. Average is not enough. We have to be the best!"

"Do you want to come with us?" asked JC.

Derrick shook no. "I have to speak with a project client at the design service desk."

"Why don't you have Debbie do that? She's the PSM."

Derrick scoffed. "It's a customer complaint, and the last thing I need is for her to muddy up the waters with her abrasiveness."

Nancy giggled. "You haven't even been here a week and already you have her pegged! I guess you were ready to be promoted."

"Lucky me." Derrick grew serious. "Listen, mystery shops and online feedback about businesses have changed retail in every way. We can't afford a single customer complaint to reach the public on the internet or we'll get killed."

"I don't think a lot of people read that bull"

"That's not the point, JC," cut in Derrick. "If we lose one customer because of an online complaint about our store, or a poor mystery shop score, it's game over."

He watched them to see that they understood. This had to be said, he knew. "I don't like this any more than you." He hesitated. "Just see that we fix this."

Derrick wondered if JC and Nancy were capable of handling this as he walked away. But he'd have to make do with what he had. After all, he couldn't do it all alone.

Chapter 82

Derrick saw Giovanni Mercado sitting across from Laura Tanaka at the design desk, watching him keenly as he approached. Giovanni had his legs crossed and arms folded, and did not have the look of someone happy.

"Hello Giovanni, how may I be of help?" said Derrick, offering his hand.

Giovanni sighed, and rose to his feet before taking Derrick's hand limply in his own. "I need to know what's going on with my project," he said matter-of-factly.

Derrick listened intently as Giovanni explained how his designer, Janette, dropped the ball at every stage. "First she ordered my cabinets wrong, then she didn't charge me for the install at least some of it," he corrected himself. "Then she went on vacation before reordering the cabinets she left out of my design, which pushed back my project start date by a whole month." He looked as spent as he sounded. "She never returns my calls, she's never here, and when I do hear from her it's to collect payment for something she forgot to add on my order in the first place."

Derrick knew this was going as far south as it could go! "Let me start by apologizing for our failure to meet your expectations," he began. No sense dodging a bullet that's already struck us in the forehead, he reasoned. "Has Debbie, the project manager, addressed your concern?"

Giovanni stared back absently. "Who is she?"

Derrick could not hold back grinning. Why am I not surprised?

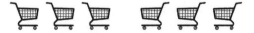

Janette wasn't happy about having to work Saturday. "I was hired on the understanding I had weekends off," she told her boyfriend as she got ready to leave for work.

"Then why go in?" Mike, her boyfriend, asked.

Janette told him about the Memorial Day sale and how each designer was required to work either a Saturday or Sunday to help collect project retainers. "At least they let me keep Sunday," she said, sounding relieved. She was an avid church-goer, never missing Sunday Mass.

"Why not call out sick?" suggested Mike.

Janette cocked an eyebrow. Not a bad idea, she thought. However, the last thing she wanted was trouble for not working her scheduled shift. "None of the other designers like the idea of working the holiday, but are going in so I'd better too."

When Janette drove into the parking lot she balked. "Look at all these cars," she said aloud. The lot was packed to the max and someone parked in her favorite spot by the tree that shaded her car. She had to park clear on the other side of the lot and did not look forward going inside the store.

I don't know how they do it, she wondered, shaking her head in reference to the associates who worked the sales floor. Like many designers she loathed working the sales floor. It was far beneath her talent, or so she believed.

Janette walked past the design service desk and greeted Laura. "Hi Lar," she said, calling her out by half a name.

Laura jumped up from her chair. "Janette, you're not going to believe what happened?"

This can't be good, thought Janette. "What?"

Laura repeated, "You're simply *not* going to believe it!"

"I got that part," said Janette, exasperated.

Laura was oblivious to Janette's sarcasm. She took a deep breath and told her Giovanni Mercado came in to see the store manager, and Laura reveled in seeing the color drain from Janette's face. Take that you skinny bitch!

Janette took a moment to regain composure and asked, "What did he want?"

Laura's lips pursed into a smile. "Like you don't know," she said with intentional sarcasm. Janette didn't have many friends on the sales floor, what with how stuck up she behaved.

After observing her sweat Laura decided to fill her in. "Giovanni told Derrick how you dropped the ball on his project. He said you don't return calls, told him how you ordered the wrong cabinets and didn't place the reorder until *after* you returned from vacation. He said you leave him with the impression that you don't give a damn about his project as much as you do your personal life." Laura laughed heartily at the last part and made that up knowing it would upset her.

Janette choked. "What did Derrick say?" she asked, her voice trembling.

Laura paused, observing Janette keenly. She looks like she's going to shit, thought Laura, enjoying the moment. Finally she filled her in. "You'll be happy to know the store manager backed you up a hundred percent, and Giovanni bought it."

Janette pondered that. "How do you mean?"

"Derrick explained how a lot happens during a remodel that can put a client's patience to the test," replied Laura. "He pointed out how product can arrive damaged and needs to be reordered, installers sometimes have to reschedule due to unforeseen issues, and that projects cost more than originally quoted upon discovery when installers find additional work that needs to be done. He basically schooled the client." She waited for Janette's reaction and finished off by adding, "In short, the store manager did what the designer should have done from the start."

Janette cocked an eyebrow. "And that is?"

Laura smiled condescendingly. "He set the right expectations."

An awkward silence followed. "What did Debbie say?" asked Janette.

Laura shrugged and shook her head. "She was nowhere to be found. That's why the customer asked to speak to Derrick."

Janette nodded in thought and asked about the rumor of the store closing, so Laura repeated what Derrick said in the morning meeting. "And do you believe him?"

Laura shrugged again. "Who knows what store support will do? Those people are wired funny."

Janette went to the design room feeling uncertain. She didn't like others meddling in her projects, not even managers. Debbie usually threw back any and all issues on the team, claiming she was not paid enough to babysit. She would not have thought so much of this if synergy between the designers and managers existed. Debbie had done a lot to build a wall between her department and the rest of the store that no one wanted to help projects with enthusiasm.

"It's us versus them!" Debbie declared time and again. "Don't trust the associates to properly qualify the customer. They don't get paid enough to put their heart in their work, which is why they work the sales floor. Each of us needs to take the bull by the horns and run the show. I don't want managers or associates pissing in our pond."

Janette sat at her desk pondering what Laura told her and what she knew Debbie would say once she learned Derrick got involved.

"What's wrong with you?" said a voice from behind.

Janette swiveled around in her chair and saw Susan looking over her shoulder. "Oh, I didn't hear you come in."

Susan put down her purse and briefcase and sat at her desk. "How goes it?"

Janette told her what Derrick did and Susan beamed in reflection. "If we had him as PSM, we'd be number one in our market for sure," she noted with conviction.

Janette had no love for Debbie either. She knew a bitch when she saw one too. However, her curiosity was piqued. "Why do you say that?"

Susan filled her in on how Derrick handled Justine Hildeman, praising the SM for his tact and professionalism. "I mean really," continued Susan, "can you see Debbie going the extra mile for any of us?"

Janette didn't think so either. "I don't know what to make of this guy," she admitted. "I heard the rumor of the store being closed."

"That's bullshit!" Susan said curtly. "Our manager wouldn't be that diligent if he knew they were shutting us down. Instead he'd be kicking up his feet, marking time."

Janette wasn't so sure, but she did agree on one thing. The new store manager seemed to be exactly what their store needed.

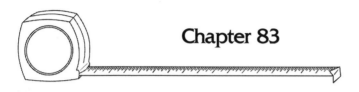

Chapter 83

Sunday 8:00 AM

Derrick walked the sales floor to ensure the store was up to par for the new day. Saturday had been busier than expected, which was good, but it meant the closing team had a lot to do before going home. The associates would start arriving at 9:00 a.m., so he had paper and pen ready to jot down notes of areas in need of attention before the store opened.

As he stood in the main aisle of the store he reflected on yesterday's events. The mystery shop didn't sit well with him, and the fact that word got out about SSC possibly shutting them down didn't help much. What really riled him was the online internet complaint about his store. They were blasted by a customer claiming to be mistreated because they were declined a refund for a refrigerator.

> *Don't shop here! They have poor service. My fridge went out of service and store refuses to repair or replace. I'm never shopping here again! Once they take your money, they leave you with the bag of goods. They don't return calls either! I had to make many trips to store for help and MY FRIDGE IS STILL BUSTED!*

Talk about vague, said Derrick silently. After doing research Derrick learned the customer's refrigerator was three years old and out of warranty. At the time of purchase the customer declined purchasing a four year extended warranty plan, and the vendor did send a service technician to repair the icemaker and water dispenser. But the customer refused to pay, so the tech refused to service the refrigerator.

"My fridge should last longer than three years, don't you think?" asked the customer.

"Warranties are offered to cover issues such as these, sir," explained Derrick, trying futilely to reason.

"After the standard one-year manufacturer's warranty expires, it's up to the owner to pay for any parts and labor required."

But the customer was having none of it. "You people are something! You take my money willingly enough and expect me to pay for damaged goods. If you don't give me a new refrigerator I'm going to write a scathing review online and tell all my friends not to shop at *The Design!*"

Derrick did not believe the customer had many friends, if any, but did not doubt that the man would write a poor review. At 5:00 p.m. the customer resolution department contacted him about the online review to confirm the customer followed through on his promise. At 5:10 p.m. Derrick contacted the customer to inform him he would order him a new refrigerator.

The appliance DS, Jesus, was up in arms over the SM's decision. "I remember this guy," he claimed. "He's a sneaky prick looking to get something for nothing!"

Derrick agreed the guy sounded like a prick to him too, but, "Online reviews have changed how we handle customer issues," he explained with regret. "We can't afford to have that out there for the public to see whether it's true or not."

But that was not what bothered Derrick most about yesterday. It was Jesus's follow-up comment over the customer incident. "Sounds like you're covering up complaints so as not to give store support a reason to shut us down after all," he said, sharply.

Derrick was not about to talk Jesus out of believing what he wanted, but made damn sure he would hold him accountable for spreading negative rumors. He went to great length to convince associates all was well, and figured he was fifty-fifty with most. We'll have to wait and see, he figured.

He walked through outdoor seasonal when his phone rang. It was Judy.

"I thought one of the perks as DM was having Sundays off," said Derrick cheerfully.

"I only have the perk of keeping my job, so long as my district performs well," replied Judy abruptly.

She didn't sound at all happy, and she got straight to business. "I received a call from Connie Palin. Do you know her?"

Derrick didn't know the woman personally, but he recognized the name. Connie Palin was the Human Resources Vice President for the company, the HRVP. Any conversation that began with her name was not going to lead in a good direction.

"I haven't had the pleasure," he said.

Judy snorted into the phone. "You have another harassment complaint against you."

Derrick leaned back in his chair and rubbed his temples. "What is it *this* time?"

Judy's voice had a hard edge. "You have a Sylvia Sanchez in your store?"

Derrick's heart nearly stopped at the mention of Sylvia's name. His close encounter with the young female associate was still fresh in his mind. But his half-second grope of the woman's tits had been a complete accident. An unintended collision of body parts... Nothing more.

Derrick listened to Judy recite the witness's account of the incident. The overall content was fairly factual. Only the cause and intent were off the mark.

Judy ended by asking, "any comment?"

"It didn't happen like that," Derrick said.

"Do tell."

Derrick sighed, and explained the Sylvia encounter in detail, including the part where she had essentially stumbled into his outstretched hands.

"It was a complete accident," Derrick said. "About six months ago, my wife, Jennifer, tripped over a carpet molding at the theater and fell into the lap of a complete stranger. It's the kind of dumb thing that happens to all of us."

"Okay," Judy said. "You've convinced me, Derrick. But it's out of my hands. Connie insists on moving forward with an investigation."

Derrick swore under his breath. It didn't make sense that Sylvia would make a complaint. She *knew* it had been an accident.

Derrick sighed. "What happens now?"

"Tasha Holguin and I will be down on Tuesday," Judy said, "to discuss the matter with you and those concerned."

Tuesday... *After* the Memorial Day sale. Judy definitely had her priorities.

"What does the district HR manager say about this?" Derrick asked.

"Just focus on the upcoming sale," Judy said.

"I'll do that," Derrick said. "And thanks for the inspiration."

He hung up the phone before Judy could say anything else.

Chapter 84

9:00 AM

The cool wind felt good against Derrick's face as he stood outside of returns, holding the door open for associates arriving for the morning shift. "Thanks for coming in," he said cheerfully.

Each of them smiled back, nodding their heads and replied, "You're welcome."

The strategy seemed to be working. If everyone saw that Derrick was in good spirits, maybe they'd believe that all was well. He was going to show them that everything wasn't falling apart, and that he had the upper hand.

Tina was responsible for spreading the gossip; Derrick would have bet his paycheck on that. And he had no doubt that Tina had weaseled Sylvia into making that sexual harassment complaint. The bitch was definitely playing hardball.

Once the opening crew was inside he locked the door behind him and continued walking the sales floor to check signage, displays, and make sure the go-backs were returned to each department. When he finished his morning walk Derrick stood in front of the main doors looking back in the store. "Are we spinning our wheels?" he wondered.

"Come again?"

Derrick spun around, surprised to find Mary Hines standing behind him.

"Mary...I didn't see you."

"Sorry, I didn't mean to scare you."

Derrick flushed with embarrassment. "You didn't scare me," he lied. She asked what he meant by spinning wheels and wondered if he should tell her. Aw, go ahead and tell her. "We've been working our fingers to the bone this past week," he explained. "A lot depends on having a successful sales day."

He caught the curious look in her eyes and thought, shit! I went too far. "Don't get the wrong idea," he continued. "I'm referring to the hard times we're in, what with the *Great Recession* and all."

The look on Mary's face told Derrick she wasn't buying it. "We'll be fine," he added. "I promise I won't let this store fail."

After a moment of staring deep in his eyes Mary looked him squarely and said, "I believe you."

Nancy, Dan, and Vanessa stood at the front desk in trade office pouring coffee and munching on donuts. It was their daily ritual only today seemed different because trade associates worked Monday through Friday, never Sunday.

"What do you think?" asked Dan, chewing obnoxiously on a jelly-filled donut.

Nancy hated the way he talked with his mouth full. "Why do you do that?" she asked, challenging him again.

"Do what?" he mumbled between bites.

"You know what."

Vanessa jumped in before Dan could do more damage with his sarcasm. "The last thing we need is to be fighting amongst each other, Dan, so why don't you try behaving like a grownup?"

That seemed to lighten the mood so Vanessa took the opportunity to change the subject. "How do you think we'll do today?"

Nancy cocked her head and raised an eyebrow. "Weekends are usually busy, so I'm sure we'll do good."

Dan laughed mockingly. "What difference does it make, if they shut us down?"

Nancy shot him an irritated glance. "You heard what he said in the morning meeting. The company is *not* closing the store, so don't go spreading rumors for the sake of trying to be funny."

Dan caught the significance of her tone. "Do either of you believe what he said yesterday?"

Now, it was Vanessa's turn to laugh. "I'd rather believe that, than run around with my head chopped off."

Nancy sat down at her desk. "I think he's on the level," she said. "He's a lot more inspirational addressing the store than Rob was."

"Yeah, but you didn't like Rob, so that doesn't count," interjected Vanessa.

Nancy frowned, but could not argue. It was common knowledge she disliked Rob for passing her over twice for supervisor. Only when she filed a sexual discrimination complaint to HR did they make her DS over trade.

Dan said quickly, "I think Nancy's right. Derrick carries himself better than Rob and other managers I've worked for." A moment later he added, "But that doesn't mean I'm sold on him telling the truth about store support's intentions."

Vanessa started to speak. "He said he would—"

"I know what he said," interjected Dan, cutting her off mid-sentence. Then he reminded both, "When have you known a manager to tell the truth? Or better still, how many managers you think are in the know with the DM on up?" He watched their reactions carefully and could see he had them thinking. "Being a manager today isn't what it used to be," he pointed out. "They're not as trained or skilled and don't keep their mouths shut for the life of them. That's why store support doesn't fill them in until the eleventh hour on anything they desire to be kept secret."

Cynical as Dan sounded, Nancy and Vanessa could not help thinking he was on to something. In today's world getting ahead was more about having a decent network versus job skills. That's why so many idiots get promoted to manager, thought Nancy. If the company was going to close down the store it was likely they'd wait until the last minute to key in the manager, but then...

"It makes no difference," Nancy said sharply.

Dan and Vanessa glanced at each other.

"What if they *are* going to close us?" she continued. "Do we throw in the towel before the fight is over? Maybe you're ready to give up, but I'm *not*. I'm putting my best foot forward, because—if store support is watching us—I want them to know I'm the kind of person they need to find a place for in the company."

Dan and Vanessa jumped from their chairs to face Nancy. After uncharacteristically saluting her they placed their right hand over their heart and began singing in unison.

"GOD BLESS AMERICA, LAND THAT I LOVE. STAND BESIDE HER, AND GUIDE HER, THROUGH THE NIGHT WITH A LIGHT FROM ABOVE. FROM THE MOUNTAINS, TO THE PRAIRIES, TO THE OCEANS, WHITE WITH FOAM. GOD BLESS AMERICA, MY HOME SWEET HOME."

Associates throughout the store heard the singing and joined in, too. When finished, the store errupted with laughter as everyone clapped.

Tina was walking out of her office when she heard the commotion and asked Emily, who was smiling as she returned to the phone room, what brought that on. "I don't know," replied Emily, "but I hope they share more of it."

"What do you mean by that?" asked Tina, curtly.

"Considering the rumor spreading through the store, I think we could use good morale, don't you?"

Tina flinched. Emily's sharp response caught her off guard. Up to now she had thought of Emily as a mousy, quiet person, incapable of challenging anyone. She decided to dig deeper. "What rumor are you referring to?" the HR asked abruptly.

Emily made a face and replied, "Take a wild guess." Then she closed the door to the phone room behind her, leaving Tina standing in the hallway with her mouth gaping.

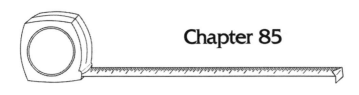

Chapter 85

9:30 AM

Throughout the store, associates were busy getting their departments up to par before the doors opened. Some of them worked feverishly, stocking the shelves with product, making signs, and wiping displays clean of the ever-present dust bunnies. Others were despondent, plodding mechanically through their morning tasks, as if every ounce of hope had been drained from their bodies.

Despite the differences in how they were reacting to the strain, everyone in the store shared a single common thought. They were all wondering whether or not they would have jobs in the coming weeks.

"They wouldn't really shut us down, would they?" asked Tiffany at the cash registers.

"They can't," replied Florence. "They'd never overcome the negative publicity."

There was a tinge of panic in Tiffany's voice. "What if they *do* shut us down? Where would we *go*? The job market is not exactly overflowing these days. And the jobs that are out there don't pay enough to cover the bills."

Florence gave her a sympathetic nod. "We'll just have to hope for the best."

Tiffany sniffed. "Hope is not a strategy. Isn't that what the bosses are always telling us?"

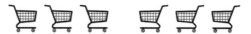

In flooring department Kelly and Felicia reorganized the rug samples.

"So what do you think?" asked Felicia.

Kelly shrugged. "Hard to say. It doesn't make sense for the company to shut down the only store of its kind in northern San Diego. A lot of customers won't bother to drive from Encinitas to Kearny Mesa. They'll just go to one of the big-box retailers, and save themselves a trip."

He straightened a stack of carpeting. "Still... You never can tell what the company suits are thinking."

Felicia raised an eyebrow. "How do you mean?"

"Well, the CEO isn't paid for his performance," Kelly said. "Neither are the high-ranking members of the board. Their salaries and bonuses are guaranteed by contract."

Felicia gestured for him to continue. "*And...*"

Kelly moved to another stack of carpet samples. "And that means whatever they decide won't affect their paychecks. Good decisions or bad, they'll still get their millions. So whatever happens to us is irrelevant to them."

Felicia clearly didn't like the sound of that. "You're a bit overly cynical, don't you think?"

"Maybe I am," Kelly said. "I hope to high Heaven I'm wrong. But let's face it... This wouldn't be the first time a CEO and members of the board made a bad call."

Felicia still didn't like what she was hearing. "I can't argue with that, but you don't have to sound so glib about it. If they shut down this store, you'll be out of a job just like the rest of us."

Kelly laughed. "True. But working for *The Design* is not exactly my lifelong ambition."

He grinned. "Unlike you, my average hourly rate is bottom scale."

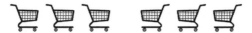

In bath showroom, Leonard, Barbara, and Andrew sat at their desks talking and reviewing orders. "I think he's on the level," said Andrew, speaking while typing away on his keyboard. "He's the best speaker I've heard for a long time, and he makes himself available to us when we need him."

"What's the big deal about that?" asked Barbara. "He's *paid* to be available."

Andrew looked up from his computer. "All managers are paid to be available, but how many of them actually do it? You've been around long enough to know how hard it is to get a manager to answer their phone, return a call, or talk with a customer."

"It's like pulling teeth!" he said. He turned to Leonard, who was silently reviewing orders on his computer. "Isn't that right, Leonard?"

Leonard looked up for the first time. His expression remained non-committal. "I don't want to be quick to judge," he said.

Andrew laughed. "Hah! I can't begin to count how many times I've heard you bitch about being unable to get a manager to answer his phone."

"What's your point?" Leonard shot back.

Andrew looked over his shoulder and decided to tone it down. "I'm only saying that our new manager seems to be the kind of guy we can trust."

"Are you saying you can't trust a *woman*?" asked Barbara, smiling.

Andrew gave her a withering look. "Of course not. I'm saying Derrick does all the little things that managers are *supposed* to do, but don't."

"Such as?" asked Leonard.

"We all saw him greet us at the door this morning," said Andrew. "When's the last time we had a manager do that? He also makes a point to address us by name. He makes time to listen to us, and he asks for our advice. Most managers act like they know everything, and they don't want our opinions."

"Good point," admitted Barbara. "So you think the rumor is just a rumor? And the company isn't going to shut down the store?"

Andrew knew what she wanted to hear, but the last thing he wanted was to mislead anyone. "I don't know what they're going to do," he said. "I *do* know that our new SM is probably the best we're gonna get. So we may as well put our best foot forward, and have the best fucking sales day we can have. If the company is going to shut us down, at least we'll show them they're closing a store that has its shit together."

Barbara and Leonard exchanged looks, and nodded approvingly.

Derrick was throwing trash down the compactor in receiving when Gina walked through the double doors pulling a load of trash on a pallet jack. "Hi Derrick," she called out.

He turned to see who it was. "Gina, how are you?"

Gina looked at the clock on the wall. "Cutting it close, aren't you?"

Derrick knew she was referring to the morning meeting. He smiled. "I didn't realize you enjoyed my speeches."

Gina stopped and looked him squarely. "We all appreciate what you said yesterday, and how you said it."

Derrick put down the trash can and faced her.

"I think we needed to hear that," she continued.

Derrick looked around to make sure they were alone. He seemed to be judging whether or not to ask her something. Fuck it! What did he have to lose? "Who do you think started the rumor?"

Gina didn't hesitate. "Tina."

Bingo! "Why do you say that?"

"She wants your job," Gina said. "She's always wanted her own store, but she doesn't want to follow the process. She wants to go right from HR to store manager, just like that." Gina snapped her fingers to emphasize her point.

Derrick nodded. "What do you think of her?"

Gina raised her eyebrows. "Can I speak frankly?"

"Of course," Derrick said.

Gina took a breath. "I think she's a lying, back-stabbing bitch, and I wouldn't trust her as far as I can throw a forklift."

Derrick grinned. "Don't hold back. How do you *really* feel?"

"I think Debbie is cut from the same cloth," Gina said. "And Kim isn't much better. If there was such a thing as an evil-female version of the *Three Stooges*, their names would be Tina, Debbie, and Kim."

Derrick checked his watch. "We'd better get to the rug department for the morning meeting. I'm sure the associates are expecting me to continue with the damage control thing."

Gina grabbed him by the arm to stop him. "Wait! I want to tell you... I want to thank you for not terminating me. I know you could have. And I appreciate you giving me another chance."

Derrick knew sincerity when he saw it, and felt a surge of positive energy flow through his veins. "That's okay," he said. "I know talent when I see it."

He was almost to the door when Gina called out to him again. "Derrick, no matter what happens, I think you should know that this past week has made a helluva difference to a lot of people in this store."

Derrick smiled again. "Thanks," he said. "I just hope it turns out to be enough."

Chapter 86

10:00 AM

This was ridiculous! It was all Derrick could do to keep his temper in check during the morning meeting. About a third of the designers had failed to show up, and the number of sick calls had jumped from an average of five a day to fifteen.

Didn't these people understand that their jobs were on the line? No... Come to think of it, they probably *didn't*. Derrick had laid on the 'everything is fine' routine at yesterday's meeting. Maybe he had bullshitted a little *too* well.

He chose to keep his morning pitch limited to yesterday's success stories. "We ended up at one hundred and fifty thousand," he said. "Up thirty thousand from last year's sales, and exceeding plan by fifteen percent. We also picked up two kitchen retainers, and one bath retainer, so we're in line to have a stellar week."

He took a moment to let that sink in. "Now, we need to focus on the next two days. Remember to follow the basic steps of the sale. Sick calls are higher than usual today, and that will hit us hard in the middle part of the day, when we get busy. Adjust your lunches with your supervisors, so we can maintain good coverage. Be sure to call the MOD first, when you have a customer looking to speak with a manager."

Derrick saw a rumble go through the group.

"What is it?" he asked.

"The MODs still don't answer their phones," shouted a voice in the back.

Derrick looked at Steve and Tim who were standing off to the side. They flushed with embarrassment and lowered their heads. The last thing he needed was for his ASM team to lose face.

"That changes from this point on," he said. "I assure you they're as committed as I am to answering the phone."

At that exact instant, Tim and Steve's phones both rang.

The two managers glanced nervously at Derrick, and then answered their phones. The callers immediately hung up.

Derrick grinned at the assembled group. "I guess that was our first test," he said. "And we passed it. Now, let's keep at it. I've gotten so many calls that my cell phone battery is ready to explode."

Everyone laughed, and Derrick used that moment to dismiss the meeting.

As the group began to disperse, he walked up to his two ASMs. "Where are Tina and Debbie?"

They shook their heads.

Derrick sighed. "Okay, I need you two to be on the floor all day."

The ASMs scowled, but Derrick wasn't going to have any of that.

"You saw what happened," he said. "If you want the associates to respect you, you're going to have to learn what's important to them, and be consistent in answering your damn phone."

The managers still didn't like what they were hearing.

"I'm not asking you to stand on your head," Derrick reasoned. "I can't be the only one the associates call when they need a manager. So, answer your damned phones. Is that clear?"

They nodded reluctantly, and Derrick sent them on their way.

He was off to find the Wicked Witches of the West. He had a bone to pick with them.

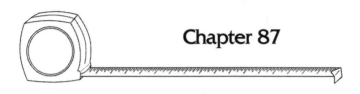

Chapter 87

Tina sat in her office and listened carefully to Tasha Holguin on the phone.

"To be frank, we don't know how this is going down," admitted Tasha.

Tina did not like the sound of that and told her so. "Sexual harassment is not something we can take lightly," she said, irritated. "If we let Derrick Payton off the hook, people will wonder what use they have for human resources managers."

"This is not about human resources," reminded Tasha. "And we aren't taking this complaint lightly, which is why I'm coming down with Judy tomorrow. But I want you to understand there are two sides to every story."

Tina had a sinking feeling in the pit of her stomach. "What do you mean? Of course I know there are."

"You can cut the crap," Tasha blurted. "I haven't read Derrick's statement, and he will of course have a statement denying any wrong-doing."

"How do you—"

"I said cut the crap!" repeated Tasha, abruptly. "Derrick and Judy have had discussions about your level of commitment to his leadership. Apparently your dissatisfaction with him has grown to record levels in mere days. Congratulations! You've really made a mark for yourself in the eyes of the associates at your store."

"What are you—"

"Don't make me say it," Tasha interjected, icily. She explained how her office at store support received anonymous and numerous calls from associates expressing disappointment at the behavior of Tina Nodzak. "Specifically, the associates are upset over your behavior in the presence of their store manager. They say you make mean faces at him behind his back, shake your head disapprovingly when he conducts the morning meeting, and leave associates feeling you don't approve of him personally.

I personally received two of these anonymous calls, Tina, and let me tell you this does not sit will with Connie."

Tina turned to stone. The last thing she wanted was to lose face with her superiors, but that's how things were shaping up. Don't say a word, she told herself. Listen.

"Are you there, Tina?"

"Yes, I hear you," she replied, feebly. "How would you like me to move forward?"

"I would start by suggesting you remember your role in the business unit. An HR manager is supposed to protect the assets of the store. You are responsible for ensuring managers consistently uphold company SOP. Keep your personal feelings out of it, because this is starting to look like you're setting up Derrick."

Tina could not stand being accused. "I assure you I am not."

"The only assurance I want from you is to tell me you understand Derrick Payton is store manager, and not you."

An awkward silence followed. Finally, Tina said, "I understand."

"Good. Now my last piece of advice is for you to stay clear of Derrick and don't provoke him, because when I show up tomorrow he won't be the only one under investigation."

That said, Tasha hung up without saying goodbye, leaving Tina to wonder how things could have turned for the worse so quickly. She replaced the phone back in its cradle and sat down heavily. For the first time she could recall in a long time, her hands were tied and she didn't know what to make of it.

Right when she began piecing things together in her head she heard a voice call out on the overhead page system. *"Derrick, you have a store manager call on 856. Derrick, please pick up 856 for a store manager call."*

The mention of Derrick's name and his position caused Tina to shudder.

"This is Derrick," he said into the phone. The last thing he wanted was a manager call. He wanted to find the Wicked Witches and put them in their place now!

"Derrick, this is Tim," said the voice on the other end of the line. "I have Mr. Juan Casillas here, and he wants to pay twenty thousand in cash for his order, but he refuses to fill out the Form 8300."

Not again! This is the second time this week. Like any businessman, Derrick was willing to take a customer's money, but the law was the law. The IRS dictated businesses accepting cash payments over $10,000 be reported on Form 8300, no ifs, ands, or buts.

"You explained we have no alternative?" Derrick wanted to know.

"He doesn't care. He said if we want the sale we'll have to forego filling out this form."

Derrick sighed. "I'll be right there," he said reluctantly. The Wicked Witches would have to wait.

🛒🛒🛒　🛒🛒🛒

Debbie looked Janette in the eye and wanted to know why she didn't resolve Giovanni Mercado's issue herself. "You know I require my team to take care of their customer issues personally," she said adamantly.

Janette sat across from the PSM in her office. The door was closed, but the designers observed the scene through the window to Debbie's office from their desks. Debbie intentionally left the blinds open. She wanted her team to know if you broke her rules there would be hell to pay.

"I know," Janette said, defensively.

"Then why did you have Derrick do your job?"

Janette shook her head. Fucking bitch! "Why the act? You know the customer asked Laura to call the store manager because I wasn't in the store yet. You assigned me to work the closing shift on a half-day schedule, remember."

Debbie did, but wanted Janette to sweat. "Do you expect someone else to handle your clients?"

She was true to form as always, thought Janette. "If a client wants to speak with the store manager I'm certainly not going to stop them. Perhaps if you made yourself available to us he wouldn't need to be."

Debbie stiffened. "Don't get sassy with me!" she hissed.

"Everyone in the office knows your rules," replied Janette with distaste, "and we also know you don't like helping us when we need it."

"How dare you!" shouted Debbie, sounding angry.

"No, how dare *you*," Janette retorted. "The role of the PSM is to step in when a client wants to speak with our direct supervisor, but you never want to."

Debbie didn't like where this was going. Her eyes shifted to the designers looking on through her office window. Why the hell didn't I close the blinds, she wondered. But that would have been a first for her seeing as how she relished in demonstrating authority.

"The issue here is the client complained how you dropped the ball time and again on his project." Debbie consulted her notes. "Failure to answer and return calls, failure to reorder product, failure to be available when the client wanted to discuss issues with you regarding his project."

Janette was quiet. Though she would never admit it, this was not the first time one of her client's blasted her for failing to meet expectations. Time and again she sat in the PSM's office to listen to another client's complaint over her performance. It wasn't so much her ability to present a good design in tune with what the client wanted. She actually was a good designer when it came to understanding the design process. But her time management and follow-up skills were lacking to the point of nothing short of being comical.

"You simply don't get it," continued Debbie in full swing, and grateful she was able to throw Janette's verbal attack off track. "You're constantly late, you're not making your sales goals, and your design mistakes have cost us over five thousand dollars."

At this Janette found resolve to defend herself. "I never ordered any cabinets incorrectly," she said, angrily. "My client changed their mind *after* I placed their order and it was you who agreed to not charge them for the design change."

"I don't see it that way," replied Debbie, waving off her feeble explanation. She paused, observing the designer closely. When she was satisfied Janette sweated enough she finally said, "I want you to clear out your desk and leave. Your position with this company is terminated as of now."

Janette froze. So this is what it's like? You're fired! Despite her quirks Janette managed to dodge that bullet her entire professional career. Now she found herself at a sudden loss, but not for long. She got up from her chair, glaring. "You've been nothing but a pain to us all," she began. "You don't make yourself available when we need you, you don't offer to help, and you're lousier as project manager than you were a designer." Before turning to leave she added, "If you had any dignity *you* would be the one to leave. This place would be better off without you."

Debbie scalded her with a glare of her own. "I still want you to clear out your desk," she said frostily.

Janette was going to do just that, but not before opening the door and saying one more thing. "You know your problem, Debbie?"

Debbie looked on wanting very much for this to end.

Then Janette said, "You need to get *laid*!"

She said it loud enough for the designers to hear, and Debbie could not help glancing in their direction.

"That way you won't feel the need to fuck the people you work with."

Chapter 88

1:00 PM

"We've been over this before, Juan. The IRS dictates cash payments in excess of ten thousand dollars require Form 8300 be filled out by the paying customer, and reported by the business accepting such payment." Derrick was exasperated from repeating this a third time. "There's no way around it."

Juan jumped in before Derrick could finish. "I know, you told me that twice already."

He spoke in broken English, but Derrick sensed he spoke better than he let on. The asshole probably thinks if he plays dumb he can get away with this. Not today.

"Why not open a line of credit and make your payment that way?" suggested Derrick. Juan turned away, shaking his head. Derrick looked at the time. "Juan, you've got to decide because I have other customer issues to tend to."

"What? You don't want to work with me?" he shot back, angrily.

"What kind of question is that?" challenged Derrick. "We're in the business to help customers, but cannot randomly change rules because you don't like them. The law is the law. If you don't want to pay by cashier's check or credit, you'll have to fill out—"

"IRS FORM 8300," Juan said in unison with Derrick.

Derrick wanted to say, 'we do things differently here,' but thought better.

Juan sighed heavily, showing signs for the first time he wanted this to end now. "They've done this for me at the Kearny Mesa store without having to go through this trouble," he continued, pleading. He was not going down for the count. "If they can, why can't you?"

Yeah, right, thought Derrick, rolling his eyes. "I'm not violating the law to make a sale."

"They don't have to know."

This guy doesn't know the IRS. "Juan," began Derrick, struggling to keep cool, "I don't have enough friends in the right places to cover my ass when it's on the line."

Juan shrugged as if to say, it was worth a try. He reached into his pocket and pulled out a piece of paper. "Will you at least match this price?"

Derrick unfolded the paper. There was a picture of a stainless steel refrigerator, French door style, advertised at $1,799.99 that included free shipping. "This is an online quote," Derrick pointed out.

"Will you match it?" repeated Juan.

This guy loves throwing curve ball after curve ball. "You know I can't match this."

"Why not?" Juan did his best to appear insulted, but not enough to fool Derrick. Maybe it was the perspiration beading on his forehead or his inability to stand still and keep eye contact? Derrick couldn't put his finger on it, but knew this guy was playing him. His behavior was too obvious.

Derrick started to speak when he noticed someone from the corner of his eye. It was JC standing at the special service desk. There was something about the way he watched them that caused Derrick to frown. What the hell are you looking at?

JC motioned with a nod for him to come here. Derrick excused himself to Juan's surprise and walked over to him. "What is it?"

The ASM glanced at Juan to make sure he was out of earshot. "Take the sale," he said in a low voice.

Derrick's brow furrowed and his face flushed red with anger. "What are you saying?"

"We need to have a big weekend sale to impress the company and keep them from shutting us down, right? *So take the sale!*"

Derrick shook no. "I know what you're thinking," he admitted. "Take the sale and look like heroes, right?"

JC bobbed enthusiastically. *"Right!"*

Derrick shook his head again. "Wrong! That price is below cost, and in case you forgot, we're in the business to make money."

JC reached out and took Derrick by the arm, surprising him. "Derrick, we need every penny," he said, fighting hard to keep his voice down. "We can worry about gross margin later. For now we need—"

Derrick stopped him before he could finish. "No. We're not selling below cost. We're here to make money." He looked at the hand JC absentmindedly used to hold him by the arm, and then back to JC. "Do you mind?"

JC released his grip. "Sorry, I didn't mean to—"

"It's okay," cut in Derrick, waving him off. He checked the time. "Shit! I've got to find the Wicked Witches."

"Who?"

Shit! "Never mind. You take care of Juan. I've got to go."

Derrick left JC with Juan watching from the service desk, curious over what they discussed. JC started to approach him, and then stopped suddenly. He looked over his shoulder for Derrick, who was nowhere in sight, and then back to Juan, still observing him curiously.

Finally JC shrugged. He did tell me to *take care* of the customer, he remembered. Suddenly JC was beaming. "Juan," he began, walking the remaining distance to him, "I understand you have a competitor quote you'd like for us to price-match, yes?"

Juan looked truly surprised. "Yes."

He handed the quote to JC, who unfolded the paper and studied it carefully.

"Well, Juan, under normal circumstances, we don't price-match online quotes." He paused and looked over his shoulder again. "But these aren't normal circumstances, and we're celebrating Memorial Day with a *huge* promotional sale."

He paused again.

Juan looked at him expectantly. "So?"

JC took a deep breath. "*So...*"

Chapter 89

Derrick was determined to confront the Wicked Witches and remind them who was in charge. I don't give a damn how this looks, he told himself. Win or lose, I'm gonna give 'em a fight they're gonna regret.

When he rounded the corner in plumbing he ran smack into Janette, spilling the contents in the box she carried. "JANETTE!"

His eyes practically popped from the sockets. "Are you okay?"

Janette sighed. "Sure, being fired is a great way to lift my spirit."

Derrick's heart rate jumped a notch. Did she say *fired*? "What are you talking about?"

Janette studied the look in his eyes and thought, you're not kidding are you? She told him what took place in Debbie's office and Derrick suddenly found himself losing balance.

What the fuck else can go wrong today, he wondered. He looked stoically at Janette and said, "You're not fired, but," he glanced over his shoulder checking for anyone within earshot, "I don't want to talk here. Let's go outside."

He walked Janette carrying her box of belongings while she lugged her heavy briefcase by the shoulder strap and her purse in her free hand. As they walked past a throng of customers and associates Janette had the look of someone leaving for the last time, and their stares reminded Derrick how easily rumors bore fruit.

That's all I need, more gossip!

When they reached her car Derrick placed the box in the trunk. "I want you to promise not to worry," he insisted. "Tina doesn't have the right to terminate anyone."

"No, that falls under *your* right as manager," was Janette's comeback.

Derrick stopped. She's still not convinced, he knew. Let's try another approach. "I was chosen to turn things around and I can't do that by replacing people. That would take time we don't have." He observed her reaction keenly and the look in her eyes told him she got the hint. "I'm going to take a chance, but what the hell?"

Janette never took her eyes away from his. "The rumors are true." She wasn't asking a question and Derrick's expression was all the confirmation needed. Janette let out a laugh. "You're a pretty good actor!" she said quickly, and followed up with, "You have everyone believing they're jobs are safe."

"Would you prefer otherwise?" Derrick retorted seriously. "I don't believe for a moment you think it's in anyone's best interest that I tell them what's at stake. You know what'll happen. Some will put their best foot forward; others will throw in the towel. We can't win with half a team." Derrick was adamant.

This was too much for Janette to take in. First she learns she has to work the weekend including Memorial Day, and then she gets fired; now she learns the store was closing. And I haven't even had lunch, she thought.

"Why tell me?"

Thanks! This was the opening Derrick had hoped for and he could not help but smile. "I said a moment ago, I—" He stopped, catching his mistake in choice of words, "We can't do this with half a team. It's all for one."

"And one for all," interjected Janette.

"Right."

Janette shook her head. "From what I know the designers aren't coming in," she said dismissively. "Look at all the sick calls you received already."

"That's why I need you to call each of them and ask them to come in."

"Me?" She was indignant as much as surprised. "You want me to tell them if they don't come in they'll be out of a job because the store's going to be closed?"

"Under *no* circumstances can you disclose what I told you." That wasn't an option he banked on. "I need you to inspire the design team by telling them what happened here today. What they lack is a *desire* to be here."

"That shouldn't be a surprise considering the PSM we have at the helm," said Janette, with disgust. Her distaste for Debbie was more than obvious.

Derrick watched her carefully. "That's going to change. Imagine the feeling they'll experience when they learn Debbie fired you, I overturned her decision, and she's being placed on administrative leave for gross insubordination."

Janette beamed at the mention of Debbie getting what she had coming.

"And all we need to do to keep the pressure off us from store support is for them to come in tomorrow and drive sales."

He prayed for the effect he needed. "Won't that be something?"

Janette nodded mechanically. Why the hell not? "I suppose I have nothing to lose," she replied without thinking.

"Nothing to lose your job over, right?"

Chapter 90

2:30 PM

What else can distract me, Derrick wanted to know.

He took a chance confiding in so many words with Janette what was at stake, but figured it was worth the gamble. After all, he reasoned, hard work isn't the only thing you need to get ahead. And right now he felt more like behind the eight ball versus the top of one's game.

When he returned to the store he was glad to see the floor packed with customers. Everyone seems to be engaging them with enthusiasm, he thought. Good. I don't think I have it in me for another pep talk this time of the day. He still had the Wicked Witches to deal with and was hell-bent on finding them.

On his way to the offices he passed the closet between flooring and décor departments and could not help stopping to listen for any heavy breathing. He looked to his right and left to make sure no one paid him attention. The last thing he wanted was to be caught in an embarrassing moment. When his fingers touched the door handle he got a chill running up and down his spine. Do you really want to do this?

He didn't, but what the hell? Get it over with.

He opened the door and was relieved to find no one inside.

"Derrick, can I help you?" someone asked, seemingly out of nowhere.

He turned quickly, displaying surprise. "Hannah, what are you doing here?"

Hannah frowned. "I work here," she replied quickly.

Derrick cocked his head. "Yes, you do," he said carefully.

Hannah looked inside the closet and realized what was probably going through his mind. Her face flushed red with embarrassment. She obviously had to get something from the closet, but with Derrick standing there thought better of it.

"I'll come back later," she said flatly.

"That's okay! I was just leaving." Derrick walked past her wishing his imagination had not gotten the better of him. When are you going to learn to leave well enough alone? he asked silently.

When he walked past the receiving door he heard his name called out. "Derrick, I've been looking for you." It was Emily, and she waved a manila folder at him. "This came for you marked *urgent.*"

Derrick thanked her and took the folder, opening it. When he read the tab on the top right of the file inside he struggled to maintain composure. "Great I've been waiting for this!"

"What's so special?"

Good job in keeping your cool, he chastised himself. He put the file back in the folder, smiled at Emily and said, "Manager stuff." And then Derrick was off again.

It was close to 3:30 p.m. when Janette arrived home. She found Mike alone watching college football on TV, drinking beer and eating pizza the perfect by-yourself food to eat when you have the house to your lonesome.

"Hey babe, what are you doing home so early?" he said, walking over to her.

Janette shook her head. "I need one of those," she said pointing at the beer in his hand, "before I relive today's events."

She followed Mike into the kitchen where he grabbed a bottle of beer from the fridge and started to pour into a chilled glass from the freezer. "Never mind the glass," she said quickly. "I'll take it straight from the bottle."

After two gulps and removing the ribbon from her ponytail to let her hair hang loose she told her boyfriend what happened.

"I think *I* need another beer," said Mike, shaking his head in disgust.

"I still have my job," Janette reflected. Then she smiled and added, "And the rest of the day off."

Mike's brow furrowed.

Janette said, "Don't look so glum. In the end I landed on my feet."

"Not necessarily," Mike said abruptly. "You have to call your coworkers and talk them into working tomorrow." He grinned mischievously. "How hard do you suppose that'll be?"

He had her there, she knew.

"Are you going to tell them what's at stake?"

She mulled it over and replied, "Derrick doesn't think I should."

Mike laughed. "I'll bet! But I don't see how you're going to convince anyone to come in on a holiday unless you come clean."

Janette cocked her head, reflecting. "Don't be so sure."

When a slight smile pursed the corners of her mouth Mike suddenly grew curious. "What the fuck are you going to do?" He was smiling when he asked.

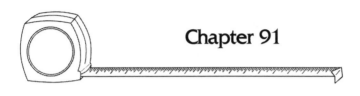

Chapter 91

"We have to do this," Janette stated with conviction. Robert was the third designer she called and so far the most difficult. "Memorial Day has always been an all-hand on deck sales day," she continued. "How's it going to look to the associates if we don't come in to help drive retainers?"

"I don't care what anyone thinks," Robert retorted. "I don't work weekends and I don't work holidays. I made that perfectly clear when Robert hired me. Family is important to me."

"No shit!" Janette exploded. She was near her wits end. "Everyone has family and everyone enjoys weekend and holidays off, but this is different."

"Not to me."

Janette thought how good it would feel to tell him if they don't pull off a great sales day he was going to have more time to spend with his family than he cared for. In another life, she told herself.

"I spoke with Marie and Susan and they agreed to come in."

Robert scoffed. "Ha, they would."

"Don't be a dick!" Although I'm sure it comes easy for you, she thought. "Derrick has done a good job this past week demonstrating good will. We've all seen the lift in morale among associates. People are working together, talking up design and installs. The rest of the company isn't faring as well, so if we lead the pack it'll keep store support out of our hair and no reason to peel back the onion, which is the last thing we need."

"The only one who doesn't want an audit is Debbie, and I'm not sacrificing my personal time for that bitch."

Janette heaved a sigh. "I don't like her any more than you," she began.

"No one does," Robert cut in.

"Fair enough, but that does not change the fact we need to be there tomorrow."

"You're barking up the wrong tree."

She was beginning to believe him. Don't let this asshole off easy. Make him fight! Janette ran her fingers through her hair, trying to think what to say that would convince him to come in.

"I know what you negotiated when you came on with *The Design*," she started, "but that was then. You know I appreciate my personal time too. When was the last time you saw me work the weekend or a major holiday?" She had him stumped, so she kicked it up a notch to keep him on edge. "You got the weekend off by calling out sick again. Don't let down the design team by failing to come in tomorrow."

Robert cleared his throat, struggling for words. He was actually embarrassed, not an easy thing to do to him. He didn't want to work the holiday, but he liked Janette. She'd supported him in the past and helped him with his clients when asked.

"I don't wanna work the whole day," he said adamantly.

Janette smiled. "Fair enough." She knew once he showed up it would be hard for him to leave anyway. She followed up with a grateful, "Robert, this really means a lot. Thanks." She hung up, exhausted.

Mike walked over, beer in hand. "How many more calls to make?"

"Five too many," she replied, reaching for the bottle and taking a long drink.

Derrick closed the door to his office and tore open the manila folder. He sat down behind his desk, excited over what he held in both hands. He reviewed both files and knew this was all he needed.

Action this day, he said silently.

He walked down the hall and ran into Emily from phones. "Derrick, I've been looking for you."

What, again? "Yes Emily, how can I help you?" This girl is like my fucking shadow!

Emily shook her head disappointedly. "We had another sick call. This one from bath showroom."

"Doesn't anyone work weekends here?" He regretted saying it, but couldn't help it. That made 16 call-outs for the day. "Don't these people need money to live on? How do they pay their bills?" He didn't expect Emily to answer, but those were questions he'd often asked himself when the same people called sick time and again.

"There is some good news," Emily said beaming.

"Good news would be welcome."

"A lot of people are saying what a good job you've been doing. You answer your phone, you listen, and you get people to help in other areas, all of which none of the other managers do." She stopped when Tim Lyon walked around the corner.

"Hey all, what's up?"

Derrick saw Emily flush with embarrassment. "Oh Tim, we were just talking about you," he said, slightly smiling.

Tim stood proud. "Really? Nothing bad, I hope?"

Emily jumped in before Derrick could continue. "I was telling Derrick how pleased everyone in the store is with him. He answers his phone, listens, and has people helping in other departments. I've been hearing people say good things about you Derrick, and thought you should know."

Derrick looked appreciative. "Thank you Emily, we don't hear enough of the good, and always too much of the bad."

Emily returned to the phone room and Tim followed Derrick down the hall. "Where are we going?"

Derrick looked at Tim. Who said anything about We? He stopped midway, looking thoughtful. "I need you to do me a favor," he demanded.

"Sure."

"Get Tina and tell her I want to meet her in seasonal." Better to meet her in my area than the confines of her office, he thought.

Tina came with Tim in tow. Derrick motioned for them to take a seat in the outdoor vignette where he waited. It was a nice ensemble, displayed under a gazebo, complete with table, chairs, and an outdoor barbeque set. They were in view of customers and associates, but out of earshot.

Derrick chose a chair, laid a file folder on the table, and got right down to business.

"I've been reviewing the hiring practices of this store," he said, "and I've found some discrepancies." He used a serious tone of voice, appropriate for the seriousness of the topic.

Tina looked pensive. Good. She *should* be .

'For instance," Derrick said, "I notice that Debbie's background check came back *yellow*."

The color-coding system was common enough for Tina to know the meaning of yellow. If an applicant's background check came back *red*, they were ineligible for hire. *Green* meant the applicant could be hired. *Yellow* required further review before a determination was reached.

For instance, if an applicant's driving record or credit rating was questionable, they would show up yellow. A yellow applicant could only be hired with the a vice president's approval.

"Debbie had a minor discrepancy on her credit rating," Tina explained icily. She did not like having to answer to anyone, especially someone whose days were numbered.

"I see," Derrick said. "What I *don't* see is the VP approval, authorizing you to hire her. According to the records, Debbie's hiring was a violation of company policy."

Tina glanced at Tim, who looked curious, as well as nervous.

The expression on Tim's face showed quite clearly that he had no idea why he had been called to this meeting.

On the other hand, Tina knew *exactly* why Derrick had asked Tim sit in on their little discussion. Derrick wanted a witness to everything that was said and done.

Tina obviously chose her next words carefully. "Debbie has been working for *The Design* for..."

Derrick cut her off in mid-sentence. "We'll get back to Debbie in a minute. First, I want to talk about some discrepancies in the way you handle T&A issues."

Tina cast an angry glare. "What the hell do you think you're doing?"

"My job," Derrick replied, sharply.

He opened the file folder, and examined the document on top. "You've been lenient with the design team's tardy and absenteeism," he said. "But store associates have not been receiving the same consideration."

He lifted the one-page document from the file, and held it up so that Tina could read it.

Tina's face turned white. The document detailed tardiness and absentees for every store associate over the past six months. The worst offenders were at the top of the list, and it was no surprise the designers led the pack. In addition to sick calls and tardiness, designers had more miss-punch slips than any associate in the store. Apparently, the designers frequently didn't bother to punch in and out on the time clock.

"This is a serious violation," declared Derrick. "If people don't punch in at the time clock, it's impossible to verify that they are working their scheduled shifts."

Tina gave him a look that was pure poison. "What's all this about?"

"You're not the only one cleaning house," Derrick said. "On my first day here, some of the associates complained to me about ongoing favoritism toward the design team."

Tina looked like she wanted to say something, but she kept her mouth closed.

Derrick glanced down at the file. "Although there's no love lost between you and the designers, it hasn't escaped anyone's attention that you and Debbie are very close."

He let that sink in before continuing. "It also turns out that you and Debbie had prior history, before either of you came to work for *The Design*."

Tina stared at him.

Derrick flipped a page of the file, and examined the page beneath. "I see that the two of you went to school together."

He flipped another page. "And Debbie listed you as a reference on her job application."

Tina reached for the file, but Derrick pulled it away. "Not so fast. This is *my* investigation."

"This is retaliation!" Tina sneered.

Derrick shook his head. "Tasha doesn't think so. And neither does Judy."

He watched Tina fume for several seconds before continuing.

"I'm a pretty fair judge of character," he said. "I knew from day-one that you and Debbie had an agenda. It didn't take me long to realize that you wanted to get rid of me."

Tim made a strangling sound, as if he were choking on something. He made a feeble waving gesture. "Sorry..." he gasped. "Swallowed wrong. I'm okay..."

Derrick looked Tina in the eye. "The human resources manager is responsible for T&A issues and hiring practices, so I didn't feel it was practical for you to investigate yourself. In view of the seriousness of these issues, I asked Tasha to look into them, to see if there was any misconduct on your part."

Tina's expression went instantly from angry to frightened. "You can't do this..."

"It's already done," Derrick said.

He closed the folder. "Frankly, Tina I never thought things would go this far, especially in only six days' time. To tell you the truth, I almost didn't follow through with it."

Derrick nodded toward the file in his hands. "I was hoping that we could work together to build up the morale of this store, and maybe develop some real synergy."

He shook his head. "But you know what they say... Hope is *not* a strategy."

Tina rose from her chair. "You've just given me all the ammunition I need," she hissed. "Retaliation is a serious offense. This company comes down *hard* on people who retaliate, and so do the courts."

"I agree completely," Derrick said. "Retaliation *is* a serious offense. But what makes you think this is retaliation?"

"Don't pretend that you don't understand," Tina snarled. "You found out that Debbie and I filed harassment complaints against you, and now you're retaliating against us by starting your own private inquisition!"

Derrick shook his head. "Sorry to disappoint you," he said, "but I forwarded my request for this information on Tuesday. In other words, I started this investigation *before* you made your bogus accusations of harassment to Judy and Tasha."

The blood seemed to drain from Tina's face.

Derrick tucked the file folder under one arm. "Say... Do you know what just occurred to me? I start an investigation that involves you and Debbie, and then... Out of nowhere, you both spontaneously decide to lodge formal complaints against me."

Derrick smiled. "What do you think, Tim? Does it sound like Tina and Debbie filed those complaints to retaliate against me, because I was having them investigated?"

"I... I... I don't know..." Tim stammered.

"Of course, you're right," Derrick said. "That's not really the kind of determination we can make at the store level."

He turned his gaze back to Tina. "It's really up to the senior company executives to decide whether or not these ladies have been conspiring to commit retaliation."

Derrick shrugged. "Or maybe that's a decision that should be made by a court..."

"You have no right to do this!" Tina bellowed. "You have no right!"

Derrick looked at her sharply. "I have every right. In case you haven't noticed, I'm the store manager."

Tina stiffened. "We'll see about that!"

Without another word, she turned on her heel and stormed away.

A few customers and associates looked up to see what all the fuss was about.

Tim whistled softly. "How in the hell did you just do that?"

Derrick pushed his chair back under the table. "I learned a long time ago to cover my bases."

"But how did you know they were out to get you?"

Derrick ran a hand through his thinning hair. "Some people get ahead by supporting their coworkers, and helping the entire team to succeed. And some people think they have to cut your throat to get ahead. After a while, you learn to spot the ones who are sharpening their knives."

Chapter 92

6:30 PM

Derrick walked the floor one last time. He was tired beyond words, mentally and physically. Things looked good so far as he could tell. So what am I missing? He was sure there was something, but couldn't put his finger on it.

When he walked through kitchens JC came running up to him. "I've been looking all over for you." He was out of breath, huffing and puffing.

"I never thought I'd be so popular." His voice was laced with sarcasm. "What's up?"

"Actually, you are."

"I'm what?"

"Popular!" JC filled him in on the scoop spreading throughout the store. Apparently some associates witnessed the scene in outdoor seasonal and the story grew way out of proportion. "Everyone thinks you fired Tina."

"That's nonsense," Derrick retorted.

"Don't feel bad," JC replied quickly. "Most people would be behind you all the way if you did." He watched Derrick closely and thought he looked to be distant. "What's wrong?"

Derrick shook his head. "I can't put my finger on it, but we're missing something."

JC glanced at the surroundings. "Do you mean the store?" It was a stupid question.

"What the hell else would I be referring to?"

JC took it in stride. "We've done everything possible. The store is signed, all displays are up, and we're staffed to demand."

"That's where you're wrong," Derrick said with restraint. "How many sick calls did we have today?"

JC knew, but didn't want to be the one to confirm it.

"Fifteen," Derrick blurted. "How in hell are we going to have a great sales day if our designers don't show up?"

JC didn't know how to respond. "Debbie will be here," he said lamely. He followed up with, "Look, it's been a long day, a long week even. Go home and be with your family. We'll close the store and make sure all is ready for tomorrow's opening. It's not like we haven't been through a major holiday sale before, you know."

Home sounded good to Derrick. But having a beer before hitting the road is what I really need!

Tim and Steve sat with Derrick at *Joe's Bar & Grill*. They were having their second round of beers at the bar, reassuring the store manager all that could be done was in fact done.

"Now all we can do is wait," said Tim, confidently.

"Not true," Steve said. "We can finish drinking."

Even Derrick couldn't help smiling as he took another swig straight from the bottle. He hated drinking beer from a glass. It just didn't seem right.

"Those sick calls are going to kill us," Derrick said, irritated. His voice was hard.

Steve and Tim glanced quizzically at each other. Right when they thought they lifted the manager's spirits he threw a curve ball at them.

Derrick thought they looked as though they had been slapped across the face. "I appreciate what you've done, don't get me wrong, but let's face it" He took another drink. "Unless we have the designers on hand to collect retainers the associates won't put their best foot forward. They need to see everyone working same as them, especially when so much is at stake." He took yet another drink, finishing it. "After all, who wouldn't want to have a holiday off?" He signaled to the bartender to bring another round.

Tim shook his head disgusted. "I hear ya. It's not like the old days when you could fire someone for not showing up to work. Nowadays it takes a shit-load of paperwork and permission from the powers-that-be to hold anyone accountable for performance."

Derrick knew that was an exaggeration, but it still held some truth.

Steve watched Derrick, his suspicions confirmed. "You speak as though a lot more depends on tomorrow's sales."

"You could say that again," replied Derrick, speaking urgently. He followed up with a sarcastic, "No one's job is safe in these times. Am I the only one who knows that? Don't people realize we're in a recession? Jobs are hard to come by, and yet we have people calling out sick at the drop of a hat!"

Tim and Steve squirmed in their chairs, and they motioned for Derrick to keep his voice down when heads from nearby patrons turned in their direction.

Derrick waved them off. "Maybe it would serve everyone right if they closed us down," he mumbled.

Steve and Tim did a double take. "What's that supposed to mean?" demanded Tim.

Realizing his mistake, Derrick seemed to sober quickly. "I'm drinking too much," he said, unconvincingly. He got up from his chair and reached into his pocket, pulling out two $20 bills and tossing them on the table. "This is on me," he said carefully. Before leaving he turned to them and said, "You all should be proud of what you've done this past week. I've seen a lot of people pull together when so much is at stake, but not like I have at this store." He cast a slight smile and finished off with, "I'll see you bright and early tomorrow."

Tim and Steve watched him leave, pondering the manager's behavior. "What do you suppose he meant?" asked Steve.

Tim shook his head. "I wouldn't want to guess, but..."

Steve cocked his head. "But what?"

Tim turned his head and stared at him. "I think we've got a long night ahead of us."

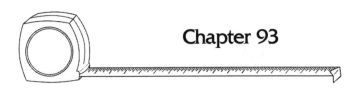

Chapter 93

8:00 PM

"You know I don't like for you to drink and drive!" Jennifer looked as angry as she sounded. "Why do you do this?"

Derrick brushed past her in the hallway and to the kitchen. He poured himself a glass of water, drinking it quickly. "Come off it," he said, lamely. "I'm not drunk."

"The hell you aren't!" She glared a look that could kill. "My father was a drunk, and I am damned well not going to be married to one."

Derrick froze. He didn't want to go there, especially while caught in the act. He turned slowly to face her. After taking a breath he said, "You're right, Honey. I've been drinking. It was stupid of me and—"

"You're damned right it was stupid!" she cut in.

Etienne appeared from nowhere. "Mommy, are you and Daddy fighting?"

This was the last thing either wanted. Jennifer turned to face her son, forcing herself to smile. "It's okay, Sweetie," she said, walking over to him. "We were talking too loud is all." She bent down to pick him up. "Let's put you to bed."

Derrick stayed in the kitchen, drinking two more glasses of water to sober himself up. You're such a fucking idiot, he told himself, angrily.

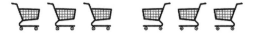

He entered their bedroom and found Jennifer reading on the bed. She didn't bother looking up at him. I'm in deep shit, he knew.

He walked into the closet and changed. When he came out she was still reading, acting as though he was not even there. I may as well be dead, he thought.

Maybe if she knew what was at stake? No, why worry her? She doesn't deserve that. But then, maybe it'll help me to talk about it. Derrick shook off that thought. Don't be a selfish prick! he scolded himself. You wanted to be store manager, which means taking all the baggage that comes with it.

Derrick climbed into bed and switched off the light at the bedside table next to him. Right when he settled in Jennifer looked at him. "Wanna talk about it?"

Derrick jumped upright. "Yeah. You sure you wanna hear?"

She smiled and nodded.

This woman gives a whole new meaning to support, thought Derrick.

Jennifer stared a long time at Derrick, doing a good job of hiding her emotions.

"I hate it when you do that," he said wearily.

"Do what?" She intentionally sounded dismissive.

"You know what."

And she did. Jennifer chuckled and moved close to him, putting her arms around his neck. She leaned into him, kissing him long and gently. When she pulled back she said, "I think what you've done is wonderful."

Derrick looked confused. "What exactly have I done?"

"All a body could." She sounded convincing. "They had you take over a store that was already marked for closure. Still, you went to work every day upbeat, putting your best foot forward to inspire your associates and do all that's needed for a successful sales day." She threw up her hands and tilted her head to the side. "If they want to shut down the store after all everyone has done, it's their loss."

Derrick mulled it over and said, "I don't know that I did anything special. After all, going to work with a positive attitude is what I'm expected to do."

"Yes, but not everyone does," Jennifer came back quickly. "Why do you suppose manager turnover is so high?" She answered before he could. "It's because not everyone takes their job seriously."

He agreed with her there. "But what if we don't have a good sales day tomorrow?" he asked, despairingly. He didn't want to believe it, but even after all the hard work he and his staff had put in, failure was still a very real possibility.

Jennifer threw up her hands acquiescingly. "Then you'll have the satisfaction of knowing you've done your best under the toughest circumstances." She stared at him a long time before finally adding, "We'll just have to wait and see."

Derrick stared back and eventually smiled. "How did I ever get someone so special like you?"

"I don't know," replied Jennifer, suppressing a smirk. "I'm still wondering when I'll ask myself the same question about you."

Derrick reached for her hungrily, pressing his lips hard against hers. Jennifer matched his urgent desire, holding him tightly. He lifted her shirt up, pulling back long enough to toss it off her before kissing her full force again. Jennifer slid a hand inside his pajamas when suddenly...

"Mommy, I can't sleep." It was Etienne. He stood in their doorway with Gnarly wagging his tail.

Jennifer screamed, disappearing beneath the covers while Derrick fell off his side of the bed.

"Are you okay, Mommy?"

She didn't answer.

Derrick got up and walked over to him. "Yes, Mommy is fine. She's just tired." He lifted up Etienne and walked back down the hallway to his room. "Daddy will put you to bed, okay?"

"Can Gnarly sleep with me again?"

"Yes, Gnarly can sleep with you, but promise you'll go to sleep."

"I promise."

"Good."

"Why is that good, Daddy?"

"Because I don't think Mommy and Daddy can take another surprise like that."

Chapter 94

Memorial Day
6:00 AM

This is it, thought Derrick. *It's do or die!*

He had planned to be the first one at the store today, but—to his surprise—Tim, Steve, and JC were waiting for him in the returns office when he arrived. Tina and Debbie's cars were already in the parking lot.

This didn't look good. The SM should not be last one to arrive on a day that could make or break the store.

Derrick entered the returns office, briefcase and coffee in hands. "I didn't expect to see all of you here so early," he said cheerfully.

"We gathered that," said Tim.

"We wanted to make sure that no stone was left unturned," added Steve.

Derrick turned to face the parking lot. "I see our PSM and HR are here too."

"Yes," said JC with a touch of sarcasm. "They're around somewhere. Busy doing *whatever* it is they do."

Derrick nodded. "Okay. Let's get on with it, shall we?"

Things went smoothly, and by the numbers. Receiving took deliveries without a hitch; the morning crew did last-minute down-stocking to fill in the shelves; trade associates made calls to clients, to verify pre-scheduled appointments; and the cashiers brought their tills to their registers.

At 9:00 a.m., the floor staff arrived and went to their assigned departments. The design desk remained deserted, a detail that escaped no one's attention.

Everyone in the store was mentally asking the same question... Will the designers be here, or *not*?

The smart money was on *not*.

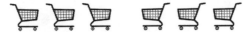

Derrick walked the floor, pleased to find his associates giving their departments a last-minute once-over. Signage looked good, as did the displays. They even had balloons all over the store, in commemoration of the holiday.

When he walked past the main entrance, he saw a large group of customers forming in front of the store. That was a good omen.

"What do you think?" asked a voice from behind.

Derrick turned and saw Nancy, from trade.

"Looks like we're in for a busy day," said Derrick.

Nancy turned her head in the direction of the design desk. "Everyone's not here yet."

Derrick knew what she was referring to. No designers.

He checked his watch. "We still have time."

9:30 AM

Derrick was having a cup coffee in trade, talking with associates when JC entered.

"Derrick, I just saw Judy pull into the parking lot," JC said. It sounded like a warning. "Tasha is with her, too."

The room fell silent.

Derrick suppressed a sigh. What the hell did they want?

"Fine," he said, "let's go meet them."

Judy was waiting at the door to Derrick's office when Derrick and JC arrived. Tasha was nowhere to be seen.

"Looks like you've got quite a crowd outside," Judy said with satisfaction.

Derrick opened the door, and gestured for everyone to enter.

"You all did your part," he said. "Your local advertising campaign is reeling in the customers."

Judy laid her briefcase and purse on Derrick's desk. "We like to think we're part of the team too. Speaking of which... How's *your* team doing?"

Derrick started to speak, but JC beat him to it.

"Most of the associates are here, but the designers haven't arrived yet." He sounded as grim as his choice of words.

Derrick flashed him a disapproving glance.

Judy looked surprised. "Aren't they scheduled to work?"

Derrick nodded. "I instructed Debbie to ensure that her team was scheduled to work, and I asked Tina to verify, since the HR is in charge of schedules."

There. He'd dodged the bullet, and dragged the Wicked Witches into the crosshairs at the same time. If Judy was going to hold him accountable for schedules, she was going to have to go after Tina and Debbie too.

Judy wanted to walk the store before the morning meeting, so Derrick led her back out onto the sales floor. They walked the aisles, inspecting the vignettes, signage, and pretty much any and everything they came across.

Judy scrutinized everything, but for the most part, she seemed pleased with what she saw.

At 9:45 a.m., she joined Derrick in the rug department for the morning meeting.

The associates were already gathering.

Judy looked around. "Where are Tina and Debbie?"

Derrick scanned the growing assembly for the Witches. "I'm not sure," he said. "I suppose Tasha is having a few words with them."

When everyone arrived, Derrick stood before them, motioning with raised arms to quiet down.

"Good morning, everyone," he said. "Thank you all for coming. As you can see from the growing crowd outside, we're in for a busy day. I want to thank each and every one of you for all the hard work you put in preparing for this moment."

Derrick gestured toward Judy. "As you can see, we have a guest with us this morning. Please give a warm welcome to our district manager, Judy."

The associates greeted the DM with applause and Derrick stepped back to allow her the floor.

Judy stepped forward with the confidence of a person accustomed to standing before large crowds.

"Thank you everyone, thank you. I'm glad to be here, and I want to congratulate all of you on a job well done. Your store prep is outstanding, and I'm sure we're in for a successful sales day."

This brought a polite smattering of applause.

Judy continued. "As all of you know, major holidays are some of our biggest selling days. One of the primary tasks is to collect as many project retainers as possible, because kitchen and bath remodels are our bread and butter. Please be sure to properly qualify all customers, and don't forget to talk up our design and installation services. The design team has been scheduled to assist in offering free consultations, so if you see any customers with project needs, don't hesitate to point them toward the design desk."

She nodded toward Derrick, and he nodded back.

Good. Short, sweet, and to the point.

Derrick took the floor, and picked up where he left off.

"Okay people, it's close to show time! We have bottled water, coffee, and pastries in trade. Let's remember that the goodies are for our *customers*, not for *us*. But I don't want you to feel too left out, so we're ordering lunch for all of you."

The associates broke into applause. Free food was always a crowd-pleaser.

Derrick finished off by saying, "Let's have a million bucks, with a million smiles!"

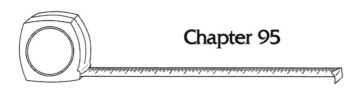

Chapter 95

10:00 AM

Derrick unlocked the main entrance and opened the doors. "Good morning," he said cheerfully. "Welcome to *The Design*."

A throng of customers brushed past him, most not bothering to acknowledge his greeting. So much for customer service...

But Derrick continued to welcome the incoming customers, whether they returned his greeting or not. He had given himself the task, and he was determined to do it well.

Mary Hines came running up to him, slightly out of breath. "Derrick," she said, "you've got to see this!"

"See what?"

She grabbed his arm. "Come on!"

Derrick allowed himself to be led.

Mary pulled him past the customers, through the front doors, and out onto the sidewalk.

She pointed down the length of the store front, to the parking lot by returns. "Look!"

What Derrick saw practically floored him.

The designers were getting out of their cars and heading for the store. Each of them had a briefcase in one hand, and the ever-present coffee mug in the other. They looked like the twelve Apostles, coming to save the day.

"I'll be damned," Derrick said.

Mary laughed. "You almost *were*."

She tightened her grip on Derrick's arm. "Follow me. There's more." She led him back inside the store.

They reached the front end registers near the returns office, in time to see Tasha escorting Debbie and Tina out of the store. The Wicked Witches carried what appeared to be their personal belongings in boxes, with their briefcases strapped over their shoulders. Both women glared at Derrick, before turning their eyes away in disgust.

"Looks like good things come in threes," Mary said. She was grinning from ear to ear.

"What's the third good thing?"

Mary swept the store with her arm. "We've been open less than five minutes, and we've already got wall-to-wall customers."

Just then, Janette walked past. She caught Derrick's eye, and gave him a thumbs-up.

Derrick returned the gesture, and smiled.

When things quieted down, he'd have to ask Janette how she had managed it. Every designer was here, and they were all happily engaging with customers.

Mary laughed again. "Way to go, Boss! You beat the Wicked Witches!"

Derrick's eyes practically popped out of their sockets. "Where the hell did you hear that name?"

Mary shrugged, still grinning. "A woman never talks."

Derrick laughed. "My ass, they don't!"

They remained at the entrance, greeting customers, and thanking them for coming.

"So, what do you think?" Mary asked. "Can we *do* it?"

Derrick shrugged. "We're damned well gonna find out."

He was grinning when he said it.

Author's Notes

The character Derrick Payton is fictional, but I did have the pleasure of working with someone of the same name at one of the largest home improvement retailers in the U.S. I want to extend another thanks to the real Derrick, for allowing me to use his full name in my book. Coming up with character names is always challenging and fun, and his name had such had a nice ring to it that I couldn't resist.

I was inspired to write this novel shortly after my first book, *THE SANDMAN*, was released in 2009. I wanted my next book to strike a chord with many readers, and I realized that writing about life in a retail store would do precisely that, because just about everyone winds up taking a job in the industry at some point in their life.

Some people may wonder if a promotion to store manager can happen in the manner described in this book. All I can say is, 'always expect the unexpected.' A friend of mine was asked to help out in another store, while the company was 'cleaning house' of its management team. The moment he walked through the doors, he was handed the keys to the store and told, "You're it!" So, this can *definitely* happen in real life.

Today, many companies follow a process of interviews before a promotion is offered. But in my experience, anything can happen when the 'powers that be' decide to take an occasional shortcut. This being the case, I have learned to watch my back, be careful who I trust, keep a positive attitude, and know when to be seen, but silent. (Okay, I'm still working on knowing when to be silent.)

The customer scenarios described throughout my novel are only slightly exaggerated. Thankfully, in my own career as store manager, I haven't come across as many crazy customer encounters as my main character, Derrick Payton. Even so, I've certainly had my share.

The employee-manager politics described in this book are right on the mark. I wish I could say that I invented the back-stabbing, sick calls, tardiness, and petty jealousies woven throughout this story. Unfortunately, this kind of stuff happens every day in retail stores all over the country, and—I suspect—all over the world.

Despite these challenges, people in the industry do eventually develop trust in their fellow workers. There's really no other choice. You can't accomplish anything on your own, and you need the support of your associates in order to do your job. I'm glad I was able to describe that in my story, because it emphasizes the importance of relationships, and how they define who we are.

Recently, I ran into an old coworker whom I hadn't seen in years. Looking back at our time together, he said, "that was the best group of people I ever worked with."

I had to agree with him there. Although the industry has changed considerably, I look back at those first 17 years in home improvement as my absolute best. I went from an inexperienced and sometimes disillusioned kid, to a seasoned professional with a reputation for trustworthiness. I'll be the first person to admit that I have many (many) flaws, but my people have learned that they can rely on me. And that, for me, is priceless.

I'm still lucky today, as I continue to forge new relationships in the home improvement industry. I'm glad that each of us still has the opportunity to make a difference to the people working around us. The industry is not perfect, but camaraderie is alive and well, and all of us have a bright future if we continue to work together.

— **David Lucero**

About the Author

Award-winning author David Lucero lives with his wife, Martha, in San Diego, California. He has worked in the retail industry for more than two decades, and is currently a store manager of Pacific Sales Kitchen, Bath & Electronics, located in Chula Vista, California.

His first novel, THE SANDMAN, was the Military Writer's Society of America's First Runner-Up for Best Fiction in 2009.

Books the Author Recommends

If you enjoyed *WHO'S MINDING THE STORE?*, be sure to put these books on your must-read list:

'*CONFESSIONS OF A CONTRACTOR*' — by Richard Murphy

I found Richard Murphy's book to be more than an inside look at the life of a contractor. It's engaging, witty, and on-the-mark. I can easily relate to the scenarios encountered by his character, Henry Sullivan. I've worked in the home improvement trade for over twenty years, and I can tell you that Murphy knows his business.

'*SIDEWAYS*' — by Rex Pickett

You've seen the movie, now you've got to read the book! I saw the movie by accident, when my sister in-law stayed over with Martha and I, and brought the DVD claiming, "You've got to see this movie!"

I didn't think it was my style, but found myself laughing the moment Miles and Jack hit the road (pun intended). I enjoyed the movie so much, that I just had to read the book. Rex Pickett crafts his characters with imagination, depth, and a superb sense of comedy. We've all known a guy like Jack, and too many of us—including me—are probably a bit too much like Miles.

'*KITCHEN CONFIDENTIAL*' — by Anthony Bourdain

This professional chef-turned-TV food critic explains how (and *why*) he became one of New York's most popular chefs. It's a no-holds-barred look into cook schools, restaurants, and food service unions. If you're anything like me, you'll come away secretly wondering if you might have missed the calling to becoming king (or queen) of the kitchen. Martha and I love Anthony Bourdain's television show, *No Reservations*, and his entertaining nature transfers easily to the written page. If you read this book, you'll never look at your kitchen the same way again.

16131968R00223

Made in the USA
Charleston, SC
06 December 2012